LITTLE PILGRIM

KOLIYA

SHAKYA

• Lumbini

KOSHALA

• Kapilavastu

KHASHI

• Shravasti

Kushinagara

• Sarnath

Ghaghara River

• Vaishali

Jumna River

Ganga River

Patna

• Rajagriha

Son River

Gaya •

MAGADHA

Mahanadi River

Bay of Bengal

Godavari River

Deccan Plateau

Arabian Sea

Krishna River

MADRAS

MYSORE

(Tamilnadu)

• Cochin

Indian Ocean

CEYLON

(Sri Lanka)

ANCIENT INDIA

Approx. 500 BCE

Map Not to Scale

KOLIYA	Country
Lumbini	Ancient Name
(Tamilnadu)	Modern Name

LITTLE PILGRIM

KO UN

Translated by Brother Anthony of Taizé
and Young-Moo Kim

Parallax Press ✦ Berkeley, Ca

Parallax Press
P.O. Box 7355
Berkeley, California 94707
www.parallax.org

Edited by Rachel Neumann.
Cover and text design by Gopa & Ted 2, Inc.
Author photo by Lee Sang-Wha.

The original text in Korean is 532 pages. This English edition has been edited
and condensed with the author's permission. The translators and the publisher
gratefully acknowledge the support of the Daesan Foundation (Seoul, Korea).

Library of Congress Cataloging-in-Publication Data
Ko, Un, 1933-
  [Hwaom-gyeong. English]
  Little pilgrim / Ko Un ; translated by Brother Anthony of Taizé
and Young-moo Kim ; [edited by Rachel Neumann].
     p. cm.
  ISBN 1-888375-43-4 (pbk.)
  I. Anthony, Brother, of Taizé II. Kim, Yong-mu, 1944-
III. Neumann, Rachel. IV. Title.
  PL992.42.U5H9413 2005
  895.7'14—dc22
                                              2005019262

1 2 3 4 5 / 09 08 07 06 05

CONTENTS

EDITOR'S NOTE

OR THOSE OF YOU who like to "get right to the good part," I encourage you to skip these notes and jump right in. Some ancient ruins are best appreciated by simply walking among them first and then later figuring out what you saw. So it is with *Little Pilgrim*, a book that is both humble and rule-breaking, funny and profound, adventure tale and spiritual teaching. Based on a 1,600-year-old text, one of Buddhism's oldest and most complex sutras, it is also a thoroughly contemporary tale, filled with quarrelling lovers, stubborn children, shouting giants, and dangerous adventures.

Ko Un has set his novel in India before it was known as such. His main character, the young boy Sudhana, travels deep into the South, then returns North and follows the Ganges river as far as the sea. On his journey he meets fifty-three teachers, some human and some spirit, whose methods of teaching are as diverse as their appearances.

Ko Un wrote the book for Buddhists and non-Buddhists alike, and no prior knowledge is necessary to enjoy the adventure he retells. But if you are someone who likes a little *amuse bouche* before the main course, I recommend Ko Un's own Author's Note. Ko Un is Korea's conscience and muse, a learned monk and irreverent poet who brings to this novel the full force of his intelligence, spiritual understanding, compassion, and wit. His own humorous retelling of how he came to write *Little Pilgrim* will assure you that you're in good hands.

For those who prefer to travel with guidebook out, map in hand, I direct you first to the end, where Gary Gach, Francisca Cho, and Brother Anthony of Taizé provide some historical and literary context for this work. Whether their thoughtful essays are read before or after the novel itself, their love of the book and their knowledge of its place in the Buddhist literary canon, is enough to inspire a second reading to find themes and treasures missed the first time along the path.

Twice nominated for the Nobel Prize in Literature, Ko Un is a gifted writer whose epic novel is a treasure far too-long unavailable to English readers. As one of the only Buddhist novels available anywhere, its publication is of celebratory significance for Western Buddhism in particular and spiritual literature in general. Enjoy!

—Rachel Neumann, Parallax Press

AUTHOR'S NOTE

OMETIME IN ABOUT 1959, while I was a Buddhist monk engaged in Son (Zen) Meditation, a senior monk, the Venerable Unho, told me I should read the Avatamsaka (Garland) Sutra. In those days I was young and brash; I felt that I knew it already, having studied it with the Venerable Myongbong in a recently published translation.

But when Master Unho told me to read the Avatamsaka Sutra, he really meant that he wanted me to compose a long epic poem on the endless wanderings of the child Sudhana in his quest for truth, described in the Gandavyuha that forms the last book of the Avatamsaka Sutra.

He spoke warmly: "The novelist Ch'un-won intended to write it, but couldn't. If only you could take his place." But in those days I had no interest in writing epic poems, so I did not take up the task that Ch'un-won had left unfulfilled. I merely made a noncommittal response and left it at that.

Looking back, I can see two reasons for my lack of interest. First of all, I did not believe that I could portray Sudhana properly with my limited poetic skills. Secondly, it was a time when I was far more attracted by the Prajñaparamita (Transcendental Wisdom) Sutras, especially the Diamond and Heart Sutras, than by the complex, fundamental principles of the Avatamsaka. I could not feel any enthusiasm for the Gandavyuha and was not interested in Sudhana.

It was only after I had gone much further in my own life's wanderings that I realized how close Sudhana's quest was to my own. I had left the monastic life by that time, but not the Avatamsaka Sutra. In 1969, I began publishing regular installments of a tale entitled "The Little Pilgrim" in the Dok-so newspaper, not an epic poem but a tale in prose. Once publication there ended, the text was published in book form in 1974. That volume contained the first thirty chapters of the present work.

I ought to have gone on writing, but at that time I was going through an irreligious phase. Friends and former colleagues kept encouraging me though, and at last it is finished, twenty-two years after I first began.

According to the traditional account, the Avatamsaka Sutra belongs among the earliest teachings of the Buddha but was at first transmitted in a number of separate sections, only being brought together as a unified work long after the Lotus Sutra had been compiled. Later, the original Sanskrit version was mostly lost. The Gandavyuha is reputedly the oldest extant among the sutras.

At first, we are told, the Avatamsaka Sutra was a total failure. It was so far removed from the commonly received Buddhist ideas of the times that it could not be easily understood. Seeing that it would not do as a starting point, as a stopgap measure the Buddha preached sutras with other subjects. Even such leading disciples as Shariputra and Maudgalyayana, though they were present when the Sutra was preached at the Jetavana monastery in Shravasti, were unable to grasp the truth contained in it, for "their eyes were covered with thick darkness." A later Chinese commentator compared them to deaf mutes. Since all who heard it were deaf and dumb, preaching the Sutra had apparently been a waste of time.

In Sanskrit, "avatamsa" means a garland, used as a general image of the Buddha's teaching. The "garland" here represents the realm of Vairochana, the transcendent Buddha, adorned with lotus blossoms and jeweled flowers of all kinds. The Gandavyuha is the record of little Sudhana's quest. Once his heart has been awakened, he sets out on a journey through southern India in search of the deeds expected of a bodhisattva (an awakened being who awakens others). In the course of this, he visits fifty-three teachers. With the teachings he receives, from his first teacher, Manjushri, to his last, Samantabhadra, he attains the high state of bodhisattvahood he had been seeking.

Yet some of his teachers have almost no connection with Buddhism; among them are brahmans, slaves, merchants, boatmen, children, prostitutes, and heavenly spirits. This is an expression of the conviction that truth can be gained from anybody. Sudhana discovers that the whole world is full of the truth, which the Buddha realized, and this endless pursuit of truth has influenced the thinking of many who lived long after him.

All through the Avatamsaka Sutra, not only the Gandavyuha, there are constant references to the sea, both the Arabian Sea and the Indian Ocean.

It looks beyond the borders of India from its very beginning. There is even said to be a relationship between it and the Koran. It is clear that the Avatamsaka Sutra has been read and has shed its influence on an international scale; not only India but also the West, as well as China, have learned from it. With the whole world as its stage, the pilgrimage of Sudhana covers a vast area. As it shows that truth is limitless, the world of the Gandavyuha is naturally of tremendous scope.

In the course of writing, I reflected my own states of mind in this work. Inevitably, then, the beginning, middle, and end vary as I varied. This can most easily be seen in the lyricism of the early chapters, the social awareness of the middle section, and the more specifically Buddhist language I employed towards the end. This work may constitute the best expression of my own life's progress.

Quite frankly, the story of Sudhana's travels related in the Gandavyuha cannot be read without long periods of considerable boredom. If the present work reproduces this effect, the fault lies with my limited literary skills.

The Venerable Unho, who first proposed the task, died many years ago. I end with a final thought for him.

LITTLE PILGRIM

1.

DAWN OVER THE SON RIVER

HE RIVER WAS BEGINNING to loom into view beyond a cluster of hibiscus trees hanging as if in a drunken stupor. It flowed quickly in the early morning light, the sound of its rippling subdued. For little Sudhana, that glimpse of the river constituted his first awareness of the world as he regained consciousness.

"He's alive!" Manjushri rejoiced. The old man had rescued the child the evening before, as the boy floated close to the riverbank. All night long, the aged Manjushri had kept watch beside him on the sandy shore of the vast triangular reach where the Son River united with a small tributary before flowing down to join the Ganga.

They were in the northern regions of what is now called India. All the nation's frontiers and fortresses were in a state of unprecedented alert. King Virudhaka had determined to wipe the entire Shakya clan of Kapilavastu from the face of the Earth. The barbarity with which he conducted his campaigns had left the shores along the tributaries of the Ganga littered with corpses. All the farmland had been laid waste, every building razed. Walls that had taken generations to build were toppled, broken fortifications lay spread across the region. Every night the ruins rang with fearful screams. Theft, rape, and murder were commonplace among those who survived.

The whole Son River valley was once a thick forest of sal trees but they had all been burned to ashes. Sudhana had been born and raised at an estate deep inside the sal forest. As the fighting neared, Sudhana's nurse had bound the sleeping child to a raft made out of some bits of rough wood and set him floating down the river. Sudhana's entire family had perished in the flames that consumed their great manor house.

Sudhana's body might have washed into the sea, if not for Manjushri.

The old man had been out admiring a spectacular sunset. The seventy-two-year-old Manjushri had once seen the Buddha himself touched by the beauty of a sunset, and he was seized with emotion at that memory. The ultimate beauty of that fading light gave him yet deeper faith in the truth of the Buddha's words: "All things vanish in splendor. All things in themselves are evanescent." Just then, his old companion Parthivi had come rushing up. Parthivi fell on his knees in front of the aged sage, rose, and stood pointing towards the river. Manjushri followed Parthivi with the slow steps of an old pilgrim. The monsoons had set in and the river had swollen, spreading wide beyond its banks. It was flowing very fast. Darkness was spreading over the twilit Son basin.

"Over there, Master!"

Parthivi pointed towards the sandy shore further along the river's edge. The plank-built craft was no masterpiece of shipbuilding, to be sure, but it seemed sturdy enough. Still, the little boy who lay tied on top of it appeared to be dead.

"I saw it being swept down," Parthivi whispered. "So I swam out and brought it in. I could hear a faint sound of crying coming from the boat, you see. And look, he's still breathing!"

Manjushri peered at the small boy. "Ah, what a jewel of a child! Let's carry him into the quiet of the camp. He needs to be cared for."

An all-night vigil kept Sudhana warm. Then, in the dim light of early dawn, he opened his eyes.

"The world's all dark," he murmured. "The Himalaya's snowy peaks must have died!" He gazed toward the river. Manjushri's companions were busily rolling up the tents of their little encampment, but stopped when they heard the boy speak.

"This little fellow knows all about snowy peaks!" One of the men laughed. "Mountains dying! Who ever heard of such a thing?"

Manjushri stayed silent for a moment, then replied: "A child knows everything, just as a river at dawn knows everything. The reeds and trees along the banks of the Son know that the far-off Himalayas are dark. To know one grain of the sand on this shore is to know the whole universe." He spoke in a low voice, as if eager not to interrupt the river's murmur.

"What's your name, Grandad?" the little boy whispered, his voice hoarse. "I'm called Sudhana."

Manjushri contemplated the child. "I'm called Manjushri."

"Do you live near here? Why is there no hair on your head?"

"I always live by the roadside."

"By the roadside? With no house?

"No, my home is in the sleeping fields, under the sleeping trees, beside the sleeping river."

"Where am I, Grandad?" Bewildered, Sudhana tried to clear his eyes.

"Well," Manjushri said gently, "this is a sandy beach at the lower end of the Son River. I was here only once before myself, about ten or so years ago. But the fighting hasn't reached here, so it's quiet. In the days to come, we're hoping to care for people who have suffered from the war."

"I want to go home," Sudhana cried out in the ringing tones of the Son Valley. "There's plenty to eat there, and lots of servants, and elephants to ride on." Sudhana tried to sit up. "Where am I?" he asked again.

The old man had a vision of Sudhana's home—the palatial mansion built of stone blocks carted down from mountain quarries, filled with every kind of treasure—turned to a heap of smoking rubble. He opened his eyes and the vision faded, replaced with Sudhana's weary young face.

"No," Manjushri said quietly, "there's no call for you to go back there. I'll show you the way you must go." He pulled Sudhana to his feet. Sudhana stumbled slightly and then was astonished to find that he could stand perfectly well. He had regained his full health and strength. Manjushri took his arm. "Look at that old sal tree branch. That branch is showing you the way. Now go, Sudhana."

The sage bowed towards the tree with joined hands, whispered a few words in Sudhana's ear, and then he gave the boy a gentle shove in the back, as if pushing a boat off from the shore. Morning broke, and Sudhana the orphan found himself alone in the world.

2.

THE LITTLE PILGRIM'S FIRST STEPS

OR ALL HIS WARM and generous heart, the old man had abandoned Sudhana in the middle of a completely empty beach. Sudhana was overwhelmed with intense loneliness and did not wipe away the tears that slid slowly down his face. He could not believe the aged Manjushri would have pushed him away without a purpose.

The Son River came flowing down through vast stretches of swamp, yet the sand on the beach was bright and clean. The fateful branch of that morning's sal tree was casting a clear shadow across the sand. The branch's shadow was pointing toward Ajay Ferry, where the roads from Rajagriha, Jetavana, Magadha, Koshala, and Chalnadu met before turning north and west along the Ganga and on towards other kingdoms. So Sudhana set off in the direction indicated by the tree, and pursued his path weeping, his loneliness glowing warm between the tears.

As he walked, his past in the stone mansion faded until it disappeared from his memory completely. All Sudhana could remember were Manjushri's last whispered words as he pushed Sudhana away: "We'll surely meet again." Those words remained a secret embedded deep in Sudhana's young heart.

Houses lay in ruins along the roadside, and in places the oleander trees of the windbreaks had toppled, but the road stretched into the distance, white and endless. Beyond the grassy plains, it continued as far as Ajay Ferry, a flourishing center of civilization in those days, the main trading-point for the whole lower Ganga Valley. There were normally huge flocks of tropical birds here but the recent fighting had driven the birds to seek other havens; all that remained were a few black-headed herons, perched on one leg near muddy pools in the fields, distracted and dazed. Even when

Sudhana threw stones at them, they would merely flap one wing idly, making no effort to fly away.

Sudhana soon sensed new energy flowing through his limbs. He set out through the vast, midday solitude. Nobody was in sight as far as the horizon in any direction, and after a while he felt he was the only person alive in the world. No longer crying, he began to strike up a friendship with the road, talking to the various objects he met along the way.

"Tell me, tree," he said to one old gnarled willow, "I'm almost ten, but you're at least fifty; so why are you still like a child?"

"When I'm with you, I'm nine years old, too."

"Do you know the Himalayas?"

"No. But I know all the animals hereabouts. They gather here and howl when the moon rises."

A big yellow flower hanging on one branch of the neighboring tree intervened. "You two are having a nice time. Let me play with you, too."

A palm tree across the road spoke up and scolded the other trees sharply, "Stop chattering! There's someone waiting for Sudhana in the camel trainer's house at Ajay Ferry. Go quickly. If you stay here, you'll get caught in the monsoons!"

At that, all the other trees, the leaves, flowers, and grass in the fields, even a grasshopper sitting beside a dead snail's shell, urged Sudhana to hurry.

"Very well," he sighed. "Trees, holy trees, until we meet again, goodbye."

As he set off along the road, Sudhana gazed towards Ajay Ferry. In the wind he could smell a compound of human griefs and joys, poverty, disease, and cares, mixed with the laughter of young girls who laugh for no reason. He hastened on towards the sweetness.

It was early evening by the time Sudhana arrived at Ajay, where all the fruit on the trees hung glowing green. Candles were guttering on the streetside stalls, and every street seemed to leap and dance by their light. There were trees everywhere! Slow, plaintive melodies rang out, sacred scriptures sung to harp accompaniments. Sudhana could make out some of the words:

> Darkness does not linger
> but wanders to and fro.
> Flowing from dark frangipani leaves,
> the darkness becomes

the whole world.
Darkness is the wheel of darkness,
all the world is the wheel of the world,
as darkness wanders to and fro, here and there.

Cows wandered aimlessly along the evening streets. Sudhana went on, looking for the camel trainer's house down near the ferry landing, where the sound of the river was loudest. Candles burning here and there inside the houses kept the darkness at bay. The night was being forced back, pierced with shining holes. Arriving at the house, Sudhana stood at the gate. The stillness of the light that filled the wide courtyard left him unable to speak.

Squatting in front of the flickering candles, little Sudhana closed his eyes for the first time since he had opened them that morning and seen the venerable old Manjushri. In relief, his closed eyes filled with the wandering darkness.

3.
NIGHT AT AJAY FERRY

EFRESHED BY THE BRIEF RESPITE with his eyes closed, Sudhana looked around. The garden was enclosed by a living fence composed of bamboos and sal trees and was drenched in the rich scent of sal flowers. Someone was weeping, a young girl by the sound of it. "Is anybody there?" Sudhana called towards the light-filled courtyard, "Is anyone home?"

The Son could clearly be heard flowing nearby. A young girl emerged wearing a white sari that left one of her shoulders exposed. Night nestled on her brow. She was no longer weeping, but the wetness of her cheeks glistened in the light of the candles.

"Is this the camel trainer's house?" Sudhana asked.

Her eyes widened and she stared at Sudhana. "You must be the child the Master sent? Am I right?" Sudhana stayed silent.

"Father has passed into nirvana," she continued. "He was still breathing until a moment ago, waiting for you."

Opening the gate, the barefoot girl led Sudhana to the room where her father lay dead. The room was filled with the scent of flowers and the candles inside were steadier than those in the wind outside and shone humbly with a steady glow.

"I am Iryon," the girl said. "Father was wounded in the side, resisting soldiers in the war; his wound wouldn't heal, and now he's dead. Father entered into nirvana with his eyes open, hoping the promised child would come. Will you close his eyes, please?"

She bent gracefully and uncovered the body. The dead man's staring eyes were grotesque, but Sudhana closed them with a light gesture, and the body became just an ordinary corpse.

"It's nearly midnight. We must bring father to the riverside for cremation. The bearers have been sleeping, but they'll soon be here. Even without Manjushri's holy presence, you've arrived, so father's spirit will not be sad."

People could be heard approaching the house. Going out, they saw the bearers bringing a bier adorned with lotuses. Following the dead man's wishes, they omitted all the rites of the brahmans and simply loaded the body onto the bier, which set off with the little pilgrim leading the way. Walking behind the cart, the girl was composed, her face calm and solemn.

A single candle lit their way, burning with such intensity that it was not dimmed by the fresh night breeze. Passing through the still-crowded market area around the ferry stage, the mourners followed a dark path upstream along the riverbank, moving through the night without waking any sleeping creature. Other workers had already arrived and pyres were burning brightly at the cremation site. All around the circular clearing, trees reared high into the night sky, forming a dense wall.

The old man's body was solemnly fetched down from the bier and placed on its pyre. After a few minutes the smoke from the body formed a column rising towards the dense treetops. The still-hot bones were collected from the ashes, placed in a stone basin and reduced to powder. The workers left after gulping down the wine they had brought with them. Sudhana handed Iryon the coffer holding her father's ashes.

"Come on," Iryon said. "These ashes must be scattered on the river. The Son has received the remains of this town's dead for centuries now."

"Right now?" Sudhana asked. He was exhausted.

"No. First we'll go home and prepare things for the journey. You and I have somewhere to go today, a place father told me about before he died."

Sudhana followed her. It was early morning by the time they reached the house. Reverently placing the box containing her father's ashes on a pedestal in the center of the yard, Iryon went to her room and emerged quickly carrying carefully wrapped bundles. Sudhana strapped them on his back. Iryon took up the coffer. Holding it level with her forehead, she blew out the candles that were still burning brightly here and there. The whole house grew dark.

Sudhana walked ahead, carrying a candle. The previous day he had covered ten miles and still had not slept, yet now he felt full of energy, as if invisible pinions were bearing him on, despite the accumulated fatigue. He and Iryon untied the rope holding a skiff to its mooring-post and got in. It was hard work crossing the dark river. Iryon manipulated the oars with a skill that seemed to derive from long practice, nudging the nose of the boat back upstream whenever it began to turn downstream. She furled the oars and Sudhana handed her the casket. The boat began to drift down on the current. Iryon opened the box by the light of the candle and sprinkled handfuls of the dust on the water. The ashes slowly mingled with the stream. When the box was empty, she sent it floating away as well.

Iryon spoke to Sudhana, her face reflecting the beauty of the light shining across the water. "Now father is united with the Son. The Son is nirvana." As she rowed, Sudhana moved closer to her. "Where are we going?" he asked. "Aren't we returning home?"

"We've left home, just like father. There's a place father told me about."

The night began to withdraw from the river. They heard foxes barking; a swarm of fireflies approached across the water and vanished toward the distant shore. The river grew wider as dim light spread all over it. Low down in the sky above the plains to the east, the pink of dawn was peeping from between clouds shaped like fearsome blades; the newborn morning seemed to be bringing great sorrows in its train. A few fish rose to the surface, churned the water, and disappeared again. Iryon skillfully brought the skiff to the shore.

But Sudhana was unaware they had reached shore. Lulled by the river, he had fallen asleep. When he awoke it was already broad daylight and rain was falling. Along the wharves, women were up and about, drawing water. Iryon forced the still sleepy Sudhana to walk. They washed in a side-stream, then Iryon produced some dried fruit from her bag. They sat by the stream and ate together. Not looking at Sudhana, Iryon spoke: "Father asked me to tell you something. If you want to find the Truth, first you must meet the monk Meghashri in Sugriva Mountain. He asked me to be sure to tell you that, then he died."

These words brought Sudhana fully awake. "Truth? Sugriva Mountain? Where's that?"

"If you go that way to the forest surrounding the city of Patna, there's a fork in the road. While we're on our way there, think carefully: is it to be the mountain, or me?" She pulled Sudhana to his feet and got him walking, like a mother teaching her infant child its first steps. "Look! The spot where the road divides!" They walked on towards it without any further words, each one absorbed in secret thoughts.

When they reached the crossroads, Iryon asked, "What have you decided, little Sudhana?"

"I like you!" he blurted out. She smiled. But then he added, in a louder voice, "I'm going to the mountain. I want to learn what I don't know." Her smile faded but she nodded. She took off a bracelet and handed it to him. "Off you go then. We'll meet here in two years' time at the Fish Festival! I'm going to Rajgir to find the crown prince. Perhaps I'll marry him instead."

She did not linger. Sudhana took the left-hand fork, leading towards the highlands. Far away, Sugriva Mountain towered, caught in a mass of clouds.

4.
CLIMBING THE MOUNTAIN

HEN SUDHANA REACHED THE FOOT of the mountain, he saw a group of peddlers and hunters gathered. One of the huntsmen, who had a hawk perched on his shoulder, called out: "Hey! How does a kid like you come to be traveling all alone?"

"I don't know," Sudhana replied curtly, put off by the hunter's manner.

The hunter poured a measure of water from a leather pouch and gave it to Sudhana.

As the young boy drank, the hawk gazed at him. It looked older than Sudhana and bigger too.

"Would you like to see my hawk fly?" the man asked.

Sudhana nodded. He was interested in anything to do with the hawk. A cold smile appeared on the hunter's lips.

"This hawk has lived with me so long, it'll surely die with me. I think of it as my wife. It's caught me all sorts of birds and wild animals. Just take a look at the muscles here in my arm; all that comes from eating the meat this hawk has caught."

One of the peddlers, who had been playing a flute with no great skill, butted in: "A fine wife you've got, to be sure, hunter!" The old huntsman made no response but merely looked at Sudhana and shouted an order to the hawk in a tongue Sudhana did not recognize. The hawk sprang from his shoulder and went soaring off, its wings stirring up a breeze like that from the fans around an empress's throne. The hawk drew the crowd's eyes higher and higher, rising until at last it seemed poised, a single dot, motionless in the void.

Its owner looked smug and murmured: "That's fine, fine! But sometimes it goes even higher, until these old eyes of mine lose sight of it altogether. There are times when I leave it flying high above and go on; a few days later, while I'm walking along a road in some quite different place, it'll suddenly land on my shoulder. It never fails to catch something, even if it's only one small chick."

"How many years have you and the hawk been together?" Sudhana asked.

"For a long time, now. The year my wife died, I was in the forest at Kari; it had hurt its wing and was flapping around on the ground so I caught it, cared for it, then tamed it."

The hawk shifted its position in the sky high above them, came hurtling to the ground not far away, then rose again. All the power of the hawk was expressed in that movement. It had brought them a wild hen in its talons. The hen's comb was already drooping, its eyes were covered with a kind of white membrane, but it was still alive. As soon as its master had taken its prey, the hawk flew lightly into the branches of a dwarf gum-tree nearby and perched there.

"Let it go free, mister!" Sudhana cried, unable to help himself.

"What did you say, boy?"

"It's wrong to kill wild animals. Don't we all share this Earth together?" Sudhana addressed this last question to the hawk, then snatched the hen away from the man and hugged it to his breast. "Hey, hawk. While you're around, this hen will be scared. Get away from here."

At once, the hawk spread its wings and flew off, sending a few leaves fluttering to the ground. The hunter and the peddlers were dumbfounded. Sudhana put the hen down. It glanced fearfully around, then scuttled away, tottering on wobbly legs.

"You know how to talk to hawks, too! Where did you learn that kind of magic? You sneaky little rascal!" The hunter addressed Sudhana with greater circumspection than before, but with open hostility.

Sudhana braced himself and then spoke. "From now on that hawk will go flying after truth, it won't kill any more animals." On hearing that, the hunter sprang up and knocked Sudhana to the ground. He dealt similar blows to each of the peddlers in turn, sending them all sprawling.

"You bastards!" the furious hunter cried. He called after the hawk, "Darling! Sweetheart! You bitch! Come back here, at once, come back or I'll..." and he went running off in the direction the hawk had flown.

"Hey! This young man is special!" one peddler exclaimed. "Let's get out of here before he brings a curse down on us!" Luckily some of them knew Sudhana's native dialect fluently, while the hunter knew only a few words. The peddlers scattered, leaving Sudhana alone with the mountain. He began to climb a sheer path that rose almost vertically up the cliff. The valleys grew deep, ridges towered aloft.

"Why doesn't Meghashri come down into the world with all its suffering, put wrong things right, serve as guide to the wretched?" Sudhana wondered as he began the arduous climb. "What's the point of being all alone up in the clouds? I really can't understand grownups at all!"

As he approached the midway plateau, completely exhausted, the air grew thicker. What had first appeared as mist was really the cloud that always shrouds Sugriva Mountain. Sudhana touched the silver bracelet circling his wrist. He felt lonely and afraid.

He was so weary that he had no idea how long he had been wandering in the clouds. He wept, thinking of Iryon, whom he had left behind. He called her, afraid of the mist. "Where are you, Iryon? Did you marry the prince?" But the clouds only swallowed his voice.

He climbed frantically upwards. The cloud belt ringing Sugriva Mountain ended not far from the spot where Sudhana finally collapsed. In the sleep that came to him he dreamed of Iryon. He saw her beauty veiled in thin silk.

He woke to feel something clawing at his shoulder. It was the hawk! It struck him once more on the shoulder with its wings, then flew up into the air. Sudhana slowly came to himself. Below, all was wrapped in an ocean of clouds; above him soared the mountain's five great peaks, jutting sharply into the cold blue sky. He rose with new energy flowing through his veins. The hawk guided him from above, slowly moving ahead of him. Sudhana felt that its guidance was something sacred.

"Thank you, dear hawk, thank you."

He climbed each of the first three peaks that towered above the highest point of the plateau, but Meghashri was nowhere to be seen. He lost hope. He stared up at the hawk, as it too looked for the monk. Then it flapped its wings and flew like an arrow straight toward the foot of the fourth peak. Seeing that, Sudhana climbed on despite the wounds on his legs caused by falling rocks. At some point in his climb, the hawk left him.

The path up the fourth peak was different than the others. Where before

there had been nothing but ordinary mountain tracks, now Sudhana was forced to climb steep stairways of piled rocks. The path wound up across the high cliff that formed the base of the northern face of the mountain's main peak and ended in a huge cave.

A white vapor wafted gently from the mouth of the cave, rather like the beard of some ancient mountain spirit. The old monk was seated in the lotus position on a pedestal placed in front of the cave, plunged in deep meditation.

Sudhana called out, "Master!"

There was no reply. Wondering if perhaps the man was a statue, Sudhana threw a stone that struck the monk's chest. The monk opened his eyes and glared at Sudhana, who had endured such great torments to reach him.

"The old camel-trainer's dead, Master! He asked me to come tell you."

No reply.

"Master Meghashri?"

"I heard you. Come on over here."

The stern expression melted into a warm smile. "You're a remarkable fellow, little Sudhana. Many have aspired to reach this place, yet only you have succeeded."

"I've come to find the truth about everything, Master."

"Fine. But we can talk about all that stuff slowly later, after we've had something to eat." He giggled and made a soft whistling sound. As if in response to his call, a host of raccoons and squirrels, hares and unicorns, wolves, leopards, lizards, and wild horses emerged from the seemingly empty mountaintop stillness. Sudhana tried to hide behind the monk's tattered robes.

"It's alright," Meghashri comforted him. "I call these my children."

The animals produced a collection of chestnuts, mangoes, and fruits Sudhana had never seen before. The young boy and the monk ate well. After eating, they, along with some of the smaller animals, retired into the cave. The vast evening sky was hung with stars. There they lay down to sleep.

"Everything in this world is sacred," the monk murmured. "All things are truth and teachers of truth. These animals asleep beside us are your masters, too."

Sudhana had no sooner heard these words than he fell asleep.

The next morning, Sudhana awoke to find himself alone with the old monk.

"Where did the animals go?" he inquired.

"They've either gone to the meadows lower down, or up to the high ridges, Sudhana. Why don't you go and spend some time with them?"

"Won't they gobble me up?"

The old monk laughed and shook his head. Sudhana took his morning meal of fruit and water, then ran out in search of freedom in the marvelous beauty of the high pure mountain.

5.

ALONE BESIDE THE BRAHMAN SEA

UGRIVA MOUNTAIN is rugged and harsh; its icy upper reaches are so bleak that even alpine plants find it hard to flourish there. Meghashri led a life of utter solitude that at first seemed tedious to little Sudhana. Yet after being with the old hermit for only a few days, he found himself accustomed to it.

"Teach me! Teach me something!" Sudhana would wheedle each day after returning from his sojourn with the animals. But the old monk's eyes would be closed, and he would sit plunged in deep meditation for the rest of the day. Apart from the mere fact of spending the days together, Meghashri never taught Sudhana anything. Yet Sudhana absorbed each and every thing that emanated from the monk, like a chicken pecking eagerly at scattered grain. After all, once wine has matured, it becomes fragrant; its scent travels far and permeates deep into everything around. Meghashri's whole being had so matured that not only Sudhana, but even the mountain highland mists were affected by the truth emanating from him.

Sometimes, Sudhana would get so frustrated, he would tickle Meghashri's back with an elm twig and beg, "Teach me!" But Meghashri would only shout: "You little mustard seed of a brat! What could I ever teach you? Look at those hills and clouds, look at those red and green plains beneath the clouds. Look your fill! Look until you can't close your eyes even when you sleep, until your eyes are gone forever. Heaven and earth are beautiful, aren't they?"

His shouting would gush out like water forcing its way through a dam. Then he would seal his lips with profound significance. In those moments, Sudhana had the impression that it was not Meghashri speaking, but a spokesperson proclaiming a message on his behalf, then vanishing again. Without being taught, Sudhana learned many things from the monk's silence.

The wind blowing over the mountain often turned into a veritable tornado—the birds and animals living there, even the smaller rocks, found themselves whirled up into the air. When the gardenia flowers blossomed, a special gardenia wind blew. Not a single petal would fall to the ground, instead they would be swept up into the sky and their scent would fill the air.

One day, Sudhana was whirled up into the air by such a wind. It hurled him about, as if he was a ball, then returned him to the ground with luckily only minor injuries. Back at the cave, he found Meghashri cutting off his little toe using a knife of his own making. The toe had been festering for quite a while.

Meghashri looked up when Sudhana came in. "It hurts a bit. I've got nothing to teach you," he continued as if in the middle of a long conversation. "I once met a noisy drunkard called Sagaramegha at an inn down on the river; you ought to go and look for him. My truth isn't a touch on his. He's a remarkable old fellow; not a day dawns but he's sobering up from the night before." He spoke indifferently. "Yes, it hurts. It hurts just a bit."

"I don't want to go!" Sudhana stamped his foot. "I won't! Up here I feel like I'm way above everyone else."

"You little rascal!" The monk's eyebrows were trembling as he spoke, "You little mustard seed of a brat! What a fool!" He handed him a slip of paper with a few words written in Sanskrit, then landed him a wild kick with the foot from which he had just removed the little toe. Sudhana went sprawling.

For all his fussing, the little pilgrim did not overly resent being kicked out like that. He knew it was time for him to go.

The great difference between his ascent and his descent was the difference between not knowing the way and knowing the way. The road dropped down the slope at the end of the plateau and stretched across the southern plains. He walked on for a time, then turned his head. Something had changed. At first, whenever he looked back, there had been the eternal soaring stronghold of Sugriva Mountain comforting him with its mysterious beauty; but now the mountain had vanished! All around, as far as the eye could see, was an endless expanse of grasslands.

Sudhana began to feel lonely again, but there was no one he could turn to for company. Holding Meghashri's scrap of paper tight against his breast, Sudhana murmured an incantation to the wind that he had heard Meghashri reciting to himself.

The few days spent in the mountain had given Sudhana sufficient strength for his long journey; he walked with no effort. Even in the midst of the darkness that began to spread at sunset from the western forests across the plain, he walked on and the road remained obediently beneath his feet. The presence of this child, walking onwards even in his sleep, seemed to send the night itself to sleep.

He traveled on for three days and nights, resting under trees or sleeping for short periods in fields of reeds or under dried lotus leaves. Now, the sea loomed before him, covered with myriad tiny waves. A single boat floated on the indigo water. As the little craft drifted closer to the shore, Sudhana could see its sail was in tatters. It looked as if it had only just managed to reach land after being caught in a violent storm.

"Ahoy, there!" Sudhana took off his white turban and waved it at the boat. The ship was heading for a natural breakwater. Sudhana hurried toward it, reaching the boat just as a young man climbed out with an old man, apparently quite ill, across his shoulders. The young man lowered the elder to the ground.

"Where have you come from?" Sudhana asked. But the young man did not look around or give any indication he'd heard a voice. He split open a coconut and held it for the old fisherman to sip the milk. It was the old man who noticed Sudhana first.

"Who are you? Where did you come from, child?"

"I've come from Sugriva Mountain."

"And where are you going now?"

"I don't know. I'm on my way to look for an old drunkard called Sagaramegha. Do you know who he is?"

"No, I only know the sea, nothing else. My grandfather and my father both died at sea and I only barely escaped the same fate."

Sudhana pulled out Meghashri's paper and showed it to the old man.

"Why, this is the kind of writing that I learned as a child. It says, 'Hereby receive three tonic pills from this child Sudhana. I gave him three pills' worth of health, help, and dreams, so you can take those three pills off your drinking bills.' That's what it says! Oh, ha ha ha!" The old fisherman laughed until his sides ached.

Abruptly, the young fisherman spoke up, "I have heard of Sagaramegha.

He lives in the desert not far from the city of Sagaramukha, but he's never at home. He's always on the move."

Sudhana was startled to hear the young man's voice. The youth continued, "He's been living there for twelve years now, in a house out in the desert near Sagaramukha; I hear he just sits, staring at the sea. I've never seen him. They say he's always drinking and that if he runs out of wine, he throws a handful of sand into the sea; then the whole ocean turns into wine and he laps it up. I've heard that when the sea is wrapped in darkness or whipped up by a storm, he roars at it like a lion, all night long. I plan to meet him sometime, too. If you'd like, I'll take you to the harbor at Sagaramukha tomorrow in our boat." Sudhana nodded eagerly. They replaced the old torn sail with a new one made of Sudhana's white turban and the plan was set.

Sudhana slept by the sea and the next morning he took leave of the old man and sailed off with the youth towards Sagaramukha. It was Sudhana's first experience of the midday sea! The clouds were as white as arsenic and the water so blue it seemed resolved to color the innermost recesses of Sudhana's body. The sunlight poured down, turning the innumerable crests of the indigo waves into flashing blades and splintered mirrors. Behind the city walls rose white domes, watchtowers, and roofs. Soon, they would arrive at Sagaramukha, the city known as the Ocean's Door.

6.
One Grain of Sand

S THE YOUNG FISHERMAN'S BOAT sailed on, Sudhana gazed at the extraordinary spectacle of the shore and opened his heart to the first stirrings of the monsoon, for a sea breeze had begun to blow from the south.

"Look! There are sea birds following us over there!" He pointed behind the boat.

"They always do." The young fisherman allowed himself a small smile. "Those birds know me well. Yesterday, before I ran into that storm out in the middle of the Bay of Bengal, they warned me by wheeling around my ship's mast. Is this your first time at sea?"

Sudhana nodded. "You know, out at sea like this, human beings seem very small. People appear insignificant, compared with the sea and the sky."

The youth tightened the sail, then turned the bar to change the boat's direction. Once the sail took the wind, the fisherman relaxed. He grabbed a long spear and plunged it into the water. A few moments passed before they saw a great silver fish flapping on the surface, pierced by the spear. The young fisherman drew it up, scraped off the scales and cut it into thin slices. Then he opened his monkey-leather pouch, brought out some salt, and sprinkled it on the raw fish.

"Eat up. You won't come across anything as tasty as this again. Eat your fill." They devoured the fish with gusto.

"Why do people kill fish and eat them?" Sudhana wondered.

"All life is the fruit of death. But here we are, little pilgrim! Get ready to disembark!"

A host of sailing ships, skiffs, and rafts floated in the harbor. On each vessel, sailors were dancing strange dances and singing incomprehensible tunes. Sudhana was arriving in a land where he could not understand the language. It made him feel nervous. The young fisherman's kind attitude seemed to have vanished the minute they reached dry land. He brusquely pointed out the road leading to the desert beyond the city walls where Sagaramegha was said to live and turned the boat back in the direction they had come from without a single word of farewell.

Sudhana found himself alone at the harbor. Although the city was still some way away, the landing itself was a flourishing market village, a place where goods from every part of the country were brought and traded. It was crammed with jewels and cereals, exotic fruits, fish fresh from the sea, meat from the mountain regions, bamboo wares, musical instruments, carpets from central Asia, all kinds of perfumes, incense, herbal tonics, and more. The market was the place where life happened.

A fruit vendor shouted at Sudhana to buy her wares, then tossed him a sweet fruit. Although she spoke in a Garinga dialect he couldn't understand, he knew she was telling him to eat the fruit. She was a beautiful woman, with a long scar down the side of her face. Thanking her for the fruit, Sudhana headed westward, following the fisherman's terse directions. The market and lanes around the harbor formed such a large town that no matter how hard he walked, it was some time before a clearing appeared.

Finally, Sudhana emerged from the port's crowded market area. The desert began on the far side of a strip of land occupied by sparse plantations of coconut trees, followed by stagnant marshlands. The desert was hot, even in the evening. The soles of Sudhana's little feet were scorched by the sand, in spite of being protected by shoes made of wild boar leather from Sugriva Mountain.

The still desert shone white. Strewn with crab shells and conchs, it stretched sparkling as far as the distant coast. Sudhana turned his back on the last glories of lingering twilight floating on the darkening sea. Finally he reached Sagaramegha's cabin. It was built of lumps of volcanic basalt. The doors had fallen off and lay scattered by the sea. It was more an open-sided shelter then a hut. Still, the solid stone walls kept it from being as hot as the desert outside.

"Is there anyone home?" Sudhana called. "Is the venerable Master Sagaramegha at home?"

The hut was empty except for the bones of a dead bird that lay in one corner of the sandy floor. A wine flask was hanging on one wall; it had long been drained but Sudhana could still smell the faint odor of the alcohol that had once filled it.

"Where can he have gone?"

Sudhana felt defeated. Now he could not even deliver the message from Meghashri. With no other ideas and no one to take care of him, he decided at least to spend the night in the hut. The echo of the waves crashed against the stone walls. In the southern sky, a new moon had risen and was shining on the sea. Sudhana murmured comfort to himself and finally began to cry. Light from the city's watchtowers could be seen in the distance, but the stone house where Sudhana lay was still and dark as if dead.

At dawn, the waves fell asleep. Their noise hadn't troubled Sudhana's sleep but the stillness when they stopped woke him at once.

He realized on waking that even without Sagaramegha's presence, he had learned all he could from the drunken sage. "This house is still his house, even if he's not at home. It's the body for a spirit that comes to dwell for a short moment in this world. The body is inhabited by the spirit, then falls vacant and rots away." Sudhana left the house without regrets.

He had gone about four miles across the desert when he felt something lumpy under his feet. He dug down into the sand and uncovered the body of a tramp stinking of wine. The tramp's identity struck him at once.

"Venerable Sagaramegha?"

"How dare you wake me up?" The body came alive and began to roar at Sudhana. A few days before, Sagaramegha had got completely drunk. Before falling asleep he'd covered himself with sand to keep warm. "Where the hell are you going, you rascal? This desert will make a skeleton of a mite like you in a flash. A fearless rascal you are, too, or perhaps just a rascal!"

Sudhana handed Sagaramegha the note from Meghashri. The tramp made as if to throw it away, then unfolded it and peered at Sudhana.

"Mmm...This fellow Meghashri is a mean kind of friend! To think he's so scared of what effects karma may bring! Sending a little rascal like you to write off my debts? The rogue!"

The drunkard's ranting seemed to invigorate him. He tapped Sudhana on the shoulder. "You little rascal! You're quite something, you know!"

Sagaramegha led Sudhana along the beach. The waves came rushing at them full of vigor, but left nothing more than a patch of weak foam behind. Sagaramegha took a handful of sand that he tossed into the sea; where the sand landed, the water turned into wine. He waded out into the water and began to drink.

"Hey, you rascal, come and drink, too! Drinking is the only thing you'll ever learn from me." Sudhana took a mouthful and, drunk and staggering slightly, he walked on along the desert shore with the vagabond Sagaramegha.

Sagaramegha ate nothing, merely filled his empty stomach with alcohol. Sudhana had no chance to eat any of the dried fruit in his traveling bag. He was obliged to travel onwards sustained only by mouthfuls from Sagaramegha's bottle.

"I'm drunk all the time," Sagaramegha babbled as he walked. "Liquor is fool's medicine. You can become a fool, too, if you drink. All wisdom and the roots of wisdom, the very roots of compassion will die, your heart will be filled with utter folly. Yet folly is like a Buddha's enlightenment."

"Did your Venerable Drunkenness ever meet Siddhartha walking along the shores of the Ganga?" Sudhana asked, echoing something he had heard from the monk Meghashri.

"Never. But he's not the only Buddha, you know. There have been other Buddhas in ancient times and in other worlds. If Siddhartha's really the Buddha, he came into this world much too soon. He should have abolished sorrow first. Since we are still in a world of suffering, the Buddha is a suffering Buddha too. But the Buddha is not, was not in the beginning, and is innumerable, not one; I and you, we all are Buddhas."

Sudhana said nothing.

"Still, if he has come, he can't really have come too soon," Sagaramegha continued, correcting himself. "When anything comes or appears, it comes when it has to come, appears when it has to appear. I feel bad today. I've drunk too much; my body isn't obeying orders. Rascal, give me your hand."

The tipsy Sudhana walked on, supporting the drunken Sagaramegha's weight until they reached the desert's lowest point. There, Sagaramegha collapsed. There was no one near, no sign of life. The desert formed a universe composed entirely of white sand, utter silence, a scorching space. Sagaramegha was dying. His fingers were dying one by one. His hands, his arms, his feet, his shoulders, his waist, all were dying. "If you cross this desert," he murmured, "you'll find the region of Sagaratira on the banks of the river Godavari. We've gone about four miles so you only have another two hundred or more to cover. There you'll find the temple of Supratishthita, a most humble man. Take me there."

But Sagaramegha didn't survive that long. He had no sooner stopped talking than he became a lifeless corpse. Little Sudhana gazed around. All he could see in the desert valley were some bones half buried in the sand. He shook Sagaramegha, who had lost the smell of wine at death and was already beginning to smell rotten. His rigid corpse showed no signs of movement. A corpse quickly rots in the fiery heat of a sandy desert. It rots in solitude, unvisited by even a single fly. Sudhana covered the body with sand. He took with him the wine bottle that Sagarmegha had carried.

"Silly old sage," he sniffed. "What a silly way to die. He left his bottle behind and quit this stupid place..."

Sudhana was faced with a very long journey. He thought of returning to Sagaramukha and its adjacent harbor, but the desert stretching around him seemed to forbid him to turn back.

He tried to reassure himself. "There's a fine place out there ahead. It has clouds that can't be seen anywhere else, and heavenly flowers, and heavenly songs, and in the midst of it lives the ascetic Supratishthita in a temple set in the sky."

He recovered as best he could from the effects of the wine; he gathered his wits and made a sign of reverence in the direction he was heading. In his heart he prayed for guidance.

Sheltered by his prayer, little Sudhana walked for six whole days without getting caught in a sandstorm. He was almost out of drinking water, so from his pack he drew out a coated dew-cloth that Iryon had given him and unfolded it to collect the great nighttime dewdrops, the tears of the stars hanging clustered in the sky. They would evaporate as soon as the sun rose, but as long as he did not sleep too late, he would find a few drops of dew collected in the hollow center of the cloth.

Filled with new energy, he walked on for another three days. He saw dry lightning playing in the clouds. Despite all his efforts, it became harder and harder to resist the fatigue that threatened to bring him to his knees. He bent over, resting his forehead on his knees. When he looked up and out at the desert horizon, he noticed a drawn-out cortege snaking along. He ran towards it. It was one of the Garinga desert caravans that set out directly across the great desert whenever the usual routes were closed by floods of the Manadonajay River. While some caravans were composed of camels and others of horses, this one was clearly a caravan of camels, indicating its travelers were prepared for a long trip. Horses were quicker but might run short of food and water; a caravan of camels was a moving oasis.

Sudhana waved as he ran toward the camels. He collapsed before he could reach the band of travelers, but a woman dismounted her camel and came to him. She pulled him to his feet and, when she saw he was too weak to walk, took him in her arms. Once Sudhana was mounted on a camel and had drunk some water, he soon regained his strength.

The seaside town of Kina, with its green trees and bustling crowds was a relief after the long desert crossing. Sudhana was freed from the great burden of the empty desert. What new and lovely life! The soaring coconut trees, the sal tree flowers with their delicate scent, mysterious melodies played on unknown instruments, people greeting one another, laughing, the smell of living human bodies, and—fresh water! After his long journey through the desert, Sudhana experienced all these things with a feeling close to tears.

He filled Sagaramegha's empty wine bottle with pure fresh water. From now on, he decided, he would live on the road. He would cling to no person and no moment of happiness, but frequent only the ways of one who walks the unending paths of the seeker of truth. No one could change Sudhana into someone else.

Sudhana slept deeply in one of the inns of Kina. On rising the next morning, the peniless pilgrim swept and cleaned the wide inn yard and the floor of the vast halls. When he had completed the work, payment he'd negotiated with the innkeeper the night before, he left.

7.
A SECRET LAKE

HE TEMPLE of the venerable Supratishthita was just a few hours away, but Sudhana kept losing himself in the thick forest. It was evening when he finally reached the walls of the dilapidated monastery and he found the gates tightly shut. As he stood fretting outside, flowers began to rain down from the sky, and the clouds grew dazzlingly bright. Supratishthita and a whole train of devotees were returning to Earth after a walk through the heavens. Sudhana was spellbound. He fell prostrate, stretched full length on the ground in reverence before the descending sage.

Upon seeing him, Supratishthita said, "The venerable Sagaramegha was my friend in many previous lives. He would drink while I sang. My songs moved the heavenly gods. I sang for his heart and when he drank, his heart was different from that of all the other drunkards in this world. And now he has entered nirvana out there in the desert."

"How do you know that?" Sudhana asked, his head still bowed.

"I knew you'd come," Supratishthita said. "Thanks to my unhindered wisdom, I can walk through the heavens and see the comings and goings of the people below." He spoke kindly as he adjusted his robes.

The little pilgrim followed Supratishthita into the extraordinary temple compound. The temple was divided into different sections, one for the highest monks, one for their assistants, and another for the ordinary laity. It had one main shrine, and many rooms where devotees could practice meditation. Sudhana found a number of novices his own age who had left home to enter the monastic life. As soon as the venerable Supratishthita presented Sudhana to them, they gathered around, their questions tumbling over each other.

"Did you really come from so far away? Did you come across the desert? Are you an infant Buddha?"

Their eyes were bright and clear, their skin was soft, their voices pure. Sudhana went with them to their clean quarters in the novitiate. After that, he had no chance to meet Supratishthita. For a devoted seeker of truth like Sudhana, with the thirst burning within him, the hours spent in the company of the young novices seemed like wasted time. Still, Sudhana easily returned to the ways of childhood, spending time with them without the least pretense or insincerity. They were busy learning by heart lines from ancient scriptures composed high up in the Himalayas, and they could already recite a good number. Moreover, it seemed that they were skilled in meditation.

When it was time for sleep, Amidahwa, one of the wisest young novices, came to Sudhana and pulled his pillow away. Sudhana's head hit the floor.

"Sudhana! Are you asleep already?" the novice whispered.

"You aren't keeping the rules about sleep?" Sudhana challenged the boy. Amidahwa was the son of a merchant from the land of Chu, beyond the Himalayas. His face was white as the snow-capped mountains, his eyes dark brown.

"Come on. I've got something to show you," Amidahwa whispered. Sudhana followed him out into the dark moonless night. Amidahwa laughed and grabbed his hand. Cautiously, without waking the other novices, they crept out of the room and entered the temple's portrait hall.

In the portrait hall a candle, never allowed to go out, was glimmering faintly. Eerie portraits of aged brahmans, devout and stern, were displayed along the walls of the hall's galleries. Amidahwa came to a halt before one of the portraits. Unlike the others, it bore no halo.

"This brahman was an expert in astronomy and geography," he said. "I learned a lot from him until last year. If I failed to study properly, he used to flog himself. It hurt me as much as if I was being whipped. He was really an original teacher. Just before he went into nirvana, he told me something when we were alone together."

"What was that?"

"He said that there is a huge lake hidden underneath this temple."

"What?"

"Wouldn't you like to go down and visit that lake?" Amidahwa turned and left the hall. Sudhana followed.

Passing through the long galleries of the portrait hall, they crossed towards the oldest of the buildings. It dated from the very foundation of the temple. Only the highest of the brahmans went there to offer special prayers and rituals and they always went alone. No one else could enter it without permission. Utterly still and dark, the ancient shrine was like a treasure chest hidden in the very heart of the temple. After Amidahwa made Sudhana swear not to tell anyone that they had been there, they entered. Passing through several rooms, they came to one where they pulled up the floorboards and a bitterly cold breeze came gusting up.

"Follow me! No one can see now if I light a candle," Amidahwa said, and a flame sprang up, revealing his face and the excitement shining in his eyes. He transferred the flame from the tinderbox to a candle. They cautiously set foot on a subterranean stairway that began immediately below the floorboards, and began their descent with a growing sense of tension. They continued down for so long Sudhana lost track of time.

When they reached the foot of the stairs, they found themselves in an open space and set out along a stone-paved path. That path led down into the far depths of the earth. Sudhana began to wonder if Amidahwa was some kind of goblin. It felt as though they had walked on for so long that day had already broken above ground.

"Sudhana! Sudhanananana!"

Amidahwa's cry rang out, only to be taken up and amplified in a great booming echo. Sudhana jumped.

"Shut your eyes!" Sudhana duly shut them.

"Right. Now open them."

He opened them. "Ah!" Sudhana exhaled. As Amidahwa had said, a lake lay spread before them, vast as the sea. He could not understand how the lake had been hidden by darkness and only appeared after he had opened his eyes.

"My teacher discovered this lake. In the last of the worlds to preceed this present world, there was a beautiful lake that is now the site of the Kina temple. When that world was annihilated according to the laws of universal destruction, the lake remained buried below the ground, surviving beyond its age into the present," Amidahwa explained. "Not even Master Supratishthita knows about it yet."

The words reverberated loudly and were hard to understand. The lake was utterly dead. Its beauty was not that of the world above. There were no people in sight, no fish rippled the surface, no trees grew thickly. It was a fossil.

Without warning, Supratishthita appeared in front of them.

"Why, Amidahwa, did you really think I was unaware of the existence of this lake? Of course I know about it. There's no halo painted on that teacher's portrait because he was too attached to this place. It cast such a cloud across his detachment and untrammeled freedom that he did not deserve the honor of a halo."

He turned to Sudhana. "Keep on along the shore of this lake, and you'll find another way back to the upper world. Once there, make your way to Vajrapura. It has a neighborhood, the Healing Village, where a healer by the name of Megha is busy saving all those with leprosy and deformities, mad people and mad dogs too, as well as everyone suffering from fevers. You must visit him." Master Supratishthita took Amidahwa's hand and led him back toward their temple.

Obedient to Supratishthita's command, Sudhana walked on along the shore of the lake on the stony path. His shadow stretched out over the water. The path beside the underground lake was as long as any road in the world above and it wearied him. Sun and moon had left this underground world. The dim luminescence emanating from ancient ruins gave off a glow that scarcely sufficed to relieve the darkness. Sudhana tripped. He looked down and was amazed to discover he'd stumbled over a young girl, stretched out on the ground where a house had once stood. Sudhana had grown used to the lake's eerie stillness, but somehow he felt that the girl's presence was at odds with the reality of this underground realm.

He bent down and shook her shoulder gently. "Can you understand me?" he asked.

The girl nodded. Her fine eyebrows outlined delicate eyes from which hope had ebbed away until only despair remained. She had a small scar like a slight wrinkle on one side of her broad forehead. He could tell at once she was sick, yet she seemed compelled to tell him her story.

"I was born on the shores of this lake, the youngest daughter of a wealthy father, a doctor. But the kingdom of Indra became infected with a mysterious disease and many people died. I should have died, too. When all had been annihilated, the world of the kingdom of Indra came to an end, leaving me here like this. I was meant to die but I did not, and survived into this new world. I am sick with a disease that can never be cured. Tell me, what country are you from?"

"Well, I don't..." He felt ashamed. On her disease-ravaged face he detected the traces of a very ancient beauty. "Come with me, up into the present world. I'm on my way to the world in which you are meant to be reborn."

Sudhana raised the girl up and set her on his back. She was so light that she added nothing to his weariness as he walked. Once settled on his back, she fell asleep.

Up ahead, Sudhana caught a glimpse of sunlight and let out a sigh of relief.

"We've made it!" He roused her. "Once we leave this lake behind, there's a doctor called Megha who can cure every disease. I'm on my way to meet him. He'll be able to cure you, too."

They climbed a long flight of stairs. Finally they emerged from the doorway of a cellar. The stifling heat of the sunlit world greeted them and they were assailed with the nauseating stench of life and every kind of piercing noise. They had come back into the world and for a moment felt such sharp pain that they seemed to have been struck blind and deaf.

After setting the girl down, Sudhana gazed out at the vast cloud-covered city of Vajrapura. Neatly joined to the great walled city was a smaller city, with a third beside it, and trees could be seen growing thickly inside the city walls. The country was prosperous.

"Come on!"

The girl's body had been like a fossil but now life had returned to it, and for the first time she hesitated to let Sudhana carry her. They entered the third of the cities. Compared to the other two cities, Vajrapura seemed to have enjoyed great good fortune. It overflowed with an ancient peace. The girl was breathing in the city as if it was her life's breath. Sudhana marveled as she became more and more at home.

8.
SEIYA RETURNS TO LIFE

MEGHA'S HOSPITAL was at the end of a gallery built of white bricks on the far side of a vast courtyard full of carts bringing new patients. A guide had come out on to the gallery and was waiting for Sudhana.

"This way," the guide said, but the girl shook her head. "No, it's this way," she said, leading them towards a smaller gallery to the left of the hospital building. The guide did not know whether to stop them, for the girl and Sudhana were heading towards a hallway that had once been the hospital's main entrance. It was now only used as a passage for Megha himself.

For most of the journey, Sudhana had been leading the girl; but now he found himself following her increasingly energetic steps. Megha had his residence in the most secluded part of the hospital. As she headed towards his room, the girl walked more and more like one possessed. Her face shone with joy. The guide had no choice but to let them continue.

Megha had just finished treating an old peasant for swamp fever and was taking a drink, when the girl came hurrying in, Sudhana following behind.

"Here we are, this is the place," she exclaimed. "My room was right next to this one. Yes, this is the place. I spent a whole month lying sick in here. But the bed's gone."

The girl was muttering to herself, unaware of what she was saying. Megha motioned for Sudhana to sit down, then asked him who the girl was. Sudhana said nothing.

Megha turned to the girl and, examining her closely, noticed a faint mark on the girl's forehead. Could he be dreaming?

He shook his head slowly. "It can't be! Are you Seiya?"

The girl just stared at him. She had no recollection of her name. Yet looking at her closely, Megha was sure she was his daughter, Seiya. Five years ago, she had died of a disease he couldn't cure. He had cremated her body in a remote forest clearing above the underground lake. Now, Megha gently rested his hand on her brow, needing to touch the evidence he saw with his own eyes. After these five years of mourning, she had come back to him!

Megha felt he should have been skillful enough to save his own daughter from disease. Soon after his daughter's death, the Buddha and his disciples had passed by Vajrapura. Megha had sought refuge in the Buddha and become a Buddhist. He had erected a shrine to Seiya on the hospital grounds and fervently prayed for her.

Yet although Seiya recognized her father's room and the hospital, she did not recall her father. Megha did not want to tell her yet, afraid it would be too much of a shock. Instead, he offered the travelers dinner after their long journey. He led Sudhana and Seiya to a dining patio in the garden. Seiya hastened on ahead, obviously familiar with the place. Megha, Seiya, and Sudhana sat in bamboo chairs around a small table. The garden was full of every kind of flower and tree. Butterflies fluttered low over the green lawn. While Seiya and Sudhana savored the most sumptuous food Sudhana had eaten since his journey began, Megha just watched, content to observe his daughter.

The room prepared for Sudhana that evening was on the upper floor of Seiya's private pavilion, on the far side of the garden's woodland grove. Although the outer door was simply woven reeds, the room itself was magnificent. The floors were covered with rugs from central Asia, and there was a stove set in the wall burning cow dung to offset the evening chill.

Late that night, Megha came to Sudhana's room. Sudhana, still awake, welcomed his host.

"Why are you not asleep yet, little pilgrim?"

"The evening is so beautiful," Sudhana said. "On such a night, even without sleep the body craves no rest, sir."

The old man was silent.

"Do you know this child who came with me?"

"Yes, I know her. She is my daughter. My dead daughter come alive again."

"Perhaps she returned because there is a task remaining for her in this world."

"Where did you find her?"

"Beside the underground lake."

"The underground lake?"

"That's right, sir."

"What land are you from? Why have you come here?"

"I came to meet you. I do not know where I was born."

"Really? Why did you want to meet me?"

"Because the venerable Supratishthita told me to."

"Supratishthita? Why, it's been so long since we met! I treated his hand when he hurt it once, many years ago. You, young pilgrim, are a good child. The truth stays in no place. Whoever journeys in quest of truth already has the truth. The truth is found in hearts like yours, little pilgrim, like flowing water, as they move on and on in quest of it. I have to teach now," Megha sighed, "but I hope we have a chance to talk more tomorrow."

Megha went back to his room on the other side of the wood. There was a full moon tonight and each full moon people would gather in the doctor's shrine for what was called "Megha's night watch."

Megha faced the assembled crowd and began to speak:

"Bodhisattva awakening means releasing all beings from their sufferings, becoming a fire to burn away avarice and self-love, becoming a cloud bringing rain, becoming a bridge so that all sentient beings and all living creatures can cross the river of life and death. Behold. I enter the sea that contains all these properties of bodhisattva awakening and lay down my name within the sea. I lay down all my words within the sea. What became of the diseases I have cured, once they have left the bodies they were tormenting? Where did they go? Behold. I lay down all diseases in the sea, too."

Megha's words rang out from beside the shrine's high altar, which was ablaze in the darkness with great candles. The unexpected arrival of his daughter and his visit with Sudhana had given the old man the urge to speak with all the passion and intensity of youth.

The next day, Megha asked Sudhana to stay at the hospital for a while. He offered to teach Sudhana his healing skills. Although the boy recognized that it was a supremely holy task to heal diseases and lead those thus cured towards truth, he knew he could not accept Megha's offer.

Megha shrugged, as if he already knew what Sudhana's answer was going to be. "If what I suggest is not agreeable to you," he said, "you should go southward, on a journey long enough for you to grow more. When you reach a place called Vanavasin down in the south, you will meet a great man by the name of Muktaka, who has completed all his tasks."

When Sudhana found Seiya and told her he was leaving, she cut his arm with a sharp knife. "I believe that in this world there is no body and no spirit that does not bear a wound," she said. "I want you to give me my wound."

She held out her arm to him and he cut it lightly. Bright red blood emerged and a few drops fell on the ground and mixed with the blood from Sudhana's wound.

"Sudhana, you can never settle anywhere." Her eyes seemed empty and dry and Sudhana was reminded of how lifeless she had appeared when he had first encountered her at the lake. "You will always be a pilgrim, I know. This wound is a sign of our parting."

Sudhana left Megha's hospice. As he set out from the city of Vajrapura, the monsoon season now over, he gazed southward to where the line between sky and earth stretched as clean as if he had drawn it himself. There was a long journey ahead. The cut on his arm reminded him of the sadness in leaving Seiya, but he had no regrets. Megha had said that Master Muktaka had attained a final freedom. For Sudhana, it was worth almost anything to see this.

9.

A SAD SONG

UDHANA PASSED THROUGH many provinces and king-doms. One night he stood in the moonlight outside the city of Ijan, sunk deep in melancholy. The rice rose thick in the outlying fields, ripe for harvest. Cold moonlight was pouring down and hosts of insects were chirping in the moonlight. Sudhana could hear a song in the wind. He had heard that song once before, sung by Laritha, an old blind woman he had met outside of the port of Sagaramukha on his journey to find Sagaramegha:

Moon, moon,
you know everything.
Tell me now:
Where is the love my heart is seeking?
I grow sick and old. Where is he?
Flowers, drenched in dew,
you know everything.
Tell me, for I am alone.

It was a sad song, almost sad enough to drive sorrow away. He felt that he could not stand hearing that song again this evening. The life of the old, blind singer at Sagaramukha was the saddest story Sudhana had ever heard in his life. Laritha was the only daughter of a poor farmer from the *sudra* caste. Her father had died of a snakebite when she was four years old and when, soon after, an official from the royal music department passed by in search of girls who could sing, she was sold to relieve her mother's poverty.

Laritha had gone to live as a slave in King Yuma's singers' compound. It was a desolate place, full of grief-stricken women with the saddest voices. One night, when the moon was full, the official told her, "Listen, my girl. This is your last moon, so look your fill at it!"

She had gazed up at the moon. She was at an age when human memory and knowledge are just beginning to awaken. She felt tears flow from her young eyes; then suddenly, someone grabbed her from behind. She could not move. An iron skewer, heated red in the fire, gouged out her two eyes. She screamed with pain, then fainted. When she came to her senses again, she was blind.

"Here you have to sing sad songs," the official had said. "If you are going to sing sad songs, ordinary sorrows will never be enough. Sorrow at a father's death, sorrow at losing a home are not enough. You need an overwhelming gulf of sorrow. Henceforth you will draw your sorrow from darkness and despair, the enduring bitterness of being blind. Now you can sing the saddest songs in all the land."

For the next two years, Laritha learned to sing under a constant rain of kicks and blows. When she was seven, she appeared before the king for the first time and sang for his birthday. It was the middle of the day when she sang, yet the sorrow in her childish voice was such that the daylight grew dim; even the animals in the palace came to hear her.

When she was fourteen, she was destined for the king's bed. For the seven nights preceding the full moon, she was forced to lie with the king. Afterwards, her body was mutilated with a sharp knife. Singing became her entire life. Fifty years of song went past, and she grew old. After King Yuma died, there was no one left to hear her sing. Laritha had found her way to the port of Sagaramukha, where she sang for coins and where she had come across Sudhana and told him her tale.

"In my singing, it has been my fate to be blessed," Laritha had said. "I am happy in my songs."

Laritha had become an artist and spoke as one. Hearing her sing, Sudhana was able to rid himself of all the illusions he had been harboring. It was as if dawn's azure darkness had come to lodge within his ears. Songs emerging out of deep sorrow can give rise to tremendous joy.

It seemed a long time had passed since he had stood on the shores of Sagaramukha and heard her song. Hearing it again in the moonlit night outside Ijan, he felt tears sting his eyes. Her songs had reached him in this distant land. Songs are quicker than the wind.

Sudhana awoke the next morning when the shadow of the sal tree moved away from his face. It was already midday. He set out for Ijan. Sound asleep, the guards at the city gates did not even realize that a stranger had entered the city. The officials were asleep, the people were asleep, even the priests were asleep. If ever a foreign army entered Ijan, they would probably fall asleep, too, felled by osmosis. It was a land full of sleep.

Sudhana walked on alone through streets full of silence. It was scorching midday. A solitary elephant was trundling down the middle of the main street. It walked along with an air of immense stupidity, appearing to know nothing at all, when in fact it knew everything. Sudhana, dripping with sweat, went running after it and pulled its tail. The ungainly beast wrapped Sudhana in its trunk and swept him up to the *howdah* on its back. Sudhana had no choice but to sit there and let the elephant carry him where it would.

"You must be bored, young pilgrim. I know I am." The elephant glanced round at him as it spoke.

Sudhana nodded. "I'm on my way to Vanavasin."

"That's still a long way away."

"I don't care. Nowhere is near or far for me. Wayfaring is my goal."

"Why are you going there?"

"You already know. You know where I came from. If you know that, you know everything."

The elephant gave a shrug. Sudhana nearly fell off.

"I'll take you there. I'm getting old. I've lived at least a hundred and sixty years in this world of pain. Once I've brought you there, I'll go into the forests of Vanavasin and quietly leave the world."

They traveled in silence for a little while, enjoying the journey and the way time and space flowed on around them, until the elephant remarked, "I rarely carry people. My grandfather was the king's elephant, but I've never even seen the king. That's why I'm wandering on my own through the world like this—though I did once carry a girl, called Iryon."

"Iryon? Did you say Iryon?"

"Why?"

"Where was it?"

"Up in the north, near the city of Rajagriha."

"Was she alone?"

"Yes. It was just after she had danced before the crown prince and he wanted her for his bride, but she ran away. The palace guards were after her. So I galloped off with her on my back, then I tossed her into the lake. A

crocodile carried her to the far shore on its back. I don't know what became of her after that."

"Iryon!"

"Is she a friend of yours?"

Sudhana felt homesick for the north, yet the elephant was carrying him even further south. When, if ever, would he see the rivers, the lakes, and

the kingdoms of the north again? Perhaps he might perish by some southern roadside. Would he ever see Iryon again? The sight of the haze shim-
mering on the horizon filled him with despair.

"You're sad," the elephant murmured.

"Do you, an elephant, know how to be sad? But of course, you have to
feel sad. There's no living in this world without sadness. Even Siddhartha's
compassion comes from sorrow."

"I saw him and his companions once, you know," the elephant said. "The
king and his court were all on their knees before them. There must have
been nearly two hundred disciples following Siddhartha."

"So where is he now?"

"He's like you; he never stays anywhere long. They're always on the
move; I don't know where they are now."

Sudhana enjoyed his conversations with the elephant. The huge animal
knew everything, yet deliberately kept the knowledge concealed and did
not boast. Through small fissures like a little stream, the elephant revealed
how much it knew.

They ambled along for quite a while, Sudhana growing sleepy with the
steadiness of the elephant's gait. The elephant began to sing him a lullaby:

> There was never a moment
> When I was not wildflowers in the field.
> There was never a moment when I was not water babbling.
> There was never a moment when I was not birds or beasts.
> There was never a moment when I was not a weary seagull
> forced to fly from island to island.
> There was never a moment when I was not a beggar.
> I am father, and stars, and the bright morning sun.
> I am a rainbow after rain.
> And like all these things
> There was never a moment when I was not an elephant.

Those were the lines the elephant sang as it plodded along toward
Vanavasin, as though its whole body was filled with thick black blood.

10.
A VERY LONG JOURNEY

T LAST THE FIRST of the cities of Vanavasin appeared on the far side of a river. They advanced upstream along the riverbank. Water buffalo were wallowing in the river to escape from the heat; people were swimming and playing. Sudhana longed to join them, but the elephant headed for the ferry, where a great log raft carried them across.

"Where does the venerable Muktaka live?" Sudhana called down to some children playing by the roadside. Their small fingers pointed the way. Sudhana looked at the children and did not recognize himself. He had come across high mountains and over deep rivers. He was still young, but his heart was deep and he had left behind his childish ways. He headed for Muktaka's house with a grave expression on his face. The house stood in a forest the size of a small country.

Sudhana wondered how long he had been traveling, for it seemed his journey down to Vanavasin in quest of Muktaka had really taken twelve years. It wasn't possible, and yet he felt sure it had taken him that long. The journey had been so full of vicissitudes along the way. The reason why he was making the journey had grown vague in his mind, rather like the way the eyesight of an old man weakens until he can no longer distinguish clearly the outlines of things. Surely, the journey had been that long.

"What am I doing here?" Sudhana wondered.

While he had been resting, the elephant that had been his companion for the last ten months had somehow disappeared. Sudhana did not remember him leaving and his absence left Sudhana despondent.

He arrived where the good master lived. He had to meet him, yet his hand could not open the closed door; his feet seemed stuck to the ground where he stood. At last, the door in front of him opened and a man appeared. The man placed his hand on Sudhana's shoulder and drew him inside. The room was a solemn space full of vast pillars. The air was cold. Sudhana shivered.

"You have been traveling a long while, huge aeons of time. Come and sit down."

"Are you the master?"

Muktaka's eyes laughed. The wrinkles surrounding them spread in a fine lacework. How could an old face be so like a flower? The whites of his eyes remained as clear as those of a child who had not been sullied by the dust of time or of life. His was the highest innocence, clear and calm, never once troubled by anger. Yet it seemed to Sudhana that if anything fell under the scrutiny of Muktaka's eyes, no secrets could stay hidden. His whole body was one vast mirror.

"You've come all this way, yet I've nothing at all to show you. Try looking at that blank wall," he suggested, shrugging toward the large wall behind him. "There are all kinds of pictures that can come out on a blank wall."

He had no sooner spoken than a woman's face loomed up on the wall. It was the old blind singer Laritha. Her pale jade-like blind eyes seemed to shine brighter here than when Sudhana had met her in person.

Mukata looked at the vision on the wall. "This mural represents the woman's songs that you treasure so much. But now you must get rid of all that. Never treasure a song for too long. Songs are real songs when they are sung once or twice, then forgotten."

Sudhana lowered his head.

"Look. Look at the blank wall again, young pilgrim."

Laritha's face vanished and the whole course of the ten directions of the universe appeared. Sudhana could see fragments of the journeys of Siddhartha with his disciples and of his innumerable past lives. Time passed. Once again the wall was bare.

"Young pilgrim. Many people strive to form attachments and possess things. Now is the time to set all that aside and travel onwards. I never leave this spot, yet here I can encounter all the Buddhas everywhere in the ten directions of the universe. Yet the Buddhas do not come and I do not go to them. Your coming here, too, is not a matter of your coming here. Neither have I gone to you. The Buddhas are murals, the bodhisattvas are murals, perhaps you and I are murals, too. All things are painted murals and dreams."

With these words, the melancholy occasioned by Sudhana's long journey melted away like Himalayan ice in a tributary of the Ganga. Sudhana took his leave and gazed out across Vanavasin. The landscape was utterly devoid of any person or sign of human labor. A single human figure would have destroyed its beauty. Muktaka gave Sudhana his next instructions—to search for Saradhvaja in the southern realm of Milaspharana—and Sudhana took off.

Once past the plains, the road entered the hills. Birds from further north flitted across the hills and Sudhana guessed that winter had come to the Himalayas. Sudhana recognized himself in the migrant birds, and gave them one last long glance, before following the hill path deeper into the forest.

Once past Mount Sadal, Sudhana cautiously set out on his journey through the marshes. It only took him three days to emerge at Milaspharana, although Muktaka had warned him it might take a month. Perhaps he was in the wrong place. Sudhana asked a passing pilgrim if this was the only place with such a name.

"You mindless numbskull! Another snake with ten heads, yes, that there may be; but there's only one Milaspharana!"

He roared out his reply. Sudhana enjoyed his roaring.

"Look, it's my destiny to live like this," the traveler said. "But how come a little fellow like you is out on the road? Where are you from?" Sudhana gestured towards the far north.

"Hmm. They say there's another weird fellow up north calling himself the Buddha. You northerners must be a wretched lot!"

"Have you ever been up there?" Sudhana asked.

"When could I ever go that far? Perhaps in my next life. But why have you come all the way down here from the other end of the world?"

"I don't know."

"You stupid vagabond, get out of here."

Despite such rough jokes, Sudhana liked this shabby pilgrim. He seemed deliberately to be masking a very noble mind. Sudhana ventured a wild guess.

"You aren't by any chance the venerable Saradhvaja, are you?"

"What? How do you know Saradhvaja?"

"Do you know the master Muktaka?" This time the pilgrim looked hard at Sudhana. Sudhana knelt before him.

The older pilgrim nodded. "Indeed. I am the Saradhvaja you are looking for. You've come to beg for truth. But I don't know any truth. I don't know women, or money, or fields, or orchards. There's no reason why I should know any truth. People looking for truth are all mindless dolts like you. Go on, get out of here!"

Sudhana gazed sadly after the old man as he hurried off. Why was he so unkind? Saradhvaja turned round and shouted. "Go and visit my wife. I've cast her off. She's full of truth!"

11.
LOVE IN THE MIST

SUDHANA GAZED after the retreating figure of old Sara-
dhvaja and then began to make his way up to Sarad-
hvaja's hillside lodge. Saradhvaja had been one of the
richest men in the land. No one could understand why
he had suddenly dressed up as a shabby pilgrim and
gone rushing away.

Sudhana was ushered into a guest room in an isolated woodland pavilion. He asked to meet Saradhvaja's wife but the servant instructed him to
wait until the next morning. The sea could be seen in the distance reflecting the shine of countless evening lamps. In the middle of the night, the
lamps vanished from view and the air grew suffocating, thick with a sea mist.

All night long an ox could be heard lowing a lament for the death of a
beloved cow. The sound made Sudhana feel sad. Nobody he knew had ever
died; the death of his father and mother and all the others had left no trace
in his memory. Yet this sadness seemed to suggest that someone close to
him had died. Iryon? Meghashri? Laritha? He shook his head. Sleep refused
to come, as if it had lost its way in the fog and could not find him.

At daybreak, Sudhana walked out into a mist that was no longer last
night's stifling blanket but now offered him the freshness he desperately
needed. The forest floor was strewn with white sand. The fog had infil-
trated its way between the trees, filling every space beneath them, and
was eddying thickly. He walked toward Saradhvaja's manor house, and
soon lost track of his route.

Sudhana became aware of a woman standing beneath one of the dead
trees. He composed himself. Perhaps this was a spirit, or a homeless phantom; unless ancient southern animals could transform themselves like this?
As he approached, the woman's figure became more distinct. Once he

could see her more clearly, he lost all power of decision. His mind was dependent, no longer his own, to the point that it had quite left him and now seemed to depend entirely on the woman.

"I am so fond of mist at dawn that I came out before you," she said. "In these parts I am known as Hehua, which means 'Sea Flower.' Follow me now, please."

She was dressed in a thin sari of an azure so delicate it seemed almost white. Her face and breast were golden in the mist. The rules Sudhana had been living by, reinforced by all of his travels, collapsed in a heap. He fell deeply in love.

Hehua was in her thirties. Her body emanated a fragrance of gardenias. They walked away from the ocean towards a grove of black sea pines that rose ahead of them like a cliff. There they found a stone-built cottage covered in ivy. Entering the cottage, Sudhana was startled to find it full of the most priceless treasures. It seemed remarkable that such things could be left there without anyone coming to carry them off.

He sat on a couch covered in silks from the west. It seemed remarkable that such things could be left there without anyone coming to carry them off. At his side was a glass of wine and a piece of dried bony fish. He drank, gnawed, and felt himself filled with tremendous strength. His empty stomach was completely filled.

Hehua let her sari drop to the ground and slid down beside him. A long-buried flame seemed to burst from his heart. As the sun rose beyond the sea and the mist was struggling to contain its light, Sudhana and Hehua fell into each other's arms. There, each of them experienced love for the first time.

Hands and breasts, valleys and hills, all came alive, moved, rose, grew thirsty. He wrenched her ecstasy from her and made it his. She drew his passion out of him to make it her own. Replete in the union of their bodies, the whole world was theirs.

Morning had fully arrived and on the bed sheets there were stains of fresh blood. Their bodies were crusted with salt. A chill still clung to the mist and the most perfect peace swept over them, as if to remind them of the similarity between peace and death. Sudhana had a fleeting impression that he could once again hear the ox lowing.

"You're the first person I ever made love with," Hehua smiled. "My husband never touched me. Shall I cover you up? Are you thirsty?" Sudhana shook his head.

Pale sunlight was weakly entering the cottage through a window. "I don't come from here, I was sold up in the north. My husband bought me to be his wife with thirty gold rings. He grew up in poverty but then became the richest man in Marikara. For most of his life, he could think of nothing but amassing money and land. That's why he never laid a finger on me even though I was his wife. Then, yesterday, he left home, leaving all of his riches. If something is to be done properly, that's how it has to be done, it seems. That's how you should make love." Sudhana lay silent.

"A few days ago my husband said that a visitor would soon be coming, sent by an old-time friend of his. He asked that I greet this visitor warmly."

Sudhana now understood what had happened. With this understanding, sleep overtook him. The woman also fell into a deep slumber. At noontide, the mist vanished like a reptile sliding into its hole. The deep blue sea lay quiet.

In their sleep, Sudhana and Hehua clasped each other's hands and dreamed the same dream. The woman was leading Sudhana here and there through the estate, in which there were many villas. There were also shrines consecrated to the king of the heavenly musicians. Plants from north and south filled the flowerbeds. Hehua taught Sudhana their names one by one as they walked, hand in hand. Just as they were crossing a stream at the far end of the estate, Hehua slipped and fell in. The water was deep but Sudhana leaped in after her. They both sank. As they sank, they each gave a piercing scream and woke up. They embraced.

"Ah! It was a dream, wasn't it?" Hehua said.

"You dreamt it as well, about falling into the water?"

She nodded. They rose and gazed out at the sea. On the dining table outside the house, servants had already prepared a meal. They sat down together.

"I don't suppose you've ever met Siddhartha?" Hehua asked.

"No, never."

"I have never seen him either. And yet..."

She asked nothing more about Siddhartha. Perhaps she had decided to wait until Sudhana said something more about him. Hehua was amazed by her overflowing love for Sudhana. Her love was such that she might have hurt him, simply to be able to treat the wound.

From that day, Hehua threw open the ponderous gates at the entrance to the estate, went to the great central house and, having summoned all the poor, began to distribute to each the riches and lands accumulated by Saradhvaja. Heavenly divinities and spirits came down wrapped in clouds and took part in the distribution.

"It's what my husband wanted. He used to say that riches were like the rise and fall of the tide. He reckoned that once they had been accumulated they had necessarily to be dispersed again."

She laughed as she spoke. Hehua was attached to no treasure apart from Sudhana and had decided to join him in his travels. After giving away all of her husband's goods, she gave away the entire estate to the servants who had worked there. Sudhana was deeply impressed by the dramatic way she rid herself of everything. They were oblivious of everything except their love and hastily set out on a pilgrimage through the southern kingdoms.

12.
THE SLEEP I PRODUCE

S UDHANA AND HEHUA LEFT, walking along the shore to avoid the curious stares of the townspeople, and set off towards the forests in the land of Samudravetadin.

"At last I've got rid of everything!" she shouted.

"No," he replied. "You've not rid yourself of me!" His heart raced at the way this woman had come bursting into his life. He believed he had shaken off all of love's constraints, yet he had not considered preventing her from coming with him.

The shore was at first composed of sand but soon they found the way blocked by white cliffs and the path became rugged. They walked on, until they arrived at the top of a steep slope.

"If I should die," Hehua said calmly, "I want you to throw my body into the sea to feed the fishes. I want to share my flesh with the fish."

Sudhana was disturbed by her words, but he nodded. She no longer seemed the same woman he had met in the garden a few days before. She seemed inhabited by a vague renunciation. In spite of her boldness in setting out with him, she was casting a shadow over the blue sea.

"Why do you keep heading south, ever further southward, when Siddhartha is in the north?" she asked.

"Truth is not only found with the man who speaks truth, it can be found in every place. I have been following this path since I was a small child. South or north mean nothing to me."

She did not reply, instead she joined her hands and bowed towards the ocean. As Sudhana was leading the way up the rugged slope, Hehua stepped on a piece of weathered rock in the cliff face and slipped. Her hand escaped from Sudhana's grasp. In one breath, she fell into the sea far below at the

foot of the cliff. By the time Sudhana reached the edge of the cliff, he could see nothing but the thrashing waves.

Sudhana screamed. He paced back and forth, unwilling to believe that she was gone. A strong gust of wind lifted Sudhana upwards and tossed him onto a rock.

His elbow was bleeding and the bones in his shoulders were throbbing, but Hehua's words pierced through the pain. "All things are the same. All things are transitory. My love has attained the sea."

He wept and banged his fists against the rocks. In the distance, dry lightning flashed across the parched sky and vanished. The far-off sound of thunder reached him. He stayed rooted to his spot on the rock.

He beat at his body with a small stone as he cried. He struck hard and soon his breast, shoulders, and legs were covered with deep wounds. Blood streamed down. Exhausted, he sat facing the sea and prayed for her soul's happiness, then fell asleep.

He awoke disoriented. His wounds had been anointed with ointment. He tried to raise himself, but his body was in too much pain and refused to move. He looked around. He was in a sumptuous room with walls covered in jade-beaded blinds. Perfume filled the air.

"Ah, you're awake!" A girl appeared before him. "One of our servants brought you in. Your wounds were so deep and you'd lost so much blood that you were unconscious. There are lots of wild animals out there...you've been lucky."

"Who are you?"

"Hehua's friend Asha."

"How did I get here?"

"The tide brought Hehua's clothes to shore just below our house. Hehua outlived her appointed span of life by nine days and nights, only because of her fierce desire to encounter your truth and love. Wandering seeker after truth, you can stop your grieving now and drink this water."

Asha offered him a draught of pure water from the slopes of an extinct volcano. Drinking the water, Sudhana accepted that Hehua was really dead and he was still alive.

"You've traveled many, many miles in search of the truth. The things I can teach you are like a grain of sand set beside a mighty mountain. All I can offer you is one draught of water."

Sudhana shook his head. "You're already far too gracious," he said.

She bowed her head in acknowledgment. "Since you were destined to visit this place, rest here and take your fill of truth."

Her voice rang like the strings of a harp. She had ceased to speak and her words emerged now as song.

"Little pilgrim, if Hehua was only a dream, the truth you seek is also a dream..."

Sudhana fell into a deep sleep. In his sleep, he saw sea swallows flying through a pure bright sky. Asha lay her gold necklace on his sleeping breast and quietly stroked it with her delicate hand.

By the time Sudhana awoke, the sun had set behind the mountain peaks and the approaching evening darkness was bright with the glow of sunset. His sleep had been full of blossoming flowers and fledgling birds. It seemed to him an old fisherman's dream of a long-ago childhood. Asha woke him.

"Come," she said. "You can keep sleeping, but come sleep next to me so our souls can meet at a deeper level."

She led him down a long gallery, maids curtseying as they passed, until they reached her room. It was adorned with every kind of precious ornament.

"All these jewels come from every kind of mountain, sea, or rock; but they are wretched things, only useful for gaining truth. You, little pilgrim, are more precious than all of them."

They lay down together on her bed, but there was none of the lovemaking there had been with Hehua. They simply lay next to each other like a young mother with her firstborn child or like two people who've been walking side by side along the same road for a long time, knowing nothing of each other's name or home.

They had nothing to say to one another. Instead, they found the meaning that exists before and behind words. They slept and that meaning matured in their sleep like wine. In the far distance, volcanoes rumbled and produced pure water.

13.
TWELVE YEARS OF DREAMS

UDHANA AWOKE to find himself being tilted off an elephant's vast back and deposited roughly on the ground. "Ouch!" He rubbed his aching behind.

Thoroughly bewildered, Sudhana looked up. It was the elephant who had left him at the riverbank. Where had it come from? How had this happened?

"Where are we?"

"We have just passed Samudravetadin, a city wrapped in the sound of waves. You have been sleeping the long sleep such waves inspire."

"But what about Asha? Hehua? Saradhvaja?"

"Little pilgrim! You are still only a little pilgrim. Those twelve years were a dream I gave you. Since the moment you fell asleep outside of Vanavasin, you have been unable to distinguish between dream and reality. That first taste of passion for a woman was really only part of your dream."

At the elephant's words, the years Sudhana had spent in his dream fell away like branches from a tree struck by lightning.

"Now you and I must part," the elephant said kindly. "First I carried young Iryon, and now I've carried you; I will never again bear anyone on my back. Farewell. There is to be no end to your travels, young pilgrim."

Dumbfounded, Sudhana gazed after the elephant as it ambled away into the coconut groves without so much as a backward glance.

"But did my dream last twelve years then?" Sudhana called after him. Sudhana looked down at his body. He had not grown. There was no sign of his having become a young man able to make love with women. Days may have passed since Vanavasin, but not years. His arrival in Vanavasin, and his encounters with Saradhvaja, Hehua, and Asha had all taken place in a dream on the elephant's back.

Did that mean that all the distance between Vanavasin and Samudrave-tadin was a world that existed only in his dreams? He gazed at the reality surrounding him. He saw the capital city of the kingdom of Samudrave-tadin bathed in the dazzling rays of the setting sun. He thought of turning around and entering the city but the elephant had given him no instruc-tions.

"I ought not to turn back towards the past. My road always lies ahead of me."

He got up. He was starving but had nothing to eat in his bundle. He began to walk. After riding for so long on the elephant's back, his legs were shaky, but soon he was able to walk without effort. The old blind woman's song from his dream came to his mind. He tried to imitate it, but a song as intensely sad as that was beyond his capability.

Just as he took the road through the forest, striving to resist the pangs of hunger, he encountered a band of traveling peddlers.

One of them, a middle-aged man, handed Sudhana a piece of coconut. "You're starving!" He spoke with fatherly concern. "Where are you going that demands such sacrifices?"

Sudhana found himself quite unable to reply. So far, every person he had met had told him of another person he should meet, giving him the next goal on his journey. But the elephant had left him without any instructions.

"We're on our way to visit the seer Bhishmottaranir-ghosha," the ped-dler continued. "They say he's already lived several hundred years and only eats the roots of dead grass he digs up. We always offer him a share of what-ever profits we make. He'll use the money to bring up our grandchildren after we die. Come along with us and meet him."

Sudhana was happy to have a goal again. His steps became light and cheery. No longer hungry, no longer alone, he was finally sure that all this was real and his dream of Asha and Hehua faded away.

The forest was deep and the darkness of night had already filled the path-ways. Once they were through the forest full of cedars, jambu trees with their sweet fruit, flowering ulpara and patma trees, the darkness along the road grew bright with starlight. Suddenly, they heard sounds of life. The noise grew louder and louder. They could see lamps and candles shining out over a wide open space and a large crowd had gathered around.

A moment later, the sage himself appeared, dressed completely in bark, and sat on a pallet of dried grass spread under a flowering tree. The crowd bowed down before him.

The peddler stepped forward. "Master, I have brought this young way-farer with me. I beg you to strew noble aims on his life and mine."

The peddler drew out a coin.

The sage immediately handed it to a nearby disciple and gazed at Sud-hana. "You have certainly been on a long journey. And what a long dream you had as well. What do you think, have you found all the truth you were looking for?"

Sudhana could only stare at this man who knew not only his journeys but his dreams as well.

Other seers came and joined the sage. Bhishmottaranir-ghosha addressed the others. "Look at this child. He was weary but has now received new light. He will give more light than any candle or star, for he is intent on gaining yet brighter wisdom."

The sage sank into meditation for a while, then spoke again.

"Young pilgrim. Make your heart into sand, grind and grind the granite of your heart, pound the granite peaks of Mount Mara-deva that rises high by the shores to the south into sand to stifle the waves that break on the southern shores. Then break each one of those grains of sand and empty your heart completely. Fill the empty space of your heart with a voice that will cover every length of time, a single night, a single day, a century, a thousand years, ten thousand, the vast immensities of a hundred million aeons. For as you know, the voice is the origin of everything. Young pilgrim. As I am here but not there, you too are not really here. Holy indeed, young pil-grim. You have made this night holy for me by this meeting with you."

The merchants left. The candles went out. Sudhana spent that night with the seer on his huge bed of dry grass in the open air. The seer slept soundly yet Sudhana learned many things thanks to him. His smile was like the arrival of wonderful news. His sleep was like a humble guest from a dis-tant place.

Starlight flooded their sleep. Sudhana welcomed the dew that dropped along the beams of starlight. Soon, his whole body was soaked in azure. The starlight existed alone; the star itself had died many thousands of years before. Sudhana thought of how many incarnations he must have lived through during the long journey of the light to earth! And how many more awaited him!

The next morning the seer and Sudhana drank a little water from a warm spring and shared a meal of roots. The seer spoke as he chewed. "Little pil-grim, how did you enjoy your dewy sleep? We spent one whole night together! Now you must go southward to meet the brahman Jayoshmaya-tana in the land of Ishana. He's my half-brother by my mother's ninth hus-band. In his enthusiasm, he keeps hurling himself onto the rocks of Sword Mountain, then into the Valley of Fire. There's no dewy sleep for him!"

With a bag full of roots to eat, Sudhana took his leave of the ulpara flow-ers and the sweet scent of the forest. At a swampy point along the road, Sudhana hesitated, unsure of where to go next. He looked up to gauge where the sun was setting and saw a hawk making circles in the sky.

"Oh! Friend hawk! It's been so long!" Sudhana cried, recognizing his friend from its one white wing. "How is it that you did not forget me and flew so far?"

The hawk swooped and flapped its wings before setting off toward the South. The road soon stretched clearly before him. Had the hawk willed the road to appear before his waiting feet?

14.
THE VALLEY OF FIRE

SUDHANA NOW ENTERED a scorching land. His brow was soon burned by the sun and it ached and throbbed. Born on a riverbank far in the north, this was the young pilgrim's first experience of equatorial high noon.

Sword Mountain rose sharply out of the Valley of Fire, slashing the strong gales that struck it from all sides. The mountain was surrounded by volcanic fire.

Defying the heat cooking him like a pig in a cauldron, Sudhana passed between the flames and began his ascent of Sword Mountain. He walked over a path embedded with razor-sharp blades of basalt, his feet were cut to ribbons.

He stopped. A solitary ascetic was frantically tearing up the ground and trampling on the rocks, his whole body bathed in blood. That man was more terrifying than either mountain or valley. It could only be Jayoshmayatana. Sudhana's own feet bled freely, yet they did not hurt. He was astonished to find that the wounds inflicted by this mountain, which the city people never dared to approach, were quite insignificant. The eyes of the old brahman monk blazed. His whole body seemed bathed in flames.

"Master monk, your whole body is covered with blood! Come away, it's too hot here," Sudhana called. "I am called Sudhana, a pilgrim who has come far to visit you."

Jayoshmayatana briefly stopped making his jerky movements. "Don't be afraid to climb the mountain like me, don't be afraid to hurl yourself into the Valley of Fire. I've repeated these gestures more than a hundred thousand times now, and I am encountering truth."

At that, Sudhana stepped back a pace. In the priest's gaze a terrifying spirit seemed to be lurking. Among all the people he had visited, this was the first one he doubted and could not simply believe. Perhaps he was more demon than brahman?

But as Sudhana was considering the man to be an incarnation of evil, a ball of flame erupted from the Valley of Fire. From below, Sudhana had a vision of the fireball as the Brahma gods from the Ten Heavens, speaking directly to him:

"There has been nothing to scold until now, yet today I scold your heart. Child, look at this man. Listen to what he says. This man's blood gives birth to wisdom, not evil. This man's fire enlightens the homes and ways of every nation. This man has drawn fire in the Valley of Fire and he has become fire. He is a holy man, so throw away your empty thoughts and hurl yourself into the Valley of Fire. Child, after a night there, your darkness and every darkness will vanish."

Sudhana cast one glance down at the vast plain of Ishana, stretching away in an endless panorama of splendor. He saw the dead souls of all sentient beings gathering above and flocking towards him in solemn assembly. With one last resolute breath, he closed his eyes and threw himself forward, thinking only, "Burn me. Burn me up entirely." When he came to himself again, five kinds of light were emanating from his body. As the light fell on the rocky sword-points nearby, it transformed them into dazzling sculptures of fire. Astonished, Sudhana looked at the old man. The brahman's crimson eyes and body had been purified.

"Thanks to you," the brahman said, "my eyes of crimson fire, my body of crimson fire and blood have at last found sleep. I could never have attained this purified body without you. Many, many thanks indeed."

"Master, as I entered the flames, my body was filled with intense wellbeing!" Sudhana spoke in awe. Sacred bliss flowed from his penance. He no longer feared sword or fire. He knew that swords, fire, and evil spirits, too, were all love. All evil was Buddha. All fear was compassion.

He staggered away from Sword Mountain, then gazed back at it from below. The rugged mountain, with its sharp rocky spurs, was being consumed by the flames. As it burned, it began to crumble and collapse.

"Go and visit the maiden known as Maitrayani. Take the northwestern road. Henceforth my work is done." The old brahman priest called after Sudhana with these final words, before hurling himself into the midst of the burning mountain.

At the bottom of Sword Mountain, Sudhana found all the inhabitants of the nearby village gathering to contemplate its dramatic end.

An old man, weeping, spoke through his tears. "Jayoshmayatana has completed his acts of penance. He has made reparations for the adulteries of his father, the sins of his half-brothers in fighting and killing one another, the appetites of the people in his home village, and the wickedness of the nation's evil statesmen!"

Sudhana bowed his head.

Once again, Sudhana was obliged to set out on his journey. Over the first hills, the road lay like a white sash stretching to the horizon across endless grassy plains unlike any he had hitherto seen. Then it touched the sky, where a great mass of clouds towered at the horizon.

It was already night when he crossed the plains of Simhavijurmbhita and reached the city. It was a nation where everyone slept through the heat of the day and rose in the evening to do all of life's business through the night. The deep night was full of a busy hubbub and thick with fog. People made a lot of noise but they could not see one another plainly. Everything they did was like writing partially erased. Where the fog took away their sight, they compensated by developing keen senses of smell and hearing.

"I smell a stranger." Several people near Sudhana murmured. They spoke in Tamil, a language that Sudhana had not realized he knew until that moment.

"You're right," Sudhana spoke up. "I am a pilgrim from afar and going yet farther. Can anyone tell me how to reach Maitrayani?"

A voice came out of the fog. "If you would be so good as to follow those girls in front of you, you will find her."

Sudhana hurried forward, the lamplight wavering in the fog. The four girls walked with downcast eyes. Their hair hung in long tresses down their backs.

Sudhana was happy. Even in the fog, the girls' beauty was dazzling. When the five of them reached Maitrayani's home, the garden was already crowded with girls arriving from all directions. Sudhana's heart began to beat quickly.

15.

MAITRAYANI DANCES

NE OF THE GIRLS led Sudhana to Maitrayani's room and explained: "Tonight Maitrayani is going to dance for the repose of the souls of the dead, drawing dead and living into unity. After the dead spirits are all asleep, she will dance to calm the souls of the living. Dancing is the most sacred task a soul can perform. I hope you will watch Maitrayani dance."

Maitrayani stood motionless in her room, a faint smile on her face. She seemed to be hoarding every last movement before her dance. She was fifteen years old, yet she seemed ageless. Her lips alone moved as she spoke: "I once heard a report that a little boy in the north had set out on an unending quest for truth. You are most welcome here, little pilgrim."

"Mistress Maitrayani, my name is Sudhana. The brahman Jayoshmayatana sent me to you."

"Is the brahman well?"

"He is in heaven now."

"Ah, so he's gone. His task must have been completed. I still have many things left to do. As do you."

Just then a serving girl parted the beaded curtain and made a small sign with her hands. A faint shadow passed over Maitrayani's brow. She rose. Sudhana followed her out into the garden, where the mist was thick. Here and there great lamps glimmered. A crowd of young women gathered around the raised stage. Two elderly women, musicians of great skill with harp and horn, sat with their eyes closed. Sudhana looked around him. The only men present were himself and an old blind gardener.

Maitrayani threw a cloak of feathers over herself and stepped briskly onto the stage. Utterly composed, she began a low invocation, welcoming the spirits. The guiding spirit of the dance entered her body, recited the names of the souls of the dead, and then began to create a dance in the darkness within her.

Maitrayani's fingertips began to tremble. The tremor ran up her long arms and slender neck to her very hair. The sleeping harp and horn awoke, their first notes invoking a cool breeze. Their song rose louder and louder, a needle-tipped pain between the notes. Their playing followed the rhythm of Maitrayani's dance: the first part devout, the second more spectacular, and the third part attaining such a frenzied peak that the dancer no longer seemed human. Maitrayani had just reached this point, when the groans of dead spirits could be heard breaking through the silence of the young women gathered in the courtyard. Their groans pursued the melody of the accompanying harp and horn up the scale, mercilessly shaking both the instruments and the old women playing them.

As the fourth part of the dance began, the dance of the underworld, the spirits grew calm and the instruments, players, and spectators regained their previous serenity.

As the dance ended, a water lily bloomed on the back of Maitrayani's hand. The hand waved once violently in the air, then froze. Sweat broke out on the spectators' faces like many drops of rain. Their faces were pale with relief, aware that the dancer had just passed a dangerous turning point between life and death. Maitrayani's youth had ensured her survival, yet every scrap of her energy was gone. As the spirit left, all the young girls worshiped, bowing their heads to the ground. Maitrayani allowed herself a tired smile.

It was already past midnight. Maitrayani drank a glass of juice made of roots from the region of Poona soaked in fresh pine leaves. Sudhana could see the eerie indigo fluid passing down Maitrayani's throat, her flesh almost transparent. Each spectator was then offered a glass of the same liquid.

The mist had thinned and the lamplight seemed brighter as Maitrayani began the final dance, a dance for the salvation of those still alive. The dance was a single movement, the calming of a fierce wind that has blown over vast plains. Her robe flew off and Maitrayani's naked body, devoid of any shame, moved with a pure effortlessness. Watching her, it seemed as if all living people and beasts could regain their original unspoiled nature and enter a state of utter ecstasy.

Maitrayani's dance reached its climax and melted all the sorrows of Sudhana's heart, like thin, high clouds in the northern, autumn air. Maitrayani's voluptuous dance came to an end just as the first pale fingers of early dawn were lighting up the sky behind the grove of yura trees.

The girls parted, each one treasuring a great store of emotions in her breast. The lanterns they had carried on arriving were extinguished. Maitrayani's attendant approached Sudhana. "Young lord, you are to remain here. Maitrayani wants you to stay."

The attendant cast one last longing look at Sudhana and then left with the others, brushing through the leaves of the yura trees. Sudhana found a serving woman standing beside him.

"Maitrayani is waiting for you."

They passed the terrace and entered a corridor inside the house. He found Maitrayani in a simple room that contained only a bed of precious wood. "I'd like you to rest here for today. If you care to wash, there is a spring at the end of the corridor."

Sudhana realized that day had dawned and he still had not slept. She brought a cup of cold water for him to drink, a bowl of cold water, and a hemp towel.

She lifted him up and removed his clothes as if he were her son, then moistened the towel and carefully wiped his body with it. She was perfectly at ease and did not hesitate.

"Now rest. When evening comes and you wake up, come visit. My room is just opposite. Rest."

Sudhana soon fell asleep. When he woke, evening had come. He knocked on Maitrayani's door. Despite having danced all night, it seemed she'd been up for some time. There was nothing left of sleep in Maitrayani's room.

She smiled at Sudhana. "Let's go out into the back garden."

He followed her out across wide lawns shrouded in mist. Although Maitrayani seemed only a few months older than Sudhana, her happiness was that of someone who had seen and lived much more. It became contagious. Passing beyond the lawns, Maitrayani entered a grove of palms and yura trees standing on a rise. A small shrine, adorned with exquisite metalwork, stood solemnly in the middle of the grove.

"This is the shrine of Vairochana," she said. "In each of its glass pillars, its diamond walls, its golden bells, you will find the Buddha's practice reflected as water reflects the moon."

Then she continued, "I have encountered innumerable Buddhas in our Tamil lands, so I prepared this shrine. Each of them has brought me through a different gateway to the threshold of truth."

Her eyes flashed and Sudhana knew that it was time for him to move on.

Maitrayani cut off a lock of her hair and gave it to him. When he tried to refuse it, she pushed it into his bundle. "Farewell, then. No one can take hold of running water. It's time for you to visit the monk Sudarshana in the land of Trinayana. Farewell. The most sorrowful greeting in Tamil is the word we use for leave-taking. For it is hard to meet again."

16.
EYES LIKE A LOTUS

NCE AGAIN, Sudhana was on the road. Trinayana lay in a wilderness on the far side of a desert. It promised to be a very long journey and the intense heat made Sudhana wish he could dream away the passage of another twelve years.

But the desert was utterly real. Its horizon stretched on endlessly with only isolated clumps of coarse grass, basalt pebbles that hurt his feet, and the bones of dead cows to break up the monotony of the desolate plain. Worse still, not one of those lifeless things would speak to him. There were no voluble trees or philosophical elephants. The desert stretched on and on like a vast river.

Once he had passed beyond it, he found himself in a wilderness. He was as weary as he had ever been. But there was no succor for him in that wilderness. Apart from prickly cactus and bundles of weeds, it held nothing but brown rocks that looked like rusty gravel and barren earth. It was the harshest and most desolate wasteland in the whole of nature.

His flesh seemed to be melting away like the moon vanishing in clouds. Despair led him to rush wildly after mirages and go sprawling onto rocks. He knew nothing beyond the ruins of nature now and so when he saw the flourishing city at the edge of the wilderness, he forced his eyes wide open, sure it was a mirage. Only when he was sure that the city was not just his desperate imaginings did he allow himself to collapse at its edge, where he was found by a man foraging for dried bones.

The man carried Sudhana on a stretcher to the doctor at the region's hospice for travelers.

The doctor immediately took Sudhana under his care.

"It's terrible, and so young, too. Coming across the wilderness like that! This child is not human, he can't be human!"

The words woke up the little pilgrim.

"Ah! This is the land of Trinayana. Where have you come from, all that way across the wilderness?"

"I'm a pilgrim. Do you know the monk Sudarshana?"

"There is no reason why I should. Anyway, if you don't know where he is, perhaps he doesn't want to be found."

The doctor told him Sudarshana's story. Trinayana was extremely poor because of the greediness of a king who squeezed his people like so much laundry, robbing them of their harvests as well as any profit they might make, squandering everything on women. Years before, Sudarshana had tried to lead a revolt against the king and failed. He'd fled deep into the mountain. The king was quite insane and soon forgot Sudarshana, who had become a hermit living deep in the hills. A traveling monk had shared the Buddha's teachings with the hermit, who had gone on to teach himself. "Nobody knows him anymore," the doctor concluded. "And nobody knows where he is."

Sudhana received treatment at the hospice for three days. On leaving, he went roaming in search of the monk, but no one seemed to have heard of him. Finally, when stopping in to a tavern to beg for something to eat, he heard the old woman at the counter say, "We ought to sell this wretched child to Sudarshana." He immediately questioned the old woman, who pointed him in the direction of the Pathless Mountain and he set out hastily. But once he came near, he was unable to discover which direction to go.

After crossing and crisscrossing several ridges, Sudhana finally found a small hermitage, built of tree trunks and sheltered from the wind in a hollow beside the road. He hurried towards it and tripped, falling and hurting himself as he went.

There, the aging Sudarshana was staring at him in utter amazement. He was nothing more than a farmer out harvesting rice, digging up potatoes, weeding the fields. There was nothing visibly monkish about him. Yet his eyes were translucent as lotus flowers. His only distinguishing features were the three moles on his breast that could be seen when he stripped off his upper garments to work.

"Where have you come from?"

"I've come looking for the monk called Sudarshana."

"Are you on your own?"

"Yes."

"Who told you where to find me?"

"Some old woman in a tavern . . ."

"Confound the old bitch!"

Sudhana was disappointed. Was this foul-mouthed yokel really Sudar-shana?

"Go over there, cut that rice and set it to dry. Then you'll get something to eat. The rice is ready to harvest."

He spoke roughly. Sudhana longed to turn around, but he had nowhere to go and would never be able to find his way back. He took up a long scythe and began to cut the rice. As he was cutting, he slashed his hand.

"What the hell are you doing! Give it here!" Sudarshana snatched the scythe away from him and began to cut the rice, great handfuls at a time. When old Sudarshana had cut all he felt like cutting, he took Sudhana to the hermitage and they shared a meal of cold rice. Just as they were eating the coarse fare, a fox came trotting up.

"You bloody useless son of a fox!" Sudarshana yelled. "Why didn't you tell me this kid was on his way? Get out of here! Be off!" The fox slipped away.

Sudhana spent the night on the floor. The next day, he was surprised to find that old Sudarshana, who had been so violent, had withdrawn into almost total silence, as if he had been struck dumb. The mountain high-lands were quiet. Sudhana neither saw nor heard any other person all day long. Perhaps they were the only two people who had ever passed that way. The hillsides rang constantly with the songs of birds and the calls of wild animals. Sun and moon set early. The nights were long.

"Sudhana! Aren't you bored?" It was the morning of the third day and the first kind words that Sudarshana had spoken.

That kindness was sufficient to send Sudhana rushing into his arms in a flood of tears. The monk gently caressed Sudhana's back.

"Don't you want to go back to Maitrayani?" the hermit asked.

"No. I can never go back to a place I've already been."

"She's my daughter, you know."

"What?"

"That child went walking off across the deadly wilderness and I never saw her again. She's a terror, to be sure! I reckon she sent you here because she misses her dad."

How could Sudhana have guessed! He saw no resemblance to Maitra-yani in the old farmer's weathered face. Still, if it was true, he was glad. He could serve as a bridge for the affection that must have remained in the hearts of father and daughter, though both had renounced the world.

"Sudhana, we are deep in the hills up here. You may have come looking for me but I've got nothing I can teach you in just a day or two. I'm an old monk, a monk who spends all his time farming. If you farm, nothing happens in a day or two. You have to spend a year, ten years, even. It's already fifteen years I've been separated from that daughter of mine. All that while I've sown and worked the fields here alone. If I know any truth, it's only that."

Sudhana resolved to pause and stay with the farmer that Sudarshana had become. There might be a fresh, new kind of truth in a cabbage or a turnip. This lonely farmer deep in the hills working without rest inspired him and Sudhana began to put down deep roots, unwilling to leave.

17.
JOURNEY TO SHRAMANAMANDALA

HEY SPENT THE DAYS working in the fields. As they worked, old Sudarshana would tell stories. "Back when I was in exile, banished by the king of Trinayana, I made a journey to the kingdom of Shramanamandala. It's the region that produces most of south India's rice. Everywhere I looked, I could see vast fields. Yet, in all those fields, there was not a soul to be seen. The paddy fields divided themselves up of their own accord and produced a crop in the selected area. In the several months I spent there, I never once saw anyone even come close. There was no way of knowing who ploughs the ground, or who sows the seed, who does the weeding, who drives away the birds that flock there, or who harvests the crop."

"Because you never happened to see them, I suppose?" Sudhana butted in.

Sudarshana blinked sadly and shook his head. "No. I was always expecting somebody to appear. Sometimes I lost my temper and shouted out over the fields, 'Who is doing this? How is it possible for rice to be harvested without one single person visible anywhere?'"

They stopped talking for a moment. It was as if old Sudarshana had been tossed back into the empty plains of the kingdom of Shramanamandala, as his face grew tense with anguish. The moon rose. It was already late evening. The child and the old man were both struck with a feeling that they were the only two people alive that night.

"You don't have to respond to what I'm telling you. I know how unlikely it sounds. I came to realize that the cultivation of those wide-stretching fields in the kingdom of Shramanamandala was not being done by human hands. Nature was doing it all by herself. It seemed alright for people to forget for a long while about land they had cleared and cultivated. All they had to do was receive a full crop of rice and wheat and beans. The farmers didn't mind if somebody else sowed seed on their land.

"The point is, there are lots of fields all over the world, but what the farmers had learned was that there is nowhere in this world that can be considered 'mine.'" Sudarshana sighed. "If I was hunted by the king and ended up living here in these mountains, it was because in the course of my journey I learned something from those farmers who never let anyone see them."

"But do you really mean to say that you never once saw a farmer in those fields in the kingdom of Shramanamandala?" Sudhana persisted.

"Why do you keep asking me questions? I've done everything I could to keep you from doubting. Why are you asking that?"

Then the old man added quietly: "Actually, I did see someone, once, although they were not working. It was dawn. We old people wake up early. You'll wake up at dawn, too, when you're old. I had resolved to leave that place. Outside my window, a bulbul bird was singing. Wanting to see the bird, I went outside. The sky was just becoming light. There I saw an old man walking along, with the plain stretching endlessly behind him as far as the horizon. That farmer was walking along freely, walking for the mere sake of walking, free as eternity itself.

"He looked like someone who had spent the night out in the fields and was now on his way back to his wife at home. Only I could tell that he no longer had a wife, or children, no longer had the house that had been their joy. That farmer, the only person I ever saw on those dawning fields of grain, canceled out the emptiness that had filled the plains before his arrival."

"I wanted to rush towards the farmer," Sudarshana continued. "But my feet seemed fixed to the ground. So I called out a loud greeting. It was just as the sun was about to rise, the moment when the whole eastern part of the sky begins to take on tints of sunlight. The farmer simply went on walking. He seemed to be walking for some reason and at the same time for no reason. I felt that the distance between us was growing. Perhaps this farmer wasn't a human being at all. Perhaps he was just a phantasm I created to fill the emptiness. For with the rising of the sun, the light had became dazzling and I could see nothing. The farmer disappeared.

"I suppose that farmer was a product of my thoughts," Sudarshana finished his tale. "I had spent so long hoping for someone to appear, I can quite believe that I created that farmer on my last day. At that moment the idea

came to me of returning home to Trinayana. I came up into these mountains. I'm living here in imitation of that phantom farmer."

Sudhana was quiet for a while, absorbing the story. "Did you ever meet
Siddhartha?" he asked.

"Never, although in my heart I am always meeting him. It's like the love
that keeps a parent watching over a child when the other parent is gone.
It's not only Siddhartha, I meet all the other enlightened beings too."

After all of the plowing and the talking, Sudarshana's truth finally
reached Sudhana. After sowing the seed, Sudhana stayed in the hills until
the sun had ripened the harvest during the short dry season. It was time for
the rains to come again. Through daily farming, Sudhana had learned that
everyone possesses the laws of the universe within them. Between any such
person and the universe there will always be the simple words, "Come and
play with me," and the pure meeting of child with child.

It was time for Sudhana to go. The rain poured straight down, untouched
by any wind. "Sudhana, my child. How hard your hands and feet have
grown," Sudarshana said as he looked at Sudhana's callused palms. "If you
work in the fields, your hands and feet will grow hard but your heart will
stay soft. I still distinguish between body and heart; it's the only thing I can
do. Go to the land of Shramanamandala where I used to live. There's a
child named Indriyeshvara there who once looked after me when I was sick.
You and he are the same age, so you'll be able to grow more childlike and
play children's games together."

"He lives by a river, doesn't he?" Sudhana asked. "It just came into my
mind."

Sudarshana laughed. He took some of the fruit he had stored up for
emergencies and put it in Sudhana's bundle. The little pilgrim took his
leave of the mountain farm he had grown so fond of. A cluster of snakes
went with him to the foot of the mountain to see him off. Once he had
left the mountain, they went squirming back.

Sudhana returned to life on the road. As the falling rain soaked his
clothes, he was truly happy. The road lay idle. Many years ago, an army
opposed to the king had gathered near the southern frontier. Traces of the
villages the rebels had lived in could still be seen, although nobody lived
there now. Here and there between the rebels' houses the little pilgrim
glimpsed bones of men and horses, as well as fragments of bowls in stone
and metal. He spotted some elephant bells. He picked them up and shook
them. They jingled. Sudhana had no idea where the land of Trinayana

ended and the next nation began.

"What a desolate spot. It looks as though nobody's living here." He was looking forward to meeting Indriyeshvara; a child's energy would be welcome after this desolation. Sudhana followed the road through a forest, only to find beyond it a bleak wasteland where the road simply vanished. The only living things were thorny bushes, thistles, and the poorest of poor agaves. Even nature had fallen into ruins.

Shramanamandala's main city, Sumukha, dominated the sandy shores of the Aso River, standing at the meeting point of various roads that followed the deep river's tributaries. The five city gates stood open and a rich blend of people from many countries could be seen living within the city walls. Descendants of gods and descendants of demons, people from Arabia and Ceylon, to say nothing of tribes resulting from the intermarriage of divinities with brahmans, all lived together without conflict and made the city their home.

Sudhana was overjoyed to be out of the wasteland and did not even notice his exhaustion after the long journey. The river was blue, the sand white like moonlight. As he made his way to the sandbanks along the Aso River, a young musician from Ceylon, completely naked, followed along behind him, playing a quiet tune on his flute. Just as the flautist left him, Sudhana glimpsed a child playing alone on the white sand of the opposite shore. There the young lad called Indriyeshvara was busily building houses of sand, then demolishing them again.

"Hey! Indriyeshvara!" Sudhana shouted across the river.

The child startled, then waved in Sudhana's direction.

"Sudarshana sent me to visit you," Sudhana explained. "That's how I know your name."

"What's your name?" Indriyeshvara shouted back.

"I'm called Sudhana!"

18.
TWO BOYS TOGETHER

LTHOUGH THE BOY looked his same age, Sudhana had no idea of his own actual age. The dream that seemed to last twelve years had blurred his relationship with time, as if he was viewing a forgotten landscape after a long illness. He had no idea how much time had really passed. "Indriyeshvara, how old are you?"

The boy shook his head, taking up a handful of sand and letting it trickle between his fingers. "I don't know. It's like this sand trickling away if you pick it up. How old are you? We must be the same age, surely?"

"I don't know, either."

"Then our age has run away from us."

With that, Indriyeshvara flopped down onto the sand. Sudhana followed suit, and lay sprawling on the sand in the warm evening.

"How did you meet that old man? Sudarshana, I mean, " Indriyeshvara asked, then continued without waiting for an answer.

"That old man taught me many things. Once, when I was so sick that I forgot words, colors, and even my own mother, he embraced my unconscious body and prayed all through one moonless night, until my senses were restored. As I was coming round, I wondered why the world was so dark. I thought that the world was always plunged in a rainy moonless night. As my wits returned, the darkness frightened me. Without thinking, I began to call for my mother.

"That was my first step towards recovering the world and the people I had forgotten about. He saved my life. Yet he lived as though he was always hiding, on the run from something, and when spies from his own land turned up here one day, he disappeared without even a farewell. He must have sent you so that we can search for truth together. It doesn't matter how old we are."

"Indriyeshvara," Sudhana clasped the boy's hands. "When I hear you talk of the past, I feel like doing the same!"

"No need, I know you. I know your past. We're already old friends; in the centuries past we've slept on the same pallet and shared our lives a hundred or more times. Don't you remember our friendship?"

Sudhana gazed out at the darkening stream. Their bodies were covered with sand. With the flow of water, over the course of centuries, the great rocks and cliffs of the highest peaks had been reduced to sand, and the sand in union with the river, knew all that the rocks had known. In the deep evening stillness, the sand was very gently weeping. After they sat watching the water and enjoying their happiness for a while, Indriyeshvara had an idea.

"Sudhana, tomorrow's the new moon. Let's visit the plains around Surajong village across the river. There we'll be entertained all night long. We won't be bored for a moment."

"Why? What's going to happen?"

"We'll see the most ecstatic dance in the whole world."

"Let's go!"

They rowed across the river in a dugout boat made from the trunk of a nine-hundred-year-old tala tree. At first, they had to overcome the resistance of the river's current, but then, feathering the oars, they were carried by the stream to the landing.

Red curtains dangled from the market stalls, a sign of festival, and the village girls had all adorned their foreheads and cheeks with daubs of red so that their faces appeared on fire. Night was just falling. The lamps at the stalls were blazing brightly.

Sudhana and Indriyeshvara waited in a remote spot under a tala tree, until a noisy band of village children vanished in the direction of the plain. The boys followed after them. The night was cloudy, and not a single star could be seen. They kept tripping and stumbling on the unfamiliar path until, finally, they arrived at a place where they could no longer hear the river. Since the great roar of the rapids was completely inaudible, they must have come a long way. The plain seemed hardened under the tension of the night, poised for something to happen.

"There are lights!" Indriyeshvara whispered.

They were walking along a rather dull, level stretch of the plain, when lights spread thickly along the horizon, like a ghostly will-o'-the-wisp, until there seemed to be a complete wall of fire across the plain.

"I'm frightened," Sudhana murmured.

"It's alright. This is my second time," Indriyeshvara assured him. "The dance is a festival where the wills of all sleeping things enter bodies and become manifest. It is danced just once a year, on the last day of the ninth month. The people here believe that on that day the holy gods come down to be with them. As they dance, many drop dead."

Their two hearts were drawn to the flame. The deeper the night became, the more the area covered by the light seemed to deck itself with an uneasy tension. As they arrived, the leading village elder was just beginning a speech on the circular stage. He carried a small fan in one hand as he spoke. Men and women from all the different tribes of Surajong were gathered. The speech was brief and as the chieftain descended the stage, the entire assembly dropped to the ground in a deep prostration.

A girl made her entrance, concentrating deeply and bringing her whole body into stillness. Raising slender arms and lifting her head, she let her hair fall free. She looked like a statue standing there in the light from the many fires. The chieftain dropped the fan into the flames and the girl began to dance, spinning and spinning until she seemed to be made of light.

In the spirit dance she was performing, the girl's own will had withdrawn and her body was a spinning top driven by divine possession. Then she stopped.

The chieftain began to beat on a drum and her dance changed. Every villager present joined in a frenzied spirit dance. Groans, cries, exclamations, and lamentations rose above their frantic movements. Their sorrows and their very bodies were forgotten. The dance lasted far into the night, with no pause for rest.

Indriyeshvara and Sudhana stayed hidden in a nearby patch of marsh, fearful of the dance's intensity. The night grew ever darker, so full of the dance, nothing could penetrate it.

All through the night, the dance had Sudhana vibrating in terror. At dawn, he and Indriyeshvara fell asleep. When Sudhana awoke, it was already late morning. At first, he thought the clearing was still covered with people sleeping. But on closer look, he did not see a living soul. The ground was littered with the dead bodies of those whose spirits had departed heavenward during the dance.

Indriyeshvara had woken before him and was walking between the corpses. "The bodies are simply left lying here, and by this time next year only the completely clean bones are left. Then those bones are thrown down to the Dragon King's palace below the River Aso."

Sudhana came across the body of a young girl. "It's her! The girl who danced last night!"

Indriyeshvara nodded and spoke sorrowfully. "Not so long ago, she came across the river to see me. She'd swum all the way across that wide river in secret."

"You mean, you knew her?"

"Yes, I knew her. Not only that, I was very fond of her. It was because she invited me that I came here last night. She was that chieftain's granddaughter."

"You must be feeling sad."

"Yes, very. But at least I still have the song she sang to me:

A flowing river knows everything,
knows the future of everything,
while a little boat knows nothing at all.
I am a little boat,
just floating down the omniscient river.
Little boat! Tossing all it knows into the river.
My little boat just floats down with the river.

"Sudhana, I've shown you the death of the girl I loved. I've nothing else left to show you. Now you must go floating in that dugout down the Aso River. Tie up the boat at the nineteenth ferry landing and disembark at the entrance to the city known as Samudrapratishthana."

"You mean, you're staying here?"

"Yes, I'll go on living here caressing the sand. My dancing girl has disappeared and you are leaving me, too. All I have is sand."

"Samudrapratishthana is a long way away."

"Yes, a very long way. But you need faraway places to visit. You'll be meeting a beautiful woman. There's no need for you to know her name but her divine powers will guide your craft. I once met her in just the same way."

"I'm sad to leave you," Sudhana said. "But I'll do as you say."

Indriyeshvara rowed the boat toward the river shore, but then changed direction and approached a sandbank. Indriyeshvara got out and briskly pushed the craft off. Sudhana found himself alone in the boat.

Rejected by its owner, the boat selected a particular eddy in the river and began to float downstream. Sudhana waved at the steadily diminishing solitude of Indriyeshvara. Then the sandbank, too, shrank to a white streak and disappeared. The river was flowing far more rapidly than it seemed.

Sudhana wept as he tried to sing a snatch of Indriyeshvara's song. "The little boat knows nothing at all..."

Perhaps it was true. Knowing is not the same as realizing. It was necessary to float down the river, tossing away everything he knew and returning to the original emptiness of knowing nothing. A new peace came to Sudhana as he journeyed downstream.

19.
A GENEROUS WELCOME

FTER PARTING FROM Indriyeshvara, young Sudhana had ample leisure to savor solitude. He met no one else on his long journey down the serene river. From time to time, a breeze made the boat rock; that was all. Along the river-banks, manifold species of trees clustered together. Farther down, the luxuriant woodlands became a wasteland where it seemed not a single blade of grass had ever grown since the creation of the world.

Occasionally, he saw houses built out over the water, and children could be glimpsed bathing. A few times he passed old boatmen on skinny skiffs. Yet they didn't exchange a single word. Sudhana merely waved a hand at the children, the boaters, the leaves on the trees, the cliffs along the river and their shadows. Then he left them behind.

He passed rich areas where trade was flourishing and regions so poor not a single fish seemed to pass by. He passed boats drifting downstream and others struggling against the current on their way between ferry-stations. He passed nineteen ferry-stations in four different kingdoms before reaching the kingdom of Samudrapratishthana on the coast of the Indian Ocean.

At the landing-stage, he tied the faithful boat to a stake at the ferry landing and abandoned it. The boat had already lost Indriyeshvara and now it was losing Sudhana, too. The little pilgrim recalled a saying, "Once across a river, you abandon the boat you took." He remembered another of the same kind, that he also disliked: "When you point at the moon you forget the finger that points." We should value all that help us reach a goal, he felt. Sudhana poured a libation of water over the boat as a token of gratitude.

While he was doing so, a man came rushing up, carrying his young daughter. "Little fellow, lend me your boat. My daughter is sick. I have to go to Candananamu ferry-station by the sea so she can be treated."

"You're welcome to take it. I've finished with it."

"Tell me, child, you aren't by any chance on your way to visit the wealthy lady, the beautiful Prabhuta, are you?"

Sudhana hesitated before replying. Prabhuta? He didn't know the name of the person he was supposed to meet, but it sounded right. "I am indeed. Do you know how I get there?"

"Up at the inn on the jetty there, you'll find a man on his way to her manor. Just follow him."

The father and daughter boarded the boat, untied it, and floated off on the current. At a food stall on the jetty, Sudhana had his first cooked meal in a long time. Then he entered the inn.

He found the man right away, a beggar whose right hand had been amputated with an axe. The man had heard reports that Lady Prabhuta gave out free food and he was on his way now to visit her.

Sudhana and the beggar left the hustle and bustle of the ferry and set out along a quiet path over the meadows. The paddy fields were lush and the breeze sent waves racing across them. Beyond the plains, a hill rose. The hill offered a broad expanse of green shade between the forests. The path became a busy road, with people coming and going, and others resting on the roadside, many of whom seemed to be beggars headed for Lady Prabhuta's home. Sudhana's companion recognized a few of the travelers and stopped to rest with them while Sudhana hurried on ahead.

Lady Prabhuta's vast estate lay behind faded boundary signs forbidding entry, but the place was clearly open to everyone. Most visitors came to get their fill of food; Sudhana came hoping to fill up on wisdom.

Crowds were streaming in through the many gateways and the main gate swung open just as Sudhana reached it. The manor was composed of a number of immense buildings. Lady Prabhuta was in the simple main building. She was sitting casually and unadorned and her face harbored a constant smile.

Lady Prabhuta was surrounded by girls, each as beautiful as she was. Each maintained her own beauty with complete freedom. Sudhana bowed in reverence.

"I am a young wayfarer passing by. Please satisfy my starved mind as you satisfy starved stomachs."

Lady Prabhuta stood up. The small bowl set in front of her shook slightly as she rose.

"Little traveler, at last I have met you. All I can offer you is in this little bowl."

Sudhana looked into the bowl. There was nothing in it. A man who had come in and was standing behind Sudhana exclaimed:

"I was longing to eat fine rice with honeyed oysters, and this bowl is full of it. How can an empty bowl suddenly fill with the food I desire? Truly you are sacred, Lady Prabhuta."

Lady Prabhuta shrugged. "Ah, you were searching for food and so it has already appeared. Here you are, take it."

With an air of regret, she transferred the food to a plate one of the girls was holding. The man turned away and began to eat hungrily.

Lady Prabhuta gazed at Sudhana. "Young pilgrim, in your heart of hearts you desired nothing and so your wish did not materialize in my bowl. But I have new food ready for you, food never before seen, the food of the high heavens and the deep seas, of the springs deep in the hills."

She delved with her empty hands into the empty bowl and handed something to Sudhana. It was nothing. Sudhana received it.

"Little pilgrim, I can provide the food that thousands of people desire. If people need clothing, head scarves, necklaces, even carts and boats, I can supply them. All, high and low, experience a rise in position once they have received goods from me."

She continued in a low voice: "Consider these beautiful young girls. They have purified their hearts, setting aside their individual beauty and giving everybody the food and the other things they hope for, so that they will be able to journey through the limitless worlds in the ten directions in the space of a single thought. Yet the food in this bowl never diminishes. This is the bowl of bodhisattva nature that never decreases." Hearing her words, Sudhana realized that his empty stomach had been filled.

It began to rain lightly over Lady Prabhuta's vast park; the guests thronging to visit her took shelter in the various buildings or the encampment tents. Sudhana felt the urge to sing. Lady Prabhuta took his hand. "Young wayfarer, holy wayfarer, come to my home! Women, please, usher him!" she implored the young girls. The girls lit the candles on the innumerable candelabra surrounding the main building. A beautiful night descended. The young women sang to usher in the evening, their jade-hued songs lingering in the night air.

20.
THE EATER OF ASHES

ADY PRABHUTA's delicate hand guided Sudhana to the dormitory, the maidens following behind. The room was enormous. The windows had no curtains, and Sudhana could glimpse the forest canopy and the sky beyond. Seeing Lady Prabhuta and Sudhana enter, the stars in the sky began to twinkle and gradually drew closer.

Lady Prabhuta lay down and Sudhana lay beside her. All the maidens took their places side by side, like a fan unfolding.

"I am called 'Lady' because I lead these maidens, Sudhana," Prabhuta murmured. "I too am a maid, a widow with no dead husband."

Sudhana was already on his way into a deep sleep.

"Ah, Lady," one of the maidens smiled at Lady Prabhuta. "This child wayfarer already knew that! Even a passing wayfarer can tell by Your Ladyship's outstretched hand and sacred smile."

Sudhana sank deeper into a childlike slumber. He was lying close beside Lady Prabhuta, but in his dream they were even closer. They strolled through the grounds of her estate together, but even in his dream Sudhana sighed to think that soon he would be obliged to leave.

"It is not possible to restrain what flows," Prabhuta whispered in his dream. "You cannot restrain water, wind, or all the immensities of time. I couldn't force you to stay here, even if I wanted to, just as I couldn't command a bird to perch on a branch."

"For me, things that stay in one place all part from me, as I flow on," Sudhana replied. "If I decided to settle somewhere, everything else would flow away from me. There are people who live beneath trees that span a hundred and fifty generations, until the trunk rots into the ground, but that is not for me."

"Karma decides whether our lives are spent in meditation or in pilgrimage. Wayfarer, lovely pilgrim, why not visit Vidvan, who eats ashes."

In his dream, Prabhuta told him the story of Vidvan's life. Vidvan belonged to the ancient royal family of the Deccan Plateau. When the kingdom collapsed, his family became one of the poorest in the land. Most days, he had almost nothing to eat. Vidvan was reduced to pondering whether he should choose beggary or theft, the art of living or the politics of living. Begging is an art. Theft is politics. He chose politics and became a robber.

A new king had taken power in the ruined land. On the night after a long festival, Vidvan broke into the palace. No one knew the royal palace better than he. The moon was on the wane as he made his way into the royal bedchamber. The king was sound asleep, exhausted after all the festivities. Vidvan gathered together a hoard of valuable loot and was about to leave when he noticed a bowl of ashes beside the sleeping king's water bowl. Too hungry to notice what he was eating, he madly gulped down the ashes. He was free to escape with a great hoard of precious jewels, yet could not resist a handful of ashes.

Once his stomach was full, his wits returned. Vidvan looked down at his ashen hands and the now empty ash bowl. "Ah! Ashes are enough to satisfy hunger!" he exclaimed aloud.

Beside the king lay a girl's thin dress. Vidvan tossed all the valuables he had intended to steal on the dress.

He shook the king. "Sir, new king!"

The monarch woke startled and afraid.

"King, sir; take me prisoner," Vidvan begged. "I've just realized that I can eat ashes when I'm hungry. Make me your prisoner and punish me!"

But the king saw that Vidvan was sincere and gave him gifts of rubies before guiding him through the maze leading out of the palace grounds. From that moment, the king began to govern wisely. Vidvan lived a newly consecrated life, homeless and eating ashes, and became a saint.

When Sudhana awoke, the story of the ash eater stayed with him. He could even taste the ashes on his tongue. Beside him, Lady Prabhuta's sleeping face was beautiful.

"Even asleep, your compassionate wisdom knows everything!"

He bade her good-bye as she slept. Then he crept out of the dormitory and went wandering off through the dark gardens. The supplicants had retired to the estate's various big houses or returned to their homes. The luxuriant garden lay empty. As he looked out, the whole world seemed empty.

"There's no need for me to stay here any longer. Only I don't know where to find Vidvan." As soon as he said the words out loud, he knew where to find the ash eater. As she had filled his stomach when she knew he was hungry, Lady Prabhuta sent him in the right direction, even as she slept.

Her guidance propelled him out of the great gates. In the early daylight, an iguyol tree rose high as a hill in the level plain. An old tramp was squatting alone under the tree.

Just as Sudhana was passing, the drowsy tramp stretched and got to his feet. "Where are you going so early? Early in the day, you have to let the road go on sleeping a bit more. You're too impatient."

"Why are you sleeping here, old man? There's too much dew. There are plenty of tents in the camp, yet you sleep under a tree!"

"I'm a leper. People drive me away."

"What?"

"Yes, they call me Vidvan the leper."

"You're Vidvan? I was on my way to look for you."

"You've found me." The old leper's voice was dull as he rose. He had cut off a rotten toe the previous evening. The severed toe lay by the roots of the tree. He and Sudhana left the outer gardens of Prabhuta's estate and headed inland.

"You're not as I expected," Sudhana said. "I didn't know that you were sick like this. Do you know Lady Prabhuta?"

"Is there anyone she doesn't know? She is loved by every man, every male animal; even the male trees love her. Shall I tell that beautiful woman about my being a leper? Funny little wanderer!" Vidvan laughed hollowly. The glow of the rising sun lit up the far horizon, that gradually passed from yellow to red.

"Did she tell you I'm originally of royal blood? Ha ha! Who isn't of royal blood, after all? I've lived my past and present lives without any division between them. The rubies the king gave me I gave to the poor. Then I met Siddhartha and built one wing of his monastery. He said that in order to enjoy a bodhisattva's bliss, you first have to experience one kind of human suffering in your own body. So the reward I got for having built a wing of his monastery was the most painful kind of leprosy. Funny, isn't it!

"Ah well, that's how it goes. How could I ever experience unending bliss without undergoing the Eight Sufferings? Birth, age, disease, and death are

the first four, of course. Then there are the last four: parting from what we love, meeting what we hate, failing to attain our aims, and all the ills of personality, the five *skandhas*. As I cut off my toes one by one I'm gaining my joy. You have to know that truth, don't you?"

Hearing Vidvan's story, Sudhana was ashamed of his initial reluctance to walk beside him.

Vivdan stopped. "Listen!"

Far away, a song echoed and the majestic pinnacles and temples of Mahasambhava rose into sight.

"Let's go to Mahasambhava together," the leper said. "Look how the light shines on the temples. My temple of Seven Treasures is waiting there with its empty darkness. When I open the doors, the darkness comes rushing out and, weeping, perishes in the sunlight outside. My leprosy is like a suit of clothes; I must quickly go and take it off."

Sudhana followed Vidvan into the temple and was astonished to find all the treasures and riches of the whole world. Jewels rose in great heaps and elaborate ornaments decorated every surface.

"I am a bodhisattva who makes bodhisattvas. Look. The darkness is going to come out weeping, you'll see."

He heaved the doors open, the darkness duly came rushing out and perished. Old Vidvan stroked the empty air, as if to comfort the dying darkness.

"Look! Fix your whole heart on the center of the empty air. See how all creatures become bodhisattvas in the empty air. Look! Look!"

As he gazed into the air where he was pointing, Sudhana saw that the empty air was seething with sick, poor, angry, sorrowful people, hosts of people wounded in wars. Thanks to the welcome Vidvan offered, they were becoming bodhisattvas and they danced as they sped away in all directions.

"I help people rid themselves of their desires for love and food and sleep. I was the one who made you wake up early back there in Lady Prabhuta's room. But you're too impatient. That's why I told you to consider the sleeping road. I can only perform my task for each person once. Look, they are turning into bodhisattvas, then as bodhisattvas they are reborn and take on the sufferings of life again. It's a life of greater suffering they take on now. There is no bodhisattva life without living creatures. Without sentient beings there can be no bodhisattva and no Buddha."

Sudhana realized that Vidvan himself had become a bodhisattva and had enjoyed unending bliss.

The airborne festival that had materialized so splendidly before his eyes vanished again, and with it the temple of the Seven Treasures. Sudhana found himself walking over an ancient battleground, strewn with rusty fragments of swords, human bones, and bits of shields. Vidvan was limping. Another toe had fallen off.

"Off you go now. Southward, go south. I really don't know why you chose a life heading southward. It's a shame."

"Where should I go? Who should I meet?"

"Ha, you little leper! Now you take my leprosy, and off you go. It's a shame you asked me to teach you that." As Sudhana left, Vidvan sang:

> All suffering is known by one suffering.
> Taking one suffering on yourself,
> you affirm the world of suffering
> by your suffering self.
> So suffer,
> then cast off that suffering.

21.
NO MEETING WITHOUT FIRST PARTING

FTER PARTING FROM VIDVAN, Sudhana went on his way in deeper solitude than ever. He had become a leper child; his eyebrows had fallen off. He was surprised to discover that his fingers no longer obeyed him, because of the sickness. In a few days' time he would be cutting them off. Vidvan had gone scuttling away after giving him this new suffering, like someone freed from a great burden. What was this leprosy he had inherited? Who was Vidvan? What had been accomplished at their parting? He had become a suffering pilgrim, obliged to follow whatever path seemed to offer a way of overcoming his sufferings.

"My path exists," he thought, "even if no one tells me where it lies. I have to make my road as I go. For me, every road is newly made."

Once past the inland grasslands, he found himself passing through vast ruins along a path made by wild animals.

In the midst of those inland ruins, Sudhana let drop one of his fingers; then, crossing the brow of a hill, he came upon a coastal region dotted with windbreaks of coconut and oleander trees. There one woman called out to other women:

"Ratnachuda is about to leave the world!"

The message was repeated by those women to others farther on, transmitted from one field to the next beneath the windbreaks.

"Ratnachuda? Ratnachuda leaving this world?"

Sudhana's mind had grown weak from the long journey and the pain of his sickness; the women's words filled him with horror like fresh blood spilled by an axe.

"Who's Ratnachuda?"

Sudhana had no sooner hurried up to them with his question than all the women screamed out:

"Help! Help! A leper bringing ill luck!"

And they all ran off in dread. He was a leper, unable to speak to people, or greet them, or ask them the way. Indeed, the women's husbands might very well come running along and take him prisoner. He headed for the main highway that ran past their fields. A grove of oleanders grew between the fields and the road; there the burning sunlight was filtered and turned into cool shade. But he felt uneasy. The oleanders had so far taken no heed of him, but now one branch spoke up.

"Young visitor! Visitor passing by! Leave your sickness hanging here and go on your way. How will you be able to meet the person you are to meet if you are carrying that kind of disease with you? Just leave it hanging here."

He pricked up his ears and gazed around. One dead branch was waving alone. He hung upon it the whole heavy load of leprosy he was carrying in his heart.

"No hesitation before hanging it up, eh? It must have been terribly painful."

There was nothing he could say, too relieved that all his pain had left him.

"Farewell now, little pilgrim."

Temporarily refreshed, he hurried on. He had lost only one finger. His eyebrows began to grow again. When he had crossed the fields and was near the outlying houses of the town, some men appeared and blocked his way.

"You're a leper," one shouted.

"You leper!" they all yelled.

Then one of them came up to Sudhana and examined him closely.

"Hey, your old woman made a mistake. He's no leper."

They grew calmer. There was some muttering, then the mob broke up and dispersed. Sudhana had been fully prepared for them to grab him and fling him into the sea, but he found himself able to go on living. A girl was approaching, her head covered. As he felt inclined to rest, he sat down under an ailanthus tree and watched her. As she passed, she turned and looked at him.

"Are you on your way to see Master Ratnachuda?"

Sudhana nodded, recklessly. Ratnachuda? He supposed he was. The scarf covering the girl's head swayed and waved. He had seen her somewhere before. Some far away experience was coming close. What was it? At first he could not recall. Who can she be?

"Are you not the lord Sudhana?"

"Indeed I am. And you?"

"Ah, Lord Sudhana. I am Iryon."

How long had it been? And here she was again! The earth they were walking on heaved; a passing earthquake. The whole landscape swayed. They came very close to one another, yet they did not embrace.

"I have been staying with Master Ratnachuda. He is about to leave this world. He told me a visitor was coming and I should go out to welcome him."

"Iryon!"

"I went to the capital and was going to marry the crown prince but the night before the wedding I swam across the river and escaped from the city by the waterways. I've been roaming around like this ever since."

"Just like me!" Sudhana exclaimed.

"Now we have met. We must not part again."

They rested again when they reached a place from where they could see the outer walls of Ratnachuda's city. They were obliged to walk a little, then rest, walk, then rest again. They were so happy that words refused to come. When many words are needed, words refuse to emerge.

From his hand, caught in her delicate one, sprang pearls of sweat.

22.
EVERY SONG YIELDS A FLOWER

NITED WITH IRYON, Sudhana entered the city of Simha-pota. All the people were walking about with bowed heads. Passing along the main street that was plunged in sorrow, they reached Ratnachuda's residence behind the city's principal administrative building. Ratnachuda was lying robed in violet, his hair and eyebrows shining white.

"Welcome," Ratnachuda said, "I have been waiting for you. The time has come for me to go where I must go."

He made everyone but Iryon and Sudhana leave the room. Then, in a weakened whisper, he spoke.

"This city of Simhapota was in earlier times the capital of a great nation. Regretting the destruction of that nation, my ancestors established a king-dom modeled on it. That was over a thousand years ago. If you go westward to the pine grove on the hill overlooking the sea, you will find buried there the song made at the establishment of the former kingdom and the song of the foundation of this nation a thousand years after. Or that may be a myth. People here don't believe it, so you two must go and dig up those songs. I was waiting to tell you that. Now everything is finished." Closing his eyes, he departed quietly.

Ratnachuda had been sick for the last fourteen years, and at last death had come. Those who had left the room returned. Iryon passed the tidings to the people outside. Ratnachuda's old wife and aging daughter entered, followed by his chief secretary and members of his staff.

Two days passed, then Ratnachuda was cremated on the shore at the end of a grand ceremony. His ashes were sprinkled on the sea, which grew so intoxicated by receiving such an honor that it began to roll wildly.

The new moon rose and hung suspended like an arched eyebrow. As

soon as the moon disappeared again, Sudhana and Iryon left the city and
hastened westward. The sea lay dead, untouched by the slightest breeze.
Sudhana was carrying tools to dig through earth and stones, as well as a
lantern; he and Iryon soon reached the place Ratnachuda had spoken of.
They put up an awning to keep off the dew, then rested. It was long past
midnight. The sound of the weeping ghosts of fish came faintly from the
far horizon of the ocean.

Iryon had been there once with Ratnachuda. At that time, she said, he
had seemed about to tell her something, then had not done so.

"It's here. Under these bulwarks." She pointed out the place to Sudhana,
and at once they began to dig. It was hard work. Just as dawn was breaking,
their tools struck a large metal object, a great bronze bell.

"It's a bell, Lord Sudhana! It was a bell he meant! Now we only have to
dig it out."

Sudhana and Iryon cut arrowroot vines, threaded them through the two
ears at the top of the ancient bell, and hauled it up. It was not particularly
heavy. As soon as they dug out the bell, beautiful singing sounds gathered
in a little cluster and began to rise above the ground in the empty space
beneath it.

"Ah! It's singing!" Iryon marveled. The sounds merged one by one into
a number of different songs. There was the song sung by girls a thousand
years before in the ancient kingdom, then the song that had been sung a
thousand years later when the Ratnachuda dynasty had begun its reign:

> God, I offer you my body.
> By this body,
> comfort all who are sad in the world.
> By this body's song,
> comfort the world's wretched folk.
> Who can do that?
> None but a god can comfort the world.
> A god, and all gods.

Then:

> I am mother of the moon.
> Giving birth to the moon,
> I brought light to dark paths.

Now, you wayfarers,
wash your weary hearts
nineteen times in moonlight.

And next:

Every bell's sound,
after sleeping a while,
will one day blossom as flowers,
will bloom as white camellias by the sea.
Ah, renew.
Yes, renew this world.

Those ancient songs, long buried silent in the ground, had lain there fossilized; who can express the emotion the two experienced that morning as the melodies turned into songs again? Once each song was out, it would never be heard again. Each vanished into the morning sky, a song already heard.

Every bell's sound after sleeping a while
will blossom one day as flowers.

Sudhana realized that the sound of the bell and its songs had all turned into flowers. This thought struck Sudhana and he looked about him. There were white camellia flowers everywhere.

The grove of ancient trees was blossoming with camellia flowers, in quantities such as had never before been seen along that coast. The echo of the bell and the songs from a thousand years before had remained enclosed in the ground as a pearl enclosed in a shell, and had at last emerged. In all that time, so many songs had flowed on and away. The wandering poets who had composed the songs, and all the girls who had sung them, had all flowed on and away. Yet these fossil songs, buried beneath the bell and rusty as only songs can become, had at last echoed in the open air, then had turned bud by bud into pure white camellia flowers. In bestowing those songs and the scent of the flowers on the young pilgrim, the dying Ratnachuda had fulfilled his task.

"Iryon! For the coming time, let's travel together. The soil here is fertile and produces abundantly, but we have to make our hearts more fertile still, and more abundant. Let's go down, drink one sip of water from Ratnachu-da's well, then leave."

They passed the ancient palaces of Simhapota city and entered the home where Ratnachuda had lived. Iryon told the people there to build a pavilion for the bell they would find lying on the hill, and let the ocean hear its tones. Iryon had been living as Ratnachuda's adopted daughter and had monopolized his last reserves of love. She urged her older siblings to build the pavilion quickly to fulfill Ratnachuda's last wish.

After drinking a mouthful of water, she and Sudhana set off to the farewells of all the city's nobles. They refused the many gifts villagers offered, filling their bundle only with dried fruit from a tree that Rat-nachuda was said to have planted himself.

Walking along with Iryon beside him, Sudhana felt far happier than when he had been alone. Previously he had been obliged to walk wrapped in his own silence, unless someone or something happened to address him. Iryon had been his first love, the first person he had met after being rescued by old Manjushri and his company; and now here they were, walking together after a long parting.

"Here the road divides. This road is the one I came by, this is a new one," he said.

They set off along the new road he had pointed to. Before they had gone very far, they encountered a storm moving along the foot of a mountain and were forced to seek shelter from it. It turned into a torrential deluge and if they had not succeeded in finding shelter in the mountain's grim caverns, they would have been swept away. They were obliged to shelter in separate caves, for each was scarcely big enough to contain one person. Sudhana found himself alone, squeezed into a narrow cave. He could not even call out to Iryon.

As the downpour grew more fierce, he heard a sudden cry. Iryon!

Defying the danger, he made his way to her cave. It was a perilous undertaking. A great boulder offered itself in Sudhana's place, and was swept away over the precipice. Iryon had almost been forced from her cave by the storm; the wind was so strong it had edged its way under her and was sucking her out. Sudhana threw himself on top of her and their senses came alive. Previously, they had been afraid of the storm, but now, overpowered by sensation, they lost all fear.

They wedged themselves firmly against the little cavern's rocky vault and sides, and held each other tightly, until their bodies became one. Desire took control; an immense surge of power flowed between them and blotted out the storm. Later, soaked in sweat, they let their bodies dry in the sound of the receding wind, still locked in an embrace. As their inner maelstrom came to an end, the storm too moved away. Outside the cave, light drizzle was falling, trembling in the breeze that had replaced the gale.

"It's alright now. There's danger in staying here any longer. Lions will be coming soon." She urged him up, then they crawled out of the cave. The storm was over.

"Sudhana...let's settle down together somewhere," she said. Her hair was blown about from the wind and the dust of the cave was on her face.

"Settle down? No, that's impossible."

"One danger gives rise to even greater dangers. Since I escaped from the crown prince's fortress, I've encountered nothing but danger."

"Have you already forgotten Master Ratnachuda's wish? You mustn't. We have to walk on endlessly, continuously renewing our strength."

"What is there ahead down the road? Is there anything but storms? And even if you find the truth, then what? Think how many there are who search and search and fail to find anything."

"Siddhartha seems to be a single person but there are as many Siddharthas as there are innumerable living beings," Sudhana replied. "For every human being there is necessarily a bodhisattva."

"But what have you discovered so far?" she persisted. He remained unmoved. "Sudhana, you are my husband."

"Not so. I am no one's husband," he argued.

"Your seed has already entered my womb."

"Not so. The seed of the storm has entered there."

"The seed of the storm? Impossible!"

"My seed is only in myself. You must give birth to a storm and so govern the evil in this world."

Iryon stared at him, but Sudhana could no longer think or speak. He simply drew her to him as they walked on along the storm-cleared road.

23.
OLD MYOHYANG

T HE KINGDOM OF SIMHAPOTA city and the nation of Vetramulaka are neighbors, but since each has wide territories, the two capitals lie far apart. The two young pilgrims had great difficulty in reaching the city of Samantamukha. Iryon's feet had swollen until she could walk no farther. When she saw an elephant being led by a boy as they neared the city, she mounted the elephant for the rest of the way.

Once the long journey was over, Iryon quickly recovered her spirits. In her womb, the little pilgrim's seed had begun to grow. She descended from the elephant in front of a shop selling fragrances, perfumes, and incense. The city rose like a hill, dominating the smaller townships around it.

"Why, it's a couple of little pilgrims! How tired you must be! Just look how pale your faces are! Come in and rest." The storekeeper's wife carefully guided Iryon into their house.

In that region, wayfarers were completely safe; for the punishment for failing to welcome travelers properly was extremely severe. The woman could quickly tell that Iryon was pregnant: "You should stay here for nine or ten months. We only need sell a little of this fragrance and we'll be able to look after you properly and you can give this land a fine baby. Home is wherever you're born, after all."

Iryon was given stewed plums to drink and put to bed. Once Sudhana and Iryon were in their room, they were left to themselves for the night, like any newly-wed couple. Sudhana was sunk in deep melancholy.

"Spend ten months here?" He shook his head.

"Why not live here? Lord Sudhana, once you've seen the baby born, you can leave or do as you like. You're tired from so much traveling. Sleep now," Iryon said.

"You sleep first." Sudhana went outside and walked restlessly up and down near the city gate. A cacophony of flutes was coming from a cluster of nearby taverns, each marked by long white banners, where soldiers and travelers and the local youths were busily drinking. Sudhana ventured inside one. He had no money to pay for a drink, so he simply sat down at an empty table and looked at the people around him.

"Pilgrim, have a drink," an old man tossed Sudhana a bottle. He drank. He had sometimes drunk wine produced by fermented fruit but this was the first time he had ever drunk liquor produced from grain. His head reeled. He seemed to be spinning.

"Where have you come from?"

"From Simhapota city."

"You seem to be from farther away than that," the old man said.

"Perhaps so."

"Why did you come here?"

"I'm just roaming from one place to another."

"Right. I understand. This handsome young man is a wandering ascetic, a homeless pilgrim in quest of dharma, the teaching of truth. That's it, isn't it? I'm right. Ah! A sacred task. I too..."

"Are you a pilgrim too, sir?"

"No. Nowadays...But my older brother, he's eighty-nine, he's up in Mount Samantanetra. I was with him for a time but then I became a drunkard and ended up here. I enjoy drinking, I'm a master drinker. Ha ha. Whereas you...on closer inspection...hee hee...you like a bit of skirt, I see. And with your peachy complexion, too. Ha ha."

The old man's laughter only slipped between his teeth but it rang out loudly.

"Who are you, old man?"

"Me? No need for you to know that. Go and visit my brother, old Myohyang."

Then they both got very drunk. By the end, Sudhana was in no condition to know how intoxicated he was. That night, Sudhana left Iryon behind and followed the old drunkard outside the city and up into the harsh and lofty heights of Mount Samantanetra. The path they took formed a stone stairway stretching on up into the dark sky. As he climbed, the fumes of alcohol began to clear and with sudden intensity he remembered Iryon, and his seed contained within her womb. For the first time, he realized how cold he had been and he suffered as a person, as a husband, as a father.

"Hey, you think you're having a hard time now, with only enough suffering to make the ground sink a bit?" the old man said. "In times to come, you're going to have to bear suffering heavy enough to bring down heaven and earth, paradise and hell, if you're going to save all the world's beings, innumerable as grains of sand? And you worry about trifles?"

"How do you know about my sufferings?"

"Ha ha ha. It's not me who knows, it's the drink. Try a drop of this." He handed him his liquor, which was making a sloshing noise in the flask. The full moon was shining brightly, the mountain was very high. The moon seemed to be floating below them.

"Liquor's a fine thing. Leaving a wife and kid behind is good, too. Your wife can meet any number of other men. The kid will grow up okay without a father. If it has a dad, it grows up stupid in its father's shadow. Better grow up alone from birth. Ah, I'm drunk, I'm very drunk. You go on alone. There's no need for me to go any farther—I prefer drinking. If you meet my brother, give him my best regards. Scold old Myohyang on my behalf: tell him to get off to heaven. What's he think he's doing up in this mountain—unable to get rid of attachments?"

Sudhana found himself alone on the dark mountain slope, dumbly gazing after the retreating figure of the old drunkard until he vanished. He longed for Iryon and decided to go back, but the moment he made a step on the downward path, a rock came rolling down onto the path, blocking it. Sudhana's whole body shuddered. Just then, the moon rose.

"Who's there?" He pricked up his ears. "Who's there and where are you from?"

Sudhana felt relieved, recognizing that booming sound as a human voice.

"I'm looking for Myohyang," he said.

"Ho, and so late at night....Come on up here."

Just as day was breaking, he reached a small hermitage, perched below the mountain peak. It was farther than the sound of the voice had suggested. Up there, it was already early morning. He had spent the whole night climbing the mountain. Old Myohyang, so old that he seemed near death, was waiting. His eyes were bright and steely; a mane of white hair hung down to his shoulders.

"Young pilgrim, you must rest. You have come a long way. Who would have thought anyone would come as far as you have? Get some sleep first. Those you left behind down there are alright, so get yourself some sleep."

Sudhana did as he was bid and fell into a long, deep sleep. The whole mountain fell asleep with him. The morning sunshine began to stream down brightly on Sudhana, and the mountain, and old Myohyang, who had gone back to sleep too, but their sleep with its deep darkness kept the sunlight at bay. A single hawk, with burning pinions, was hovering in the sunlight.

As soon as Sudhana awoke, he could not contain his inquisitiveness. "Holy master. How can I attain enlightenment? How can I achieve bodhisattva nature and follow the path of enlightenment?"

The old master replied sorrowfully, "Everywhere in the cosmos, everywhere in each clod of earth, even one small as a mustard seed, everywhere in the air, even a spot small as a mote of dust, in every place a bodhisattva is sacrificing its life for the sake of all living beings. All is full of growing enlightenment, as all living beings encounter bodhisattvas and they suffer together. Consider the air. Consider each clod of earth, each pebble. They are all bodhisattvas. If they are not, what is? Ah, young man, your awakening cannot be like mine. How could my bodhisattva awakening be like what you are destined to find through your long journeying? You are my teacher."

"How could I ever presume such a thing?"

"Not so. Not so. Once I knew the diseases of all living beings and I learned how to vanquish them. I burned my fragrances for everything troubled by wind and cold, by heat and every kind of sickness, by spirits and poison and magic spells, washed them with fragrant water, dressed them in fragrant clothes, and restored them to life. I brought cooling to those consumed by passion, compassion to those without compassion. By the encounter of all living beings with fragrance as I burned my fragrances, the worlds in all ten directions became full of bodhisattvas and I was permitted to see them. But I am no better than my brother, and now I am no better than you.

"Ten kinds of wisdom are not worth one seed of practice, while without practice ten kinds of wisdom are pointless."

For several months, Sudhana lived with only his teacher and the mountain. They lived on a diet of pine needles and milled mountain rice. During that time, he learned something of his teacher's earlier life. Unlike Myohyang's younger brother, the drunkard down in Samantamukha, Myohyang had a young wife whom he had truly loved. She died in a plague and he had become a healer as a way of praying for her soul's repose. His intense love for that one woman grew into a love reaching out to his neighbors and far beyond. He devoted nearly ten years of his life to roaming the vast southern regions, treating the sick.

Finally, Myohyang became so ill it was hard for him to continue. He had caught various diseases from people he had healed and he dragged his disease-ridden body up into the fastnesses of Mount Samantanetra, where no one could see him. Once there, he was drenched in storms for forty days and slowly recovered. Apart from the time a few years later when his younger brother stayed with him for a few weeks, he had severed all ties with the world and never left the mountain again. It was there Sudhana had found him.

From Myohyang, Sudhana learned how to pray for all living beings. Soon he was praying for sky and clouds, moon and stars, as well as for the rocks around him, for fir trees and old trees, and for animals' bones. He prayed for Iryon and their child in her womb and he prayed for the spirits of the dead.

The old man would praise his disciple just as the evening sky was aflame with dazzling splendor. They loved one another and by that love, they were able to experience an incomparable bliss. By that love, they were able to know all things. Wisdom is nothing other than the fruit of love. If they had not loved one another so deeply, their sharing of wisdom would have been in vain. They loved, and love made everything known.

"I am glad to be here, " Sudhana would tell his teacher. "By your prayers, many bodhisattvas are made happy, many living creatures are being released from their inherited karma."

"Ah, now go to sleep," Myohyang would respond. "Even the stars are full of drowsiness. All that remains is for everything to sleep like us."

Sending a laugh ringing out into the night, old Myohyang used to throw himself down where he was, and Sudhana would likewise flop down.

Several months had passed since Sudhana had climbed Mount Samantanetra. The sky was damp with a thick mist; the whole countryside below the mountain was veiled from view by the same mist. Old Myohyang's white hair hung damp around his scalp. He spoke what seemed to be a prayer to Sudhana.

"The world comes into being through loss. You have lost the girl and the seed you left at the foot of the mountain. All things must be lost. And you have lost them. You have lost what you had to lose. How could you fail to lose those things that you can never take care of?"

Sudhana showed no surprise at the old man's words. He sat there stiffly, as if struck deaf. Only the sound of rain falling on leaves and grass pierced his deafness.

"You have lost much and by that loss you have gained much," the old man continued. "The time has come for you to leave this mountain and set out on a very long journey. This is the moment for you to lose this mountain while I lose you."

Finally the little pilgrim replied, "I am a migrant by nature, and yet it seems that I ought to stay longer in this place. There is more I should learn from you, Master."

"Not so. Not so. What makes you think you can only learn from me? You must learn from many people, many mountains and rivers, trees and stones, from each crumb of each clod of earth, from every grain of sleeping sand. There is nothing that is not your master, even the least grain of dust."

Old Myohyang shook Sudhana once with his bony hand, then turned away resolutely and went into his cave. There was nothing more Sudhana could say.

The rain-shrouded mountain was hidden; there was no knowing what lay in which direction. The mountaintop cave was already invisible in the rain and mist, as he began his journey down, step by step.

When he reached the city of Samantamukha at the foot of Mount Samantanetra, it was cloudy but not raining. He headed for the perfumer's shop.

As soon as she saw Sudhana, the woman at the shop said, "At dawn yesterday your baby died and was cremated. The baby's mother scattered its ashes on the sea and left for who knows where. Why are you so late returning?"

Sudhana began sobbing. The woman gave Sudhana something Iryon had given her before leaving. It was a handful of ash, wrapped in a white cloth. The ashes were nearly pure white.

Sudhana took the little bundle and went out to the place where the dead of the brahman caste were cremated. The sea was a dark ash hue, reflecting the cloudy sky above. Waves were breaking in white surf. Sudhana scattered the ashes there. Instead of being swept away by the waves, they came flying up into his face, making him choke.

After standing vacantly for a while, looking out to sea, he bade farewell to the city of Samantamukha and walked on along the shore where he once again found Myohyang's drunkard brother.

"You've just come down from the mountain," the brother said.

"It's been a long time since we met," Sudhana said. "Why aren't you drinking?"

"I've forgotten all about liquor. I've nothing left to forget. Nothing left except staring hard at the sea."

"Master Myohyang says..."

"Shut up. No need for that kind of message. Aren't you curious about your wife Iryon?"

"What do you mean?"

"That young woman will always be somewhere out there ahead of you. Hurry after her."

"I'm not someone to go running after a woman," Sudhana replied.

"Follow what you like, the dharma or the woman. No point in distinguishing between them. I don't make any distinction between the dharma and liquor. None at all."

The old drunkard collapsed onto a sand dune, apparently drunk even without drinking. He waved Sudhana on with one hand. The little pilgrim took up a handful of sand, scattered it on the old man, and set out. The shore stretched endlessly away but he did not follow it; instead he directed his steps toward a road that led off from there. The previous day's rain had stopped; Mount Samantanetra looked very far away. It rose faintly in dark green hues and it seemed unreal to think that his old teacher was living up at the top of that mountain. He set off along the meadow road after bowing several times towards the mountain.

24.
THE EXECUTIONER

UDHANA WALKED ON for a long while among fields that had been abandoned and left fallow, recalling one by one all the teachers he had met. Keeping company with the past, drawing the past into the present, he was able to go on walking while the teachings of his former teachers of truth murmured all together in his heart.

He recalled the hawk, whom he had first met while he was with the band of hunters, when he was about to climb Sugriva Mountain. They had met again once after that, when it had shown him the way. Where was it now that he was again aimless? Had it died? Was it no longer able to dominate the air, to soar hour after hour through the vast, lofty skies? Ah, if it had completed its destined course in this world, to what other world might it have gone to continue its free soaring?

As he reached the depths of that memory, something suddenly dropped spinning a little way ahead of him. Merrily spinning with light flicks of its feathers, it came dropping down from high above. As soon as he saw it drop, he raised his head and stared skyward. The hawk had returned.

It hovered motionless in the sky. Sudhana waved; at once it made a turn and dropped lower. The hawk circumscribed a slow circle down through the sky and settled in front of Sudhana on the branch of an old tree. The branch broke; it flapped its wings fiercely, changed position, and settled cautiously on the remaining stump. It had grown very old. The hawk furled its wings, pecked at its claws with its beak, and stared piercingly at Sudhana with obvious signs of joy.

"What a long time it's been, hawk. How old you've grown. I'll be old like you one day."

The hawk said nothing.

"Where have you been traveling around until now…" Sudhana had scarcely spoken when the old hawk flapped its ancient wings, soared into the air, and began to trace a huge circle.

"I know, you've traveled a lot, too, like me, and likely met a host of teachers of your own."

They traveled on together, one on the ground, the other in the air. Their journey went on for many miles, until they reached an encampment of nomads not far from the city of Taladhvaja. It was on a coastal plateau, where wildflowers were blooming in profusion. At the far end of the plateau rose white city walls, with towers and spires soaring above them.

It looked like a happy place, but when Sudhana reached the camp of the nomads, they explained, in a dialect he could not fully understand, that inside the city of Taladhvaja, an atmosphere of terror reigned. They urged him not to go there. If he so much as went into the city, they warned, he would be taken prisoner and executed.

Sudhana was utterly weary after so much walking, and so he stayed the night with the nomads. The old hawk flew on over Taladhvaja and disappeared. The sun set and the western horizon seemed ablaze with red flames. Gradually the rising tide of night surged over the desert. The nomads chattered and a woman came in, bringing Sudhana a tray of mutton. The smell of it assailed his senses. For so long now, he had lived on a diet of raw vegetables and grasses, but he broke off a fragment of the precious food and ate it.

As day broke, Sudhana left the still-sleeping camp and reached the city gates. There were soldiers there on night watch; others were posted on guard duty at the watchtowers along the city walls. Yet Sudhana did not receive the rude welcome he had been told to expect; he avoided the guards, and made his way into the city through an unwatched postern gate.

The city lay under curfew until sunrise; no early-rising women could come out to draw water at the wells. Even the livestock were still asleep as Sudhana made his way down the main street alone. From time to time he had to hide under the streetside stalls while a watchful squadron of troops rode by mounted on elephants.

As soon as he had hidden beneath the market stalls, a hand grabbed him. "What are you doing? If you walk about the streets now, you'll be executed. Come inside quickly…" Sudhana soon learned that the citizens were not asleep; they had been awake since daybreak and were alert, peering through cracks in the walls.

He waited inside until the sun rose. When it was already broad daylight and perfectly legal to walk about, he walked through the area until he reached the gates of the ruler's main residence.

"Who goes there?" a sentinel asked roughly.

Sudhana made a gentle reply, "I have come to pay my respects to King Anala, the ruler of Taladhvaja. I have come all the way from the distant north at the risk of my life, in order to catch one glimpse of His Majesty."

The man seemed to be an officer in the palace guards, for he personally gave Sudhana permission to enter the palace.

"If you want to have an audience with His Majesty, you'd best go to the execution grounds at midday; seventy-seven criminals are due to be punished," he said. "Turn left at the main palace, then go on until you see a black banner hanging on a high pole. Head for that. That's where the sentences will be carried out."

Sudhana shuddered. The nomads had been telling the truth. He wondered why he had come. From the moment the nomads had told him not to go, he had resolved to enter the city. If the king was guilty of dreadful crimes and put many people to death, what call was there for Sudhana to meet him? What could he hope to learn from such an evil ruler?

He reached the black banner and found the executioners, all dressed in black, dancing a grim dance. On the central terrace, King Anala was sitting on the royal throne, gazing down at the dance. The area was marked off by luminescent pennants, and surrounded by a host of ministers, generals, and soldiers. A truly dreadful atmosphere reigned.

First, an executioner read out the crimes of each one, then carried out the prescribed punishment. Some were rolled in mattresses soaked in oil and burned to death, others had both eyes put out. Some lost ears and nose, or had all four limbs chopped off with an axe, while some had ropes tied around their wrists and ankles, then the ropes were tightened and they were torn apart in a gory punishment that left the executioner covered in blood.

Some died with their eyes shut, some spat towards the throne where King Anala was seated; some died gazing at the soldiers with hate-filled eyes, while others died shouting.

"It's not possible. It's not right. Why ever did I come to meet this wicked king?" Sudhana was on the point of withdrawing when a voice fell on him from the empty air.

"Young pilgrim, you have to learn that even the wickedest king in the world can be your teacher. Don't leave. Go and meet him."

Sudhana looked around. No one was there but the voice had sounded oddly like old Myohyang from up on Mount Samantanetra. He looked again towards the scene on the execution ground. The executions had been going on without interruption since midday; now evening was arriving. With nightfall, torches and candelabra had been lit. The place reeked of blood. As it grew darker, the number of soldiers increased, and their surveillance over the crowd at the site doubled and tripled. Just as the seventieth of the criminals had been dealt with, Sudhana lost consciousness, overwhelmed by the cruelty he was witnessing, and collapsed. He was carried out onto the execution area by several soldiers.

The silence was immediately broken by a loud clamor. One of the soldiers spoke in a loud voice, "This child is a stranger here. Perhaps he's a spy for the neighboring kingdom of Keema."

King Anala sent the captain of the palace guards down to see who had caused such a commotion in the grim silence of the execution area. Now Sudhana lay at his feet, waiting for the royal command. Everyone was holding their breath. With the exception of the dead bodies of those who had been executed, even the criminals who had received their punishments were staring in frank curiosity at this child who had suddenly plunged into the midst of their dreadful torments.

"Child! Where did you come from?" King Anala questioned Sudhana himself.

"I am a passing traveler. For those already punished, there is nothing to be done, but I beg you to pardon at least some of those still waiting."

"You wretched, presumptuous child!" On hearing his words, the captain of the guard seized his scabbard, drew out his sword, and prepared to behead Sudhana. The king made a sign with his hand. "We'll take this child into the palace. That's enough for today. Put the remaining criminals back into prison."

King Anala led Sudhana into the main palace building and sat facing him; the awe-inspiring, princely appearance he had hitherto harbored had changed into a most affable manner. "Where did you come from, young pilgrim?"

"I am a mere foolish traveler, knowing neither where he has been nor where he is going," Sudhana replied in clear, steady tones.

"What was the reason you bade me cease punishing wicked men?"

"In order to prevent you from becoming even more wicked."

"Hmmm." The king ordered the captain and the rest of his escorts to leave the room. The two of them were alone. "Little pilgrim, won't you stay here with me?"

"I am a wandering pilgrim. How could a wanderer ever stay for long in one place?"

"No. You can live here."

"Listen. You refuse to recognize those who do not obey you. Therefore the unhappy spirits of the unjustly executed throng round that execution place like so many drops of dew. Those who don't obey you are still your subjects. All who submit to your every word are not on that account your true subjects. You must listen to those who oppose you."

The king listened silently, his eyes shut. "That is true. What you say is right." He tore off his resplendent robes as he spoke, "Young pilgrim, your words are amazing and true. But know that I caused that atrocious spectacle on the execution place by the laws of illusion and transformation. It was not intended for you, but for the eyes of wicked people. I confect the illusion of criminals, and the mere sight of their punishment causes many people to abandon their evil ways. I don't have it in me to kill so much as a single ant, let alone another human being. Those seventy people who have undergone punishment since midday were not human beings at all, but emptiness robed in human form. Now do you understand what I am, young pilgrim?"

Sudhana was amazed. The ruler watched him with amusement.

"Am I not King Anala, the lord of this place?"

"You are King Anala, sir, I know."

"Not at all. I am not really King Anala of this city of Taladhvaja at all. I am that aged hawk that has been traveling along with you. I am no king; I don't kill innocent people as criminals. Go and look. I am merely a roaming beggar bringing this world's evil to its senses by the laws of illusion and transformation. I am really nothing more than an aging traveler, no different from you."

Sudhana left the palace and hurried towards the execution ground. What previously had seemed a ghastly spot where ghosts might appear at any moment, was an utterly peaceful expanse of meadow. The sight gave young Sudhana a shock. No corpses. No reek of blood. A gentle breeze was ruffling the grass. He went back to the palace.

"Look at my palace." It was a magnificent building, adorned with gold and silver, rubies and every kind of jewel. "My accumulated karma of merit enables me to enclose myself in this kind of splendor. Yet since my karma is an empty thing, this too is empty. Behold."

Before Sudhana's eyes, what had been a resplendent palace turned into an empty ruined hovel. And there was no sign of King Anala. All he could see was a hawk, that seemed to have flown out through a hole gaping in one wall of the tumbledown shack. The bird caught the light in such a way that it seemed to be leaving a trail of fire, as it vanished into the distance.

Sudhana turned his back on that ruined hovel without the least regret and hurried off down the unending road in the direction the hawk had flown. He passed the emptiness of Taladhvaja city, walking fast yet with less fatigue than usual. Glancing behind him, he found no trace of the imposing city anywhere. All that remained was the encampment of the nomads, receding over the skyline. The nomads, like Sudhana, had been deluded by illusion into thinking they could see the city of Taladhvaja before them.

All night long, Sudhana walked between the fields without taking rest. He pushed on through the darkness with rapid steps as if something was pursuing him. Then, just past midnight, he collapsed.

It was morning. Sudhana was awakened by the sound of a woman's voice questioning him. "Pilgrim, where have you come from? This is Suprabha city." He opened his eyes; the road sank down under seven levels of fortifications until it passed into an underground cavern and divided in a maze of tunnels. The houses were richly adorned with white silver and shone so brightly that no darkness could ever come creeping down the streets where they stood, on account of the silver's brightness. It was a magnificent sight. Oxen with horns of pure gold wandered freely up and down the underground streets, gently drooling white foam. Passersby collected the foam and drank it.

With the woman as his guide, Sudhana continued farther downwards until a marvelous temple rose in the very heart of the subterranean city. With the help of a few of the citizens, he made his way to King Mahaprabha of Suprabha.

"Let's go in. Anyone can meet our country's king whenever they wish." Sudhana's guide led him along blithely. Entering a glittering pavilion, they found the young King Mahaprabha sitting alone, without any guards, harboring a beautiful smile.

"King Mahaprabha, I am a passing traveler."

"You are welcome, young pilgrim. I am glad, very glad."

"You must possess great spiritual knowledge to have established so vast an underground kingdom. I beg you, impart a small portion of it to me, even though it be but one ten-thousandth part. I am hungry for spiritual knowledge; I starve for want of truth."

"Pilgrim, what do you think of this kingdom?"

"Truly, it is sublime."

"Yet this underground kingdom is a place which different people see in different ways. To wicked men, white silver and pure gold look like cow dung, while the people look like blood-soaked phantoms. You have seen things as they are; you are like one of us. All the people of this land have attained the broad vision of the great heart, living in unity and trust, with no strife among them. They see all that exists with purest eyes, knowing silver as silver, gold as gold, and milk as milk. They see things as they are."

At a sign from the king, flowers blossomed in the underground plaza, clouds drifted by, music rang out, and the people joined hands and began to dance.

"Behold, young pilgrim. In this way all things existing turn into dance. But that dance is not something arising lightly; each heart has to grow deeper and deeper until it becomes the dance of a complete full moon. Every least turn in the lightest dance is the manifestation of a divine inspiration emerging from within, transcending the ecstasies of the deepest wisdom. Now you, too, young pilgrim, should go outside and join in the dance."

Listening to the king's words, Sudhana saw clearly that this dance by the citizens that he and the king had been watching together was not something that could be expressed or performed by just anyone. It only occurred because the whole subterranean world was full of the broad vision of the great heart. He seemed to glimpse something of the reason why this underground city was buried so deeply. Sudhana, joining in their dance, turned round and round the city plaza. He felt infinitely happy. In the midst of the dance, a girl came up to him and took his hand.

"When you go out from here, head for Sthira city. Visit my sister—she's a devotee there."

Goodness knows how long he danced. The dancing did not tire him. It felt like a breeze rising above a lake. Finally, Sudhana took his leave of the beautiful, young King Mahaprabha. The king offered him a pair of newly-made sandals.

"If you wear these shoes as you walk, they will know where you want to go and take you there accordingly."

Sudhana left behind his old shoes of arrowroot vines, and put the new shoes on. At once, they began to walk with quick steps, as if in a hurry to get started on the journey. He returned upwards to the surface of the world. Above, it was as bright as it had been below. But unlike in the streets below, it was uncomfortably hot.

"That's right," Sudhana murmured to himself as the shoes hurried along, "I have to walk on in this hot and painful universe, feeling heat and pain with all who live."

> Where have you gone, old hawk?
> Dear old hawk,
> you turned into an imitation king for me,
> then into a youthful king—
> so where have you gone? Where are you?

But the destiny drawing the hawk into Sudhana's travels was now complete; it never appeared to him again. Encountering is the mother of parting, and sometimes parting's son. The experience of meeting followed by parting is the shape endlessly taken by this world's unfolding course. Such were Sudhana's thoughts as he walked along.

25.
FREE YOURSELF FROM LIFE AND DEATH

T THE END of several days of hard walking, Sudhana reached the city of Sthira. Since ancient times, Sthira had been a trading center, exchanging with the lands to the west in one direction, and with the remote northern ports in the other. As a result, traders from the north had settled there. Sudhana entered one house and rested a moment in the citrus-scented shade of the garden. An old man approached him, his large eyes full of melancholy and seemingly fixed in meditation.

"You're not from these parts, are you?"

"No sir, I am a pilgrim."

"That is what I thought. Are you not from the north?"

"Yes sir, I am."

"Then you have come a very long way. I too came a long way, by sea." The old man addressed the young pilgrim gravely. Although he was a trader, Sudhana was struck by the way he seemed deeply immersed in inner reflection. "So where are you going now? Don't you ever think of going back home?"

"No sir. I have left home for good."

"Ah, a homeless ascetic, a homeless sage. In that case, I hope you will meet a beautiful devotee living here before you leave. She is young and holy. I have often seen her bathing in the forests. Her body does not awaken any desire; it always seems only to reveal heavenly beauty."

Hearing the old man's words, Sudhana grew curious about the devotee. But he was so tired that in the end he simply fell asleep. In his dreams, the devotee spoke to Sudhana: "You have come a long way." She had been born out of a vast lotus blossom, two hundred and fifty *yojanas* in diameter with eighty-four thousand petals, each one holding a million drops of dew that each radiated a thousand rays of light. She was a young woman who had severed all attachment with this world and dwelt only in the imagination or the world of concepts.

Many years before, she had undertaken a long journey to a temple in the central highlands, where dwelt a venerable master whose mother had died in childbirth. He grew up in the temple, where he lived until now he was over ninety years old. Thanks to his lifelong practice of meditating on a skull, he had attained the power to see Paradise as a land composed entirely of glass. The glass composing it was everywhere flawless, with no trace of darkness at all. He saw that the road to Paradise was marked by a golden cord. People from all over the Deccan Plateau came to visit him, venerating his transcendent wisdom, as the devotee had done.

When she arrived, the old brahman master did not meet her as he did all the others who came. Instead, he hid and refused to see her. Just before that, while walking in the grove of jewel trees, he had glimpsed the beautiful devotee as she descended from her palanquin and walked towards the temple; his faith in the Pure Land Paradise, which he had spent ninety years developing and perfecting, crumbled and collapsed completely at the sight of the woman's beauty.

"Beautiful. So beautiful. How can I call that beauty illusion and falsehood?" the old monk lamented, as he hid watching her. He had never even looked at a woman before, certainly never embraced one, so completely had he cut all bonds with the present world. He was utterly unworldly, considering women to be merely one kind of object pertaining to the world. The appearance of the devotee brought the old monk into direct relationship with the world for the first time in his life, and also the last.

That old monk, who had until now had so deep a sense of the world beyond, whose only thought had been for that other world, suddenly saw his entire universe fall apart because of one woman. He was at last reduced to the ordinary, lonely, human being he had been born to be.

Although the devotee knew the monk did not intend to meet her, she did not leave at once. After all, she had risked death in order to come and meet the venerable master, so steadfast was her devotion to the Pure Land. Night fell. The old monk suddenly appeared in front of the lodging that had been assigned to her, looking rather like an old tree stump. The woman came hurrying out and knelt in reverence at his feet, which were nothing but packets of bones. As her brow touched his feet, a fire sprang up and began to burn the old man. She was amazed at the sudden conflagration, but as the old monk was consumed in the flames, she saw unfolding in her own heart the vast lotus blossom of the Pure Land Paradise with its eighty-four thousand petals.

After that, the woman made pilgrimages to various lands, sowing seeds of the joys of the world beyond in this sweltering, painful, present world. Then at last she returned home to Sthira. As Sudhana dreamed, he heard the woman speak to him:

"Lose this world's evil passions, pilgrim. Lose its life and death. Yet those passions, and even that life and death, are the first steps towards Paradise. The desire that gives rise to evil passions is at the same time the source of Paradise. I have nothing else to show you. You have seen my beauty, that of Paradise, and I have seen your sacred wisdom."

Sudhana was unable to hear all that she said, for in his dream he tried to seize her hand, failed, and awoke. He had slept for a long while. The old merchant from the north had waited beside Sudhana as he slept and now he spoke: "First you must wash, then let's go to meet the maiden."

Sudhana shook his head. "It is not necessary for me to see the devotee. Many other encounters are waiting for me in my next destination, so I must set off for that."

"Surely you don't mean to leave yet?"

"Yes. Many thanks. I must be leaving now. That will be the same as seeing the devotee."

The old man tried to restrain Sudhana, but despite his efforts, Sudhana shouldered his bundle, casually stood up, and went out mumbling, "It is hard to encounter the good in this world, but still. . ."

The old northern merchant felt sorry for Sudhana but he hastened on through the hinterland of Sthira, intending to meet the devotee alone.

The city of Tosala was famed for its community of unorthodox ascetics and Sudhana hoped he would meet them on reaching the city. He knew that although truth is revealed by contact with truth, it can also be discovered through encountering attitudes opposed to truth, as well as in things having no apparent connection at all with truth.

What would those mysterious ascetics prove to be? They were apprehended by people viewing them as unity in multiplicity, appearing sometimes as one and sometimes as four, sometimes as a crowd that broke up and went each one his way. Yet no one knew if really they were one or four or a crowd. Sudhana felt no need to know whether they were one person dividing into many or many becoming one. Beside a stream, he reckoned, it is enough to know the stream.

Long before, a volcanic eruption had devastated Tosala, which had previously been the most flourishing city of the whole southern region. With the destruction of the city, the people had gone to live in the nearby lowlands. Seeing that no one was returning to the city, a group of ascetics and strangers had come along and established a nation with neither king nor army. The lowland area in which the ascetics chose to live lay behind the sea wall, below sea level. If ever the sea wall were breached, there was a risk it would be flooded, but the ascetics were far beyond being troubled by concerns over any such danger.

When Sudhana reached Tosala, he saw the city was in ruins. Within the city there existed no government, no king, no soldiers. Yet the inhabitants were living without disorder. The young pilgrim had never even known such a nation existed.

"Where is the king's palace?" he asked one of the many people walking by.

"There's no king here, so naturally there's no king's house either. Here everyone was a king in a previous existence, so it's impossible to choose one person to be king; all are equally untitled citizens. Ours is a very proud nation, high beyond compare with any other nation."

Sudhana recognized that the peace arising from this land's lack of a governing body was a splendid thing. He had seen that kings and rulers, rather than fostering harmony within a nation, were often the main reason why a nation could not enjoy peace and stability. When no one is higher or lower, when all are close, when all are equal in solidarity, then all are closely united side by side. Yet the ambitions of living things always struggle upwards, while those who have taken the upper places try to keep control over the others in order to preserve their superior position.

Sudhana saw for the first time that in order for people to be free of this world's evil desires and free from life and death, first and foremost the distinction between the governing upper and the governed lower class has to be abolished. The unorthodox ascetics were people who did not accept the idea of particular, individual sanctity, but preferred to appear as a crowd, or three or four, as a communitarian incarnation of truth. Feeling he had learned what he had come to learn, he turned to leave the city.

26.
YOUR LIGHT'S TOMB

UDHANA WAS SUDDENLY challenged by harsh voices: "Where are you rushing off to like that? A fine pilgrim you are, tramping through all the wide world to your heart's content with those tiny feet."

"Are you the ascetics of Tosala?"

"It's true that we're ascetics. But we're not the only ones. You must know that the whole of nature, as well as each and every person and animal in Tosala are all ascetics."

"All ascetics?"

"Of course; everything in the realms of the lower, middle, and upper heavens is engaged in spiritual training. All at some point or other become bodhisattvas, so that the title bodhisattva is unnecessary. If all are becoming Buddha and bodhisattva, surely there is no reason to make a distinction between 'Buddha nature' and all living creatures? At this moment you, us, and the ground we are treading on, all of us are in a process of striving and growth. The very motion of the whole universe is a process of profound spiritual growth. All change, all life and death, loving and hating, all is training and growth. Isn't it? Isn't it?"

They addressed him in voices that echoed in the hills ahead.

"Like everybody in this city, we have become one with the whole of humanity and with an appearance like theirs, with their voice, we live in quest of truth."

Sudhana asked, "Master ascetics, why do you stay here? Why don't you come walking with me round all the lands here in the south, teaching the ways of ascetic living?"

"That's a very good question. But everything has already attained a state in which those ways have been taught and learned. There is no empty place anywhere. There is not one empty spot in all the wide universe. Everywhere is full of encounters between bodhisattvas and beings. That is where truth arises. Here in this city where we are, as well as in all the places you visit in search of wisdom, there is the Buddha nature and the Mahasattva bodhisattva nature proper to that place. No matter where we are, we are present to all the worlds beneath the four heavens. You are living in just the same way, little pilgrim."

"My name is Sudhana, and I must leave Tosala city."

"You mean to leave so soon? You leave one, you meet another; you exchange a few words in the time it takes the heavens to let drop just a few pearls of light, then you leave again. And that is a fine thing, indeed. Why not pay a visit to Utpalabhuti in the land of Parthurashtra? She's an old woman who sells blue lotus perfumes."

Sudhana left them and began again to walk along the far-reaching road. He advanced alone like a solitary wild goose that has lost its flock flying through the far-reaching immensities of heaven.

Here I am on my way towards Utpalabhuti's house in the unfamiliar land of Parthurashtra, he thought. What am I going there for? Does that person really have anything to teach me? Does anyone have anything to tell me, to teach me? So far, I have learned nothing at all. I have heard nothing at all. I have nothing at all to give. It was all mere illusion. Surely my world of experience is the scaffold where illusions are put to death. Yes, I have nothing at all. Nothing. Just then a song drifted toward him, sung by Utpalabhuti, who was waiting for him:

> I know every perfume.
> Since the time I was four
> until now my hair is white,
> I have been selling all kinds of perfumes.

> I know the perfumes in the dragon's store.
> If you burn just a little of the perfume
> that arises when two dragons battle,
> a vast fragrant cloud will cover the sky
> and for seven days it will rain perfumes.
> If you get wet in that perfumed rain,

your clothes will become flowers of cusma and sunama,
attracting the bees that frequent such flowers.
After one breath of the perfume from those flowers,
for a week your whole being will brim with joy.

I know every perfume.
I know the sandalwood perfume from Mount Maraya.
Anointed with that oil,
you may enter a furnace unscorched.
I know every perfume.
I know the perfume of invincibility.
Apply that fragrance to war drums or conchs,
it attaches itself to the sounds they make
and fills the enemy army with thoughts of love.

I know every perfume.
I know the aguilaria perfume from Lake Anabadala.
All crimes are abolished by its scent.
I know every perfume.
I know the nomiforma perfume from the Himalayas.
It provokes deep meditation of a pure woman's beauty.
I know the bamboo perfume from the heaven of Nirrti.
Only apply it and you become free as the birds in flight.

I know every perfume.
I know how to grind them, burn them, apply them.
I know the perfume of perfumed majesty
from the prayer halls in the heaven of Indra.
I know the perfume of pure offerings from Suyama Heaven.
I know the sontabara perfume from Tushita Heaven.
I know the perfume of Fragrant Flower heaven.

I know every perfume.
Through them I bring into being
the bodies of Buddhas
and enlightening Mahasattvas.

As he listened to the words, a faint perfume filled the air. As her fragrances spread with the song, Sudhana's mind was delivered from the melancholy inspired by his long journey, and he found himself once again overflowing with joy.

When he finally reached Utpalabhuti, he knelt at her feet. "Ancient lady, many thanks and thanks indeed. How can I ever repay you for having bestowed on me the gift of this most sublime fragrance?"

"Not at all, young pilgrim. I have longed to learn one truth, ten billion truths, following you. I am weary of this perfume business and find no way to the truth. I beg you, go in my place along many roads, meet many bodhisattvas, many creatures, many evil spirits, receive their truths, and burn this perfume, apply this perfume. Sacred monk of the road, holy, holy, holy young monk of the road.

"With this old body of mine, I speak many words. I have simply produced perfumes and sold them. But perfume's wealth is not worldly wealth. Now I am content. I have drawn my perfume songs out of this aged breast of mine; now there is nothing left there. It is I who should be thanking you."

"Lady, I shall never be able to repay you for your kindness—not in a future incarnation, not in all my future lives."

Utpalabhuti left him with a piece of solid perfume called the Heaven of Skillful Transformations and this final word: "Soon you will reach Vasita River. You should cross that river by the ferry and find Jayottama."

Now, whether the sun set and night fell, or night passed and daylight rose, as moon followed sun and sun followed moon, all things appeared to him in a dazzling light; nothing in the world was hidden.

Following her instructions, he pursued his path towards a place where the river valley was luxuriant with reeds. The river was flowing white, empty. At the ferry station, one ancient boat with a single oar was tethered to the shore and faced into the current as the river flowed. Everything was very quiet, as if a loud noise had never once been heard there.

It had been a long time since Sudhana had encountered a river. It was so wide that it gave the illusion of being a lake. The water was dazzling. All the previous night's stars appeared to have fallen into the stream and lay floating there. A strong breeze scoured Sudhana's flesh.

A quiet song reached his ears:

Float down this river...
float down in this old boat...

every river reaches the sea...
where upstream and downstream meet...
reaches the darkening sea...
is left as a crust of white salt on the shore.

So float on down the river...
eyes closed... lips shut...
every scrap of dharma set aside.
Float down alone...
winds will blow...
night will fall and float down with you.
When you reach the sea...
Proclaim...
there is no one in pain...
anywhere in this world.

The low melody reached Sudhana's ears from a simple hovel beside the ferry landing. He could hear the song faintly, as if it had long lain buried underground. Just as the song ceased, he reached the place from which it had originated. There he found a man lying plunged in sorrow, one hand clasped to his brow.

"May I...may I come in?"

On hearing his words, the man rose silently and gazed at Sudhana. He spoke: "It has been a very long time, little pilgrim."

"Do you know me?" Sudhana asked, startled.

He shook his head. "I always say that to everyone...I am the ferryman here on this River of Liberation. But since there hasn't been anyone headed downstream for months now, I just wait here in silence like this, day after day. Where are you going?"

27.
JOURNEY DOWN
AN ETERNAL RIVER

UDHANA LOOKED at the middle-aged ferryman and slowly began to smile. The ferryman's face grew bright with an identical smile.

"My name's Vaira, what's yours?"

"Sudhana."

"Let's get rid of names. Names are a great hindrance to people." The ferryman pointed at the river and laughed. "The hosts of nameless bodhisattvas are free of that."

"I've got a name, but it's never been used much," Sudhana said, "No one ever got tired of speaking my name."

"So much the better. Cast any name that has no one to speak it into this white River of Liberation. Ha ha ha." His laugh was slow, like a swelling wave. "Where are you headed?"

"I have to keep going with nowhere to go. I have to go where the ferryman decides, where the ship's bow decides, where the river decides."

"Ah, that's good. It's been worth waiting a long time for such a passenger. It's good, very good."

"Have you been ferryman here for very long?"

"Oh yes, I have been ferrying people here for a very, very long time; since before I was born, before my parents were born, before the Buddhas of ancient times were born. Only look at this age-old oar. It is all my parents and teachers."

"You must know the river very well."

"I still don't know it so very well. The course of the stream changes all the time; it is always turning into a new river. That means I keep turning into a new ferryman, too."

"I find everything in the world flows like this," Sudhana said slowly. "Everything changes in the same way as this river."

"You know, when I look at the river, it's not the water that's flowing, it's me. I'm ceaselessly flowing on."

Vaira the ferryman reached out his hands from within the long sleeves of his coat and untied the boat. After Sudhana had boarded the craft, the ferryman got in, seized the oar, and entrusted the vessel to the current. They began to float rapidly downstream as the boat moved into the center of the river, where it was gently borne along. The ferryman reclined in the bottom of the boat.

"With the fares I get, I buy clothing and fruit for the poor. Then I teach them the river's wisdom. If you want to go all the way down this river, you have to stop and rest at several ferry stations. I buy fruit and cheap cloth as I go. Then I ply the oar and remount the river, or go across to the landing on the opposite bank. I have been ferryman in the fair land of Amrita, and in the land of Sumiya across the River of Liberation."

Ah, dear waters of Liberation! Carry us quickly down to the sea,
to meet the ocean's dragons and their newborn babes.

As if struck by a sudden thought, Sudhana drew out a dry reed flute Iryon had given him and tried a few notes. Songs drifted near and were absorbed into the flute. He did not at once blow on the song-filled flute, but replaced it in the darkness of his bundle.

"Ah hah, you've made a good catch of songs." The ferryman watched him. "There'll be sounds of the river forming part of those songs, I reckon."

Then they both fell asleep. The sleeping boat, bearing its sleeping passengers, wafted on untrammeled by dreaming ripples. The river, apparently eager to prolong their happy journey, grew deeper than before.

Sudhana was awakened by a song emerging from the flute he had put back into his bundle. At first it was a girl's voice, but as the song went on it turned into the low rough voice of Vaira the ferryman. Just as the song was ending, the boat reached some rapids where the river's murmur grew into a roar. The ferryman opened his eyes and looked hard at Sudhana. Sudhana had become one with the river, and attained the river's deep wisdom.

"Are you not human?" Sudhana asked the ferryman.

"Ha ha, if I'm not human, those river birds are not river birds. But I have no idea if I'm human or what I am."

A mist swiftly covered the whole area.

"Ah, the mists of the land of Nandihara. They're designed to welcome travelers," the ferryman said.

In the mist, the smell of the river was thickly mingled with a kind of drowsy perfume.

"How old are you, ferryman?" Sudhana asked.

"Me? The same as you, little pilgrim."

"That's not possible. I'm still a child."

"Once I'm reborn in the next world, I'll be younger than you, won't I? Therefore there can be no question as to which of us is younger or older. We're the same age."

"But in that case, this river is the same age as we are, too?"

"Surely, surely. What you say is right."

Their conversation lulled, and the river that was bearing them along began to sing to them. Sudhana had the impression that he had cast away the long journey he had hitherto made, all the way from the north after his escape from death down to this southern land, and was just now starting out for the first time. That filled him with a fresh happiness as he gazed eagerly around him. Out here on the waters of the River of Liberation, he had truly become a new pilgrim.

A particular moment on a long journey can make us forget all that led up to that moment. In this way, beginnings arise in endings. Sudhana's journey was beginning now, at the very end of a very long road.

> Be born again.
> Be born again.
> Be born again,
> several times,
> several hundred times,
> several trillion times,
> the waves sang.

The ferryman fell asleep again. Each time they awoke from sleep, it was as if they had been reborn. As soon as the ferryman was asleep, his pilgrim companion felt terribly lonely. This time he could not fall asleep with him. Gradually, the river grew wider and the flowing stream filled his pure young eyes. Sometimes birds would fly close to the craft, settle on the stern and rest for a while.

Sudhana opened his bundle, drew out the things it contained, and began to throw them one by one into the river. No further need for the dry reed flute, the dried fruit, the hawk's feather, Iryon's ghost, the scrap of netting received from a fisherman. Throw everything away, and then the bundle's wrapping, too. He felt inclined to cast even himself into the river.

"Why are you throwing all that away? You still have to carry it with you." Awaking from sleep, the ferryman spoke sharply, abandoning his previous simple smile. "The things of this world possess a certain force, without which you will never get free of the world. If you throw your body away, who will be left to throw your heart away? You still have to carry your body about with you. A body is not just a body. Without a body, how will you be able to incarnate a bodhisattva heart? The body is the temple of the heart…"

The ferryman seized his oar, beat roughly at the waves, and brought them safely through a section of raging rapids. The river had become a vast, surging torrent, their boat something very small on the surface of its mighty flow. The river seethed, foaming and roaring. When they emerged from the regions covered in mist, cliffs and meadows appeared on the riverbanks, while white clouds drifted above their heads.

"We're almost there. But it was a long journey. Infinitely long. This river is endless."

"You're right, ferryman. We travel without end. To travel endlessly, I have to travel an endless path in this life as if I were endlessly enduring the torments of a bodhisattva. I shall never become an enlightened being. I shall just go on and on experiencing life in the course of endless reincarnations."

The ferryman embraced the little pilgrim. The boat floated on down the wide, white river. For a long while they floated on, locked in that embrace. "Truly sacred pilgrim! You speak like a bodhisattva!" The boat heard those words and rocked in response. From far below, a buried ray of light broke the surface.

28.

IN QUEST OF NANDIHARA

INALLY, THE BOAT pulled to shore. After embracing Vaira one last time, Sudhana turned his back on the river, and set out down the road the aging ferryman had indicated. He had met twenty-five different masters and learned from each of them. He was now ready to attain full bodhisattvahood. Bodhisattvahood was no longer a goal lying ahead of him but was rapidly becoming the substance of his daily life. Sudhana was no longer pursuing a road; the road was hastening toward him. It was now a living road, one that only dies when the person dies. As Sudhana advanced further and further towards the south, the road absorbed him. Sometimes the road was simply a level meadow path; other times, it had rough passages and steep ascents. Sometimes it was covered with a layer of crimson gravel.

Sudhana lost his way and went wandering for a while in the forests along the middle reaches of the River Krishna. He mistakenly followed tracks made by animals instead of human paths. For two days, he wandered, lost. Then he came across a band of savages armed with hunting spears. He gazed brightly at their white teeth and dark eyes. They seized one of his feet, turned it over, and examined the sole. They were astonished to see a bare sole that had clearly walked many thousands of miles. Their leader gave an order; a hunter hoisted Sudhana onto his shoulders and little by little forced a way out of the forest. By afternoon, Sudhana found himself standing alone on a road with a village before him.

The village was composed of a market extending along both sides of a central road. It looked like the kind of market where, if a rumor arises on either side, it spreads everywhere in a flash of wildfire. Yet, although Sudhana walked the whole length of the road, there was not a soul in sight.

All that could be heard was the sound of a cowbell somewhere and a woman weeping. Perhaps the oldest villager had just died? Or had died a year before and this was the anniversary of his death? Or was this a village of death, with not a living soul in it? Suppose the bell and weeping were mere illusions?

Sudhana firmly set all such thoughts aside. He was feeling a little weak and rather weary, but the road continued to give him joy. Once past Madras, he would reach the city of Nandihara. The remembered words of Vaira, the boatman, accompanied Sudhana along the road: "Sudhana, I know all about working my ship's wood and metalwork and sails, and judging the strength or weakness of the wind filling its sails. The people and animals I carry are able to travel peacefully. They lose all fear of the ocean of torment arising from birth and death in this world; they receive power to transform that ocean into an ocean of wisdom. Little Sudhana, you and I both have the power to change the ocean of desire, the ocean of the entire Buddha cosmos, into a blue ocean of perfect purity."

Soon, Sudhana was standing at the top of a hill near the port of Madras. From the top, the indigo ocean was suddenly visible in three directions. The sight of it transformed young Sudhana's tiny heart into a cosmic vastness, and absorbed his loneliness. Sudhana devoured the ocean with his eyes.

Madras was one of the world's great ports: fishing and trading, farming and hunting, were all flourishing there. Although he longed to spend a few days there, he resolutely pushed on. His heart ached for people and human community.

To keep himself company, he sang to himself:

> The countless ecstasies of silence
> are a garden welcoming a full moon.
> One breath of wind is surely no wind at all
> but an extension of the truth I must cherish?
>
> Behold the face of the full moon.
> Though it only brush the face,
> the wind is invisible.
> The wind is, yet is not,
> and though it is not, it passes by.
> Surely these countless ecstasies are this world's every song?

Sudhana came across a soft, moist road that was a pleasure underfoot. It was a gentle road soaked by rain brought by the last of the seasonal winds a few days prior, and now drying out. As evening came, the smell of stabled animals told him he was approaching a village. He was very weary, and walked slowly. A patch of forest loomed up, already yellowing now with the changing season. At a crossroads, he found an inscribed stone. It marked the frontier of Nandihara. As Sudhana read the stone, a young woodcutter emerged from the forest, his wheeled cart loaded high with firewood. Sudhana asked him the way to Nandihara.

"It is a vast city, without gates or walls. This forest forms the city walls. But where are you from? Are you going to visit someone there?" the woodcutter asked suspiciously.

"I am a wanderer from the north. I am on my way to meet the venerable Jayottama."

"Jayottama the venerable? That plutocrat? You can go wherever you like in this kingdom, and you will always be walking on lands belonging to him. This whole land belongs to him."

"Do you know him?"

The woodcuter shook his head. "He meets three hundred people every day. When will you ever get a chance to meet him? I reckon you've wasted your journey."

"Not at all. I'm sure I'll get to see him." He bade the woodcutter goodbye. Little Sudhana had journeyed far and wide; he had received instruction from many teachers, and had constantly been astonished to discover that everything in the world was the eternal truth he was seeking.

Here and there, the forest was interrupted by broad stretches of field and swamp; in the swamps, crocodiles lay with gaping mouths. He entered an avenue lined with stone sarcophagi facing the east. Beyond the stones rose high buildings of immense majesty. Everyone he saw was clothed in fine, soft materials. Sudhana inquired of one girl as to the whereabouts of Jayottama the venerable. She made a sign with her hand to follow her and went on ahead of him, talking as they went.

"I am Sumera and Jayottama is my uncle. Normally, people have to stay here at least five months, just to meet him for as long as it takes to blink fifty times. There are so many waiting to see him. Visitors here are never able to get a single room, there are so many waiting. But at this evening's family party, my uncle will be present without attendants or guards. I'll arrange for you to meet him briefly then."

Sudhana looked shabby after his long journey, yet she perceived something worthy in him. "You have reached this place at the end of a very long journey. This land is supremely blessed by you, traveler. I believe that my uncle will be glad to welcome you."

Sudhana followed the girl into her family mansion. She led him to one of the twelve buildings composing the compound, where he entered a room and settled down to wait. The empty room was fragrant with incense. He was served a nourishing meal. A bright light was kindled in an oil lamp as night fell. Time flowed on.

Late that evening, he heard someone coming, and the girl led a tall, elderly man into the room. Jayottama the venerable did not look like the owner of a thousand billion gold coins, of mountains of cowrie-shell cash, to say nothing of endless stretches of land. He had rid himself of everything. He was dressed in clothes of thin, coarse hemp as he was performing penance for his wealth. The man was weary. Glancing back at Sumera, he spoke:

"Truly, it is as the delightful Sumera has said; among all the countless people I have so far met, this young seeker of truth ranks highest. Sumera, you have done well in bringing this young fellow to meet me."

Sudhana bowed down to Jayottama's feet in greeting, then rose and stood. The room had grown warm with truth and compassion. The whole cosmos, brahmans, and atmans, all burning in a single mass, trembled and swayed.

Silently, he wondered, "Holy master, I have come thus far in quest of enlightening ways and bodhisattva works and now I have met you. Tell me, I pray: by what means may I be enabled to stir the leaves on the trees in the forest with bodhisattva wind and breath?"

Jayottama replied to his silent, heart-sprung question. "Child, little Sudhana, you have already penetrated deeply into the realm of truth. I have bought lands and earned fortunes, not only in this kingdom of Nandihara but in every kingdom, until I need envy no king in this world. I have established no less than nine new kingdoms with my own hands; but for a long time now I have found my main pleasure in meeting people of every nation and speaking to them, not about money but about truth and universal justice. I only wonder why I did not do so from the start.

"Doctrines that are no doctrines must be thrown aside. If there are any people advocating ways that are not the Way, they must be converted and brought to knowledge of the rightful Way. And since the most precious thing in the world is peace, it is better that you and I should be killed before we fight, so that peace can be reborn. Once minds are fixed in that direction, all mankind will live as bodhisattvas in a life of complete detachment, as if all the prisoners in hell or in the stinking prisons of the western land of Muro had been set free and were singing praises to heaven."

"You are a high and most high master," Sudhana said.

"Not so," Jayottama replied, "I am low as the ocean floor. I have not yet said everything; let's go out and pass the night beneath the old lailai tree where I always sleep and watch. We could spend three whole days and nights just talking of the merits and virtues involved in bodhisattva living."

The aged master invited his niece to accompany him and they went out into the early dawn, where the morning star was about to rise. Sudhana followed them. Jayottama spoke to the dawn:

How good you are, first dawn.
Deepest night is good,
midday by lotus ponds is good,
the red glow of dusk at twilight is good,
but you, first dawning, son of truth,
you are best of all.
The sage from the north
perceives the truth of dawn
and declares you are best of all.

Following them, Sudhana saw that although the venerable Jayottama had spoken of going beneath the lailai tree, the place was more like a vast cavern; for the light of heaven could not enter, sunlight had never penetrated there. Jayottama sent away the various servants who were waiting in the tree's cavernous shade and addressed Sudhana and his neice. His words created a whole new cosmos, one established between their three hearts, that had the power to expand the sacred relationship uniting the old sage, the young boy, and the young woman to the infinite.

Before the sun rose, Sudhana was briefly able to close his eyes. While he slept, Sumera left the shelter of the tree and returned to her home. Sunk in delicious slumber, Sudhana dreamed he was once again on his way to meet Jayottama.

In his dream, he saw agaves everywhere. Before him stretched a silent desert in which the agave spikes seemed to have slashed all the sounds of the wind to death. He felt his spirits leave him and go scurrying over the desert vastness. He was empty. All the truths that Sudhana had heard until now were utterly useless. Previously on his journey, every time he had heard a truth, his heart had leaped for joy and he had felt as if he had become the greatest man in the world. Now not a trace remained of any of that joy. Tears welled up. He found himself lamenting that the ferryman had sent him on such an utterly desolate road. Even if the path had been gentle and easy, even if it had not led across a desert, he would still have hated this life spent wandering at other people's behest. He yearned to turn into a tree. He yearned to become a house, to become a village and its inhabitants, a kingdom's population.

Yet although he grumbled about his path, no hatred or resentment entered Sudhana's heart. He felt like a fool. There was not a hope of seeing a single tree anywhere in this desert, not a single bird. Yet, desert though it was, there was no sign of camel bones emerging from the ground, not one human skull belonging to some poor wretch who had expired with a final rictus. The path was so remote. He recalled little Seiya, Maitraiyani, and his dear Iryon in turn. He even recalled Sumera, although she still lay in the future, like a bright moon.

Without waking, his dream shifted. He had been in an unending expanse of desert, but now, looming before him was a grove of sal trees that still lay far ahead.

Sudhana dreamt that he finally arrived on the grassy plains of Nandihara, the city that the ferryman had told him about. He inhaled deeply the sweet fragrance of the grass, but it was already withering. The landscape surrounded Sudhana in a solitude it had shown no one else.

Sudhana's innocent steps led him on toward a place where the meadows were cultivated. There he hesitated, as if struck by the smell of men. The leather slippers he had received somewhere along the way were worn out. It was a pity, as they had been good for walking. How far had he come?

Someone was coming towards him, dressed in tattered long-sleeved clothes, priestly robes. It was an aging wandering monk with a rough beard and piercingly bright wild eyes. Quickly, the light faded from his eyes, his swaggering gait faltered, then seemed to collapse. He began to mutter in a low voice.

"Fancy letting such a kid out in these plains. How could such a thing happen?"

His voice began to shake. "Here. Would you like a drink of water?" He

drew a leather water pouch from the belt of his robes. The water was tepid and tasted strongly of wild animals. Sudhana took just one sip and handed the pouch back.

The old monk questioned him: "Where have you come from? Where are you going?"

Sudhana made no reply. The old man commanded again, this time without speaking a word, as it happens in dreams: "Tell me."

"Surely the answer lies in what you have said, water-giving sir," Sudhana replied. "The answer is fully contained in your question. I am on my way to meet Jayottama the sage in Nandihara city."

"Jayottama the venerable? Who rid himself of the art of becoming rich and mastered the art of the wind's blowing, of the water's flowing, of breathing in harmony with wisdom? You don't want to go running after that kind of fellow, with his bony scrap of learning; come roaming with me, I'll teach you the art of sleeping and having fun.

"You surprised me," the old man continued, "I was even frightened. There's nothing more frightening than something looking like a person in a vast open plain with not a soul in sight. You gave me such a fright, it blasted my sleep to smithereens and muddled my sense of emancipation. You're a fearful creature, you know. Or rather, more dazzling than fearful."

"For a thousand billion aeons we were one, for all the ages of eternity," Sudhana said, "Living creatures are not separate entities but are all returning into imminent oneness."

The old man replied, "When I was a child, I traveled from place to place like you. I followed fire worshipers and went gadding about with old Jains. But all I got out of it was diseases; I found myself alone in the world. What I'd lost was life. So nowadays I reckon nothing's better than sleeping in the shade after a meal. Sleep is peace and freedom. And there is nothing as new as waking up from sleep."

"So in the future you intend to sleep for a few million hours?" Sudhana asked.

The old monk's eyes flashed wildly and then he sank into deep reflection. Time passed. Abruptly he began to laugh until he was drooling. His whole body was full of laughter. He must be mad, Sudhana thought. Then he realized with a shock that no, he was laughter incarnate. He felt a glimpse of the intensity of the level of power reached by the old man, who had attained heights he could never aspire to.

"Who are you, sir?" Sudhana spoke aloud to the old traveler for the first time.

"Who, me? I'm the Old Sleeper of Nandihara, Old Sleep himself, everyone knows me."

"Where are you going now?"

"Me? A long way away. To bask in the sun during the dry months and sleep a bit."

"Have you no home?"

"None. Maybe I'll build myself a house one day, as the men of the west build themselves big tombs."

"Isn't a house the beginning of all forms of attachment?"

"It certainly is. And to the fool, the hills are water. A house likewise. But you can't trust a houseless person. No way of knowing anything. Without a home, he'll vanish although he says he loves you. He leaves his country, he leaves you and me. What's left once he's left everything? Is that where truth is? What's the use of that kind of truth? I'm a wanderer myself, but I dislike wanderers. Not worth a single firmly rooted nettle. A house is where you go back to. No truth without a home. That's dharma."

The Old Sleeper picked a wayside flower and began to roll it between his long-nailed fingers. Sudhana sensed that the old man could never fit into ordinary society and had ended up offering a vague caricature of himself. Perhaps he had lived for a time with a beautiful girl, then been rejected by her. Essence had been defeated by forms!

Little Sudhana felt happy at his intuition. In that happiness, the old man became more likeable. He rather wanted to live with him, to be able to eat and sleep whenever he pleased, like a fat pig.

"Off you go now. My path is calling me," and with those words, the old man sauntered off out of Sudhana's dream. Sudhana set off again, alone. He encountered woodlands and tranquil streams, the scent of human life grew stronger. From the forest emerged the rustling sound heard just before a breeze passes, causing the breeze to arise and in a flash turning woodlands into a windswept forest. Birds could be heard singing here and there above the sound of the wind. One old snake had been about to move out from the shadows into the sunlight but changed its mind and settled down in a coil. It made no move to intercept Sudhana as he passed by. All the world's creatures were in harmony.

As soon as he left the forest behind, he found rough houses scattered around and shacks perched in trees with ladders hanging from them. The children came crowding around Sudhana, and a few adults trailed along behind him. The sight of a strange boy like Sudhana was a great event. Children and adults alike were utterly poor but each and every one wore a cheerful smile. Poverty lodged in sincerity is the mother of all joys.

An adult addressed him. "Just ask us the way. We'll tell you exactly."

"I am on my way to the place of instruction far from sorrow and anguish in the grove of trees near Nandihara."

"Why, you speak another language from ours! You don't need to ask the way, just keep walking straight ahead."

"Many thanks."

"On the contrary, it is we who should thank any traveler deigning to pass by our wretched village. Farewell."

Sudhana realized that with the passing of time and the multiple changes it brought, poverty could be abolished completely. The contention that poverty would never be dispelled from this world was a weak one, for he kept discovering that the truth he was seeking and the solution to the problem of poverty were one and the same. The truth belongs to the earth, not to heaven.

At last, the gates of Nandihara opened wide. A few wild fowl were idling there, and three oxen sprawled motionless: a scene of utter lassitude. Then abruptly the three oxen rose and came charging towards Sudhana, breaking his dream.

He awoke in the vast cool shade of the lailai tree. This long dream was leaving him. The sage was already awake, deeply immersed in his daily meditations.

"You're awake. Little pilgrim, Sudhana. You have spent one night here. This place is yours; make yourself at home, have no cares, do what you like. Wash in the running water, walk three score paces to the outhouse and relieve yourself." They ate a light breakfast of fruit. Then Sumera came out to them. Her dark hair was not yet dry.

"Sudhana, in my dreams last night I was you, and had lived my whole life on the roads."

For some reason, he felt embarrassed. "Oh, I merely dreamed that I was still on my way here to meet the sage Jayottama. Passing over a desert . . ."

"Sudhana, my uncle says that each and every grain of sand in the desert of Nandihara is a diamond seed of the world to come. It means you walked over diamonds to reach us."

"I saw poor people, too."

"The day is surely coming when we will live in a Pure Land Paradise and the poor and those who are rich like my uncle will no longer be enemies. That is my dearest wish."

At the far edge of the shadow, a group of people had gathered to seek Jayottama's private advice. Jayottama's servants were admonishing them and sent them back the way they came. Sumera spoke. "Sometimes you cannot hear the teaching you came for. The teaching you have to wait longer to hear is the one that penetrates most deeply in the end. Something you get easily is more likely to slip through your fingers. If you try to pick up one handful of sand, it all slips away."

29.
SUMERA AND SANUITA

AFTER LUNCH, Jayottama made his way to a vast garden. A crowd had gathered to hear his afternoon sermon. Sumera stayed with Sudhana.

"They say that my name comes from long long ago, from Mt. Sumeru, set between west and north." Her words sounded like a modest reply to a serious question he had not asked. "When Sumer collapsed, its people were scattered eastward, southward, and far to the west. Sumer manifested the truth of the four stages of life: rising and flourishing, decaying and death. Now, only the name remains."

Sudhana felt that he should be ready to move on, but he didn't want to leave. The grove inspired people to speak truthfully and Sudhana longed to talk to everybody who entered it. Although language barriers prevented Sudhana from talking with all present, he could tell that everyone, not only the sage Jayottama and his niece Sumera, belonged to the clan of wisdom and compassion.

Sudhana was soon lost in thought:

Leave the grove,
leave the shade and darkness.
There is a joy,
pierced by arrows of sunlight,
where you and I are abolished.

"Why are we born into this world of torment, pain, and sorrow?" Sudhana wondered. A poet, inspired by this grove, had once pointed out that its inexhaustible magnanimity could only be encountered by leaving it. A world of torments was the mother that gave birth to Lord Indra's paradise.

If this dark world is a place of pain, it is at the same time a world where suffering is endured. Tyrants cause others to suffer needlessly and perhaps bodhisattva nature even involves provoking armed uprisings, in order to reduce the tyrant's wickedness to ashes.

Sudhana had drifted away in his own thoughts, and he was surprised to find that Sumera had vanished and a young boy was sitting in her place, preaching a strong sermon that drew Sudhana out of his own reflections.

"I do not simply live here," the boy said. "Like you, I am a wanderer with the whole world before me. I have spent time in distant galaxies, constantly on the move through the whole universe's realms of form and formlessness. Boarding a shooting star, I have traversed the dark voids of space. I have ridden on the wings of the wind and crossed the great southern ocean for a full forty-nine days. I knew you from the moment you entered Nandihara. We are brothers."

Sudhana interrupted curtly, "Who are you?"

"I am known as Sanuita."

"But then what happened to Sumera? If you aren't Sumera, where did she go?"

"Whether I am Sumera or not is not an important question," the boy replied softly. "What matters now is simply that you and I are together, united as brothers in truth."

"You matter," Sudhana conceded, "but for me Sumera matters, too."

"Everything in this world is vanity; all is lies." The boy continued his sermon. "Yet we are not the only ones to consider that it is wrong to despise even the least of this world's motes of dust or scraps of refuse. This world is a strict school, where every single thing without exception is a master, faithfully observing the Way. Even if a person has committed a heinous murder, that person still possesses Buddha nature. Sudhana, you know the girl called Maitraiyani don't you?"

Sudhana was displeased by this business of Sumera and Sanuita. He was insulted by the way Sanuita had taken Sumera's place and now he had to endure this boy talking about Maitrayani. Memories of Maitraiyani remained buried deep in his heart, and were now returning to him like water overflowing from a bucket. Rippling on the surface of his liquid memories came the thought that this present moment must surely be the result of his dazzling encounter with her and all that she had taught him.

Sanuita looked him in the eyes. "Sudhana, I was born as Maitrayani's twin sister, but I was destined from birth to a life of wandering. At last, I found myself here, where I was adopted as a foster daughter by Jayottama's sister. After my foster mother died, I came to serve my uncle in this grove. Now that I have met you, however, I want to accompany you so I prayed to change into a boy's shape and have become Sanuita. My uncle has charged me to go with you further and further south. We will reach a great river. Across it, we will find the nun, Sinhavijurm, in the city of Kalinga-vana. If you are willing, my uncle gives his blessing for me to stay with you forever on your pilgrimage."

Sudhana was growing accustomed to confusion, but still he had to struggle to comprehend Sumera's transformation. But sitting next to Sanuita was quite natural. With Sanuita as his companion, Sudhana felt life would be happier than when he was traveling alone.

"Very well," Sudhana said, pleased to be free of his previous life of lonely journeying. "Birds in flight prefer to fly together, too. In order to keep from hindering the beating of the other's wings, they always fly slightly separated. Let's travel together in the same fashion. Our sweat will dry together in the heat of the sun."

"Uncle Jayottama has already taken his leave of us. Let us leave now, without disturbing him in the middle of his sermon," Sanuita said.

"Fine," Sudhana shrugged. "Farewells are superfluous."

They passed through the woodland universe out of Nandihara, their splendid shadows following faithfully behind. With the shaded grove behind them, it took all of the two boys' energy to grow accustomed to such fiery heat. Sanuita was well-equipped for a long journey with a water bag and a pouch full of powdered dried fruit. Sudhana, who had always lived on the road, carried much less.

They set off up a hill road as the sun was setting, their journey knowing no distinction between day and night. Their mountain path was already wrapped in darkness. Sanuita's feet soon began to trouble him. A few birds were still flying in the quickly darkening sky, chattering scolding complaints to their companions already settled to roost in the woodland branches. Sudhana felt a bird's droppings fall on his forehead.

To pass the time, Sanuita sang a song of Sumer:

Sumeru, Mountain of the World!
Blazing Sumeru, imbuing with dazzling brightness
all those that come flocking to you!
Brightness of that blazing host!

Brightness such that prohibits night
from birthing anywhere in this world!
Sumeru! Not mountain now, but brightness!

The hillside road lay dark but Sanuita's song brought sunlit day bursting from their hearts. Gradually, though, their journey began to fill with the aches and pains that naturally come to those who travel. For Sanuita, the pain brought unfamiliar discomfort. For Sudhana, it was like coming home.

One rainy dawn, a few days after they had hailed the second full moon of their journey, they reached the Boundless Stream, the great river they had been searching for. In the early light, the water sounded like the clashing of swords. Sudhana and Sanuita were completely exhausted. They soaked their aching feet in the water and were at once made well.

Day was just breaking in the east. The rain had stopped. The hills on the far side still lay under the power of darkness, the night's obscurity not yet fully banished. The eastern sky shone solemn as this world's first steps. Sudhana breathed deeply. The world is destined to vanish in the space of a single breath.

Sanuita spoke. "Sudhana, I have completed my task. I must now entrust this world to you and close my eyes forever."

"No!" Sudhana was unsure what thunderbolt had struck him. One of Sanuita's legs had already begun to stiffen. Sudhana massaged the leg with all his strength, but his effort was in vain. Still, he continued to rub, trying to keep Sanuita's other leg from stiffening in the same way.

"You'll recover. Brace up. The forests of Kalingavana are not far now. Look at the river. See how powerfully the water is flowing." Sanuita handed him the pouches he had been carrying.

His dying eyes and Sudhana's lonely ones stared together at the pale river.

"I changed into a boy and came all this way with you out of love. In the midst of vanity, the world is true, and I, Sumera, was false in the midst of truth. The magic spell by which I transformed myself tarnished the truth and made me ill."

Sanuita's eyes closed. His living light was extinguished. Sudhana desperately shook the corpse. It had ceased to be a person more quickly than the time it had taken for Sumera to speak his last words.

Sudhana lay his companion's body, now reduced to a mere object, in a grassy meadow. The ground was moist after the rain. It took him half a day to gather enough dry firewood for the pyre. As the sun stood high in the zenith, Sudhana heard a bell tinkling and found an elderly tramp. The tinkling sound had come from a little metal bell dangling from the belt that held his tattered clothes together. The tramp helped Sudhana set about the cremation.

They worked all day. By evening, the body was reduced to ashes and a bundle of bones, returned to its components of earth, water, fire, and wind. Sudhana and the tramp offered worship to the sacred Buddhas and bodhisattvas of the worlds in ten directions. They prayed to receive the essence of the departed life.

The old tramp laughed: "Poor kid, you've lost your young comrade, and you've got old me, instead."

"But without you, sir, how could I ever have prepared this funeral? Thank you. It seems that not one gesture of ours in this world is possible without some kind of destiny."

The tramp asked where he was headed.

"I'm on my way to Kalingavana."

"I'll accompany you on the ride over," the tramp offered.

They boarded a ferryboat waiting by the side of the river and continued to chat to the sound of the oars striking the water.

"Ah, Kalingavana!" the tramp sighed. "That forest belongs to a wealthy witch who has forgotten all about this world's poverty. There are no beggars like me there."

"Not so. If there are poor people in the world, no place can belong to the rich. Come with me," Sudhana said.

"Why should I go someplace where one cranky bitch tricks and lies until she gets hold of people's minds with magic, then makes them mad so that they spend all day dancing in a frenzy? I'd rather go roaming up and down this riverbank, thank you all the same."

"Come with me," Sudhana persisted.

"No, I won't. I can't stand these people who are all the time talking about the Way and hell."

The oar that had been cleaving the water suddenly struck the tramp's shoulders. The ferryman, who had until then been rowing sleepily, was glaring fiercely.

"You seven hundredth avatar of an aging tramp! How dare you go jabbering away like that? I feel like chucking you in where it's deep."

"You only have to row us across—what are you hitting me for?"

"Cut the chatter and go with the kid."

"I won't."

"You will, you wretch! Truth rarely comes near any creature; how can anyone fail to seize that truth and enlighten his sad situation if they have the chance?" the boatman lamented to the empty air. He turned to Sudhana. "Do you know how to get there? If you take the left of the three highways before you, you'll arrive at Kalingavana late at night when the kugira bird is fast asleep. No matter. There, you'll find night with its songs and dances is just like day."

The ferryman had stopped at a landing stage built out into deep water. As they prepared to disembark, the ferryman looked back at Sudhana, who still clutched a bundle with the remains of his friend. "Throw those bones into the water," the ferryman chided. Sudhana threw the bundle into the river and the remains of his friend drifted away.

Sudhana and the tramp got out. The boat and its navigator drifted away. The tramp was grumbling. "I wish I hadn't come across. Food has no taste on this side. Even when you manage to get some, food has to have some taste."

30.
SUNLIGHT PARK

UDHANA FORGED ON AHEAD. When he glanced back at the tramp, he seemed to have disappeared. Until a few moments ago, his little metal bell had been tinkling as if in a dream. Now there was no sound of it. He was gone.

Sudhana wondered if perhaps behind the shape of that foul-mouthed ruffian, there was someone who had rid himself of all worldly desires. Someone for whom even Sudhana's journey in search of truth was merely one more form of desire. And perhaps the boatman who had struck the tramp was another such person? Sudhana shuddered with the thrill of the thought.

Sudhana was destined to be on his own again. The day was over, the impatient evening star already visible on the horizon. The river ran alongside the road, busy with ducks and geese heading home.

Sudhana sang to himself as he walked on until he heard the sharp cry of a mouse caught by a wildcat. It silenced him. The hunters and the hunted were out. It was not only the wildcats who were killers. This whole world and time advance through death. All living creatures come to an end.

As Sudhana reached the forest of Kalingavana, a great flood of light pierced the night. Sudhana's whole body grew empty to receive it. The heart of the forest welcomed Sudhana with song and fragrance. His eyes were blinded, his ears rang, his nostrils quivered for excess of delight. Men and women of all ages arrayed in long trailing robes, knowing nothing of sleep or repose, were living there in utter peace.

A girl sitting beside a spring saw him and spoke: "Wash your feet in this water, young guest." Sudhana bowed in greeting, then proceeded to drink from the spring before washing his face and feet. He asked about the nun, Sinhavijurm, he had come to see.

"All the visitors who come here are looking for her. A long time ago, I was the same. If you go that way, you'll find her in Sunlight Park."

"What's Sunlight Park?"

"Thirty-three years ago, a blacksmith of Kalingavana Forest equipped his young son with wings. The boy would collect every ray of sunlight that fell in the forest. Then, flying up into the sunset glow, he would gather all the departing sunbeams. After three decades, the place was full of sunshine and the sunbeams had lost all thought of leaving for anywhere else. Sometimes, without warning, this vast mass of light joins with the entire forest of Kalingavana and dances. It's an incredible sight."

Sudhana left the girl and hurried toward the park. The nun Sinhavijurm sat on a lion-shaped throne in the park's center, one of her feet poised on the ground beneath. Reverently, Sudhana circled the throne and the crowd surrounding the woman. When Sinhavijurm noticed him, she beckoned him close. "Good and most good son of this world, come here."

Her words of high praise entered Sudhana's ears and filled him with a luxurious sense of comfort. The wealth of Kalingavana Forest was such that a person was rich with nothing and full without eating. Every face harbored a smile bright as a flower.

After completing his full circle around her, Sudhana knelt before her and asked his question. "Sacred nun, my heart has been intent on seeking the way of righteousness for as long as I can remember. I am eager to know how one advances along the way of enlightenment and what works need to be done. Will you tell me?"

His question was utterly sincere. Sinhavijurm answered in song:

Child, you have turned a hundred million times.
How can you be a questioning guest and I an answering host?
Once you have seen me, do not consider my bright form.
Once you have seen the Buddha, cast the Buddha's form away.
Once a creature knows nothing of creaturely forms,
as a babe knows nothing of its own form,
all the variety of this world turns into Buddha nature.
Once you have seen the teaching,
do not look at its form
and when you come to see that all teaching is a dream,
the true teaching will appear as darkness at the end of light.
Joy. The works of enlightenment? Joy.

Sudhana savored her response even as his heart yearned to speak more. Sinhavijurm's heart spoke to his, "Child, you are light as I am light." Sudhana looked down at his body. It radiated the dazzling light of the sun. Light such as this lay hidden within the depths of every human heart, waiting for the world. Light came bursting from his hands and his breast. "Look! Look!" Sudhana cried out. "The darkness in my breast has all become light, shining bright. How can the bodhisattva way not be clear? It's brightly visible."

The nun's heart quickly contradicted him: "Not so. Not in this way. All is not yet done. There are still many places left that you must visit, Sudhana. You are a man of the road. You will live and die on the road."

Sinhavijurm invited Sudhana to sleep against her chest to absorb the peace that permeated her whole body. He awoke from the sleep of jewels to find his body light as a feather.

Rousing himself, he gazed up and saw numerous lion-thrones scattered about the forest; Sinhavijurm sat on each of them, holding a different person to her breast.

Sudhana's dark eyes grew wide.

"Holy nun, how many hundred bodies do you have?"

"Many. In ages to come, you too will encounter a host of living creatures in hundreds of bodies. Buddhas and bodhisattvas encounter one hundred billion beings in one hundred billion bodies."

"Lady nun, my body yearns to be multiplied one hundred-fold and to shed one hundred times as much light into the darkness. It is so good here, but outside of this garden lie the mortality and pain that none can avoid, the oppression and exploitation that mark the relationships between the four castes and the multitude of secondary castes. Have you forgotten that?"

"Ah, child. In times to come, this forest will fill all living creatures with the love within my breast, untying all bonds as naturally as winter passes in the north and springtime follows. Doesn't your own journey have this same aim, little pilgrim?"

"Holy nun, Lady Sinhavijurm, you are most truly righteous and beautiful."

"All thanks, all thanks. Child, it would be sufficient if by my gratitude the realm of Amitabha might be established."

Sudhana left her embrace and mingled with the other people. He began an animated conversation with one young boy and, before Sudhana realized it, he and the boy walked away from Kalingavana Forest and its park full of sunlight. They found themselves outside of the forest in the reality in which they had to go on living.

"My name is Vasumitra," the boy said. "You're Sudhana, aren't you?"

The lingering remnants of Sinhavijurm's light died with the boy's words. Sudhana nodded.

"My father's a shepherd; he brought me up as his only child. My mother died when I was born. My father always held me with one hand, even when he led his flocks. We came all this way to the land of Kalingavana because my father wanted to entrust me to Sinhavijurm so that I could become a bodhisattva radiating light like her.

"But no matter how hard Sinhavijurm tried, I was only a little boy. It was a great disappointment to my father. I stayed a full two weeks in the Sunlight Park, yet the light never entered my body.

"Finally, Sinhavijurm gave up. She said I could become a Buddha of light slowly, after stone and gravel became Buddhas first. That was when I was entrusted to you. My father and the nun together..."

"Entrusted you to me?" Sudhana interrupted.

"That's right."

"Vasumitra, then perhaps I may entrust you to someone else as well. The road I am following is not the right path for someone like you."

"Don't worry about the future now. With today's sky, there is nothing I need."

The boy spoke with such complacency that Sudhana felt a sharp pang. Within the boy lay concealed an enormous, unshakable power that no force could prevail over. The discovery emerged like a drop of blood. All the light in Kalingavana's Sunlight Park was not enough to fully illuminate this boy. The boy was too deep a crevasse for the light.

Vasumitra possessed an utterly invincible, creaturely ignorance that left those with bodhisattva wisdom, even those with supernatural light and wisdom, quite helpless. The boy's power seemed to belong to the totally empty zero prior to the emergence of one. Before the might of zero, all living creatures and Buddhas were less than nothing.

"Do you know where you're going?" Vasumitra asked.

"No idea."

"This is the way back to my home. I'll show you where I come from. Now that Father has found peace in the light of Kalingavana Forest and is free from pain, I must come out and go home."

Sudhana decided to devote himself completely to the boy's freedom. He would simply follow. Sudhana looked at him closely. Vasumitra was quite unique among all the people Sudhana had met. The boy was utterly beautiful and seemed to exhale a fragrance of unparalleled boldness.

Vasumitra noticed Sudhana's gaze. "I am a sinner; back in former worlds I robbed people of their lives. I'm only a child, but one woman was so bewitched by me that when I wouldn't do as she wanted, she took the sharp bone of a cow, slit open her stomach and put an end to herself. Then there was a woman, already married, who couldn't stop thinking of me after we exchanged a few words; in the end she fell into a decline and died. That was several lives ago. The daughter of a passing foreigner once clasped my hand for a moment; she fell so desperately in love that she went mad and threw herself into a stream. That must have been along the upper reaches of the Indus.

"My problem is I can't escape from the torment of recalling all that happened in previous existences. The sheep that nourished me with their milk in my childhood are the result of my having once or twice thrown them something to eat in long-ago lives.

"But in this world I am just a child. I have never once thought of myself as beautiful or ugly. Beauty and ugliness are both the shadows of falsehood. Even when I saw Sinhavijurm, I felt neither admiration nor wonder."

Sudhana liked listening to Vasumitra. The boy seemed equipped with absolutely nothing beyond the simple fact of having been born. He was completely free from any kind of attachment. The two boys grew closer as they talked together and when they stopped talking, walking in silence, they became closer still. As they walked, Sudhana completely lost track of time, immersed in both his own thoughts and Vasumitra's stories.

The passage of time seemed to have come to a halt for a while. Sudhana realized he was stuck on something Vasumitra had said at the beginning of the conversation.

"Vasumitra, you can't say that the death of those people was your fault."

Vasumitra laughed. "You're still thinking about that conversation? Well, losing your senses completely and then abruptly returning is one of the ten kinds of consciousness, I suppose."

Sudhana felt a fool, but continued. "It wasn't you that killed them, it was their own karma. Karma is not merely a matter of what you and I do. Karma is a sea far vaster than mere sin."

The boy stopped laughing. In his gaze gleamed a limitless understanding of Sudhana's words. An old thread had produced an ecstatic new present moment. The two boys grew even closer than before.

"When Father made me go off with you like this," Vasumitra said, "it was because he reckoned that with you alone there would be no risk of mistaken love."

"You never know," Sudhana laughed.

"You can't laugh off that kind of thing; that's why I gave up laughing. For a long time after those people lost their lives, I couldn't sleep. I would lie all night long listening to the cries of the animals roaming the hills beyond the village. Those animals were the best teachers I ever had. Once I finally slept, I woke knowing that this world is calling me."

"The so-called world is an impermanent thing designed to retain us here," Sudhana said.

"Impermanent?" The boy's voice was shrill.

"Yes, impermanent, Vasumitra. The world never stays exactly as it is. Even mothers are impermanent. Enlightened beings, too. Fundamentally, every living creature in the world was once a Buddha. Then that Buddha put on robes of karma and became the living creatures of a thousand million aeons."

For the first time in their friendship, Sudhana had become the speaker instead of the listener. In the distance, the road seemed to drop out of sight. Here the road's clay was turning to sand, turning the path back into a desert. Among all the things humans make, nothing is more impressive than a road.

The old men down south called this spot the Desert of Bones. It absorbed the children's words and they grew increasingly agitated. They had left the forest unprepared for a long journey and lacked the water and food necessary to cross the desert. Sudhana remembered that Sanuita had died partly because of lack of water. He wondered if he and his friend would survive the journey. Perhaps a dead Buddha would give birth to a new vibrant one?

Sudhana realized he had spoken the thought aloud and both he and Vasumitra smiled. The two little boys wandered through the desert, more lost than in search of truth. They had not walked for more than a day when they came across human skeletons resting in a final mocking snigger, a dead laugh half buried in the sand.

"These are the skeletons of people who started at the other end of the desert," Vasumitra explained. "Nobody dies only half way across a desert. People have to fail to attain goals they have almost reached. You have already passed many such critical points. Once across this desert you will come to a high and rugged region. There lies Ratnavyuha. That is where I come from."

A layer of clouds obscured some of the intensity of the sunbeams. Still, the sand blazed like a stove. Even Sudhana was not accustomed to such weather and could not imagine how he would endure the rest of the journey. Vasumitra touched Sudhana's hand for the first time since they had met. The touch immediately cooled Sudhana, easing the torment of the heat. Sweat oozed from his palms. What was this? Vasumitra had turned into a girl!

The boy's sudden transformation into a girl troubled Sudhana. He had come to depend on Vasumitra as he had Sanuita, who had followed him before. He wanted to ask her what had happened, but he was utterly exhausted and could not speak. His throat was burning. His legs kept threatening to give way. He was hungry. He was utterly empty, with not a scrap of anything inside his heart. Not one bird could be seen flying above them. Occasionally, desiccated forest blocked their way. The tenacious will to advance that had been so strong in Sudhana failed to manifest, although it hadn't disappeared completely. The desert was silent. Devoid of all attachment and desire, it was the immutable Buddha of ancient days, long lost in obscurity. Sudhana walked on beside the newly-female Vasumitra. As they passed mile after mile of Buddha desert, truth was born. Very early on the third day, mountains began to loom into Sudhana's field of vision, very far away.

"Sudhana. That's the mountain where the city of Ratnavyuha lies. The grassy plains at its foot are the home of all my family's ancestors. When we reach there, I will give myself to you."

Sudhana remembered that an ascetic in Sinhavijurm's Sunlight Park had told him about a wise young woman. He had heard that if anyone afflicted with passion or folly exchanged a few words with her, their intensity would melt away; if they just held her hand once, the emotions would vanish; if they simply sat down for a moment beside her, their turmoil would slip away; if they once saw her stretch, the passions and follies of an infinity of ages would all go flying away. Sudhana glanced across at Vasumitra and grew convinced. Might not the boy, now the girl, walking alongside him be that very woman? Perhaps those that died after contact with her did so because they were ready to let go of all attachments.

Heaven and earth were tinged crimson to permit the rising of the sun in the east. Vasumitra could see the image of her own past lives in the efful-gent splendor of the sun rising. In response to Sudhana's unasked question, she told him more of her story.

"In times and worlds past, I lived as a woman so poor that she had to prostitute herself. There was nothing to eat and Father was reduced to catching wildcats for food. Before I went to sell myself to a brothel, I sur-rendered my body to my own father. I recklessly cried out that since he had given me my body, I could only sell it to other men after surrendering it to him. After taking my virginity, he hanged himself in a tree. At that time, I suffered more from hunger than from grief at my father's suicide. Think-ing that I had been soiled, I rushed to the swamps at the foot of Ratnavyuha. I devoured mouthfuls of foul mud and stinking lumps of clay. I even drank the water from latrines. I lived in the stacks of rice-straw spread over the fields until my body was free of the toilet stench. After that I became the plaything of every man who came along.

"A few lifetimes later, I became my former father's wife. He was rich, with vast estates and crowds of servants. My husband was old and I was young, yet we lived in harmony. Then one day, as I was out buying a mass of gold, I saw a band of a hundred beggars passing by. I threw them the mass of gold. Without realizing it, I was performing an act of almsgiving.

"In another past life I was among the followers of a sage who crossed the Ganga up in the north proclaiming the truth about shunning pain and enjoying bliss, as well as the truth concerning the vanity of all that exists. We were no different from that band of beggars. Afterwards, I kept search-ing for truth until I came to a point beyond which I again began to live in lust and greed. Finally, I was born as the daughter of my present father, and we lived as workers on a cattle farm. One day I set eyes on you and changed into a boy for the first time."

"Vasumitra! You are that wise woman, aren't you?"

"I am a mere girl, that's all."

"Lady!"

"In my last life, a very handsome customer gave me his seed and I had a baby. I brought him up with what I earned as a whore, but when he was five, he fell sick with cholera and died. After that I went mad, giving myself away to drunkards, peddlers, thieves, beggars, and all, without taking a penny."

"Oh, holy bodhisattva, desireless desiring." Sudhana screamed out the words, unable to endure the pain the girl's words were provoking in his heart and stomach.

In the heat, her story had completely overwhelmed him. "I'm sick... Lady! I can't...go...on any farther." Sudhana collapsed at the edge of the desert.

"Sudhana, do you want to add to the skeletons in the Desert of Bones?" The girl challenged him where he lay. "Don't you want to encounter the truth in Ratnavyuha? The pain you feel is good, it is the pain resulting from the elimination of the last dregs of desire remaining within you. But you must get up."

A flock of birds flew past, the first birds they had seen for a long time. The sun burst out of the ground and rose crimson. Darkness fled and Sudhana's pain began to fade away. The girl pulled him up. They stood together. Their long shadows stretched as far as the grassy meadow that lay at the end of the desert. They drank from the spring that bubbled there and began to walk again.

That evening they reached Vasumitra's home village, also named Vasumitra, at the foot of the citadel of Ratnavyuha. They went to one wing of the empty house on the farm where Vasumitra had lived before, where they slept profoundly.

When Sudhana woke, it was night. Vasumitra's face was visible in the starlight. He felt that there was no beauty in the world, save that of newly opened flowers and that of this girl. In the ground beneath the place where they lay, a new stream of water had opened and could be heard gurgling as it flowed. A new world would surely open beneath the ground. At the same time, he could hear the sound of people in the heavens calling for a new world to open in the heavens, too. Ordinary ears take that sound for the wind, but it was the night of the Garland Sutra meditation.

31.
A HAIRY FELLOW

HE SUN ROSE. High in the air, the leaves on the trees formed layer upon layer of wide-cast shade. Vasumitra's face shone full of darkness, more beautiful than the most lovely, divine being in the entire Buddha cosmos. She brought her hands together for a moment, in the direction of the sun. They strolled from the open shed of the farm towards the mossy brink of a small spring nearby. As they sat, village women brought them cold ewes' milk, which they drank while dangling their feet in the river.

"Sudhana! Embrace me. Then all your desires will be consumed in flames."

Sudhana surprised himself by shaking his head: "No. I want to dream about you, love you, stay with you forever, but I must leave. If I kiss your lips, passion will rise; if I embrace you, I will sink deeper into the mire of desire. Perhaps in some distant future, I will come to visit you. But I have to pursue the road toward enlightenment. I cannot stay with just one teacher or one single world."

"Good. I'm pleased. Now you have nothing more to hear and learn from me."

"That's not so. Even now, your beauty blinds me so I can scarcely see the morning light of the sun of deliverance reverberating on the heavy leaves of those trees. I am the very least of your disciples in this world."

"Ah, young master Sudhana! You have learned what you needed from me. If you keep heading south, you will reach the land of Shubha-param-gama, where the hirsute hermit Veshthila lives. He is completely unworldly and owns absolutely nothing. Visit him and receive his guidance in bodhi-sattva living. He is a teacher whom I myself followed for a long time.

Though I was his pupil, he kept bowing down before me, like flowing water always seeking the lowest place."

Even though he was to leave, Sudhana wanted one more night with Vasumitra. He decided to spend the day exploring the city of Ratnavyuha and to leave the following day. A child from one of the village farms served as his guide and showed him all the corners of the city. The sun was already sinking low when Sudhana returned to the village outside the city walls. But Vasumitra wasn't there. Sudhana waited. Perhaps she had deliberately gone away somewhere in order to permit this departure. Beauty demands resolute departures. As the sun was setting, Sudhana rose to his feet, and set out along the twilit road.

The night clung closely to him. As soon as he left Vasumitra's beauty and freedom, his own heart felt completely empty. It was as if he'd callously parted from his own self as well. "Leave the lovely lady behind, off to the hairy fellow," he murmured.

Sudhana had parted forever from his twenty-eighth teacher, the boy-girl Vasumitra. He entered a new world. Night was vaster than day. Sudhana entered a state of single-minded concentration, called *samadhi*. Samadhi is the holiest form of journey possible in this world.

Sudhana's journey pursued its way along a tranquil night road. He was able to walk as cheerfully as an old lullaby or a practiced, well-mastered dance. Finally, he reached Shubha-paramgama. The journey had been an easy one and he hadn't once stopped to ask the way.

The city of Shubha-paramgama possessed neither gates nor walls. A twelve-foot-high stone set in the highway, dividing it in two, served as the city gate. Children were playing around it. It seemed there were no sleepy-heads among the city's children. At the crack of dawn, even before day had banished night, the children would rush out of doors. In Shubha-param-gama, the saying that a person "hadn't stirred a leg at daybreak," was another way of saying they were dead.

Sudhana approached the children. "Do you know the hermit Vesh-thila?"

A few of them nodded slowly.

"How do I get to his house?"

One boy with shining black eyes spoke up. "Our hairy teacher lives in a shanty down at the far end of the town. If you go straight down this road, you can't miss it. If you go there, he'll give you something to eat."

As Sudhana walked through town, he saw it was run down. The people were poor with the kind of generalized poverty that is the price of a few people's great wealth. The road led between houses with no doors. Sudhana slowed down, carefully studying each shack he passed. He was immensely hungry and devoured handfuls of dried mango flour from his bag as he walked.

Shubha-paramgama's name meant "that which has reached the opposite shore," but it didn't resemble nirvana in the least. The ruler was appointed as monarch for life by the emperor of the neighboring kingdom of Jong-vaidurya. He had been reigning for the last forty years. Everything worth having had been carted off to the capital city of Jong-vaidurya, be it sheep or fruit. Shortly before Sudhana's visit there had been a large-scale revolt. A band of poor people had stormed into the royal palace, where they had all been slaughtered. That day, the number of those "not stirring a leg though it's daybreak" was at least five hundred.

He arrived at the shack at the far end of the town. Beside the shack rose a tall tree virtually devoid of branches, enjoying its loftiness.

"Anyone at home?" he called out. His voice echoed. There was no door, so he entered. The house had not been empty long; there was no dust on the floor, no spider webs dangling along the walls.

Sudhana sighed. "This would be a good place to spend the rest of my life. It's good enough to keep out the rain and wind in the monsoon season. Good enough to ward off epidemics during the rains. Good enough for me to grow old in, like other grown-ups."

He made himself at home, stretching out on the floor. He stretched out his legs and arms. Soon, he was asleep. Sudhana never slept on his right side in proper ascetic style; he curled up just like any other young urchin. His sleep was a form of self-abandonment. Occasionally, his mouth moved as he slept, as if he was playing all alone.

It might be said that sleep is the death separating two lives. Awakening is a rebirth. Perhaps the sum total of our daily repetition of such deaths and rebirths is what leads us to leave this world forever. Sleep and death can be considered ports, moments of rest in the wheel of life that is *samsara*.

"What sluggard's come crawling in here? Get up! Get up!" Sudhana felt a kick. He opened his eyes. The hermit Veshthila was staring down at him, the lower part of his face completely concealed by a thick black beard. A smile spread over his savage-looking face. "Who the heck are you?"

"Hermit, sir, you know very well who I am, so why ask?"

"Ha, what a chap! I took you for a kid playing on the ground and you're a kid playing in the heavens." He clicked his tongue in wonder.

Sudhana jumped up, then knelt at the hairy hermit's feet in a display of respect. "I've come to learn the deeds a bodhisattva should perform. I have heard that Your Holiness's great works are as profuse as your beard."

"You brat! Now that you're awake, go out and have a good piss, then come back. Bodhisattva, Mahasattva, what does it matter? We'll lie here for a time, then you can eat until your stomach's so full it booms like a drum."

Sudhana was surprised the hermit knew about his aching bladder. Of course, it was normal for people to urinate right after waking up from sleep, but Sudhana was sure the hermit's power of insight went deeper than that. Relieving himself in a field not far from the shack, Sudhana felt like a small boy again.

When he came back in, the hermit said, "Brat, this hairy Veshthila has one thing he's proud of. What? The fact that he's reached *vimukti*, and liberated himself from the cycle of life and death. But the name I've taken to mark my emancipation is 'Not-Entering-Nirvana.' Not a graceful name, I'm afraid. Not dying, not entering nirvana is the name of my liberation and its very essence."

Sudhana's face reflected his confusion.

"Listen, idiot. There is no final entering of nirvana for a Buddha or all the Buddhas of the world. They only make a show of going into nirvana, in order to help living creatures live better lives. Real Buddha nature is a matter of not having any such thought as 'a Buddha has entered nirvana,' or 'a Buddha is now entering nirvana,' or 'a Buddha will later enter nirvana.' Every single thought of mine reveals the works of the Buddhas of all the worlds. Have you properly understood my boast?"

"Not completely," Sudhana admitted. "What level of thought have you attained?"

"That's a prickly artichoke of a question. When I attain vacuity at the heart of thought and all worlds and all things are forgotten, at moments like that it's possible for me to see the many Buddhas of this world being born, one by one. I have seen the ancient Buddhas Kashyapa, Kanakamuni, Krakuchchanda, Visvabhu, Shikhin, Vipashyin, Tishya, Pushya, Yashottara, and Padmottara, and besides them, in a single moment, I have seen one hundred Buddhas, one thousand Buddhas, one hundred thousand, one hundred million, a billion, a trillion, a quadrillion, a quintillion, more, far more, as many Buddhas as there are motes of dust in the world.

"But that's enough chattering for today, let's go out. Once you've seen this country, other countries have nothing to show. In this country the entire human situation is completely recapitulated. Suffering, poverty, and ignorance persist. So what's the use of seeing all those Buddhas?"

The hairy hermit and Sudhana left the shack and went wandering through the city's back alleys. "But don't many more Buddhas need to come into being in such a place?" Sudhana asked.

"How right you are. You've got good questions, young man, and that's the most important thing. You have a real right to be here. You are good, like an oasis after a desert crossing."

Everywhere Sudhana and the hermit walked, they could see the king's palace, towering in its golden splendor. Yet the streets felt like death. There were no people strolling. Every street and road in the kingdom could be monitored from the watchtowers of the palace, and nobody was allowed to move around without permission. As they were passing in front of a house in a back lane two soldiers from the king's palace guard came hurrying up.

"We can't have people just roaming around this country at will," one shouted. "Go home, young boy, you're not invited here. As for you, hairy fellow, I don't know if you're some kind of Buddha or wild dog, you're all the time roving around wagging your head and raving, chattering away then begging, or talking nonsense to kid pilgrims like this. You're the worst good-for-nothing in the whole of Shubha-paramgama. Get home with you. Get home."

The old hermit, who was all the time guffawing and putting on fearsome airs, was circumspect. "Let's be off," he took Sudhana's hand and they started back the way they'd come.

As soon as Veshthila was well clear of the soldiers, he burst out laughing again. "I wanted to go through the gate that you came into the city by, but I can't. Such is life. There are children waiting for me there, it's the only place where my pupils can gather. Those children live in the city orphanage. One time a day, I collect food and clothing to give those kids. Then I teach them this world's basic principles out in the fields; they're clever enough to grasp what I say."

Veshthila began to sing, his heart swaying:

Where the sea secretly ends, it knows a river's touch;
ah, the touch of waters salt and fresh!
Beyond that water, a mountain rises.
What beauty in Mount Potalaka's buried treasures!
In that Mount a holy creature lives amidst flowing waters,
udumbara trees and crab apples, all the beauty of this world.
Beauty! Dancing layer on layer of beauty.
That holy one is the bodhisattva Avalokiteshvara.
Cross the sea and visit him.
Ask him about merit, the greatest merit.
He will instruct you, ah, all night long like the waves,
like the bright sunset shining over the waves.
He will instruct you like the bright full moon shining over the
waves on a moonlit night.
Compared to him, I am less than a cesspool.

Sudhana realized the hermit was telling him the route he would need to follow.

They returned to the shack, sat down on the floor and stretched out their legs. The hairy hermit went and fetched two ears of boiled corn. He sniffed them. They were a bit stale but still edible. Sudhana greedily devoured his. The long day was drawing to a close. A few carrion crows were flying through the red twilight glow. The hermit spoke.

"I used to be able to see lots of Buddhas. This world is so full of Buddhas, there's not one empty spot. And there's not a single place where there isn't a bodhisattva offering itself for living creatures. This world is sacred. There is nowhere left to spit, nowhere to piss that isn't Buddha. I came to see that here in Shubha-paramgama; the lepers, even the wicked king, even the king's soldiers, are all Buddhas and bodhisattvas. When I'm out in the field pissing and shitting, I see Buddhas there, too."

"So why is the world still so full of evil and suffering?"

"Sickness, exploitation, and oppression do not disappear so readily. Yet the karma of those responsible for them has its own limitations. If you believe that, these ills will soon disappear. You create the power to eradicate them."

"Hermit master, I am not on this long journey for myself. I travel for the good of all those I meet and all those I'll never know. Each living person fortifies my resolve to continue on."

"This world's Buddhas are just the same. I have seen all the Buddhas, from the first to the last. I have been enabled to see everything, from the first setting out of a bodhi heart, the planting of *bodhi* roots, the acquisition of awakening and supernatural gifts, the establishing and fulfilling of the Great Vow, the entry into the place occupied by bodhisattvas. Once a person becomes a Buddha, I see the world purified and glorified with and for the sake of all living creatures. I remember all that each Buddha has done. Only..."

"Only...?"

"Only I have done nothing myself, except open the liberation of Not-Entering-Nirvana. The liberation of all living creatures in the cosmos, not just of myself, has not been granted to me. Go south. Remember my song and go to Avalokiteshvara in Mount Potalaka."

Sudhana set out the next evening to avoid the worst of the daytime heat. Before he left, he swore to Veshthila that he would come back to do something for the people of Shubaha-paramgama, people so sunk in poverty they scarcely knew they were alive.

To the southwest, beyond prairies and marshes, lay the Sea of Indra. Once across that sea, Sudhana would have to follow the banks of the river he found there. He was always beginning again.

32.
THE SONG OF AVALOKITESHVARA

MOUNT POTALAKA, in the southern Indian realm of Mari-gukta, was surrounded by a whole community of thickly clustered towns and villages. It was more a towering world than a mountain. Sudhana arrived at an ancient village on the mountain's southern side, flanked by ancient trees of vast girth. The whole area radiated a spiritual aura. In the village, there were quite a number of people older than ninety years old. The villagers were so old that when a child was born there, people said its face took on adult features immediately. Villagers claimed that no newborn baby was ever heard crying in their town.

Sudhana considered growing old there, before reminding himself that the hermit had given him a mission. "I'm not going to grow old here. I'm on my way to meet the bodhisattva Avalokiteshvara."

An old servant in the village directed him a little farther to the west. He asked some washerwomen in the next village. They replied that he should go just a little farther. Since "a little farther" proved to be quite a distance, he had the whole day to prepare for his meeting with Avalokiteshvara.

The long walk made him thirsty, and he started walking toward the sound of running water. A stream flowed through a ravine on one side of the mountain. Pushing through the brush, he drank a few gulps. He would have liked to drink more, but he recalled a tramp's advice: a traveler must never fill his stomach with water.

A shadow was floating on the rippling stream. He turned and looked up. The bodhisattva Avalokiteshvara stood above him. A tangled mob of other bodhisattvas clustered behind. Over the bodhisattva's shoulders hung a shawl of simple woven cloth. Sudhana joined his hands in greeting and bowed low.

"Welcome."

Avalokiteshvara spoke: "Last night in a dream, a hermit from the north came and told me your name. So you are Sudhana."

Sudhana rejoiced.

"I am a flower, you are a flower bud. Welcome."

The hermit had warned Sudhana that Avalokiteshvara might appear in any of thirty-three different forms. Avalokiteshvara was an incarnation of the compassionate love that delivers all creatures from suffering, the hermit had taught him. If the bodhisattva Mahasthamaprapta stamped his foot once, the entire Buddha cosmos trembles, but when Avalokiteshvara revealed himself to living creatures, he adjusted his form to the ability of each person he met. By the multiple forms of his various incarnations, he showed how light, sound, smell, taste, and each phenomenon were all sources of bodhisattva enlightenment. With his thousand hands and thousand eyes, there was no place in this world that he couldn't touch and see. In one head he had eleven faces, so that he could perceive at the same time the world in all six directions—above and below, before and after, left and right. Such is the bodhisattva Avalokiteshvara. He is at the same time present in the faraway Western Paradise and in this world. He was also a poet singing in the last limitless regions of southern India. Sudhana encountered the bodhisattva in his most essential form, known as the "Sacred Avalokiteshvara."

After praying to the bodhisattva in his heart Sudhana spoke: "Holy bodhisattva, how can a bodhisattva achieve enlightening works and advance along enlightening paths?"

"I abolish people's fears," Avalokiteshvara answered, "I stand at the left hand of Amitabha in that world beyond, to ensure that when creatures fly from this world to the world beyond, no fear remains. Equally, for all this world's creatures, I banish fear in terrible situations, banish fear from extreme situations, banish fear of death, fear of wicked kings and powerful lords. I banish fear of poverty, fear of sickness, fear of shame and disgrace, of idleness and darkness. In addition, I banish fear of the way things change and are changing, lovers' fears of parting, fear of encountering an enemy, fear that makes heart and body tense, all the fear felt as anxiety and concern, the fear of not having what one longs for, and the fear of wandering in bad places. I banish them all."

As he heard these words, Sudhana's whole body was filled with new strength. He longed to repeat the words he had just heard and make them his own. But the bodhisattva began to sing:

> You have reached this place, son of the wind,
> child whose heart and body are unclad.
> You are circling around me. I am ever in this mountain.
> If I am not utter compassion, I am not who I am.

> I am in this mountain, in its diamond caverns.
> My body empty yet full of every kind of pearl.
> Hosts of heavenly gods, the dragon god, Asura demon,
> the ghosts of Chin and Garura and Najol,
> those kith and kin keep me company on my lotus-flower throne.

> You, young pilgrim, breath of wind,
> with your heart now prostrate at my feet,
> have come all this way to meet me
> in order to float on the ocean of virtue like a sailing ship.

> To learn enlightening deeds from me,
> to gain the enlightening deeds of the northern bodhisattva
> Samantabhadra,
> you never weary in distant journeys.
> I am duly bound to learn from you
> the practice of pure, deep, intrepid compassion.

> Look, what seems a net of light, light spreading far,
> broad, broader, spreading wide, spreading wide as the void:
> that wide-spreading my power bestows.
> Blessings, a hundred-fold, at once majestically adorn this world.

> You have come this far, breath of wind,
> you have come here with your heart profound.
> I touch your brow and at once, like you, like a long-traveling
> pilgrim,
> I long to throw open wide for you the gateways of liberation.
> We two are together here in the midst of truth.

Tell me, where can a doorway be a doorway?
The doorway too is merely a cloud.
Majestic cloud, regarding all living things with pity.
Vast cloud, open wide.

Having completed every vow,
I long to become one with every human sorrow,
to sacrifice myself for love.
I undergo endless pain and distress,
yet whoever calls my name is delivered of all pain.

Listen, pilgrim child.
In prison or fettered in chains,
shackled, face to face with an enemy,
those who invoke my name
will find their sufferings vanish like the wind.

Listen, all who are condemned to die.
When the executioner wields his sword,
and your soul is about to leave the body,
if you invoke my name,
the sword will melt and turn into water.

When a close friend or neighbor suddenly becomes your foe
and turns against you, invoke my name.
Then all bitterness melts and flowers bloom on riverbanks.

Little pilgrim child, breath of wind,
when life in this world is ended
and you are born into the Pure Land Paradise,
if you want to move without constraint, invoke my name.
Invoke my name a single time, pilgrim,
attaining perfection of desire.

As for you, my child, Sudhana, breath of wind,
long ago I was like you.
In order to help and save all living creatures

in every world under three thousand skies,
I formulated great vows and daily fulfilled them.

Sudhana,
your task is to move through all the worlds in ten directions,
attending each master you meet.

Listen with ears of wisdom,
behold with eyes and body full of compassion,
and if this task brings you joy,
you are already a son of truth.
Sudhana, little breath of truth's own wind.

When finished, Avalokiteshvara was silent for a while, then beckoned
Sudhana closer. The bodhisattva began to talk quietly, like a grandfather.

"As I was singing, you received all my teaching. I have entered the gates
of bodhisattva liberation but could not pass beyond the works of a bodhisattva Mahasattva. How can I live forever in accordance with the teachings of the Buddha? I came from other places and only very late came
rushing into the Buddha's teachings. How can I always be practicing Buddha works?"

Sudhana perceived the bodhisattva's immense virtue; he had set aside
all his majesty and with complete humility of heart put himself lower than
all living creatures to serve them all. Sudhana's heart was full of joy after
hearing the bodhisattva's song and he longed to respond. He rose, then
knelt with his right knee on the ground and bowed to touch the bodhisattva's feet. A poem came bursting out of him:

Beings of this world, the six worlds,
the heavens, too, all together,
the demon asuras, the host of bodhisattva Mahasattvas,
all together, join in praise, give praise and say:
"Holy Buddha's wisdom is vaster than the ocean."
Bodhisattva Avalokiteshvara, my master,
succoring all living creatures everywhere equally,
before you, all suffering is mere dew.
You can carry the earth away.
You can dry up the seas.

You can break down great mountains
and spread out plains.
Oh, holy, compassionate Bodhisattva Avalokiteshvara,
how with this worthless infant heart
shall I ever praise enough
such great wisdom and such virtue?
Bodhisattva Avalokiteshvara, my master,
joining with all who have been brought to understanding,
I will praise your exalted majesty.
With all my heart I serve and I revere you.
When Mahabrahman was in his heavenly realm,
Mahabrahman's light set fire to his whole heaven.
Now your essential nature rises in full splendor
in the midst of this world's living creatures.
Face like the full moon rising,
appearance like the rainbow after rain,
like Mount Sumeru soaring,
like the morning sun rising above the southern sea,
dazzling joy of bodhisattva being,
of deer running in meadows in the Deccan Plateau,
Bodhisattva Avalokiteshvara, my master,
like campaka and golden flowers growing together,
like white pearls strung on a necklace,
you are a flower, a flower.
In union with you
we cannot help but obtain incomparable bodies,
the whole world cannot help but hear
the sound of Buddhas and bodhisattvas breathing.
Others, coming after me,
have already entered truth
so I have this task of praise.

The moment Sudhana's poem ended, the bodhisattva leaped up and caught Sudhana's light body in his arms. In embracing that one small boy, he was embracing the whole world. The bodhisattva's joy was a heaven born of earth. If sorrow is the tears of earth born in heaven, that joy is the bliss of the bodhisattva who loves all creatures. Sorrow is the pain of the bodhisattva who loves all creatures. The bodhisattva's joy is at the same time his sorrow. Such is compassion.

Sudhana and Avalokiteshvara walked together through the mountain's glorious flowers, with the bees and butterflies. They were making their way back to the bodhisattva's lotus-shaped throne when an earthquake shook the mountain.

"He's coming!" the bodhisattva said, gazing up into the indigo-colored sky. "The bodhisattva Ananyagamin must be on his way. He always arrives like this."

Coming to this world from the empty reaches of space to the east, Ananyagamin touched the earth, landing with one toe on the loftiest summit of Mount Cakravada. The bodhisattva of the new world in the eastern reaches of space had arrived. Ananyagamin had the power to put to flight the six worlds' trillion aeons of sufferings and seeds of pain. Avalokiteshvara addressed Sudhana: "Did you see Ananyagamin the bodhisattva come into this world?"

Sudhana nodded.

"Now you must go to him and assist him, learning more of the deeds to bring enlightenment."

"I will follow what you say. When night falls, I will ask the starlight the way to find him."

Sudhana left Avalokiteshvara and walked along a narrow grassy path at the foot of Mount Potalaka. At the point where that grassy track joined a highway, Ananyagamin the bodhisattva was waiting. If an enlightened being happens to be somewhere, it is not that they are living there; they are simply waiting for someone to arrive, just as in a big marketplace you will always find water waiting to extinguish a fire.

"Teacher, teacher," Sudhana called, "I'm full of the food the bodhisattva Avalokiteshvara has just given me. But still I'm looking for more. I have passed through innumerable previous lives of gluttony, and I've inherited their effects."

"Hello, little pilgrim."

"Teacher, what world have you come from? From how far away? When were you last on earth?"

Ananyagamin spoke quietly, as if to himself: "Little pilgrim, you have already learned all there is to learn, you are fully fed. My words will make no difference. Yet saying just one word makes birds fly in the sky. Where did I come from and how long since I was last here? Those terms are foreign to me. The questions are so deep that all this world's brahmans and monks together can never find the answer. None but a bodhisattva can know. I came here from a world in space to the east plentifully supplied with good things. But since one aeon is a speck of dust, and one speck of dust ten thousand aeons, how can anyone tell how long it is since I was here before? Even I don't know. Head south from here. There's an ancient city there, where Mahadeva, the lord of heaven, is waiting for you."

Sudhana had forgotten that Avalokiteshvara had a thousand hands and thirty-three bodily forms, but he felt he had met this bodhisattva before. The same perfume emanated from both Avalokiteshvara, the bodhisattva of this world, and Ananyagamin, the bodhisattva from a different dimension.

"Two masters, each from different worlds!" Sudhana thought. But since the same perfume comes from both, they are one, after all. Fresh shoot of grain emerging, bearing two seedling leaves, the old life in that other world all done, now a new infant world has come into being.

These encounters left Sudhana exhausted and he did not at once set out southward towards the city of Dvaravati as Ananyagamin had told him. He let go of mind and body, dropping them to the ground.

"If I've not learned all the truth in this world from the masters I've met so far, I'll not learn it all from the masters I meet in the future, either. I'd like to have some fun," he thought. "Playing in this water here, I'm going to enjoy myself."

33.
CLOUD-NET THE GIANT

SUDHANA SOON FORGOT all about going to Dvaravati. A flock of birds heading homeward disappeared into the glory of the setting sun. Losing sight of them, Sudhana fell into a long dream, long like a river flowing into the sea. His dream was a world lasting one whole lifetime. In that world, he was an old man with white eyebrows, a woman of forty with a lotus blossom in her hand, and a youth on a galloping bay horse. He was also a wildflower blossoming in the fields, fluttering in the breeze, and an insect in the undergrowth, chirping ceaselessly day and night until a sound of thunder frightened him, at which point he turned into a wild dog running through meadows covered with mugwort.

At last, Sudhana awoke. Compared to the world of his dreams, reality was stale, flat, and tedious. He had forgotten the joy of meeting the bodhisattvas and had no reason to think of traveling south to Dvaravati. As he stared north and south, east and west, he knew the freedom of a child who has no direction. Going anywhere meant the eternal standstill of going nowhere. Such a standstill was the eternal motion of all journeying.

This time, even reality had turned into a new dream for Sudhana. This world had become a dream world, while the world he had dreamed about had changed into reality. The sun was shining, the clouds were gathering in towering masses as they followed the wind northwards. Now and then, lizards scurried away from under his feet. Far away, a village could be seen. As evening fell, the inevitable smoke of burning horse dung rose as supper was cooked. This was a world after Sudhana's own heart. This was what he had learned. There was nothing more to be learned. Originally there were no teachers in the world! There were no parents! No kings! No gods! Everything that exists was all the time changing randomly. Everything in the whole universe was complete impermanence. Movement and annihilation. So what was all this majestic universe, if not the music of the cosmos? Surely freedom from all obstacles was the means of getting free of one's self? He made up a song as he played:

> Forth I go, clad in bodhisattva amour!
> Then I strip off that armor,
> become a gust of wind touching a blade of grass!
> What bodhisattva laughter fills the road I follow
> with my naked bodhisattva body,
> devoid of any stain!
> Bodhisattva wisdom! Great vow!
> But then I make all those things
> less than this world's briefest dream!

At his words, the trees around grew into a luxuriant forest. It was cool enough in the forest that Sudhana stopped perspiring. For the first time since he had journeyed south, an image of the city of Dvaravati rose in his mind like a daytime moon. With that memory, Sudhana's purpose and humanity were restored and he prepared to continue his journey.

The road went on, winding along the edge of the forest, and soon he reached a sizable village. The people living there were taller than average, and in contrast, little Sudhana felt he'd returned to an earlier period of his childhood. He asked an elderly woman if this village was Dvaravati. She gathered him in her arms and swept him up into the air.

"Oh you marvelous child, seeking truth from Mahadeva in Dvaravati city. What a blessing that you should pass our village. Everyone here knows Dvaravati city; why, even the owls know it. Come and rest in our house for a while before you continue. Come along."

Sudhana was borne in her arms to her house. He was surprised by its luxuriousness. Despite the old clothes she wore, that woman was in fact immensely wealthy. He accepted a cup of honeyed water.

"Little sage, this house is too big, isn't it? I bought it after becoming rich by selling water and grain in times of drought. They say that this world's wealth is just a fine name for theft, though I gained my wealth by my own efforts. But I can't take it with me; I'll have to leave it all behind when I die.

"Before I die, I want to make this house serve truth. Of course, truth is not something owned by one person, everybody has it. Therefore, I have decided that I want the next owner of this house to be someone who will share the title of truth with everybody. I thought I might offer it to the great master Cloud-net Mahadeva whom you're on your way to visit, but he already owns the heavens, and far larger houses, forests, and fields, so I want to give it to you. If you come back here, I'll give you this house and all my fortune; what do you say?"

Sudhana made no reply. She went on talking in gasps.

"There are no worse shackles in this world than the fact of owning things, are there? That's why ridding yourself of all possessions is the first step towards enlightenment, isn't it? But getting rid of something can't be done by throwing it away; it has to be offered to someone, doesn't it? But surely it's right to say that not possessing things in this world does not mean throwing them away or offering them to another individual; it means owning them in common. That's right, surely. Just as people and animals and all of nature possess the sunlight together..."

The woman went on and on talking, repeating herself, and apparently not expecting any reply. In the end, the rich woman's hospitality was limited to that one cup of honeyed water, for Sudhana suddenly rose from his chair and made his farewell.

"Dvaravati city is only half a day's journey away," the woman said in parting. "Take the left-hand road at the foot of the nine-hundred-year-old tree at the entrance to the village. It leads straight to the north gate of Dvaravati city. Farewell, little pilgrim."

Behind the woman's many words lingered a silence deep like that in a well; Sudhana bowed in greeting, paying respect to that hidden silence, then turned to leave.

"Don't be surprised by Mahadeva's size," she called after him. "Being physically big is nothing."

After a leisurely night's journey, Sudhana reached the northern outskirts of Dvaravati city. Although the north gate was not the main entrance to the city, it was wide enough to admit one hundred people at a time with room to spare. A pure breeze blew through it. The guards directed him towards an elevated area inside the city walls. Far away, he could see the gigantic figure of Mahadeva sitting there. Sudhana headed straight toward him; it was not so much a matter of hurrying; rather it was as if Mahadeva had such a firm hold on him that Sudhana could not even struggle. The sun was high in the sky; heaven and earth stood brow to brow.

The very little child bowed to Mahadeva's immense foot, then joined his hands in respectful greeting to the towering spirit of the heavens: "Sacred Mahadeva, who comes down from heaven to fill the world. I have set my heart on attaining perfect enlightenment. Yet still I have not been able to come to knowledge of enlightened ways, virtues, and works. Therefore I have come seeking you, treading the ground with my little feet."

Mahadeva had been delivering a thundering sermon to a group of disciples. But before Sudhana had even reached the end of his greeting, Mahadeva abandoned his serious manner, sprang to his feet, opened his four hands, seized four handfuls of sea water, and washed his face. For a moment, a fragment of the sea was alive in each hand with waves that had been breaking in the ocean. Then the waves smashed against his face. The old woman had told Sudhana that physically big things are nothing, but now Sudhana felt afraid. Mahadeva, who had come down from heaven to take up residence in this world, was different from ordinary human beings. He only had to grab hold of this earthly world with his four hands and nothing would remain. It was as though a spirit left over from the age of the dinosaurs had come wandering into the human world.

Sudhana was even more astonished to hear Mahadeva speak in an extremely gentle, affectionate voice. Mahadeva's words were as much poetry as speech.

> I am Mahadeva, spirit of heaven,
> my name is Cloud-net by reason of my Cloud-net liberation,
> so speak my name aloud.
> Child, with your truth-seeking journey through endless months
> and distant lands,
> today you are indeed my joy.
> Like the morning sun,
> you are always traveling through this world's places of piety.
> Today, you bring me joy.

The giant Mahadeva, Cloud-net, filled his own heart with happiness, then taking the joy that remained, he filled the hearts of Sudhana and his disciplea.

The city of Dvaravati was full of all kinds of flowers, all kinds of perfumes, all kinds of flying banners, all kinds of gorgeous clothing, all kinds of lovely singing, and a hundred thousand million trillion lovely girls. The giant Mahadeva spoke: "Resplendent child, every aspect of reality is part of a world of extraordinary illusion. All the things I have shown you are the breath of the perfumed ocean of the Lotus Paradise. Only by offering that breath to others can a Buddha's virtue become infinite. Just as I have given this breath to you, so you too, later, must distribute it to all living creatures.

"The holiest of all deeds is the work of bestowing on others. Let your bestowing be unconscious, practice the selflessness that communicates selflessness to selflessness. All this world's joy in having is not worth one hundred thousand million trillionth part of the joy of giving.

"Vigilance, like giving, is a holy work. This world is full of desires. In this world of desire, maggots feast on dung, pigs in summer smear themselves with their shit, drunkards have to be tied up, thieves steal people's belongings, criminals are handed over to the executioner, the blind lead the blind and both fall into a pit, boats put out to sea and encounter storms. In this world where people fall into desire and cannot escape, the fragrance of the way of the Buddha is identical with the fragrance of the flowers.

"I cannot help loving all this world's living creatures with their ways of desire. That is why I employ different ways of enlightening people. For example, to one man I might first reveal myself in a girl's beautiful body. I arrange things so that he grows interested in her and begins to feel lust, whereupon I show him that same girl dying, her body rotting, being devoured by birds and wild animals, stinking so badly that if he once goes close, the stench clings to him for years, no matter how often he washes.

"After that I show him the same girl in the shape of a fearsome ghost, her red hair covering a body black as storm clouds, her belly drooping, her teeth sticking upwards, human skulls for ornaments, her hands wielding sharp knives, cursing and swearing, shouting all kinds of slander; seeing her in that shape, the man will never again be able to love another beautiful woman. It is at that precise moment that I show him the way of liberation. I may choose to show a woman the same thing about a man she desires."

His four hands once again seized water from the four oceans. This time the great god washed Sudhana's and his disciples' faces, as well. Sudhana's whole body was wet, as if he had been fully immersed. The giant returned to his sermon.

"Friends of mine. Even heavenly spirits who live without the Precepts, go to hell. The whore Marunga learned the Precepts and went to heaven. The members of north India's Shakya tribe went to heaven by the Precepts while brahmans rejected the Precepts and went to hell. King Kali turned into an animal, his sons all became wild animals, then they, too, went to hell.

"Think of the Buddha's Precepts like parents, like a torch, like a great boat on a stormy sea."

The spirit's huge finger touched Sudhana's head. "There. Now you can speak my words." Large body and little body lost their significance. Mahadeva and Sudhana were united. Now Sudhana found himself charged with the task of preaching the Cloud-net liberation.

Cloud-net listened while Sudhana preached, their roles reversed: "Heavenly spirit, Mahadeva. There are so many bodhisattvas in this world that every joint of every living creature's bones is in receipt of boundless compassion. Yet since that was still not enough, you yourself came down, spirit of the heavens above.

"Now one little traveling child will speak, having received Mahadeva's teaching. Listen with ears of earth, not heaven's ears, not heaven's cloud-net; listen with ears caught in the net of the earth. Enlightening virtue has been sown in this world's one small child.

"The proud may rave, but soon, falling on their knees, they will surrender to superior powers. Shown sights of blood being drunk, flesh devoured, they will fall to their knees. The lightning sword drops on the fool; the fool will be destroyed with sky-rending fury.

"How could it stop there? At the entry into heaven of all the works of goodness, all deeds of evil will be brought to an end like a double rainbow shining after rain."

Hearing Sudhana, the giant knelt down and turned into a vast mountain range. The mountain spoke: "Now the reason for my descent into this world of pain has been abolished. Little sage, meeting you has given me the strength to return to the heavens. Many thanks."

Weeping, Sudhana interrupted: "That cannot be, great spirit of heaven. Giant Cloud-net Mahadeva, master. You came down to this world with such an enormous body, not to show off your size, but to manifest clearly the vastness of your task and teaching. Master, in encountering you, I am not of this one world, but of five hundred different worlds. With most earnest devotion I embrace your teaching."

Child, the meaning of our meeting is fulfilled.
I, who merely obtained at length Cloud-net liberation,
I who merely managed to snap off a single branch of Cloud-net
liberation,
how should I attain the immensities of virtue
held by the hosts of great enlightenment there beyond the seas?

That power with which the heavenly lord Sakrodevendra
smote to pieces the myriad demons of evil desire—
power like the ocean,
capable of extinguishing all the fires in every single living creature—
power snuffing out all the flames of lust
endlessly burning in all living creatures—

power like storms,
abolishing all the attachments present in every living creature—
how could I aspire to possess such sacred enlightening powers?

Child, with bright eyes of enlightenment,
go now to the grove of bodhi trees
in the land of Magadha in Jambudvipa.
There, you can meet the earth spirit of the place, the noble
Sthavara.
While I am of heaven, she with deeper virtues is the earth.

In that way Mahadeva, the Cloud-net giant, finally took the lowest
place, after appearing so majestic and solemn. Out of all the immense quantity of truth contained in what Mahadeva had said and not said, Sudhana
realized that a few words, a song, were lodged in his heart like a final
bequest.

Perfumes of candana, kunkuman, agila, and musk are the finest perfumes
known on earth, yet what comparison can there be between them and the
actions and virtues found in bodhisattvas' love for every living creature?

Sudhana knelt before the great spirit in the mountain and bowed to the
ground three times. Then rising to his feet, he looked up for one final gaze,
only to find that there was no trace of the giant anywhere. There was nothing to be seen but a floating mass of low white clouds. Not a single one of
the giant's disciples was left. Dvaravati was completely deserted. The leaves
on the trees were turning and dancing to the sound of the wind, that was
all. Sudhana longed to reach the earth's underground heart. That was
where the noble Sthavara must live. Sudhana's heart was shouting: "I must
go, I must go, deep into the earth's darkness."

Sudhana was now on his way to the southern regions of Magadha, a
country inhabited by ten separate peoples, speaking ten different languages. Sudhana's goal was the place of enlightenment that lay there. On
arrival, Sudhana would have to find the hidden tunnel leading down to the
underground world. He walked quickly.

Once more, Sudhana was a pilgrim on the road. His journey stretched
on to the ends of this world's heavens and earth.

34.

THE PLACE OF ENLIGHTENMENT

UDHANA'S PATH now turned towards the northeast, toward the land of Magadha. Crowds of people were coming and going along the road. Carts left deep ruts in the water-softened ground as they passed. One skinny merchant traveling alone kindly insisted that Sudhana ride with him. Sudhana yielded to the merchant's insistence that he rest his feet sometimes on such a long journey. A mass of tropical flies were swarming over the horse's back, but it never paused in its steady pace.

The merchant was very proud of his son, who did business just outside the city walls and was a believer in the Buddha. He was equally boastful about the words of the Buddha that he had heard from his son, and he communicated them to Sudhana in a loud voice, perhaps because he wanted other passersby to hear. Gradually, though, his voice grew smaller, while his attitude grew increasingly reverent. He had begun by boasting about his son, but now he was talking about truth.

"You're very young, compared to my son. I bet you're no good at business. Yet there's something about you, something that charms even an old fellow like me."

The merchant remembered hearing how the Buddha had told his disciples that he was their friend. Suddenly he remarked to Sudhana, happy as a little child, that they were traveling along like two close friends. Sudhana was happy at the thought of friends! Friends of truth!

The merchant was perfectly sincere, and Sudhana began to feel affection for him, too. Between the two, the equal affection that exists between friends had begun to grow.

The merchant told Sudhana the story of how Buddha had said to his disciples, "I am your friend; since you have accepted me as your close friend, this mortal body can throw off death."

The first band of Buddhist believers along the Ganga, who had no Absolute Being in their creed, summed up their social morality as friendship, the fellowship throughout the cosmos between the Buddha and all living creatures, teacher and disciples. When Ananda told Siddhartha that being together with a good friend was contrary to the Precepts, the Buddha corrected him: "Having good friends and being with a good companion is all the sacred Way."

All living creatures in the whole Buddha cosmos constitute a universe that is in the act of passing from solitude to the fellowship of bodhisattva being.

Sudhana got down from the merchant's cart on the banks of a river. Each bade the other farewell with hands joined in greeting and soon the merchant's cart was moving off into the distance.

The gates of Magadha could be seen far away on the other shore. The water was a tawny color, with great floating clumps of grass. Many people were sitting with both feet soaking in the filthy water. Time meant nothing to them, as it often does to people with nothing to do. They were praying for their hearts to go flowing with the river, down to the distant sea, the sea being the great equalizer that abolishes all distinctions of class. Their lips were constantly murmuring, "Aoma. Aoma." One young man addressed the murmuring crowd. His words had the power to awaken the lethargy at the riverbank.

"There are many rivers. The Ganga, Jumna, Azerbatti, Sarabu, Maharago, Puligoni. But once each river reaches the sea, it loses its name and is simply called the great ocean. In the same way, if the four castes of *kshatriya, brahman, vaysya,* and *sudra* come together, according to the sacred teachings and commandments, all four main castes and the innumerable subsidiary castes will vanish; the Buddha's world alone will remain and flourish. Let us send all our desires, fantasies, and defilements floating away with the stream. Let us make Magadha and the whole world here into Amitabha's own world, and experience a liberation like that of the sea."

Sudhana was so touched by these words that he began to sob. He wept for a long time. Many hours later, when his tears finally stopped, he recalled that he had intended to visit Sthavara. He hurried onto the next ferry to come across.

The little pilgrim passed over the river in an ancient boat poled by a boatman so old he had lost his eyebrows, like a leper.

The city he had seen from far off seemed no nearer after crossing the river. On and on he walked, and still it loomed far away. After a passing downpour the air was cool. Suddenly, the figure of the giant Cloud-net appeared to his imagination. "Have you forgotten the way? This is the wrong road," the figure scolded him. Sudhana stopped. He had unconsciously taken the broadest path at a point where five roads met. He went back the way he had come.

A battalion of soldiers was stationed at the road junction. Their presence had given rise to a temporary, untidy settlement, full of merchants and whores. Sudhana asked one tradesman about the earth spirit preaching in the shade of a grove of bodhi trees.

"What? Why do you want to know about such things? What are you doing, visiting earth spirits and things of that kind?" He asked everyone he could find, but all he got were mocking replies.

He noticed a quiet road unmarked by the wheels of any carts, hidden behind the crossroads checkpoint. This was the road he knew he had to take, yet there was almost no trace of human passage in that direction. After journeying on for nearly half a day, he arrived at a grove of bodhi trees.

A large number of ascetics were scattered throughout the grove, sitting with crossed legs, plunged in their inner worlds. The grove was full of their deep, quiet breathing. At the sight of them, Sudhana was seized with an intense fatigue. He sank down on a soft spot at the foot of the trees, stretched out his legs, and instantly fell into a deep sleep, his first for a long time.

In his dream, Sudhana saw a host of earth spirits sitting throughout the grove, in place of the ascetics. The spirit sitting nearest to Sudhana seized hold of his clothing and said, "This is the light to which all living creatures will turn for help in the future. You are also light." Then the spirit added, "You will have power to bring all living creatures' passions to rest in a cool place like this." Sudhana knew that he was dreaming, but he could not wake up.

"You have already entered the gardens of truth, the grove of truth," the spirit said. "You will dig deep in the mines of truth and distribute truth's jewels to all living creatures. Be still. Don't breathe out, now, hold your breath. Someone's coming."

The little earth spirit appeared frightened, and composed itself into a pose of pious meditation. A moment passed, and then the whole grove rang with a great crash, as if it had been struck by a thunderbolt. Sweat pearled on Sudhana's palms. Every trace of shade and darkness had vanished from the grove and it was filled with a bright light. Sthavara, the leader of all the earth spirits, appeared. She was even larger than the giant Mahadeva. The majestic goddess's voice rang out.

"Behold. This grove is full of all the treasures of every world under the three thousand heavens. On account of this one child, the world ought to be moved to exultation. All places now are full of music. The world is one beautiful song. Those in heaven, the demons, too, and cows, elephants, lions, insects and snakes, all are rejoicing, entranced by the music. The hundreds, the thousands of rich veins of precious gems buried deep below the ground are bursting upward, beginning to dance, entranced by truth and music. Behold, rain is falling. Let the sweet-scented rain drench you. Its perfume is the breath of the most sacred being in this world, words of its simplest child. Spirits, behold this child who has come."

All the earth spirits turned their eyes towards Sudhana.

Sthavara continued, "You have done well to come here. This grove is full of the jewels of truth produced by all your incarnations."

Sthavara stamped the ground once with her great foot. The earth split open to reveal a vast store of treasures. The goddess spoke: "Young pilgrim, all these treasures are the result of the good you have done. They are yours. Take them."

Sudhana calmly shook his head. "No. These may have been sown by me, yet it is right that the harvest should belong to all living creatures. In this world my only wealth is my body, so I can travel in quest of truth. All I desire is the day when, by these treasures, all the world's poverty, evil, and discord will be changed into wealth, perfume, and song. I desire that day and nothing more."

Sudhana attended the earth spirits' midday meal. First they drew water from a spring deep in the forest, then they took roots of trees, washed them in the water, and distributed them. Sweet and sour mingled. Each spirit received a draught of water to drink. After their meal, all the earth spirits returned to their places, leaving their mistress Sthavara alone with Sudhana in the grove. She breathed deeply, a breath that seemed to be drawn from deep underground. Then she spoke.

"Because my great body was filled with the power by which I fulfill all living creatures' prayers, no matter where I lived or went, the task of grant-ing all living creatures' supplications was always waiting for me. No one could ever overpower or defeat me.

"Before I became what I am now, I lived in a world where I pursued a bodhisattva exactly like I am now, begging her to grant my prayers. Among the gods, the bodhisattvas, and the Buddhas, each without exception has at some time been demon, ghost, beast, and bug. Each Buddha has had to put off the karma that brings human beings to death; each bodhisattva has had to lose the memory of the violence of demonhood; every god has been bandit and beggar. The mother of the holiest bodhisattva was a woman of the streets. It was only in the midst of that kind of human life and existence that light could appear. You are that light. Now I will drop to the ground. I will snap like a dead branch from a tree."

Sudhana saw the goddess Sthavara as a bodhisattva incarnating a sor-rowful and gentle motherhood. Compassion emerged out of her wildness, suggesting an ending.

"From the time of the Lotus Buddha many aeons ago, I lived like a pious shadow, ever following bodhisattvas with reverence and respect, in pursuit of a reward. So a bodhisattva heart simply came to be reflected in my heart. Bodhisattva sorrow and wisdom entered my heart, where they began to grieve and shine. There was once an age, countless aeons ago, as many ages ago as there are atoms in Mount Sumeru. That age's name was the Solemn Age, the name of that age's world was Moon Pavilion World, the name of that world's presiding Buddha was the Green Jade Buddha. It was from that Buddha that I received recognition and entered the state of liberation. Since then, while as many ages have passed as there are atoms in Mount Sumeru, countless aeons have passed, continuing in this liberation, and all through this present age, I have encountered innumerable Buddhas, greet-ing them and serving them. As a result I went to live in the world of the earth spirits, dwelling amidst subterranean darkness, and earth, and rocks, and jewels, and the water that flows underground, and the creatures living in that cold water. Now for a moment of earthly time I have come out into the world, and am breathing, absorbing the light, welcoming the wind.

"There is no difference between me and any clump of grass you encounter along the road. Now you must cross this great country until you are completely exhausted. You will arrive at a river brimming with water, the Ganga, frequented by more bearers and seekers of truth than any other river in the world. Once across the river, you will come to the city of

Kapilavastu. It's a small town with low walls. It has no moat surrounding it. If you arrange to arrive there by night, Vasanti, goddess of night, will welcome you. Go to her and hear all that I haven't been able to tell you. You'll stay in that place a long time. A few days of talking will not suffice."

Sudhana woke from his trance. This spot, where the good works of all his lives had been accumulated, seemed to him nothing more than a miserable roadside inn. Following Sthavara's indications, he set out. He walked on along the forest path as it plunged deeper into the grove of bodhi trees, brushing against the ferns. The grove was completely empty.

The forest ended and a grassy plain teeming with deadly snakes opened before him. Sudhana pulled out the shoes that he wore for rough places, pulled tight the lambskin laces, and smeared the heels with a paste made from the fruit of weeds that snakes, worms, and reptiles find repulsive.

He headed north, turning his back on the bright Southern Cross that he used to gaze at in times of hunger, turning his back on countless billions of ages, considering the past as so much wind.

The wind pressed against Sudhana's back, hurrying him on. When he washed his clothes in the grassland streams and put them on still damp, the wind dried them in a breath. Sudhana was barely half way across the grasslands when tremendous fatigue forced him to his knees. There wasn't a scrap of shade. He lay gasping in the sunlight, almost losing consciousness.

Before his final breath, furious storm clouds filled the sky. Heavy rain began to pour down, beating his face and body. Sudhana opened his mouth in an attempt to drink some of the rainwater, but the impact of the raindrops stung his tongue. Restored to life, he walked the rest of the way through the night. A single light could be seen in the distance, beckoning him toward the guard post on Magadha's northern frontier.

35.
NIGHT GODDESS

ROSSING THE VAST LAND of Magadha involved a constant fight with the horizon. As he marched on, utterly exhausted, Sudhana had to constantly resist the desire to collapse. At last, the Ganga! The southern region's hills, rivers, and unending fields, formerly the scene of pilgrim-quest for truth, now seemed like a daydream, and only this present moment, here on the banks of the Ganga, felt real. The little pilgrim shed silent, weary tears. He was empty of both sorrow and joy.

The banks of the Ganga, where hibiscus trees were pushing their branches up into the sky, reminded Sudhana of his rescue from the river and his first teacher, Manjushri. He'd been so young then. That distant past felt newer than anything that had happened since.

Evening had come. After the rain, the river was turgid and rough. The current flowed on, bearing dead animals, tree trunks, and all kinds of rubbish. This filthy river was sacred by its filth. Ganga, made sacred by everything, Ganga of ancient days. The day's last raft succeeded in reaching the shore where Sudhana sat. At great risk, it had crossed over, after being swept downstream like an arrow by the raging torrent and only gaining the landing stage with three times more pole strokes than it normally took. The wild-looking boatman called out to Sudhana.

"Are you crossing over? Come on, if you don't want to fall in and drown."

Walking over the sodden turf, Sudhana boarded the raft.

Once across the Ganga, the shade cast by the thickly growing broad-leaved trees began to cool him. After the dreary dampness out on the river, that cool shade restored his spirits. Sudhana had returned north at last. He was in the region of Kapilavastu, where Siddhartha, the scion of the house of Shakya, had been born and from where he had left home. Now

Siddhartha's father, the king Suddhodana, was dead and the land had become a fief of the kingdom of Magadha. Because the Buddha had shunned his worldly responsibilities, Kapilavastu had been brought to this miserable pass. Truth had grown, but his clansmen were wretched.

The night in Kapilavastu was bright; no watchmen were necessary. The full-moon festival was just over.

Sudhana went looking for the night goddess Vasanti, the former teacher of the earth spirit Sthavara. But nobody seemed to know anything of this goddess who presided over the night. The streets were empty. At a loss, Sudhana withdrew into himself.

Leaving the main streets, he turned aside into a lane near the city walls and found himself in a poor, low-caste neighborhood. It was a neighborhood where no brahman had ever set foot. A blind man was calmly advancing all alone down the dark street. As he walked through the darkness, far from the bonfires at the town center, he moaned.

Sudhana stopped him. "I wonder if you know Vasanti the night goddess?"

The moaning stopped.

"What a fool, to ask a human being about a spirit! Off you go to the dew-fields outside the town. Go and ask the dew."

Sudhana was captivated by the immensities of the cosmos revealed in the night sky. He could see stars he had never seen before, red, green, and silver. He had the impression that the night sky was overflowing with stars on such a glorious night.

As he gazed upwards, stars shining in the heavens were abruptly extinguished, the sky grew completely dark, and the beautiful night goddess Vasanti appeared in the air, surrounded by a bright halo. She was robed in a thin cloth of gold; her long black hair hung down her back, her eyes were blue lotus flowers. The stars clustered about her.

Every aspect of her beauty, every single pore of her skin, was occupied in bringing all the creatures in the world out of darkness into light. She was not only called the goddess of night, but also of the light.

"Sacred goddess of night," Sudhana called, "my heart is set on perfect universal enlightenment. I beg you to instruct me in the ways that lead to all truth. Let me rely on you. Enable me to gain the power I need to devote myself entirely to pure works in the heart of truth."

"When people are on the look-out on dark nights for elves, or thieves, or wicked creatures, when clouds and mists hang thick, or when storms and typhoons sweep down, when they encounter dread and disaster, I could not endure it if I did not do all I can to help.

"For creatures in difficulties, I become a traveling companion, a singing bird, or a comforting, effective herb. I shed light, too, and serve as a whore for some fellow enslaved by sexual desires. Then on the following day I turn into a mountain spring and free that same fellow of all his thirst.

"But in this world, creatures' dread and disaster, poverty and disease and ignorance, and class divisions between creature and creature, are every day increasing more and more, so I am obliged to increase too, a thousand bodies, ten thousand bodies, and have not yet accomplished it. Fire dies out under the feet of a bodhisattva. How glad I am, as Goddess of Night, to meet you. All the power of truth will fill you utterly, and the way will shine bright with light for you, since you give your life unstintingly."

She called out to the stars:

My liberation: banishing darkness.
Living beings, following their nature
all yield buddhahood.
So the more this world is full of beings,
the greater the fullness of Buddha nature.
Bodies rotting by the roadside,
bloated bodies floating down the Ganga:
amidst all that carrion, flowers bloom,
Buddha is born,
basis of the world.
I am the cause of all the phenomena in the cosmos
and the cosmos is the cause of me,
great opening of the gate of liberation
for the ten-directioned universe.
Enter by this gate,
go through this gate and far away.
Oh, pure Vairochana Buddha.
Every speck of dust,
every darkening of the air yields
liberation under sleeping bodhi trees.

Many poems have been composed in Kapilavastu. It seems as though spirits love poems as much as people do. Sudhana felt her words as if they had recited the poem together.

He called to her, "Among the teachers I visited in my travels, there were many different kinds of people. Now, I have begun to meet divine beings. It seems to me there is no difference between human beings and gods. I am afraid that if I cannot gain wisdom now, I shall never be able to rid myself of my folly. Please, tell me about your past, dear Goddess of Night. Today arises from history, the future arises from history, so I am eager to hear from you, my teacher of today, about the virtues of your past and all your incarnations."

"Long, long ago, as many aeons ago as there are atoms in Mount Sumeru, there was an age called the age of Silent Light. The world that evolved during that aeon was called the World of the Jewel of Good Fortune. Fifty billion Buddhas were born into that world. In the midst of that world's fourth heaven rose the kingdom of Lotus Flower Glory. The king was named Chakravarti, which means Hill of Marvelous Teaching. The king's wife loved poetry and singing, dancing and music, only going to sleep late at night. One night, the Night Goddess came hurrying to wake the queen,

saying that the Buddha of Glorious Adornment had attained perfect illumination in the forest lying to the east of the palace, and led her there.

"That wife of King Cakravarti began to serve the followers of the Buddha of Glorious Adornment. I am today's incarnation of that queen. I spent
the following ages, comparable to eight billion atoms of Mount Sumeru,
entirely absorbed in the enjoyment of the pleasures and good fortune I
received, so that I was not able to qualify to become a bodhisattva. In the
midst of the agonies experienced by living beings in all the hells and pur-
gatorial realms and demon worlds, bodhisattvas great and small were coming into being, while I spent every day enjoying myself, enticed by times of
abundance.

"That aeon came to an end, another ten thousand ages passed, then in
the age before this present one, the aeon of Homelessness, when five hundred Buddhas were born, I was the daughter of a wealthy family and was
again led by the Night Goddess to a newly enlightened Buddha and served
him. I would wash the Buddha with my chaste hands, then bow down
before him, covering his feet with my lovely hair, until with the wisdom I
acquired, I was able to look back over all my past lives.

"Little pilgrim, now I have come to live on the riverbanks outside this
city in this small land to the south of the great snowy mountains in this
world of pain, turned into a goddess of night, my beauty surrendered to the
darkness, and here I live helping all creatures escape from danger, lighten-
ing their darkness with love and wisdom. But for me as for you, there comes
a time to leave this place. That will be in good time."

The goddess's musical voice brought the dawning of a new day glowing
in the east. The dark was withdrawing from Sudhana like an aging animal.
Vasanti spoke a final message with dignity:

"Good youth, you must cross the Ganga and head south again. At the
bodhi grove in the land of Magadha there is a great night spirit, Samantagambhirashrivimala-prabha, from whom you must receive instruction as I
myself did once. There you will find the great night spirit who leads all the
rest of us."

Sudhana felt his boyhood leave him with the Night Goddess. He was a
young man, fresh as if just emerging from water.

When Sudhana and morning met outside Kapilavastu, he was asleep.
For the first time in a long time, he has missed the dawn, sleeping the sleep
of someone who has come back to old haunts after long travels through
unfamiliar lands.

36.
THE GROVE OF
NEVER-CLOSING EYES

WHEN HE WOKE and resumed traveling, the road leading away from Kapilavastu was crowded. All were equal on this road, traders heading for the various branches of the Ganga, pilgrims, ascetics, members of the four castes. Not, of course, quite equal in the law. The low-caste people couldn't keep their heads held high as processions of strongly-built brahman priests passed by, but once the brahmans had passed, members of the lower castes took the same road with heads raised boldly.

Until now, Sudhana had taken three kinds of roads. There were roads where, after he had met a teacher the teaching simply continued. There were roads where, once Sudhana's heart had digested that teaching, he could go on by himself. And then, finally, a road that promised to lead to the new master he was to meet and that master's teaching, finally leading him to the master.

Everyone Sudhana had met so far had passed him on to their teacher. In this way, Sudhana had visited his masters' masters, adding to the number of his own masters as he went along and advancing farther out into the depths of the ocean of truth. With Vasanti, he had now met his thirty-third master. He had ventured out into the thirty-third ocean of truth, and reached a center from which he couldn't turn away. The very center of truth! The remotest seas in the midst of the ocean! It made no difference that the highway leading from Kapilavastu towards Magadha felt familiar to him; with a deep sense of solitude his journey was sustained by Vasanti's poem.

Ordinary people walked along the road, nobles traveled in carriages, and soldiers were borne in war chariots. The merchants had innumerable teams of pack animals. Sudhana was frequently covered in the milky clouds of dust left by speeding carts.

Someone walking close behind him addressed Sudhana. "Hey, there, you young man." Before he could turn round, the man had caught up with him. The man was delighted to see him.

"It really is you! I met you once before. Down south, it was. I'd fallen among thieves and been robbed of everything. With nothing to eat for several days I was sick, I collapsed and just then you passed by and rescued me. The dried fruit and the draught of water you gave me saved my life."

Sudhana couldn't remember ever crossing paths with this man before.

"Back then, I wanted to know at least your name, since I owed you my life, but you just gave me two little coins and went away. It was in the shade of a two-hundred-year-old palm tree."

"If you say so."

"I'm glad to see you. At last I can repay the kindness you did me."

"There is nothing you have to repay. I have never done anyone a kindness."

"No, no, you saved my life. Tell me your name."

Sudhana felt embarrassed.

"There is a name I use in my quest for truth, but I don't have any name for someone who wants to repay a kindness. I have never helped anyone like you."

The man was dumbfounded by Sudhana's cold words.

"What?"

The fellow examined Sudhana once more.

"You mean, it wasn't you who saved my life?"

Sudhana spoke even more icily.

"That's right. I have never once done anyone a kindness." Sudhana realized that this fellow trailing along beside him, wanting to repay a kindness, was a metamorphosis of the night spirit Vasanti.

He addressed the man again, "Go back. I am quite capable of meeting my next teacher on my own. Go back. In Magadha, the Night Spirit of Magadha is all I need. Here you're no goddess at all, you're just a cloud of dust."

Impatient with what he saw as a ruse, Sudhana had just called a teacher he had deeply revered a cloud of dust! But the Night Spirit, in the guise of the man in tattered clothes, was not saying that she had been saved by

Sudhana earlier in this life. Some hundred or so incarnations before, she had been saved from the agonies of death by starvation and sickness by a previous incarnation of Sudhana.

Every lie spoken in this world has been true at some point in the turning cycles of our reincarnations. In that sense, every lie is true. Suppose that man had told Sudhana, not that he was his benefactor but that he was his enemy, that too would have been true. In some previous existence the two might well have met in the role of enemies.

The man dropped back and, as soon as a side-road presented itself, took it, vanishing like a cloud of dust. At present, Sudhana had no inclination to be with her or with any other teacher. He had needed her poem, but he had no need of her in any additional transformation.

As he walked, Sudhana entered a fantasy in which the spirit Samantagambhirashrivimala-prabha was already standing there before him.

"Holy being, I have attained perfect universal illumination, but I do not yet know how bodhisattvas enter the position in which they should live, or act within it." This question emerged from Sudhana and immediately vanished.

"Little pilgrim, I can see I'm going to have to put up with a deal of sorrow on your account," the spirit roared. "I am a god of darkness and night. By my darkness and night, I abolish from every last corner of this world the difference between high and low, noble and base. There is no more rich and poor. Much more than that, if a bodhisattva chooses its enlightening position and sees it as something high and noble that all ordinary creatures should look up to, that is not bodhisattva living at all. Bodhisattva living would be great winds and furious waves sweeping that position away completely. It is more like a huge pillar of fire, consuming that position utterly. Little pilgrim, if you think that bodhisattva position and form are contained in the life of wisdom and compassion you have found, rid yourself of that life here and now. Get rid of it and start to cry. Little wanderer, put an end to your travels, go home, hurl a soldier's spear into the distance, kill some creature."

As these words rang in his fantasy, Sudhana's body was covered with dew-like sweat; he realized how right the fantasy spirit was. Bodhisattva position! Dog position! Bug position!

Sudhana continued his journey. The bodhi grove of Magadha lay on the far side of two large walled cities the size of Kapilavastu. Magadha had many of these cities, yet the king was still always trying to annex small, weak lands. Several times, Sudhana had to pass identity check points. Soldiers were on guard at the crossroads, glaring as they scrutinized all the people passing.

"Where are you headed?" They asked him. "I'm on my way to meet this country's Night Spirit."

The soldiers laughed at Sudhana's reply. "You must be a bit weak in the head, kid. How else would you ever have the idea of saying you were off to meet the evening ghosts or whatever?"

"There's a spirit in this country's nights."

"You idiot. Even if there used to be such night ghosts, they took to their heels and disappeared at the first sight of war. They're gone!"

"No. They stay through times worse than war, far more dreadful. As long as night follows day, they stay."

"There's no telling some people anything. Off with you, then, to your bodhi grove. Perhaps there's a ghost or something in the forest there. Keep on down this road."

The checkpoint soldiers sniggered as they pointed the way, Sudhana was simply glad that he was able to keep on towards the bodhi grove.

The road rose upwards, up a gentle slope until it reached a vast plateau that was utterly empty. Not one single bird to be seen, the open space was simply full of itself. High above in the deep blue sky, a face was barely visible. The mirage of the night spirit was neither male nor female. As some southern god once said, "I am the ungendered god, never wearing the form of men, free of the sorrows of women."

By the time Sudhana reached the bodhi tree grove, the sun was sinking and the heat of the day had decreased. He could see a spacious main hall and other buildings behind a high wall and Sudhana searched for a gateway, at a loss as to where he should go. Doors were hanging open at regular intervals. They had no particular reason to be there at all. The local people called those doors "never-closing eyes." The doors were only firmly shut for a few weeks once every few years, when the devotees living inside the walls underwent strict training.

Most of those who came to visit the Night Spirit were people deprived of kingdoms or cities by more powerful lands, people alienated from the world. The Night Spirit hated the king of Magadha particularly. The Night Spirit said he was resolved to bestow darkness and blindness on a king so devoted to greed, domination, and inhuman repression, so bent on pillaging and destruction. But even the Night Spirit was no match for the power wielded by the king of Magadha. The spirit could only swear that the strong bear their downfall within themselves.

Entering an open door, Sudhana became one of the place's inhabitants. Nobody recognized him as a pilgrim. He was able to go quite naturally to the building where the Night Spirit Samantagambhirashrivimala-prabha was sitting. Someone spoke.

"The Night Spirit has just now attained bodhisattva heart. Let's go listen to his teaching."

Several people had gathered, although Sudhana's feet were the only ones aching with the fatigue of a long journey. As soon as the disciples approached, the Night Spirit began to speak.

"In this world, when a child does something to help its mother, people praise it by calling it good, but beyond that, the term 'good' qualifies those who are able to melt away all the inheritance of past evils and in its place instill the formless sound of the wind. To attain such goodness, in order to perform bodhisattva works in all fullness, you must equip yourselves with ten kinds of observance of the dharma. Observance of the teaching is like a floating branch encountered in a flowing stream. Thanks to that stick one can survive and not sink below the surface.

"As the first observance, enter into singleness of mind, and behold the Buddha's face. As the second observance, behold the Buddha's body with eyes free of defilement and desire. As the third observance, be conscious of Buddha bliss and virtue. As the fourth observance, observe the light of buddhahood and the endless realm of things. As the fifth observance, behold how light is emerging from each of the Buddha's pores. As the sixth observance, behold the resplendent five-hued flames issuing from each of the Buddha's pores. As the seventh observance, for at least one moment adopt the Buddha's body and bring consolation to all living creatures. As the eighth observance, receive the Buddha's voice and steer the cart of the threefold world. As the ninth observance, invoke the Buddha's name unendingly. As the tenth observance, become aware of the unimpeded power in the relationship between Buddha and all living beings. Good people, by means of these ten observances, you will be able to perform bodhisattva deeds in proper fashion."

The spirit's lips were like the place's doors: once open, there was no shutting them. The spirit continued:

"There is someone among you who has come here after meeting the spirit Vasanti. Addressing you, I find that the teaching you heard and have brought here is sacred wisdom such as I should be carrying myself; there is nothing more for you to hear from me. It is true that I instructed her before, but now she has attained such a state of advanced bodhisattva being, with those songs of hers that contain in their every word the whole of the Avatamsaka Sutra's teaching, that she is no longer my disciple but my teacher. I am an old night spirit, unworthy to touch the soles of her feet.

"Now, for you who have come after meeting her, there is a teacher you must meet after leaving here; she's a master among masters—she can string this world's ten thousand teachings on a single thread and hang it round her neck. If you go to her, a few days of instruction will not suffice at all. Time with her is infinite; it lasts like the fathers of aeons. Not far away the great bodhisattva Pramudita-nayanajagad-virocana dwells beneath a bodhi tree. In one way she is all living creatures, in another she is a bodhisattva beholding all living creatures. I have planted within you a few of my humblest words, spoken between teacher and disciple. Now off you go."

Sudhana was deeply impressed by his encounter with the humble heart of this bodhisattva who adopted absolutely the lowest position of all. Sudhana, who in his fantasy had asked how to gain the position of a bodhisattva, could only plunge his own foolishness into a feeling of intense sorrow, rather than pain, passing through a despair comparable to that felt by a stone as it plunges over the brink of an appallingly lofty cliff. Sudhana longed to forget all he had ever learned. He longed to demolish the mound of truth he had hitherto accumulated and turn the spot into a patch of level ground. He longed to become an empty plain. He had nothing to offer the Night Spirit but a poem:

Bodhisattva,
You offered the sticks of the ten observances,
offered them to me in my passage over distant seas
but I had not the strength to seize even one of them.
Bodhisattva,
you have rejected the position of bodhisattva.
Hidden in one corner of Magadha's warfare,
bodhisattva works have grown and grown
until one day such ancient wars will melt away.
Bodhisattva,
as I leave,

with all my body, all my heart,
I believe in those works,
I praise those works.

In response to this poem by Sudhana, the Night Spirit produced a hymn:

Good child,
you came with nothing to learn from me.
Your eyes are like those of Pramudita-nayanajagad, your future
teacher,
always sparkling full of starlight.
Your eyes too are full of starlight.

You are a bodhisattva.
Search the threefold universe,
wherever creatures are,
staying nowhere long.

Good child,
I'd like to give you some of the dark night in my care.
I beg you to receive my darkness in your heart.

Sudhana welcomed the spirit's darkness into his heart. The darkness was
a vessel of truth and a home of compassion, as Sudhana gazed down the
quiet garden. Darkness fell over the buildings in the bodhi grove. It was
night. Obliged to watch over all the evening's various worlds, the spirit left
the hall.

Sudhana resolved to stay there for the night. Others decided to stay with
him. They were not residents of the place, but ascetics belonging to a community of brahmans from a small country, who had come to visit the spirit.
Sudhana withdrew into his solitary fantasies. There the teacher he was to
meet next, Pramudita-nayanajagad-virocana, appeared to him like a phos-
phorescence floating on the dark sea.

37.
A Cloud Rising From Every Pore

HE NEXT MORNING dawned utterly new, full of the foresty smell of the grove of bodhi trees. In a place where a thousand billion aeons had flourished and died, its newness seemed to stand at the first beginning of the world. There was no yesterday, only today. In the midst of Sudhana's pilgrimage, a new day of this kind was a source of quite unparalleled joy. On this marvelous morning, Sudhana enjoyed a perfect, powerful joy. "How can anything be this wonderful?" he wondered. "Can there really be days dark with the outgrowths of hell, full of the sufferings of all living beings?"

Ultimately, newness is a kind of infinity. Situated in the monsoon season, this morning was filling the grove with the stillness that precedes rain. Sudhana was deep in thought. "Why do I continually force myself to meet night spirits and night goddesses like this? Because the world is dark. Because this world's suffering, its sorrows and pain are night! No, because this world's dazzling light is born in darkest night. Because in order to live in this world I have to become better acquainted with darkness."

Sudhana would meet the night goddess Pramudita once the sun had gone down, when she would be seated on a lion throne in the right-hand lotus hall. It was still midday, so he had ample time to rest. In Magadha's magnificent forests the paths were shaded and free of heat. In the forest, comprised of mingled light and darkness, there was nowhere where it could be said to be bright, even at noon. The spirit of night would be able to appear without difficulty. Sudhana rested, in order to drive the last remnants of stubborn fatigue from where they lodged deep in his bones.

As he waited to meet Pramudita, he thought of all the teachers he had met before. "Aren't my encounters with true knowledge all for the sake of courage, wisdom, vows, suffering for all creatures, and bodhisattva acts? If so, perhaps I have no further knowledge to look for? I've already laid down the firm basis of the virtue I need; from now on it's surely more urgent to set out along paths of bodhisattva being and doing good? After all, if I have too many teachers, there'll be no me left. What can I gain by meeting yet another night spirit?"

But Sudhana answered his own questions. "Together with a child bodhisattva there has to be an adult bodhisattva and an old one, too. Only then is it possible to embrace the ocean of wretched creatures that no one in this world has any thought of caring for. How could one little pilgrim solve all the world's problems on his own? I must ask and seek unceasingly. Off I go. Off to meet the night spirit Pramudita."

He straightened his legs and stood up. He left the fragrant grove and walked across a nearby meadow to the next grove. There he found himself advancing towards the lotus hall on the right-hand side, where there were fewer people. A baby nursed at a young woman's breast. An old man watching abruptly remarked, his fierce eyes flashing, that the child must recently have completed its purification in hell and been reborn into this wicked world. Ever since his own son had died, he said, he found life in this world just the same as being in hell. Sudhana listened to the old man's story. After the old man's son died and fell into hell, whenever he shed tears in mourning for his son, the old man's hot tears became a scalding bath in hell in which his son was boiled, while his wife's tears turned into ice in hell, in which their son was frozen solid. The old man felt a terrible linkage of punishments between this world and the next, and had come to visit Pramudita to ease his torment.

Sudhana looked at him and the little baby at its mother's breast in turn. He sighed. The sound of the father weeping at the thought of his son was transformed into the screams of demons and pierced the ears of his son in hell as part of the punishment for his sins.

Whenever Sudhana found joy in the truth he was seeking for, invariably suffering came to contradict it. Together with the old man and the mother, he waited for night to fall. Finally, the night spirit Pramudita emerged from among a band of the Buddha's disciples and came in their direction.

"So far I have been listening to others. Now it's my turn to speak." The woman spoke softly. She took her place in the midst of the lotus calyx. Her followers sat down. A moment of weighty silence passed. The baby's breathing was the only sound. Even the mosquitos fled. The fires were no longer burning. Suddenly, they heard a windmill turning and the sound of a water wheel. After those sounds had continued for a long while, there came the sound of a fire burning. Sudhana looked around. There was nothing on fire. The sound of flames faded, then unexpectedly they began to hear ocean waves. With the sound of the waves came cries of people in distress.

The night was deep by now. The lands beneath the sea gave voice to a rending earthquake roar. Next came the sound of mountains crumbling and city walls toppling, people screaming, and the voices of the king of the Gandharvas, of the king of the Asura demons, the lord Garuda, the king of the Kimnara, King Mahoraga, even Brahma's voice was heard. They heard the voice of Yama, the king of the underworld.

Once those grim voices were over, they heard from the heavenly realms. They heard the voices of celestial apsaras and hravakas, of pratyeka-buddhas and bodhisattvas. These were truly sacred sounds. After the voice of the bodhisattvas, the sound of maidens along the banks of the Ganga began to ring out. Their voices were the most lovely sound in all this world.

By these voices, a vocal votive offering was made to all the divinities in this world and the cosmos, invoking the consolation of the diminishing of all forms of suffering.

"Which of these voices did you like the best?" Pramudita asked the crowd affectionately.

The old man advanced and replied. "Goddess of night, more than the voices of Apsaras and Shravakas, more than the voices of bodhisattvas, I listened hardest to the voice of Yama, king of hell. The reason is that if I hear any good sound here on Earth it turns into the most agonizing torment for my son in hell, the eight varieties of cold and heat, with frost and fire, freezing him first then burning him to a frazzle."

Hearing what he said, the goddess Pramudita remained silent for a while. Tears flowed from her eyes. Her tears glowed; they were visible to the people standing there in the dark. The old man rose.

"Goddess of night. Please, do not weep. If you shed tears, that plunges my son in hell into boiling water."

The goddess rose and firmly prevented the old man from speaking.

"No. Old man, your tears and mine are no longer causing your son any pain. Henceforth let there be many tears, much sorrow, much compassion; for then not only the living creatures in hell, but all this world's sentient beings will be set free of their chains of poverty, disease, loneliness, oppression, and deprivation."

The night goddess Pramudita had no sooner spoken than she gazed up into the topmost branches of the night grove, as if seeking the heights of Mount Sumeru. All the people who gathered around raised their heads. There was nothing there but darkness. No sky was visible; yet it was not so far from there to the vastness of outer space where eighty trillion Buddhas might appear.

Stricken with sorrow, the bodhisattva Pramudita began to manifest the sign of clouds. The shapes of all the phenomena of the universe became visible in clouds emerging from each of her body's lovely pores. Words flowed gently from her lips in cosmic speech:

"I am goddess of night. I dwell in this world with human beings, with all creatures on earth and wing, in flood and wind. When any of those creatures die and cannot be reborn, but wander, lost, I unfold and show a limitless world to those wandering sentient beings. There is a heaven called Akanistha, the highest world of the fourth dhyana heavens, among the eighteen heavens in the realms of pure form."

As she spoke those lines, the remote world of Akanisthadeva was sketched in the darkness. At the solemn spectacle that rose from the pores of the night goddess's body, Sudhana was too deeply moved to speak. Pramudita had made visible in her clouds all the worlds comprising the realms of desire and pure form.

She began an incantation that mesmerized Sudhana:

> There is a heaven called Sudarsah,
> a world in which all retributions appear.
> Such is Sudarsanah heaven.
>
> There is Atapta heaven,
> a world without dependence or confrontation.
> There, cool detachment once gained, all torments melt.
>
> There is untroubled Avrha heaven
> where the sufferings of the worlds of desire are stripped away
> and everywhere is peace.

Behold, the heaven called Barhatphala.
My pores and that heaven are one.
The inhabitants there are five hundred leagues tall
and each lives three aeons enjoying human life.

There is Punyaprasavas heaven,
where lifetimes of bliss last two hundred and fifty aeons.

There is cloudless Anabhraka heaven.
Clouds may issue from my pores
but nothing can be shown of that heaven,
for it is the cloudless state above all clouds,
the ultimate freedom of heavenly beings.

There is Sarvatraga-vimala heaven,
of universal purity, a place infinitely pure.

There is Apramanasubha heaven,
where a lifetime lasts a full twenty-three aeons.

There are also Parittasubha heaven, Abhasvara heaven,
Amitabha heaven, Parittabha heaven.

There is Mahabrahman heaven,
the realm of the king who commands the first dhyana heaven,
the realm of the Heavenly King who lives in a gorgeous palace
commanding this world of pain.

There are Brahma-purohita
and Brahma-parisaday heavens.

There is Paranirmitavasavarti heaven,
the highest world in the realm of desire,
the world where Mara lives, lord of the heavens of desire—
that world where pleasures turn into human form
and grant every pleasure to your heart's content,
a world where men and women
satisfy their every lust simply by gazing at one another,

that lovely world where the thought of having a son
brings a son into being on your knees.
One day and night in that heavenly realm
lasts sixteen hundred years in the human world.

There is Nirmanarati, a world whose denizens ever emit light
and live for eight thousand years.
If male and female once exchange smiles in that place,
they consummate union and a baby is born
that is twelve years old on the day of its birth.

There is Tushita heaven,
a joyful place set a hundred thousand leagues and more
in the void above Mount Sumeru,
where a palace rises made of precious jewels
in which the denizens of that heaven live:
the Tushita heaven of the Buddha Maitreya.
There are inner and outer halls there;
in the inner hall, Maitreya teaches all who dwell there.
The outer hall is a place of delight,
the courts of joyful Tushita heaven.

Below that come the heaven of Four Kings, Trayastrimsa,
and Suyama heaven, two worlds immersed in thoughts of sex.

Nirmanarati and Paranirmitavasavarti heavens above them
are wandering worlds.

Tushita heaven alone is neither submerged nor wandering,
but enjoys the pleasures of the five desires
during lifetimes lasting four thousand years.
Four hundred years in human terms
are a single day in Tushita heaven.

You think those multiple heavens are all?
There is more to show:
King Gandharva, with his sons and daughters,
mighty Kumbhanda who sucks out human vigor,

the dragon king Nagaraja who lives beneath the sea,
Yaksa with his sons and daughters, Lord Asura, King Yama,
all the Shravakas and Pratyeka-buddhas, bodhisattvas, Buddhas,
my friends, my gods, the gods of earth, of water, fire, and wind,
the spirits of rivers, of seas, and of mountains,
spirits of forests, the spirits of this grove of bodhi trees,
spirits of day, and we spirits of night.
Behold, coming back now: a spirit of the night.

Pramudita spoke on and on without any sign of thirst or hunger. To Sudhana, she seemed like one of the gandharvas, those supernatural creatures who make music for Lord Indra in his heaven and live only on incense.

Sudhana's legs were numb but he struggled to his feet to extol the goddess. "Goddess of night, accept my praises. I am a pilgrim, ever in quest of teaching. You have made a great offering to the Buddhas of all the worlds on behalf of every wretched living creature.

"The clouds arising from each of your pores bear the entire Buddha cosmos and truly there is nowhere you have not been in so many worlds, encountering the teaching, graceful through long aeons, being born and dying in so many worlds.

"Is there anywhere you cannot go, bearing every burden of karma and all majesty? Those gathered here have been born and have lived in each of the worlds you revealed, and now have returned.

"The spreading clouds and the revealed world have all come back to sit on the lotus throne. In the space of a single night, we have heard the phenomena of the whole cosmos and returned; we have heard every voice, and returned. What more is there for us to hear? What more need is there for us to go in quest of palaces veiled in clouds? Spirit of night, you are truly holy."

The spirit of night was deeply moved by his praise. She swept down and seized him in a warm embrace. Sudhana swooned at the perfume emanating from her opulent flesh.

"You are Sudhana, aren't you? The boy who has traveled through all the lands of the south in quest of teachers?"

"Yes."

"Hearing your hymn, I saw a world full of brightness, I who ever live in darkness. All my pores are asleep, yet I see a world of brightness."

"Spirit of night, may I enter into liberation with you?"

"Most surely you may. You and I have experienced time together in several worlds in our previous lives. The shadow of your wisdom is floating quietly on the surface of my wisdom's stream."

In the heart of that night's darkness, Sudhana's heart opened wide, emitting bright rays of light. Standing beside Sudhana, the old man who was so tormented earlier felt himself freed of the suffering. During the night goddess's Cloud Sermon, his son's burden of guilt had been lifted and he had been freed from hell. The old man sensed a new joy welling up inside his heart like water in a spring. The sermon had washed over the mother and her nursing baby like a lullaby and they were now soundly asleep, perfectly content.

Sudhana and Pramudita spent the rest of the night together under the trees. As day broke, the birds began to chirp and sing. With the coming light, the spirit of night disappeared.

Sudhana found a single bodhi leaf clasped between his fingers, her gift to him. He closed his eyes and thought back over the events of the night before. The goddess's magic powers had given her a tremendous beauty. All the realms of desire and pure form she manifested in the clouds were reflected in her beauty, which was strong enough to bring each heaven out of isolation and into cosmic unity.

38.

FRUIT BOTH SOUR AND SWEET

T WAS ONE OF THOSE MORNINGS when all this world's beauty seemed immensely fragile, as if on the verge of dissolution. Sudhana felt compelled to set out on a journey longer than ever before. He rose to his feet in the indigo grove, restless. He had not gotten a chance to say goodbye to Pramudita but he sensed that he might meet her again, albeit in a different form. Truth has the power to make someone into a different person every time you meet them.

Sudhana walked into the next grove. Its thick tangle of nutmeg trees was full of ancient darkness. Sudhana quickly grew accustomed to the gloom. He pushed deeper among the huge trunks until he heard the sound of a stream. A breeze, full of the scent of gardenia, whispered past him. He heard a clamor and was unable to distinguish whether the sound came from humans, or beasts, or gods. He walked toward the sound of water tinkling in the gloom. Surely the sound was the voice of the teacher he was seeking.

Sudhana called out in a loud voice: "I am glad to meet you, holy teacher, dwelling in the liberation of this grove's inmost recesses."

A human voice rang out in response, "Who are you?"

"I am a northener in quest of bodhisattva life."

"You have come a long way, child. I am Jahshri, a spirit of darkness."

"Master, divine spirit, my name is Sudhana." Sudhana noticed that his own body was emanating the fragrance of gardenias and that his own voice sounded like the tinkling stream. He encountered his own perfume and voice, completely detached from himself.

The spirit cast off the darkness enfolding it and revealed itself to Sudhana.

"Look at me now, little pilgrim. I am Jahshri, the source of this grove's darkness."

As the spirit spoke, a bright smile spread across its utterly gentle face and it murmured, "You have had a long hard journey, my child."

The spirit was a splendid sight. Light was streaming from between its eyes. The spirit had a lonely air, like the light from a distant star. From darkness, the spirit had gathered all the world's light and was reflecting it back so it shone everywhere in the world. The light penetrated the crown of Sudhana's head, filling his whole body. Sudhana's happiness seemed to pierce the heavens and fill the seas.

"I am glad to meet you, sacred spirit." Sudhana was too happy to realize he was repeating himself.

The spirit began to dim its magnificent light.

"Child, your joy is too perfect by far. I have nothing to give you in exchange for your joy. The best I can do is show you my true form."

As it spoke, it uttered an anguished sigh. The spirit abandoned the light and beauty that had until now adorned it. All that remained was its human smile. The gloom became the green shade found in any grove and the spirit of darkness sat down with Sudhana on the ground at the foot of a centuries-old anantha tree.

The spirit brought out some fruit to share and soon, it was telling Sudhana stories, as if it were any kindly and voluble relative. "Long, long ago, many many ages before this present world, I was a young girl. I met that world's bodhisattva, Samantabhadra, and at his encouragement set off on a journey. I took with me only a precious necklace that hung around my neck. It had been passed on to me by my mother and she had inherited it from her mother, as she had from hers. It was something that I was expected to pass on to my daughter; only I gave it up in order to provide a lotus-flower throne for one of Buddha's disciples, Shariputra, to sit on.

"Thanks to that necklace, I established firm roots of good karma. I was reborn in the heavens, as well as on Earth, always enjoying a comfortable life. I become a leader of the people, but wondered if it was right that I should become so simply because of a good deed in a former life. I only had to say one word, and I received at once whatever I wanted; if I spoke, condemned criminals were granted their lives, even seconds before they were to be executed. Everyone considered my rule to be blessed and bowed down towards me every day. The treasures of mountains and oceans were offered before me. My subjects went so far as to say that the food they ate, the clothes they wore, their houses too, were all effects of my gracious rule. I was indeed a sovereign the whole world looked up to. And yet any bliss enjoyed in this world is the fruit of ten thousand people's suffering. A beggar brings more joy than a king to ten thousand lives."

When the spirit had finished, it broke the fruit in half, and the two of them ate together. The fruit was both sour and sweet and it stilled Sudhana's hunger. They rose from the foot of the tree and started to stroll slowly through the shady forest clearings. Jahshri began to reminisce again.

"I came to a decision. Late one night, I resolved that henceforth I would not be served, I would become a servant. To follow that path, I left the palace. I had scarcely begun to travel before I fell ill. I only survived thanks to the help of one humble fellow. I became the slave of a member of the warrior caste. After more than ten years, I and several others of the same lowly class escaped from the slave camp and went to live in mountains that were covered with eternal snows.

"During those ten years of life as a slave, I came to see clearly how wrong is this world's system of wealth and honor. I met many poor people who endured countless torments so that the rich and powerful could flourish. What then were the so-called roots of the good karma I had received? What was the sense of my offering up that precious necklace? What was the value of the throne of Shariputra? What was my good karma even worth?

"I wandered through the mountains, pondering those questions, until I found myself separated from my group. I could not find the way back. For three days I wandered through the trees and shrubs of that mountain's valleys. Finally, I glimpsed a kite hovering in the sky visible between the trees; I walked in the direction it was flying and arrived at the mountain village of the Allia tribe. There, I met the gentlest people in the world, among them one old man from whom I heard talk of many Buddhas.

"The old man and I went to where the Buddha lived in company with a large number of other Buddhas, bodhisattvas, and disciples. There, I became a disciple. The doubts nagging me gradually eased, and I turned back into the girl I had been before I'd offered up the necklace. There was no way I could know at the time that the very same necklace was buried deep in the mud at the roots of a lotus blooming in a pond nearby.

"I visited no less than five hundred places in all, meeting Buddhas and bodhisattvas, disciples and pilgrims of every caste. I drew water for them to wash and took care of them when they were sick in exchange for something to eat. At the four hundred and ninety-fifth station on my pilgrimage, I was praised with these words, 'Her vow made in a previous life began with the sage Samantabhadra and today has become a great river.'

"After that, I left my tasks within the shrine and went to join the humble folk outside, sharing their poverty and disease, their ignorance and violence. I tried to discourage one gangster, who raped me in response. After that I was passed from one man to another and ended up working singing in a bar. It was said that my songs could raise a nation up or bring it crashing down.

"The five-hundredth station in my successive lives was in a forest grove not far from that bar. One day, I went with the bar owner and his family to visit the nearby Buddha. I offered a song and dance to welcome the company gathered there. Delighted by my performance, the Buddha sent out a ray of light. Receiving that light, I enjoyed the Buddha's love and became a goddess."

Jahshri stopped its story and shook Sudhana's shoulder, waking him up. When Jahshri saw that Sudhana was alert again, it continued.

"I can't be compared with the night goddess Pramudita who sent you here, and I'm nothing at all compared with the goddess of darkness and night, Prashantaruta-sagaravati, whom I want to send you to. All I have attained is the right to approach the gates of liberation and tread on the grass growing outside. After you leave here, you have to visit yet another divinity; ultimately, every so-called divinity in the universe has to become human. Gods are really human forms, human words, human living and dying."

"Teacher, you've acquired liberation. What kind is it?" Sudhana asked.

"Good question. This can't be the first time you've asked it. Emancipation is love. The intense love between the giver of the light and the receiver of the light. No one has ever been emancipated alone. When an I and a you are present, then there is emancipation. An emancipation is one emancipation and a multitude, each separate emancipation reveals ten thousand other forms. Rather than entering an emancipation, I have merely sniffed the smell of one."

Sudhana slapped himself with joy; emancipation was not achieved alone! That was the brightest message he had heard so far. He made repeated prostrations at the spirit's feet. At the ninth, the spirit tried to restrain him but Sudhana refused to stop. "Please, let me go on," Sudhana begged, close to tears. So while Sudhana continued his prostrations, the spirit of darkness made prostrations before Sudhana in return. Within the grove, their prostrations were the only movement; all else stood motion-less. Even death was frozen still.

Sudhana and Jahshri walked together until the edge of the forest, where they silently parted company. Sudhana headed off to find the night god-dess Prashantaruta-sagaravati and Jahshri went back along the way it had come, wearing a simple skirt that rippled in harmony with its steps.

Sudhana had eaten nothing besides the fruit Jahshri had shared with him, yet instead of hunger, he felt heavy, as if he had swallowed something very filling. Sudhana was a youth now; there was a metallic tang to the smell of his body. Yet he was blessed in that every time he met someone new, he became a child again. Was his pilgrimage destined to continue for-ever?

Sudhana left the forest far behind him. Finally the day drew to a close; rooks were flocking together. He crossed from Jahshri's grove to Prashan-taruta's. Leaving the nutmeg trees, he entered a grove where trees of all kinds clustered in confusion. Thick forest and sparse undergrowth min-gled. This was a world where no one was in charge; all lived together in community, a nighttime world full of moonlight and starlight. It was far better suited than sunlight for gatherings of spirits of night and darkness. As he passed from one evening grove to the other, Sudhana kept his eyes firmly shut. After spending so long in darkness and thick shade, he might have been blinded if he had opened them in the sunlight between the groves.

Prashantaruta's grove was like a crowded village. People ran up to him from all sides asking, "Who are you?" "Where are you from?" "What do you want?" Even the birds perched among the branches and leaves troubled Sudhana; every single one of them was chirping loudly. Sudhana returned the birds' greetings with a bird song of his own.

A young boy was coming toward him along a sparsely-grown forest path.

39.
An Ugly Face

HE BOY introduced himself, "I'm Sanantha."

"I'm Sudhana. I'm from the north."

"From the banks of the Ganga?" The boy seemed pleased. They walked deeper into the grove, talking as they went. Each was so full of respect for the other that their exchanges had a rather self-conscious awkwardness, as if they were reading from a script. It was almost as if they were afraid that some older man, overhearing them, might mock their grave manner.

"I too left the banks of the Ganga several years ago."

Sudhana was surprised: "Really? From which region?"

"I came from Rajagriha, the capital of Magadha."

"I've been there," Sudhana exclaimed, "just after the low-lying areas had been ravaged by floods."

"When disaster comes, every distinction between good and evil ceases to exist."

Sanantha had a rapid way of speaking and he obviously enjoyed debates. Sudhana was not prepared to engage in that style of conversation. He changed the topic.

"I'm on my way to visit Prashantaruta-sagaravati."

"Oh, that spirit of darkness that talks in ten different ways? This whole forest is inhabited by spirits. I want to meet him too, so let's go together. He's just one spirit of darkness, you know, he's not their special representative, or a major focus of worship. There's no one like that here; here all gods are equal. But he is the spirit most experienced in the quest for truth. He's the ugliest one, too."

"The ugliest?"

"Early in a previous childhood, one of his father's enemies nearly killed him. He survived the attack, but grew up with a squashed face, a snuffly nose, and protruding eyes. Those have still not disappeared; so although he is now a spirit, he is an ugly, flat-faced spirit."

They walked on.

"Why does everything have to have previous lives—gods, humans, beasts, even the tiniest creatures?" Sanantha asked, not expecting Sudhana to answer. "Why do they all have to inherit vestiges of their previous lives? Why is there no end to the samsara linking past lives to this life and to all the lives still to come? Everything that happens in this world is so incomprehensible."

Sudhana sensed that if Sanantha was so fond of debating, it was because he was full of a deep sadness. He wondered why Sanantha was living in this realm of spirits, but decided to ask him a different question. "Do the spirits of darkness experience human thoughts and feelings?"

"Of course! They're human too. Aren't 'god' and 'spirit' just other words for 'human beings'? Although I'm living here in this world of spirits, I've never felt more human. Being a divine spirit may be the outcome of some kind of stress or strain in the process of becoming human, I don't know. If the real world grows harsh, they turn into empty talk; when ordinary reality grows more peaceful, they come closer to reality, they become almost a fact. But all of them, even the high god of Indra heaven and the other spirits, are just phantoms that have lost all power over reality. They're all just phantoms, the whole lot of them. Buddha's just a phantom, too."

Sanantha was silent for a moment, then confessed. "I'm the son of the man who tried to kill Shakyamuni, Sudhana. Are you surprised?"

"Is that really true?"

"Yes, it's true. Do you hate me? You may have begun to hate me. Perhaps you didn't hear about my father. It happened after Manjushri the sage had already sent you off on your journey to meet teachers in the southern regions."

"You seem to know a great deal about me."

"Prashantaruta sent me out to welcome you. I am to serve as the link between the two of you."

"The spirit knew that I was coming?"

"Of course. Jahshri sent news borne on the wind through the empty air."

"Spirits send messages through the empty air?"

"Yes, but don't be surprised; that's no miracle. They have power over the void precisely because they have no power in reality. We're nearly there now. You know, people often say they've arrived when they still have quite a long way to go. It gives comfort and encouragement to the weary, but it's a lie, all the same."

Sanantha's chatter comforted Sudhana after his endless pilgrimage and helped him adjust to this new environment. The two boys were walking through the thick shade of a dense thicket of trees. While all the natural universe is asleep, the night spirits gathered there to complete the work of caring for the lonely, silent world. The night watch is one of the main tasks of the spirits of darkness and night.

They reached Prashantaruta, who was quite as ugly as Sudhana had been led to believe. His eyes stuck out, his nose was crushed. He looked like an old frog.

"Sudhana? Is that your name?" he thundered.

"That's right."

"What's all this about bodhisattvas? You've come to find out more about bodhisattva deeds? You came all this way to ask about that? My, what stupid creatures there are, to be sure."

Sudhana was taken aback. It was unfortunate that Prashantaruta's voice was so harsh; it seemed to shout curses at everyone he talked to.

"What the hell makes people go running all over south and north India? Why the devil do they think they have to leave their homes to go looking for eternal laws? Don't they realize how useless any laws they find are going to be? Idiots! Believe laws exist and they grow infinitely big; decide they don't exist after all, and they shrink and shrink until they sink into the ground. Isn't that what's called dharma? What junk to say that by sitting in a cool breeze under a tree and meditating, one comes to a knowledge of the Way!

"Our heart is really Buddha? Our heart is really dharma? Our heart is really the entire universe? Who says this? Where the hell did that heart thing come from, then? I reckon the heart of beasts and trees and piles of rock is much closer to that bloody dharma than all those people who will fabricate anything; they have no reason or need at all for any such study or any such heart."

Prashantaruta paused. "Still, this is a really marvelous forest, isn't it? People practicing the Way keep coming here. If poor people who toil all day in dusty markets would set aside their daily misery and enter the forest that knows no worldly cares, within less than a month their weary faces would grow bright and their bloodshot, pus-blurred eyes grow clear as ponds.

"On the other hand, if you take one of the forest's most revered ascetics and just for a few days put him where the poor work, in no time at all his eyes become turgid like those of a rotting fish. Each of this world's realities, each environment, each history produces the people who live in it."

Sudhana had the impression he was being slapped first on one cheek, then the other.

"You said your name was Sudhana? It's all very well traveling around trying to find out the ways of the world, but if it's with the idea of seeking for truth or learning about bodhisattva deeds, you've been wasting your time. If you want to find out about bodhisattva deeds, go and look in a pigsty. It's pigs that are bodhisattvas. Don't they get as fat as they can, then give all that flesh for people to eat?

"People think they can become bodhisattvas by sitting in a forest? What bloody bodhisattva is that? Even hell is too good for them. Bodhisattva is the title given to those who give and give of themselves for the good of all living creatures. You think that's a common thing? Lifetime after lifetime, on and on, pouring out your blood, sweating away, and then maybe, maybe not, once, becoming a bodhisattva. Sudhana! Take your first master, the bodhisattva Manjushri. Or rather, take his master, Shakyamuni the Buddha. Do you think he became Buddha by sitting in a forest grove? Not on your life! It was one tiny drop of dew resulting from having given of himself and dying, over and over again, for a hundred billion aeons.

"Sudhana, if you really want to meet bodhisattvas, you have to meet pigs, or scorpions, or thieves who have been imprisoned dozens of times, all this world's filthiest, most poisonous, most loathsome scum. They're the ones who are on the way toward bodhisattva deeds.

"Bodhisattva means suffering. Blood and pain. Sorrows. A child crying for grief because it's lost its mother, that's bodhisattva. A widow, that's bodhisattva. You'd better be kind to some widow with that fine young male body of yours! Then the widow'll go to heaven and you'll forget hell too!"

The sage Prashantaruta laughed with his ugly face. He lifted a gourd bottle to his lips and slurped the wine made from a fruit found in the forest's hillside caves. He sighed, "Ah. Very good, very good. Have a drink, Sudhana."

Sanantha handed Sudhana the gourd. Sudhana took a mouthful and swallowed. He felt himself grow dizzy, then he became quiet. He sat down. Sleep approached. He lay down and began to doze. Sanantha slept beside him. At once, all the spirits of darkness came swarming near, covering themselves with robes of leaves. Turning round and round about Sudhana, they danced, watching over his sleep. Their hands remained still, though the dance was rhythmic. The spirits grew elated. Maggots infesting filthy places are forever wriggling in joy; likewise the forest's spirits were forever dancing and shouting. As they circled Sudhana, they sang:

> Sleep well, sleep well.
> Sleep well your avidya sleep of ignorance.
> Sleep well your bodhi sleep of awakening.
> Sleep your fill, then awaken.
> Sleep your fill, then awaken.
> Awaken and dance.
> Once you're Buddha, dance.
> Once you're bodhisattva, dance.
> Infinities of living creatures, dance.
> Sleep well, sleep well, little pilgrim.
> Sleep well, Sudhana.
> Sudhana, sleep well.
> Both eyes closed, sleep well.
> Both legs stretched out, sleep well.
> Breast, navel, windpipe, earholes, nostrils, sleep well too.
> Three karmas of old and new, sleep well.
> All the world, sleep well.
> Realms of desire, of pure form, of formlessness,
> and void beyond them all,
> sleep well, sleep well.

The spirits' dance filled the forest clearings, causing the leaves to lose their freshness and wither out of season. As the leaves were trampled in the dance, their stench filled the air. When the dance ended the spirits returned to their places. Sudhana and Sanantha woke up. The sage Prashantaruta laughed in staccato gasps, as though he were unable to laugh properly. He looked far more benign than before they had fallen asleep.

"That was a good sound sleep, to be sure. The first thing to do on arriving here is to get some sleep. Now that's done, we all three have become one family, since sleep and darkness are one and the same thing. Let's be off to the forest's Place of Silence."

They made their way towards a part of the forest overgrown with ferns and moss. Yellow goldfinches were skipping from branch to branch, chirping; one even perched for a moment on Prashantaruta's shoulder, then sped away, releasing its droppings.

"Look, it wants to play!" Prashantaruta shouted. The deeper they went into the forest, the merrier he'd become. Apparently, he preferred the company of birds and beasts to that of gods or human beings.

The Place of Silence was secluded and still, the proper place for Prashantaruta to be. In the midst of its stillness he was truly a spirit of darkness and night, able to hear the low murmurs of the sea.

"It's good here," he muttered, and straddled a moss-covered rock. The three sat in a triangle, as if preparing for some kind of discussion or debate.

Sanantha spoke up. In his innocence, he was bold—even in Prashantaruta's presence. "Young Sudhana's main question in coming here seems to be about samsara and the fruits of karma."

"Surely it would be best if he asked directly," Prashantaruta said.

"No. Sudhana and I have already talked about it in our hearts. My father is no longer alive, but I want to talk about how he intended to kill the Buddha Shakyamuni. My intention is not at all to take sides with my father and attack the Buddha. If I did that, I would soon get into a fight with Sudhana, who seems to be one of the Buddha's true disciples. I don't want to fight. Sudhana is my true comrade."

"Come on. Get to the point," Prashantaruta urged.

"No matter where you go, all over India, in the torrid regions, in the icy regions, Siddhartha alone is considered holy, while my father Devadatta is universally execrated as a wicked, would-be assassin. Now, one fundamental part of Buddha's truth is the accumulation of karma and retribution from past lives. In that case, surely it's because in one of Shakyamuni's past incarnations he intended to kill one of my father's previous incarnations, that, in this present life, my father attempted to kill Shakyamuni the Buddha.

"Why do people never mention that, and simply judge what he did as a crime limited to this present world? Thanks to my father's error, I have come to the conviction that this world's truth, if there is indeed justice in that truth, is an egalitarian truth, distributed equally to all, including the wicked and those who have fallen far from the truth.

"I have heard how Shakyamuni's disciple Maudgalyayana was assassinated by a zealot belonging to another sect. That too has to be seen as the outcome of an inherited history of retribution, involving that zealot and Maudgalyayana. It happened a long time ago, but I only recently heard about it, and it helped me gain a deeper understanding of Buddha truth. Sudhana! Surely you're not going to stay silent? You're not going to tell me that Prashantaruta is a spirit of darkness and night, and therefore doesn't give a damn about what happens in the daytime out in the sunlight?"

Prashantaruta's ugly face broke into such a broad smile that it completely replaced the ugly face with a new one. "Of course he's not!" he beamed, "but Sanantha, how is it you're arguing so wonderfully, today of all days?"

"If I'm speaking well, it's because of all the words emerging from this Place of Silence. In Sudhana's presence, rocks, caves, grains of sand, and rain still unformed in the sky all begin to talk. Sudhana's visits to his teachers oblige them to open their mouths. He cast aside everything he once knew, and turned into someone not knowing anything before he set off to travel through the hot lands of the south. That is the pure thread linking his present life with his past lives, stretching on like a road."

Sudhana was bewildered to find that Sanantha was saying things that he himself should be saying, and more. He approached Sanantha and made a deep prostration. Sanantha bowed in return.

"Master," said Sanantha.

"Master," said Sudhana.

Prashantaruta merely nodded at the sight of their exchanges. Sanantha rose and began to preach.

"Lovely master, though your face is repulsive and you curse us, this little pilgrim and I are blessed. The words we exchange hold all your teachings.

"Master, each day speaking all manner of things, how is it that here you stay silent and only nod your head?

"Liberation like a cloud! Gentle rain, pouring down on our dry ground! In order to achieve emancipation, this is what you teach:

"First, offer yourself for others; then my words, meant for every creature, will all be accomplished in you.

"Second, practice the Precepts.

"Third, persevere, endure.

"Fourth, advance untiringly, advance; for any who do not advance, wisdom is utter foolishness.

"Fifth, keep lips sealed, think quietly; then the garments of the giddy, the wind-whirled, are stilled and turned into stony cliffs.

"Sixth, practice prajña wisdom, ask where are the reefs and deeps in the vast ocean of the Three Worlds.

"Seventh, practice upaya skills; no truth can be gained without preparation—the blooming of one lotus flower at a dry stem's tip is the spreading of truth by upaya skills.

"Eighth, stir up great longing; all was nothing but breath till now, but you are advancing in a great enterprise. So dream, establish directions, take vows.

"Ninth, gain the needed strength; for how can any creature without strength cross the waters of travail?

"Tenth, purify yourself. What joy when truth is found in every place of purity!

"Lovely master, if you do not speak, I will speak. I will be you."

Sudhana listened silently. One leaf dropped to the ground.

Prashantaruta stood up abruptly. "Alright! You don't need me any more. Off you go, Sudhana, to Prabhava-ta. Go with him if you like, Sanantha. Sudhana at least has a lot of places to go. Your feet are restless, like a horse's hooves just before it gallops off. But you can't shake off the bridle of us spirits yet. You still have a host of spirits' works and games to stare at. Off with you, now, you beggar of truth. You orphan of truth. You greenhorn of truth!"

With those final words, Prashantaruta rose and left the Place of Silence, leaving Sudhana and Sanantha still sitting on the damp mossy rocks without time to even wave to his retreating back.

Sudhana spoke: "Sanantha, I'm leaving alone. You still have a lot to do here, I know." He stood up and Sanantha rose as well, tears in his eyes.

40.
A Mountain Demolished

SUDHANA LEFT SANANTHA in the vast forest and followed woodland paths for three full days. Whenever he felt hungry, he managed to obtain fruit from passing spirits. At last, he emerged from the forest and set out along a road that cut across a plain of red earth, studded here and there with solitary agaves. His eyes had grown accustomed to very dark places and deep shade and he had to close them often against the searing sun.

The weather was so hot that he came across a bird that had dropped from the sky, overwhelmed. He lay the dead bird on a hot slab of rock and soon it was half-cooked. He tore off the feathers and ate it. With the bird meat, Sudhana regained enough strength to cross the scorching plain and he set out again with slightly quicker steps.

Further along, he realized that someone was catching up to him with rapid strides. "Young man!" a voice called out behind him. Sudhana turned round. It was a woman of about thirty or so, clad in a voluminous sari.

"Where have you come from; where are you going?" he asked.

"I am following you, child."

"Me? Following me?"

"I've been wandering through the southern regions and now I'm on my way north. In the south, I had seven husbands and over twenty lovers. I've reached a point where I feel absolutely no shame, even when I talk about it. I consider that such a life is my fate. It must be fate, the outcome of all my previous lives; I don't know why it is.

"No matter where I am, men go crazy over me, like flies clustering round a piece of rotting meat until maggots appear. And I could never reject any of those men, but welcomed them and even enjoyed myself with them for a moment. Then after the fun was over, I would always suffer as a punishment and my heart would bear yet another wound. Anyway, traveling through all the southern realms, I've had my fill of joys and pains. Now I'm leaving that all behind me; I'm on my way north to the snowy peaks and the salvific banks of the Ganga, in the hope of washing away my degradation. As I came along the road I saw you ahead of me and thought that you must be the purest light of truth in the world. So I began to hurry, casting off my usual laziness. From now on, after having followed you, I mean to rise early and go out into the fresh new air before dew-fall and sunrise."

She concluded her long speech by offering Sudhana some dried meat and mangoes. Sudhana accepted both her abrupt confession and the food. Then he spoke.

"I am from the northern realms. When all the states along the banks of the Ganga were consumed in the flames of warfare, I left there and have been traveling through the southern realms ever since."

The woman offered sufficient reason for a man to lose his heart to her on sight. Her beauty was a masterpiece, produced by all the gods working in concert. She had just now attained the mature peak of her feminine charms. They outshone the road itself; even the scorching plains lost the force of their heat. As a result, the two were able to walk quickly on along the road.

Sudhana sighed. Sweat that had until now refused to emerge on account of the heat broke out on his breast. It seemed this woman was the next bodhisattva he was to visit.

"My name is Mani. My daughter's name is Gopa."

"You have a daughter?"

"I abandoned her along a road near the city of Kapilavastu when I fled from the north, years ago. If she's still alive, she'll be about your age. I was starving on account of the war, so one day, without thinking I went into the house belonging to a rich man's estate manager and stole some food. He caught me and raped me. With my hunger and my wounds, I was completely out of my mind when I got away. I left my little girl where she was and went rushing blindly off, far far away.

"I couldn't go back to look for her after that. I met up with a general who promised he would go and fetch my little girl for me in exchange for my body. But after a few months, he left me and went off to other battlegrounds. My mind was lost and I started to head farther and farther south. As I wandered from place to place in the south, my mind improved even as I disregarded my body."

Refusing to belittle her experience, Sudhana thought reverently of the distance she had covered in her wanderings. The reverence was different from what he felt when he met some saint or sage; it seemed a nail was being hammered home in his head. It was the pain we feel when empathizing with the wounds of the person closest to us.

The road ended at a small stream, which they had to cross by a bridge of logs and stepping stones. Sudhana went first. In midstream, as the woman was crossing over the stepping stones, her foot slipped and she fell into the rapidly flowing current. After a moment, Sudhana looked back; the woman was up to her thighs in the rapids and striving in vain to reach the log bridge. Sudhana ran back and seized her by the wrist; the woman scrambled up onto the logs. She was soaked almost from head to foot. Her body was clearly visible beneath her wet sari and Sudhana averted his eyes. The woman's gaze became an intense stare full of sensual energy. But it quickly faded. Sudhana's heart beat quickly.

"It must have rained a lot upstream. Come on, let's get across," she said.

Now the woman walked ahead. Her back was delightful, too. After crossing the stream, they continued on their way. The woman's clothing soon dried as she walked. At the foot of a high mountain, the road divided. A farmer's mud hut stood there. Sudhana asked where he might find Prabhava-ta, the spirit of darkness. The farmer answered roughly.

"Why there have to be spirits in this world, I really don't know. Spirits are junk. They can't sow seeds and they can't have kids with women like your beautiful companion."

He scrutinized Mani's opulent body as he spoke.

"You must go this way," the farmer said, pointing out Sudhana's direction.

"Which way goes north?" Mani asked.

"It's the other one," the farmer said. "You'll have to go on alone."

Sudhana and Mani held hands as they walked to where the roads forked. With a mutual pang of regret, they parted. Sudhana headed for the gorge leading up to the mountain area where Prabhava-ta resided. Mani stood watching him for a moment, then set out along the road heading to the northern realms. The vague sense that they might meet again lessened the sorrow of their separation.

He walked with no trace of hurry as the path led upwards. Ahead, an extraordinary, precipitous cliff began to loom, suggesting the harsh world of manhood opening before him.

He could hear the sound of a *naka-ara* drum. The drum was an instrument invented by spirits in ancient India. The drum-maker Kaneshiji
taught human beings the art of drumming. It used to be said that anyone,
human being or animal or insect, that heard the naka-ara drum would
forget all their previous sufferings. When fortifications were being built
and servants were breaking stones and performing other arduous tasks,
the supervisors would beat on a drum twice a day. If anyone died working, a supervisor would beat the drum three times before the grave was
filled in.

Perhaps somewhere farther up the quarry-scarred ravine someone had
died? There were still slaves in both the northern and southern kingdoms.
At least now when a slave died a drum was beaten and prayers were said for
his soul, something that would have been unthinkable only a few years
before.

Sudhana felt a little uneasy, but continued up the steep path. A few
dozen yards farther up, he reached the mouth of a huge cave. In the empty
clearing down in the cave, several spirits were celebrating funeral rites for
one of their companions. In the center of their circle, a body was covered
with leaves from an asukasu tree. One of the spirits still held the naka-ara
drum.

For a while Sudhana stayed where he was, observing the funeral from
above. Although Sanantha had insisted that spirits were no different than
humans, Sudhana was surprised to see that they died just as people do. He
made his way down into the cave. Nobody paid attention to the unknown
boy. Each of the spirits emitted a particular perfume and Sudhana alone
brought no scent, apart from the sweaty smell of someone who has walked
a long way.

The lead spirit advanced towards the boy and cried out in a loud voice:
"In order that you may be born a better sage than a spirit, leave Sarvana-
gararak's obscurity behind you now. Go, and no lingering along the way!
Go! Aoma. Aoma. Aoma."

Sudhana knew that the spirit talking had to be Prabhava-ta, the master
sage. He was very old, his white hair blossomed around a swarthy face that
was still vigorous. The copper knob of the long staff he was holding was
fashioned in the shape of a serpent's head. After a final greeting with hands
joined, the spirit reverently took up the staff again and struck the ground
three times. The dead spirit's burial procession began. As the procession
moved away across the stony mountainside, all joined in singing "Aoma."

The song resonated among the stones, reverberating in the ravine and sending back a solemn echo.

Soon, Prabhava-ta returned. Sudhana advanced and spoke up boldly.

"Holy sir, wise master of the great cave of Sarvanagararak, I have come to visit you here and I bow down before you."

"I am just now returning from seeing off a dead companion. Encountering you is to encounter life after sending off death."

"Wise Prabhava-ta, I have nothing to ask except the nature of bodhisattvas and the way of bodhisattva living. Have you embarked upon the bodhisattva way?"

"Young seeker, as you know, I am nothing more than a spirit of darkness. However, during this present aeon I have pronounced the bodhisattva vows and, passing through one existence after another, I have crossed the threshold of bodhisattva being. As a means of working towards the fullness of bodhisattva works, for myself as for others, I have been given charge of this world of darkness. If I once embark on bodhisattva deeds, I have no reason to express in words what bodhisattvas are, or the bodhisattva way. Once sleep and waking, birth and death, have all become part of the work of redeeming all living creatures from their defilement, there is nothing more to be said. Listen, little seeker, and I will unfold the solemn mystery of the ten *dharani* wheels:

> Dharani wheel,
> immersed in the ocean of all dharma laws.
> Dharani wheel,
> keeping in mind all dharma laws.
> Dharani wheel,
> receiving the clouds of pure dharma laws.
> Dharani wheel,
> pondering the wisdom of many Buddhas.
> Dharani wheel,
> sound of the spoken names of many Buddhas.
> Dharani wheel,
> contained in the vows of the three ages' Buddhas.
> Dharani wheel,
> entering the ocean of concentration
> that quickly yields all perfection.
> Dharani wheel,

entering the ocean-like screen
of all creatures' past karma
and washing away that karma-screen's filth.
Dharani wheel,
quickly restoring every karma-screen ocean
to pure smooth waves.
Dharani wheel,
displaying the wisdom that knows everything,
boldly advancing to attainment.
Taking these ten dharani wheels
as part of a family of a hundred thousand wheels
we speak them always
for the sake of all living creatures.
Behold, I came swimming from that ocean of dharma.

Sudhana listened the teachings of the ten dharani wheels and felt there was nothing new at all. He felt none of the deep impression made by hearing a teaching for the first time. Yet although the teaching itself did not feel new, it was made fresh by the liveliness and the power of the voice speaking the words.

Prabhava-ta made his home in the deepest part of the cave, at the end of the longest of various tunnels into which the cave divided. For anyone accustomed to plains and wide-open spaces, the cave seemed a hell. For ordinary people, the cave was darkness incarnate. The spirits had nothing to be afraid of, for they had chosen to live in this darkness. When he remembered that, the cave seemed less like a pitch-black hell.

Prabhava-ta walked with a dignified majesty. If he once uttered "Aoma," every spirit he passed would open its mouth and utter the sound in imitation. Today's funeral had been for a young spirit that Prabhava-ta had loved dearly. The spirit's time allotted to his immersion in the world of spirits had been shortened, so that he might advance on the way of bodhisattva living.

Prabhava-ta rejoiced, for in the world of spirits, death is joy and funerals are joyful celebrations. He turned to the pilgrim. "Young seeker, you have suffered much in coming here. You ought to sleep for a while."

Sudhana found it hard to get to sleep. He felt confined and claustrophobic within the cave. The darkness made him tense to the very tips of his hair and the marrow in his bones ached. He experienced a dread as if he

was suffocating. To keep Sudhana's fear from overpowering him, Prabhava-
ta sang a lullaby and soon Sudhana succeeded in falling into a light sleep.
In the dark cave, the song became a fundamental reverberation; echoes
gave birth to echoes that in turn gave birth to further echoes, until the
entire cavern became one vast echo, the cavern's own Garland Sutra.
Prabhava-ta's song continued through the night:

> Long, long ago,
> as many aeons as the square of all the atoms in the world,
> there was once an age called the Spotless Flame.
>
> The karma of the infinity of living creatures appeared,
> and the Body of Transformation,
> that fashions one by one their forms.
>
> Finally those were established as flowers
> whose ending none can know.
>
> Into that network were placed as many different fragrances
> as there are atoms in Mount Sumeru.
>
> All the vows made in former times by those who understand came
> hastening,
> formed into flowers whose end none can know.
>
> Sublime flowers, as many as there are atoms in Mount Sumeru,
> adorned with as many petals as four thousand times
> the number of atoms in Mount Sumeru.
>
> On each is heaped a hundred billion trillion cities
> in each of which as many Buddhas have been born
> as there are atoms in Mount Sumeru,
> and after each had entered nirvana,
> a thousand different debates arose.
>
> Those Buddhas' teachings were divided in ten times a thousand
> different ways

and each then, as is only natural, engendered hosts of infant
teachings,
until at last they all lay rocking like the waves of some vast sea.

Soon the last age came, and a world of defilement and evil arose,
where corrupt ascetics fought each other, caught up in tiny
questions of scruple,
so that all great virtue was utterly lost.

Kings and brigands were just the same, the dignity of a girl and a
nation just the same, human quarrels and justice just the same.
Everywhere, talking was popular.
It became impossible to live alone in silence.

Then one seeker preserving the true dharma declared:
"For countless ages now, enduring every kind of suffering,
you have extinguished every burning torch.

"I have risen far into the air—the height of seven tala trees into
the air—
and with this body have spread the red clouds at nightfall,
put to death all passions, disputes,
have attained a heart of wisdom on behalf of all living creatures.

"In this way, Buddha's truth
has arisen again for another sixty thousand years."

At that time too there was a woman, a seeker;
she and a hundred thousand women of her tribe,
entering every samadhi consciousness,
received all the different dharanis.

Good seeker,
the one who re-established the true teaching
is the bodhisattva Visvabhadra in the north.
The woman who reestablished the dharma was myself,
I, Prabhava-ta.

Henceforth there is to be a succession of Buddha after Buddha,
as many as there are atoms in Mount Sumeru.

When Prabhava-ta's lullaby ended, Sudhana woke up. As he woke, the
darkness lifted. No trace of dread remained. He realized the whole world is
always full of Buddhas. All our successive lives are periods of time linked
by one Buddha after another.

41.
NIGHT SPIRITS BY NIGHT

RABHAVA-TA walked Sudhana back into the main cavern. "Why not spend the day with the spirit Anrak," Prabhava-ta said. Anrak lived in a different part of the cavern, but when Sudhana looked for him, he wasn't there. Night spirits rarely went outside during daylight. Their eyes are only bright and real when they have the gloom of forest or cave, or the darkness of night. But Anrak had gone into the outside air. What was now the mouth of the cave had once been its center, before a volcanic eruption had split the cavern into two parts. Anrak reckoned that the place where there used to be a cave could still be considered a cave and he was one of the few who liked to go out in the open air.

When Sudhana arrived at the mouth of the cave, it was deep night. The stars seemed to have come pouring out of doors to play. A number of spirits had emerged and were lying or sitting around, absorbing the dew with their wispy robes. Sudhana spoke up.

"I'm looking for Anrak the sage."

The spirits stopped chattering and joking with one another. A youthful spirit spoke up.

"You're looking for Anrak?"

"Yes."

"What for?"

Sudhana made no reply.

"You want to learn how to eat and play and sleep? Anrak's a spirit who knows nothing besides eating and playing and sleeping, you know. Do you still want to meet him?"

"Yes," Sudhana answered firmly.

Then the spirit next to this bothersome fellow called out to Sudhana,

"I'm Anrak. Why are you looking for me? You're the kid who arrived during the funeral. So, you've met Prabhava-ta?"

"Yes, I've met him. He sent me to you."

"Well, let's see."

Anrak left his companions and took Sudhana up onto the stony mountainside.

"When the sun sets, the lotus blossom that has been wide open closes and everybody goes home; all things that have life, in mountains or water or any place, return to their homes while those that have nowhere to go are left wandering. What's your name, little pilgrim?"

"I'm called Sudhana."

"Sudhana, that's a very fine name. Everything has a name; that's the way in which everything reveals its particularity. Sudhana, why you're really Sudhana Buddha. So, Sudhana, I suppose you want to ask me about bodhisattvas and bodhisattva ways?"

"That's right."

"The bodhisattva is first of all someone able to feel compassion. In compassion, wisdom and mercy unite, abandoning everything they possess, both self and possessions. It's a mistake to adorn the Buddha world with too many treasures. It's getting to a point where Amitabha Buddha's Pure Land, the heavenly realms, all kinds of places, are all turning into expensive hells. Please, Sudhana, never look for truth in any such places. First of all, there must be no possessions. Look closely. The spirits here have no private goods or jewels, of course, and no clothes beside what they are wearing now. The world is not a matter of owning things; it's birth and death."

Sudhana listened.

"Sudhana, do you want to hear an old song?"

"Yes. If you sing, I'll listen very carefully."

The spirit Anrak began to sing with a very gentle, girlish voice. The stars in the heavens drew a little closer.

Long ago in the capital city of Sara,
before the virtuous youth was born,
everything was out of joint.
Streams, ponds, and wells had all dried up.
Fields and gardens lay barren,
nothing but a plain strewn with bones.

Then that youth appeared,
like fresh rain falling from dark clouds,
and everything in the southern climes came alive.
Diseases vanished from one and all,
hungry stomachs were filled,
captives in prison were unchained.

Thus this world gained peace;
all the many creatures of this world beheld one another like father
and mother,
loved one another like sister and brother.
All suffering was banished
and a craft lost on the widespread seas
found the pole star that it sought.

Sudhana began to sing the song together with Anrak. One person's song is pregnancy, two people singing is birth.

"Sudhana, let's be going," Anrak said a little impatiently. "Come on, let's go. I'm going to leave here with you this evening. I want to leave the sacred gloom inside this cave and become a wanderer like those stars up in the sky. Only I won't be going to visit people like you."

Sudhana followed Anrak along a hard rocky ridge path gleaming in the starlight, up hill and down, on and on. The spirit spoke more humbly now: "You are a pilgrim of truth, but you've found someone who has no truth to teach. I'll have to learn from you. Times have changed, spirits now have to hear truth from humans and go looking for it themselves. I've been listening too. Far up there in the north, there's a teacher called Shakyamuni Buddha. He goes from place to place making everyone equal, the four castes, the eight, the forty, the four hundred...I'd love to have the job of guarding that teacher's couch. But really I want to help every living creature, not just one Buddha. There are lots of people to serve the Buddha, without me. But foolish creatures and foolishness are lonely things. There's no pain worse than loneliness, Sudhana."

Sudhana found Anrak's words breathtaking. He was struck with wonder at how many teachers there were in the world. There were those called teachers and those not called teachers but teachers all the same. The world was absolutely full of teachers. Sudhana praised the spirit:

Master, wise Anrak.
In sending me off,
in taking your leave
and coming with me,
you have abandoned your post,
you have left a holy place.
As I traveled in the south
I received many favors
from a host of teachers
but how can I ever repay the favor
you have shown me here this night?
Master,
you are a father to me.
Wisest Anrak,
stay with me forever.

Hot tears flowed down Sudhana's cheeks. Starlight dropped and lit his tears. Somewhere, he could hear a horse neighing. Anrak, following behind Sudhana now, seemed to have been struck quite dumb.

42.
JOURNEY THROUGH THE VOID

NRAK WAS TRAVELING to the region where his comrade Prabha lived and Sudhana accompanied him. Sudhana had never realized that there were so many spirits of darkness and night in the world. He'd imagined that all the world's work was done by day, that at night there was nothing to be done but sleep. He'd imagined that only people unable to get to sleep stayed awake at night, that only guards on night watch stayed awake at night, that only bats fluttered among the nighttime branches. Yet the night represents half the total of our time, and if it is truly part of life in the world, it is only right that there should be tasks occupying the hours of darkness. The spirits of this place were charged with welcoming the night, taking charge of it, and savoring it. At night, the spirits of darkness embraced and were embraced by its loving stillness like a mother and child.

As soon as Prabha saw Anrak, the two spirits erupted with joy.

"Anrak! After all this time!"

"Prabha! Yes, it's been such a long time."

They began by bowing with joined hands in formal greeting, then seized each other's hands, but finding that still insufficient, they ended up with arms wrapped round each other's waist.

Their friendship knew no limits. It was Anrak who broke off their effusions and started to talk.

"Why are you strolling around down here on the ground, instead of traveling far and wide through the void? Aren't you supposed to be up there, Prabha?"

"Yes, that's right. My way lies through the void. Only if you spend too much time up there, you forget about everything except the creatures of the realm of formlessness. Yet those in the realm of formlessness are mere abstractions, unless they are related to the creatures down here on this Earth. That's why I prefer the *nirmanakaya*, the body in which the Buddha appears on Earth, to the *dharmakaya*, the true body of essential buddhahood. Yet in the end, compared with the dharmakaya, the body of the Buddhas in paradise and the body of their earthly incarnations are mere physical objects, nothing more."

"So that's why you're walking about down here in your own region, this homeland of spirits, then."

"Yes. I got bored sitting on King Mani's lion throne all the time, so I've run away like this."

"Well!"

Anrak and Prabha had forgotten Sudhana in the joy of their renewed friendship. Now Anrak presented him to Prabha.

"Look, I've brought the loveliest human in the whole world to see you. He's one for truth. He'd already gained illumination into bodhisattva wisdom, but he's set off again, visiting faraway kingdoms, asking still more about bodhisattva ways. This fellow frequents the Buddha's truth both inside and out. He's met robbers and whores, good people and bad, young girls and wizened old men. Thanks to them, he's come now to visit shady spirits like you and me."

"A tremendous fellow, indeed. Welcome."

Sudhana joined hands with a deep feeling of reverence. "Wise Prabha, having come here, I want to have you as my teacher while I am here, and even after I leave again."

Seeing the relationship between his friend and pupil established, Anrak took his leave. "Well, I'll be going back now. Sudhana, have a good stay here, and a safe further journey. I am gladder to have met you than if I had met a Buddha, gladder than a weary horse on finding water."

Prabha took Sudhana by the hand and led him up onto the spacious top of a sparsely wooded hill. There he heaved a sigh.

"You humans are so profound. I mean, there's so much truth contained in just your pretty little face."

Prabha gazed happily at Sudhana. In one breath, he exhaled into the void an image of the whole natural world, including every living creature. It was as if Prabha had painted a vast living fresco. "Sudhana, this isn't a picture or charade that I've deliberately made up for myself. It's the true picture of all living creatures. By making all creatures visible in this way, I'm able to help those who are suffering. Compared to the Buddha up there in the north at the foot of the Himalayas, you might find what I'm doing quite ludicrously childish. Yet for me, the small deeds I am doing for people's benefit are the greatest there can be."

"Wise Prabha, master, you cannot imagine how happy I am, listening to what you say."

"Many thanks. I would like to set your joy as a crown on my brow."

Prabha was a spirit of revelation as well as darkness. He exposed all this world's distinct parts and the shadows of those distinctions. He revealed the shadows of sun, moon, and stars, revealed creatures' differing images and identical images, revealed their varying hues, revealed the dignity contained in certain images, revealed images of those who could move freely at will anywhere in the ten-directioned worlds, revealed all living creatures growing from childhood, revealed images of supernatural beings speeding at random like clouds, and utterly fulfilled after being of benefit to other living creatures. He illuminated creatures' good karma merit being fostered, images of the dharma being upheld, images of bodhisattvas' extraordinary vows being made, images of light illuminating the ten-directioned world, images of the world's darkness being dissolved by Buddhas' light. Prabha revealed images of wisdom and of pure-natured bodies freshly detached from every atom of dust, images of all creatures being brought to understanding, images of distinctions being dissolved in light, images of the final stage when all passions are gone, images so strong they could never be broken, images of Buddhas' power, images of truth throwing off all constraints and exulting like a galloping horse.

Sudhana lost all thought of himself, inebriated by the sight of the realities of the ten-directioned universe. These revelations gave Sudhana more than enough knowledge for a whole lifetime about the multitude of living beings and Buddhas.

Seeing these images, ten different kinds of mind arose within Sudhana, ten different varieties of thought.

The first was a thought that the spirit Prabha was actually Sudhana himself.

The second was an insight into the fact that the spirit Prabha was thinking of himself as Sudhana.

Third, the spirit Prabha was a thought exposing bodhisattva works.

Fourth, the spirit Prabha was a thought achieving the Buddha's laws.

Fifth, the thought that the spirit Prabha was doing great good to Sudhana.

Sixth was a thought making it possible to perfect the works of Samanta-bhadra, casting off all else.

Seventh, a thought containing all the blessings and wisdom needed to follow bodhisattva ways.

Eighth, a thought that the spirit Prabha would become more illustrious than he was as yet.

Ninth, a thought that the spirit Prabha contained the roots of a new karma of good merits.

And finally, tenth, a thought that thanks to the spirit Prabha, Sudhana would gain much and be enabled to advance along bodhisattva ways.

Without speaking, Sudhana communicated these thoughts to Prabha.

"Many thanks, Sudhana." Prabha hugged him. "Thanks to you, I am now enabled to advance along bodhisattva ways. At last I shall be able to do what I have been so much wanting to do! As a token of my gratitude, let me tell you about my past experiences, shall I?"

Sudhana nodded, his eyes shining brightly. By now, he was not surprised when the spirit's story was more of a song. Spirits may begin a discussion, a debate, or any other kind of conversation with spoken words, but the rhythm of song is always contained in their words and at some point it will emerge.

Long ago, infinite aeons ago, utterly long ago,
there was a world known as the Universal Light.

In the course of one aeon in that world,
ten thousand Buddhas were born
and there was one kingdom whose king was called the Light of Monks.

That king was just but fierce and the people feared him.
His prisons were forever full.
Even for slight faults, for minor crimes, even completely innocent people
were taken to fill his prisons.

His son, Heart of Monks, felt sorry for those prisoners.
He resolved to appeal to the king: "Consider those unfairly treated, those captured,
those accused, the innocent in prison.
Hear their groans, the groans of their families.
There are prisons and prisons: all the outside world too is one vast prison.
So with a compassionate heart, behold your people's bitter tears."
Then he knelt before his father.

The king leaped up, and exclaimed impetuously:
"Seize this rascal at once, guilty of a crime against his father's laws, and kill him in the harshest way."
His father having commanded that,
the crown prince suddenly became a criminal condemned to death.

Then the Buddha of the dharma-wheel
came and loosed the chains of the prince and all in prison,
scattering them over the face of the Earth.
At which they all attained liberation
and remained as inheritors of the dharma-wheel Buddha,
serving unfailingly all the Buddhas coming after him,
serving them in successive births and deaths, births and deaths
until they, like me, became for a while the spirits of night, of darkness,
of daytime shadows, of the gloom in caves, and even in mouse holes,
before setting out once again on bodhisattva ways.

The spirit Prabha stopped his song, as if there was nothing more to be said. Then he gave Sudhana his final words. "I do not know where you are to go next. It's time that you alone must decide what you will do in these perilous lands. After your visit, the spirits in the bodhi tree groves and training places, and all the other spirits too, will stay spirits no longer. All will enter the ocean of bodhisattva being. Good-bye now, off you go to wherever it is you're going!"

The spirit Prabha left with rapid steps, as if called away on urgent business; Sudhana had no time for more than a single cry:

"Farewell, master!"

Where should he go? He was so used to a teacher pointing him toward his next destination. The early morning birds were beginning to flutter their wings, and take flight. They flew up into the red glowing sky that precedes the sunrise.

"To start with," Sudhana thought, "I'll follow the birds!"

Sudhana set off. The slopes of the highlands near the lower reaches of the Godavari River were waiting for him.

43.
RETURNING NORTH

UDHANA was finally leaving the lands of the south. The Godavari River basin formed a broad expanse of arable land capable of furnishing three crops of rice in a year, but usually the land was left fallow after being planted once or twice. Sudhana crossed a section of fields left idle. In the course of his itinerary through the south, he had rarely experienced true starvation or exhaustion, thanks to the powers of his various masters; but now he was leaving behind those southern realms and returning to the real world again.

The further he trudged, the longer the road seemed. His feet were blistered and at times his legs ached to the bone. He rested, then forced himself to stand up though he was longing to rest longer. His whole body felt heavy. Mosquitoes and other tropical insects busily sucked blood from his shoulders and legs. If reality away from his masters was like this, Sudhana wondered what must be the torments of the people living in the realities of hell.

Buddha living must involve not just spiritual preaching about helping people, but advancing along a political path, the bodhisattva path, where you were supplied with the strength it took to redress that reality. Constantly confronted with such thoughts, Sudhana acquired a new degree of fervor for the bodhisattva way.

He had reached the region where the southern tip of the Deccan Plateau rose from the plains and arrived in the town of Kurnul, where there were large deposits of anthracite and he was able to beg a lift down the river on a log raft. The river pierced its way through a thick jungle swarming with wild beasts and alligators. Without mishap, the river brought him to the main market along the lower reaches of the Godavari River. This was

Masulli, the trading port for the region of Amarabathi. The Bengal Sea opened before him.

Now that he had lost the protection emanating from his teachers, Sudhana could no longer understand a word of Tamil or Telagu. Still, since this was a trading port, he was able to ask his way thanks to a few words of the universal business language that people used. Loneliness comes at the point where language fails; when words cease, no neighbors remain.

It was just when this loneliness hit him, that he came across the lady Mani again. She had been the mistress of a local trader but had recently left him, after he had given her innumerable presents of gold and precious stones.

"Our destinies did not allow us to meet only once," Mani addressed the little pilgrim courteously and with deep seriousness. "Follow me," she said.

Sudhana followed happily, but he was also anxious. After traveling alone for a long time, anxiety on meeting someone is only natural, but this was something different. The odor of her heavy scent made Sudhana's heart race. What could be the secret of Mani's power? She had men wherever she went, yet her beauty remained rock-firm, utterly unsullied.

They penetrated deep into the port's teeming alleys before climbing up to a tall building perched on a hill with a view overlooking the whole bay. They entered a banquet hall much frequented by rich merchants, where good wines and delicacies of land and sea cooked in Bengali style were always available. Mani ordered the special party menu, where thirty-six different kinds of food were served at a vast table.

"Now, if you're going to leave the world of darkness down here in the south and head northwards to the world of light, you'd better eat some of this delicious food. There's no truth in hunger. Truth is when you can eat well and relax properly. Isn't that right?"

Sudhana made no reply, but began slowly to eat one of the many dishes that kept being served.

Mani stopped eating and gazed fixedly at Sudhana. "You're really a special kind of person."

Sudhana restrained himself. One of the guests at another table walked across. He was the vice-governor of Amarabathi and before he had even reached their table he addressed Mani in a loud voice.

"If you leave here and go north, I suppose the Aryan bastards will soon be falling for you in a big way. Those scoundrels know nothing except how to fight, steal people's land, kill, rob, and enslave. While they're busy panting in delight at the pleasures of your lovely flesh, we southern Dravidians will march in and take back the land that used to belong to us. Then we'll unite the whole world and make you our goddess. You're surprised I think of making a lovely woman from Punjab in the north a goddess in the south? But if you look at all the gods and spirits of the Earth, at the thirty-three orders of deities filling the heavens above the Earth, to say nothing of all the other spirits, divinities, gods and goddesses that exist, you'll find that they were all human beings back long ago."

Mani remained silent.

"So have a good time with your pretty boy here. I'm sure you must be fed up with old men like me. After all, you walked out on Huncha, and he's the wealthiest man in town."

The mockery was embarrassing to listen to, but Mani put a bold face on it. At first, she'd frowned, but seeing that he had no intention of stopping, she'd resolved to take all the mockery he cared to offer, and went so far as to harbor a slight smile as she dipped a piece of mutton into a bowl of sauce and nibbled at it. When the vice-governor finally left, she even laughed lightly.

"Oh dear, poor Sudhana! Come on now, eat up. All he said may be true, or it may not. A dog's bark may be truth to one pair of ears and a dog's bark to another, it all depends. Come on, eat up."

Mani poured an unfamiliar infusion into his teacup. Sudhana sipped it while tasting dishes of fish and meat. It was a rare kind of wine that was originally only drunk by the queen of the great kingdom of Ashimakha in the Deccan Plateau but was now widely drunk by aristocrats and wealthy people. Sudhana grew happily drunk. The lady Mani was drunk already. Her low voice began to flow in a captivating song:

Rolling low, flying high,
most strange, the way handless dice
vanquish people with hands.
The sight of scattered dice on the gaming table
inspires an icy feel
but the magical powers contained within them
kindle a fire in the gambler's breast
like a blazing brazier.
Such is the end of the woman
who promised a hundred years to a gambler.

Along the endless road of wandering,
her mother's heart broke in a thousand pieces
on account of her children.
The accumulated debt weighs heavily on her
as she seeks wealth down roads
she would rather not take,
plotting secret schemes of whoredom.
Such a woman glances at other people's homes by night.

She stopped, noticing that Sudhana was overpowered by the wine. Mani summoned the manager of the high building and asked for a room where they could rest.

The room was cool on account of the palm grove directly behind it. Mani sighed deeply as she embraced Sudhana's supine body.

"Purest and most handsome man! I regret nothing, though I were to be sent to hell, never to emerge again!" Tears of desire poured from her eyes.

For a long time Sudhana hovered in a state somewhere near dreaming, then he awoke. He was naked and his sweat-soaked body had been wiped clean. He began to remember. Mani was nowhere to be seen. Three golden bracelets lay at his feet. He jumped up and inspected himself. There was nothing special. He felt refreshed, as though someone had chastely washed him. The faint fragrance of Mani's perfume rose from his skin.

Sudhana left the room and returned to the tall building where their banquet had been spread. Only one group of customers was left. The manager bid him farewell as he left. He called for a carriage and rode down to the harbor, unable to stop himself from feeling lonely.

"At last, I have completed all my travels in the south. And everything I have learned has proven useless. Now I'll head north and look for more truth, then I'll abandon that, too. Along the bodhisattva way, even truth and dharma, even buddhahood and bodhisattva nature are obstacles. I'll bury myself in the midst of all creatures, racing and bounding like a small animal. Ah, the holiness of that mingling."

Sudhana boarded a merchant ship leaving for Bijaga. The wind filling the sail drummed on the canvas. The dull sound mixed with the splash of water dashing against the ship's prow as it plowed through the waves, restoring Sudhana to some sense of the sea's reality. To the east stretched the ocean that knew no end, to the west was the shore beyond which could be seen dark green forests, with the lighter green of fields between the trees, and stretches of sand. The sea in the Bay of Bengal was the same deep blue as the great ocean at the farthest southern tip of the continent, that Sudhana had once glimpsed from the western extremity of the Khoz mountain range in the region of Cochin. His eyes were full of a sky so azure it seemed to sob.

It took three days to travel from Masulli to Bijaga; they had been obliged to make a detour to avoid pirates. Torches were burning along the harbor wharfs. Sudhana took his leave of the ship's captain and disembarked ahead of anyone else. He had been suffering from sea-sickness but began to recover as soon as his feet touched dry land.

Sudhana made his way to an inn frequented by sailors. He lay down on the hard bunk and fell immediately into a deep sleep. He awoke sometime in the night and realized he was feverish and quite sick. The boatmen generously gave him medicine and Sudhana improved, but he was obliged to spend another night in the wharfside inn.

As he recovered, Sudhana listened to the sailors talk about travels to other lands. There was nowhere they called home; they had no final goal. The sailors would drop anchor in port, spend a few days resting, with wine, women, and song, then sail off across the seas to some other distant port. Among the sailors were Africans far from the land of their birth and Arabs who had left their flocks of sheep in the desert and run away to sea. Like all sailors, they had a host of tales to tell. Sudhana was especially interested to hear one of them tell how he had once seen the bodhisattva of the sea, Avalokiteshvara, rising above the horizon.

Sudhana decided to prolong his stay there by another day, less on account of his sickness than because of these tales. But the sailor who had seen Avalokiteshvara was unable to stay chattering any longer in the inn. The sailor's boat was due to leave, and there was no one else Sudhana could hear that kind of talk from. He went out onto the quayside, bought himself a bowl of stewed fruit, then returned and climbed up onto his bunk, where he lay down and sank into the dreams waiting for him. Sudhana dreamed that he had already reached the north, the land of Koshala, the banks of the Ganga, the Punjab to the west, and even, beyond Kapilavastu, the Lumbini grove where Siddhartha was born.

In his dream, the distant sal trees of the Lumbini grove looked like green clouds clustered together. In their shade it was always cool. In the grove stood one artificial tree; leaves, branches, trunk, all made by human hand. Clothes that had belonged to dead people were hanging randomly from its branches. In his dream-state, Sudhana found that very funny, like a kind of children's game.

Twenty million billion woodland spirits were gathered about that tree. The main goddess of the grove, Sutejo-mandala-ratishri, was enthroned below the tree with bright beams of light issuing from her eyes. Sudhana approached until he was standing right in front of her.

There was an enormous amount of business about. Innumerable goddesses were gathered there, and each of them was all the time hastening away somewhere at Sutejo's bidding. She was constantly talking about bodhisattvas being born in the Bengal Sea. As she did so, the goddesses around her became bodhisattvas and one by one sank into the sea. It was an immensely solemn sight.

As each goddess became a bodhisattva, she would urge it away. "Go quickly, go quickly. Someone is eagerly waiting for you. Go quickly."

Although there were thousands of transformations vanishing into the sea, still an innumerable crowd of goddesses ready to become bodhisattvas remained. Sutejo stopped speaking for a moment. The stream of goddesses stopped as well.

Sudhana came close to her and bowed low.

"Holy, most holy, you open the bodhisattva way and send bodhisattvas to their place of work. I still do not understand how to attain the fullness of bodhisattva awakening and be born a bodhisattva performing bodhisattva works. I have traveled all over the southern lands, and now I am here."

"I already know you. Your name is Sudhana."

Her voice was very bright. It was so beautiful, Sudhana longed to absorb it. Perhaps all living creatures' sufferings were abolished by the mere fact that such a beautiful voice existed in the world. The extinction of pain! Surely that is in itself a lovely song.

Sudhana's dream continued, although meanwhile in Bijaga the night was nearly over.

The goddess Sutejo was like a mother in her kindness to Sudhana. Her heart overflowed with a familiar gladness as if saying, "My son has returned!"

"My dear child, what a hard time you have had on your journeys. I made a vow in a long-ago life that means I have to take care of every bodhisattva as they come to birth. Having made such a vow, I found myself born in this lovely Lumbini grove near Kapilavastu in one small mountain kingdom,

part of Jambudvipa to the south of Mount Sumeru, below the four heavens
of this world of pain. After I had spent a century here waiting for one bodhisattva to come down, he arrived at last from the Tushita heaven. It was the
Buddha Shakyamuni.

"Just before he was born, this grove filled with omens, solemn in their
sacredness. First, the ground grew smooth. Pits and bumps disappeared; all
became an expression of equality. Second, the thorns and pebbles and
unclean things in the grove vanished, and instead there was soft ground
composed of rich humus, from which rose the fragrance of the earth. Third,
the grove's sal trees put down roots until they reached water deep underground, signifying the mind that prevents easy falls or destruction. Fourth,
the fragrance issuing from the ground indicated that the earth is the source
of a better fragrance than the heavens. Fifth, the way the forest was adorned
with festive banners, scrolls, and every kind of solemn magnificence signi-
fied that this world is a festival of ecstasy. Sixth, all the plants burst into
flower, expressing the highest beauty. The seventh omen was similar.

"Eighth, all the spirits of the realm of desire and the realm of pure form
that were in this world of pain, the heavenly beings, the sea spirits, Yaksa
demons, celestial Gandharvas, Asura demons, the mythical Garudas and
Kimnaras, the snake-headed Mahoragas and the horse-headed Kumbhan-
das, all the major divinities, gathered reverently in serried ranks, symbol-
izing wholeness. Ninth, the heavenly nymphs from the realm of desire, all
that were present in the entire Buddha cosmos, the female dragons, Yak-
shas, Gandharvas, all the female spirits stood facing the Pillakcha tree.
Tenth, all the Buddhas in the four directions each emitted light from their
navels, illuminating the world far and wide, manifesting the birth of Buddhas and bodhisattvas. Seeing these ten different portents, I was so happy
that I leaped for joy.

"At last, a newborn babe issued from the side of the lady Maya, the wife
of the captain of Kapilavastu; it all seemed like a shadow, an hallucination,
a dream, a spell. Even the newborn child Buddha's words, 'I am the greatest being above and below the heavens,' spoken after he had walked seven
steps, felt like a dream. Only after all that, did I awaken out of those shadows, hallucinations, dreams, and spells, and bowed down before the spot
beneath the tree where the child had been born.

"My dear child, I can do no more than guess at the emancipations contained in such portents; you must visit a teacher who knows the higher
things. In your presence, I am nothing more than a leaf beaten from a tree

by a slight shower. Lovely little visitor, I pledge myself to a day in another incarnation when we can devote ourselves together for the benefit of all living beings; share my pledge as you go your way."

Sudhana smiled as he slept, filled with infinite respect and affection for Sutejo, goddess of the grove that flowed around him like a stream and he sang her praise:

> Oh teacher,
> you are just like a mother to me.
> How can it be that I should learn
> dharma-teaching from just one Buddha?
> I must visit ten thousand Buddhas,
> ten billion Buddhas,
> learn ten billion dharmas,
> comprehend ten billion times.
> Oh teacher,
> I kneel beneath your skirts,
> I kneel before your foot,
> kneeling
> not in the submission of a slave
> but in love for the dharma
> and bodhisattva's will.
> Accept me here,
> teacher just like a mother to me;
> accept my reverence,
> accept my fervent heart.
> As the birds sing
> in this lovely holy grove,
> as the birds fly
> in this grove,
> accept my heart.

44.
WITH THE BANDITS

 UDHANA WOKE the next morning and heard there was a boat leaving for the north, so he hurried down to the quay. Because of all the fighting, there were few boats heading north these days. The next port was Suba at the mouth of the river Mahanadi. According to the sailors, there was unrest along the frontier with the kingdom of Magadha that ran between Suba and the various branches forming the delta of the Ganga. Magadha shared a common frontier with the kingdom of Angka on all four sides, but it was not an entirely peaceful settlement.

The ship Sudhana boarded was extremely old. It was overloaded with freight as well as passengers and, if this was not bad enough, the sea was rough. The captain had heard stories about the unruly nature of the northern parts of the Bengal Sea and was reluctant to leave port, but when the merchants who needed their goods transported offered to pay a higher rate, their boat set sail at once.

The ship's captain was an old man who had spent more than fifty years at sea, yet he was still hale and hearty, with a white beard two spans long beneath his chin. His calm manner set everyone's mind at rest.

One whole day and night passed on the rough sea. At daybreak the next morning the waves breaking against the ship's prow took on a gentler note, the sea mingling now with the fresh water emerging from the estuary of the River Mahanadi. It was still quite dark when Sudhana disembarked in Suba, together with a few other people and a team of oxen.

Sudhana wandered through the streets in the early light. The streets were deserted, still strewn with refuse left from the day before. A merchant he had sailed with had given him basic direction to Kharak, and two other merchants, heading the same direction, decided to accompany him on his

journey. Sudhana decided to take the mountain road across Magadha, descending by way of Gaya and Rajagriha. He had passed mountain forests and steep cliffs so many times in the southern lands that he had had enough of them. Once past the mountain ranges of Magadha, endless plains spread beyond. The Ganga, uniting with a host of other rivers, would become a great sacred river and flow on powerfully before once again dividing into the dozens of separate branches forming its delta and emptying into the Bengal Sea. Step by step, the little pilgrim was approaching home.

In Kharak, the three travelers hastened to purchase food and medicine as well as herbs to repel snakes and wild animals. The two merchants also equipped themselves with weapons to ward off attacks from bandits. One of them, who called himself Jihol, was on his way to Sarnath. The other was a barter-tradesman on his way to Koshala on the far side of the Hindustan plains. Yet neither was transporting much in the way of goods; their baggage must have been dispatched by another route. One of them seemed to be a drug dealer, judging from the characteristic odor hanging about him.

Jihol looked to be about forty, the drug-smelling fellow must have been around thirty; both were much older than Sudhana. The three passed most of the time in their own silence. Sudhana had a rich store of past memories; he had only to summon them up to banish boredom completely.

"Hey, young fellow! Let's rest for a while." Jihol spoke, jolting Sudhana out of his reveries.

They had been walking for a long time and were at the top of a rise that offered a good place to rest. All kinds of flowers were in blossom on the slopes. The sight of a crimson snapdragon reminded him of Mani; he shook his head. Jihol had the soft gentle face of a mountain sheep. He offered Sudhana something to stave off his hunger, and some water.

"Just take a little. Being too full when you're walking is sometimes worse than being hungry."

Where walking was concerned, Sudhana was second to none, but Jihol was also well-acquainted with the ways of the road. He had already spent thirty years as a wandering merchant, from the time he was fifteen until now, going to every possible part of north, east, and southern India, as well as the western regions along the Indus. He had never once cheated anyone.

As they set out once more, Jihol and Sudhana began to open their hearts to one another. Beyond the streets of Kharak, once past the forest road to the west, they reached the Mahanadi River again. The three travellers found a small boat making its way upstream against the current. The boatman was an old man with only one eye, someone with many tales to tell. His face and neck were deeply scarred. As he plied his pole, they could see obvious traces of iron fetters on his wrists, as well.

"And why might you all be going this way?" he interrogated them.

"Because it's the fastest way through to the plains," the drug peddler replied.

"Fast, it may be, but once you're across Shiva Lake, you're into a forest teeming with tigers. Then beyond that, the road to the north takes you up over steep mountain ridges. One prince of Magadha declared the whole region a hunting preserve and forbade anyone to enter it, so it's become a paradise for wild animals. And yet, no, as a matter of fact, up in those mountains there are more hermits than there are tigers."

Jihol realized that by hermits, he actually meant gangs of bandits. He'd been in these kind of situations enough to know that the boatman was probably charged with bringing the bandits supplies and news from the estuary and lower reaches of the river.

The regular thrusts of the pole soon drove the boat far inland. From the banks of the river there were moments when birdcalls sounding like human voices would come bubbling up, but there was no sign of human life anywhere until suddenly they glimpsed a column of pale smoke rising from a grove of trees.

"What's that over there?" Jihol pointed.

The old boatman replied, "It's a place where people live."

He headed in that direction and made the boat fast. The three of them followed him ashore. A naked youth with wild hair advanced towards them. He cast a piercing glance at the travelers, his eyes questioning the boatman.

"Merchants heading for the northern plains. I'm taking them up as far as Lake Shiva."

"Don't you know that's forbidden territory?" the young man scolded. "Didn't you realize?"

"I knew, of course. But the boss doesn't have his headquarters up there anymore. He's moved to the gold mining region down south."

"What? You mean he's just dumped us here?"

"Not at all; this is still part of the chief's territory. Only nowadays the boss doesn't purloin things, unless they belong to the rich, or government officials; he only confiscates regular tributes or stolen goods being transported out of weak countries by more powerful ones. Apart from that, he's given the order not to touch anything."

It was obvious from this conversation that the old boatman was in direct contact with the robber leader's headquarters, and that the savage-looking man had been left in sole charge of this portion of the riverbank.

The old man murmured as if to calm the young one, "They say a saint they're calling the Buddha has arisen up there in the Himalayas. Times have come when saints will even start appearing among thieves, I reckon. Our chief's a saint, a real one. He'll end up as a king, taking control of all the riches in the whole of India and using them to feed the people. He'll establish a kingdom. He's already in secret collusion with the Queen of Patna; the king up there's a mere dummy. If Patna joins with the regions controlled by the boss, even Magadha will be obliged to pay tribute at every twist and turn. He'll be sending a viceroy to take control of the kingdom of Ashimakha in the south."

The boatman's eyes glittered, his voice was sonorous. This was no runaway ignoramus; he was likely to be one of the boss's chief lieutenants. Moving all over Kharak and the Mahanadi River in the guise of a boatman in charge of a tiny craft, he kept in touch with robbers and leaders alike.

The young man and the boatman went into a hut, leaving the three travelers in the small boat. The day passed and still they didn't emerge. The remaining band of young toughs was observing Sudhana and the two merchants. Near the mud hut they could see mounds of supplies and a store of rice covered with dried grass.

Sudhana sensed the whole world was being shaken. Existing nations were declining, writhing in the throes of some kind of new power. Conflicts were arising everywhere. Life and property were being destroyed by warfare. Little Sudhana's lifetime had begun in the midst of such chaos. Now, returning northwards, he was finding the world to be a truly frightening place. Even bandit gangs were establishing kingdoms. After all, the founders of nations were all brigands anyway; kings were nothing more than bandit leaders.

A kingdom was something its chiefs played with and disposed of as they liked, Sudhana thought. There was no call to consider any nation sacred. So-called kingdoms were the first thing that had to be abolished in any truly sacred age. It didn't matter how much a bandit chieftain might favor the poor and humble; the moment he became a king he was bound to fall into corruption. Sudhana's heart, guided by truth, was unshakable but he wondered sadly how much truth could achieve in the face of the world's great disorder.

The two merchants were looking very worried. At last the old boatman appeared. The naked fellow stayed inside.

"Let's be off."

They boarded the boat. Lake Shiva was a beautiful spot. Jihol lamented over how the world could keep such beautiful places concealed, serving only as the hiding place of brigands. Sudhana merely felt himself blessed to have been born in India at all.

Unexpectedly, the old boatman chimed in with the full story of the lake: "Lake Shiva was once, long ago, the site of a nation's capital city; the spirits of the place had drawn the city down and this lake appeared in its place.

"People said that the wrath of Shiva, the god of destruction, had destroyed the city. The lake may be beautiful, yet it contains thousands and thousands of alligators; it's also known as the lake of hell."

At a wharf by the lakeside they found a relatively large boat to cross the lake in, capable of holding a fair amount of baggage. It was a rowing boat with two men assigned to it; the old boatman took charge as captain of the crew. The ripples on the lake spread brightly and a light breeze began to rise as the boat went bobbing on, with nothing to restrain it. One of the dreaded alligators scraped the boat's prow with its rugged back and vanished into the distance.

The old man laughed and he shouted out to his passengers, "Once we're across, suppose I clap you in chains and lock you up for a few days?"

"What?" The drug dealer's face turned an earthy color.

"Just kidding. No need to worry. I'll get you safely onto the northern shore of Lake Shiva. I've never once been known to harm anybody. I don't commit great sins—not like those high brahmans and soldiers, who walk around putting on airs while they have their slaves beaten to death all the time. Their sins are so heavy that very soon now they'll be wiped from the face of the Earth.

"You'll already have guessed that I'm in charge of this area, one of the leaders of the mountain hermits. As to why I'm telling you this about myself, well, there are two reasons. First, I want you to know that we're not murderous bandits, as the brahmans and ruling classes claim, and second, because the time has come when it's alright for the world to know about me. We're going to establish the greatest nation in the world, covering the whole of central and southern India. It's already been founded. One day you'll be its subjects, like me." The old bandit boatman had attained a bodhisattva heart. Any who boarded his boat attained the same heart.

On the northern shore of Lake Shiva there was a well-built wharf. Several boats were moored to it. "We'll land here," the boatman said.

45.
TRANSCENDING DEATH

HE YOUNG DRUG DEALER said he would stay with the old man, and remained in the boat. Perhaps he thought his drug dealing would be protected if he was in collusion with the bandits. He seemed to have plans regarding the distribution of drugs that were due to arrive there soon. Or perhaps he had simply been taken in and transformed by the boatman's words.

Sudhana and Jihol found themselves alone on the wharf, at the northern end of the vast expanse of water. Sudhana liked the prospect of a sturdy walker like Jihol being his companion as they crossed over to Magadha.

Jihol chattered constantly as they walked. He was particularly curious about the Buddha. Sudhana replied cautiously; some questions he avoided, others he answered with a mere look.

The woodlands along the northern shores of Lake Shiva, that lay within the frontiers of the kingdom of Magadha, were full of trees belonging to quite different species from those found on the southern shore, while the mountain path they were following was thick with moss and ferns. Birds caroled ahead of them. The sound of their footsteps ceased as they paused for a while, captivated by the silence of the deep shadows reigning in the forest.

Jihol shouted: "Look! There's a town down there. It's Gaya! Bodh Gaya!"

"Bodh Gaya!" Sudhana echoed the word in his heart. Yet there was a world of difference between the Gaya that so delighted Jihol and Sudhana's Gaya. For Jihol, Gaya had been the home of a woman whose memory was deeply engraved in his heart from the past. Her death had driven Jihol out on his life of roaming. If only that woman, whom he had loved with a deep passion, had remained alive, they would no doubt have gone to live as a happy couple somewhere on the outskirts of Sarnath in the land of Khashi. But she had fallen into the river and drowned one day, when a ferry had capsized on the Jumna, a tributary of the Ganga. Jihol visited that spot once every year. He would pray for her repose, then go on to Sarnath, where they had first met, and pray there, too. The love inscribed deep in his heart had not faded, despite the passing of time. And although he went hawking his wares through many lands, he had never once had eyes for any other woman; she had been his only love. Now they had passed the crest of the mountains forming the central massif of Magadha, and his love was brought to the boil again by the intense emotion he felt on seeing his love's former home of Gaya far below, surrounded by the groves of trees that covered the plains.

"This time last year, I was here looking down on Gaya. You might say that I exist only because Gaya exists for me to visit once a year. Gaya is my love's capital city. Ah, Gaya!"

Sudhana gazed at Jihol's face; it shone brightly, sending dazzling beams glittering between the forest shadows. He was over forty; his face was marked with a love-longing that resembled sadness; it was a blissful face. A love between man and woman capable of transcending death in this way must surely be a sacred thing. It seemed no different from an illuminated being's unbounded compassion of for all living creatures. If it was permitted for a man to stay fixed in compassion for just one woman, then that could only be a model for all compassion. Plunged in these thoughts, Sudhana looked down at Gaya again.

Bodh Gaya was where Shakymuni Buddha attained the ultimate illumination of truth. For Sudhana, it was the sacred place where the most sacred teacher in the world had attained enlightenment. He was filled with awe, as if all the teachers he had hitherto met in the course of his travels were met together here.

"Jihol, that town of Gaya is sacred for me, too. It's the place where the Buddha grasped the great dharma. My free wandering is all on account of the dharma taught by the Buddha."

"I too want to visit that man you call the Buddha. I have just one thing I want to ask him: 'Buddha, what was the world before dharma came into being? And what will become of the world now that your dharma has been made widely known, or in the distant future?' That's what I want to ask."

Sudhana longed to be able to comfort Jihol. "The woman from Gaya alive in your heart is really a kind of Buddha," Sudhana said gently. He continued in song:

> Beneath the sixty-three heavens
> below Mount Sumeru,
> amidst the host of living creatures
> that are not yet perfect in insight,
> the love of man and woman
> reaches the sixty-third heaven.
> For how could the laws governing
> this whole Buddha cosmos
> exist apart, separate from that love
> beneath the sixty-three heavens
> below Mount Sumeru?

It was the kind of song Sudhana sometimes composed and sang to amuse himself during his long travels. He had at last set foot once again on northern soil. Kapilavastu, known to him only in his dream, was gradually drawing near, although he still had a long road to travel.

The meadowlands of the great Indian plains are endless. Their rivers meander like tangled skeins of thread. The horizon, too, stretches on endlessly, seemingly intent on showing that this world itself is unending. Those meadows were the birthplace of the teaching of the equality of all things that Shakyamuni had proclaimed. Sudhana expected to see Gaya appear between the trees at any moment; yet although they had already caught sight of the city from above, they could no longer find it. The town they had thought they could reach in less than a day turned out to be a good two days' march away.

When they at last reached Gaya, the gates were open; it was time for the cows to come out to eat the grass from which the dew had just dried. The soldiers guarding the gate had laid aside their spears; the townsfolk were standing along the roadside inside and outside the city walls. Since earliest childhood, Sudhana had traveled all over the river plains, growing up in a tribal society where the cow was venerated as a sacred animal. If Shakyamuni chose the elephant rather than the cow to symbolize the dharma, making the elephant a sacred animal, it may have partly been a way of rejecting the brahmans' blind veneration of the cow. Shakyamuni had said that elephants knew their previous incarnations while cows did not.

Sudhana shook away the thoughts of animals. Arriving in Gaya, Sudhana was filled with a sense of homecoming. He and Jihol spent their first
night in a dyer's shop owned by acquaintances of Jihol's. The next day Sudhana and Jihol parted company with warm embraces.

Sudhana was eager to go on alone across the Indian plains, walking until
he reached Kapilavastu, waiting like a kind of fountainhead far ahead.
From Gaya, Sudhana headed eastward. He took various ferries until he
arrived at Patna, the capital where all the tributaries of the Ganga were
united in a single river. There, Sudhana fell sick from the fatigue of his long
journey. This disease, his second sickness since leaving the south, gave rise
to a sense of insecurity that shook his previous confidence in his own body.

Sudhana was surprised to find that the person who had volunteered to
treat him was a follower of the Buddha named Suthei. Suthei had been a
lay devotee attached to a monastery of the Buddha's followers up river to
the west in Sarnath, in the forests of Varanasi. But after the death of his
father, who had been a doctor, he had in turn become a famous doctor in
the capital city of the united river.

Suthei seemed unwilling to let Sudhana go, begging him to live with
him there in Patna in his house built over the river. Sudhana replied: "You
have left the Buddha's side, but that does not mean you have left the Buddha's ever-spreading dharma. Having once met you, I am surely destined
to meet you again but first I must visit many other lands. Patna alone cannot be my home."

A few days passed and Sudhana was still recovering, but he felt anxious
to move on. He plucked three leaves from an ash tree close to the house,
put them on his bed, and left secretly. Luckily, the house's little skiff was
there and Sudhana used it to row to the shore. From there, Sudhana turned
and looked back at the house where Suthei had been caring for him. He
was just in time to see Suthei himself vanishing behind the blinds, where
he had been hiding. Suthei had anticipated Sudhana's departure and had
even put the empty skiff ready for him to use. Sudhana reached inside the
pack on his back and found it contained rice for a long journey, medicine,
and even a splendid leather water bottle. Sudhana's heart was full of a gratitude close to remorse; he found himself unable to leave immediately but
lingered for a while looking at Suthei's window before again setting out.

He took the land route along the riverbank as far as Vaishalla, where
he took a rowing boat upstream to the port of Khushinagara in the land
of Malla. Old men and children rode for nothing, and Sudhana still

looked like a small child. On the journey upstream from Vaishalla to Khushinagara, Sudhana could not close his eyes for a second, he was so entranced by a landscape more beautiful than anywhere else in India. The old men showed no great interest in the scenery; they just sat there nodding, their faces buried in snowy beards. Perhaps beauty needs to be unfamiliar; they were so accustomed to it all, it was nothing but their ordinary surroundings.

Sudhana was fortunate to meet commoners belonging to the vaysya caste who were leaving Khushinagara and heading northwards. They foresaw that very soon the town would become the site of a conflict between the older tribal leaders and the partisans of the newly arising monarchy. The commoners were taking advantage of a power vacuum provoked by the current instability and were running away. They had split into small groups of a few dozen people each and were skillfully passing from one grove to the next, escaping from the lack of freedom they had endured in this land that they had tilled for so long. Sudhana slipped into the midst of one such group and was now walking farther and farther north, submerged in the towering grass of the plains.

On reaching the northern frontiers of Malla, Sudhana found himself confronting a vast mountain range. Had it come down from the heavens? No, it was the snowy Himalayas that all of India revered. The Himalayas! Had not the Buddha himself often come close to them and gazed at the chain of white peaks soaring heavenward, these very peaks? Nothing he had seen in all his travels could compare in majesty with the immensity of the Himalayas. They were more sacred and beautiful than anything he could have even imagined. They were a teacher far loftier, deeper, and more remote than any of the teachers he had so far met. They were no mere mountains, they were a totality that brought a sense of fullness to every person, every heart. Sudhana sang them a poem:

A
O
Ma
Himalayas
Set outside this world of pain
Himalayas
By you indeed
The world exists.

A
O
Ma
Om
Om
Om
O Himalayas!
One who beholds you
becomes indeed a person,
becomes a Buddha.
Om
Himalayas decked with everlasting snows,
Himalayas,
ruling this whole world,
home of many gods!
Himalayas turned toward the Buddha
who has come to the world escorted by those gods.
No matter where I go henceforth
I will say I have gazed on the Himalayas.
I will say
I gazed at the Himalayas and I wept hot tears
full of joy and sorrow.

Sudhana stood entranced by the distant view of the snowy mountains, until they were no longer visible in the darkness. The next day he let the other travelers go on their way and entered into deep meditation, sitting facing the mountains alone. At long last, the walker had turned into a sitter.

All the next day he sat meditating. Filled with truth's joy, he was beyond the bonds of time. He could feel no hunger, did not realize he had stopped breathing when he held his breath, felt no call of nature, so intense was the bliss provoked by the Himalayas.

More than ever before, he longed to know how a bodhisattva leads all living creatures out along bodhisattva ways. He recalled that in his dream beside the Bengal Sea in Kharak, the goddess of the Lumbini grove had told him to visit Gopa, the Shakya woman of Kapilavastu. Having now gazed at the mountain home of the gods, Sudhana was seized by a longing to meet the most noble-minded woman in the world. After three days spent sitting before the mountains, Sudhana set out along a highway arriving from the southwest. It was busy with the carts of merchants and people traveling on foot. He even encountered a man from as far away as Lahore in the western Punjab region. Sudhana joined him.

"Where are you going?" Sudhana asked.

"I'm on my way to Kapilavastu. Of course, ultimately I'll be going back to Punjab."

"Kapilavastu? That's where I'm going, too. I need to meet Gopa, a holy woman of the Shakya clan living there. I have a lot to learn from her."

"What? Gopa? Lady Gopa of the Shakya clan?" The stranger repeated. "But I'm on my way to meet that same holy and beautiful lady!"

The young man from Lahore possessed a particular grace and depth. At twenty-five, his gaze was penetrating, his expression frank and open. He and Sudhana brought their journeys together. When they reached the end of the road over the plains and arrived at the river crossing, they found the river in flood, with water pouring down from the direction of Malla. Unable to cross at once, they sat beneath a tree, watching the torrent roll swiftly past. Collecting bundles of hay, they prepared a bed for the night. The thick clouds meant that they spent the night without one glimpse of the stars. There were plenty of mosquitoes, though. Sometimes waving the mosquitoes away, sometimes letting them settle, they talked about the experiences each of them had had.

It turned out that the youth was also someone always on the move, visiting sages and ascetics with long years of study behind them. Only he had had no contact with the Buddha's teachings. He had heard something about Shakyamuni, how he had walked seven steps at birth and cried out in a loud voice that he was the most exalted person in the world. Nothing more.

The floods abated the next day and they were able to share a boat with several other travelers. At last Kapilavastu came into view. The small, tidy town seemed to be beckoning to them. Sudhana's steps were borne along by the wind.

46.
GOPA, AT LAST

UDHANA WAS NOW walking along a path in the beautiful grove lying between Kapilavastu and the Lumbini grove of his dream. He and his companion advanced toward a great crowd of young girls gathering herbs. One girl was guiding them. The lady Gopa came towards them and circumambulated them once to the left in greeting. The maiden herb-gatherers looked incredulous; it was customary for visitors to circumambulate Gopa once, moving to the right, before approaching her.

"Guests who have attained awakening are exempt from formal observances; I have performed the ritual greeting instead of you. Welcome, young visitors. Does this place please you? Kapilavastu is small and weak as a nation, but when it comes to truth it sheds light like the sun on all the world. Shakyamuni Buddha was born here; some of his family still live here. They too follow the Buddha's teaching as newly discovered truth."

Gopa's voice was gentle, as if she had never encountered any of this world's pain. A light sari barely veiled her body. Sudhana was dazzled. He could think of nothing to ask; it all remained locked in the depths of his heart. But Gopa seemed to be able to converse directly with his heart, and she spoke.

"Dear friends. You've come here to ask about bodhisattva works and the nature of bodhisattva being. You already have hearts longing for *anuttara-samyak-sambodhi*, perfect universal enlightenment. When bodhisattvas perfect the practice of the ten laws, they attain a wisdom that resembles Indra's Net, where every pearl reflects and contains every other. The first of the ten involves being attentive to the teaching of the sages, which you have done; the second is the attainment of immense faith; the third is the purification of lust into longing; the fourth is the accumulation of wisdom and blessings; the fifth is to pay attention to Buddha's teaching; the sixth is to be always closely serving in the heart all the Buddhas of past, present, and future; the seventh is the faithful performance of bodhisattva works; the eighth is to obtain the blessing of the Buddhas of past, present, and future; the ninth is the emergence of a compassionate heart from a pure heart; the tenth is to cut with a single stroke the cycle of birth and death by the power of enlightening wisdom, prajña."

"Lady bodhisattva of the Shakyas, I would prefer to do without the ten laws you have just recited," Sudhana said as respectfully as possible. "For if I become too fascinated by the details, I might concentrate on them and grow attached to the power of the ten laws. I would rather devote myself to the practice of utter freedom in detachment and be like the birds in this grove."

Gopa replied in a loud voice, "Wonderful. I have long been teaching these ten laws; at last I have found someone who really understands them. Tomorrow too will be a great day. The future stretches far away. All that remote future is this present day's blessing."

The incomparably beautiful Gopa rose. All the maidens who had been sitting around her rose too.

The traveler from Lahore spoke up. "Sudhana may be young, but as we were coming here from Khushinagara I discovered that he has attained illuminations of a depth I shall never be able to equal. Yet here in your presence, Sudhana seems to have attained one more level of splendor. I think it must be on account of joy at the teaching to which your glory has been added."

"Wonderful. Pilgrim come from afar, I cannot praise enough your truly humble heart. How long will you stay here?"

"Tomorrow, Sudhana and I must depart from here. We are heading in different directions. I am just setting out on the journey, while Sudhana has always lived on the road. I am at the beginning of the end."

Gopa sang them her response:

Innumerable gatherings of Buddhas and creatures
across innumerable aeons of time!
Innumerable future offerings of those gatherings.

See, offerings from all the particles of this world.
See, offerings from the world of the particles of all the tiny worlds
arising in this present world.
Ocean of the vows made in all past worlds.
Ocean of dharma. Ocean of bodhisattva living.
Ocean of truth like magic, most true.

Remaining here, remaining here, bodhisattvas, no matter how long
ago born, are now born for the first time.
Bodhisattvas, no matter how short their enlightenment,
pierce through past present and future and bloom as a gentian,
its perfume delicate each dawn and dusk.

Although Gopa, ruler of the grove garden of Kapilavastu, was the daughter of a brahman, here she was simply a bodhisattva, no longer a brahman or a member of the Buddha's clan. Her beauty touched all living creatures, and all the microorganisms in all living creatures. Her song was her most powerful lesson. Sudhana nearly wept for happiness.

Gopa came closer to Sudhana and spoke: "Whether you leave tomorrow or not, I want you to meet Maya, the mother of the Buddha."

"But surely, after Siddhartha was born, she was taken with a fever and died?" Like everyone, Sudhana had heard the story that Shakymuni Buddha's mother had left him motherless while he was still a newborn babe. He had grown up at his aunt's breast and had adopted her as his second mother as he grew up, until the time when he became the heir apparent.

"Her death was no death. Whenever she has something to do in this world, she comes back to life. I very much want you to see her. But first there is someone else you must meet, someone you can only meet in a dream."

Sudhana went into the quarters of the male devotees, just beside the bodhisattva's garden. He was allocated a cool sleeping space there. Weary, he lay down on one side and bade sleep to come. The songs of night birds disturbed him but soon he was asleep. He sank into a long dream that Gopa had given him.

In his dream he saw an ancient city of long ago. It was the capital of Jambudvipa at the south of Mount Sumeru, the most outstanding of all the eighty-four billion cities, holding a population equal to that of all the other eighty-four billion cities. In ponds inside the city, lotus flowers were blooming blue, red, yellow, and white, while the moats around the city were adorned with jeweled balustrades and jeweled nets. Along the wide roads leading away from the city toward other towns, there stretched orchards and groves, and clusters of jeweled ornaments. The perfumes worn by the crowds of men and women traveling along the roads blended with the scent of many flowers. That city's king had a harem of eighty-four thousand queens, concubines, and maids; he had five hundred ministers of state, and five hundred sons.

The crown prince Prabhava-ta was the son of queen Padma. Since early childhood he had the singular gift of being able to adopt thirty-two different forms. The soles of his feet were smooth as mirrors and bore marks like the print of a wheel, while his hands were soft as cotton. His fingers were long and slender, with a delicate membrane spreading between them. His heels were round, his feet highly arched. His whole figure was graceful, bright and beautiful, his body firm and well-rounded like that of a deer, though if he stretched his arms downwards, his hands came below the level of his knees, like a elephant's trunk. His sex was hidden, withdrawn inside his body like that of a stallion, and just as large if aroused. Black hair grew from every pore; the hair on his head was tawny and swept to the right, orderly like a conch shell. His flesh was golden in hue; his skin was so soft and smooth that dirt did not adhere to it. He had seven smooth round bosses on his soles and palms, shoulders and brow. His arms hung easily, his backbone did not project, his whole appearance was full and harmonious like a tree. His lower chin and breast were like a lion's. His neck bore three birthmarks; a constant radiance shone out from him in all directions. His forty teeth were pure, white, regular and closely-set, his tongue was red and long and so broad it could cover his whole face, his clear voice was pleasant to all who heard it. His eyelashes were blue, neat and lustrous; he kept blinking with the upper eyelid like a cow; his irises stood out sharply from the white of his eyes. His face was perfect like a brightly shining moon, his eyebrows fine, arching like rainbows, the down covering the center of his brow was pure white, while the fleshy bulge on the crown of his head was like nothing so much as an altar-canopy.

On a given day, the prince Prabhava-ta duly emerged from the citadel. He was riding in a chariot all of gold, at the head of a retinue of twenty thousand men. The procession was majestic to see. Just then another, equally impressive procession appeared, advancing towards it. It was led by a maiden from the capital city of Siri; the girl's name too was Siri and when she first saw the prince, she was captivated by him.

She defied her mother's disapproval to meet him.

"Mother, I beg you to let me serve him. If I can't, I'll die for sure."

It was presumptuous for the daughter of a mere commoner to wish to have as husband this prince, whose bearing was that of the great king Cakravarti himself. But her resolve was so strong that there was no stopping her. Advancing before the prince, she began to sing:

> Prince, apart from you
> there is no one in all this world.
> In all this world,
> no one kindles my heart
> apart from you.
> It is you I long to serve,
> prince destined to become King Cakravarti.
> In your infinite compassion,
> accept my heart.

The prince Prabhava-ta and the young Siri were immediately united by a mutual love so strong that no power could part them. Their eyes shone, their hearts throbbed; both were full of joy. Learning from her that the Buddha's teachings were being promulgated in one school in his land, the prince grew fascinated by the Buddha's dharma and became a Buddhist on the spot. Such was the change provoked by the loving Siri. Their love matured in the grove, and the truth they venerated together penetrated deeper into them. The prince was eager to go and inform the king his father about all that had happened. He united the maiden's procession with his own and returned to the palace.

There the king, hearing now for the first time of the Buddha's teaching, was so delighted he began to sway in a kind of dance before the prince and his lady Siri.

"I possessed everything except the dharma but now I have learned from you the Buddha's law. I will devote the rest of my life to the study of the Buddha's teaching. I and my people will believe the Buddha's teaching and practice it faithfully. What joy!"

The king surrendered the kingship to the prince and set out to join the followers of the Buddha. After a ceremony where water was poured onto the crown of the king's head, he left the palace accompanied by representatives of all ten social classes. Thus the prince Prabhava-ta became king and the maid Siri became his queen. They spent long years together, during which they had many children, devoting themselves to the truth and the nation's welfare, and their mutual love. At last they opened the gates of liberation and were admitted to the realm of emancipation, where ideas of truth and nation and even love are mere cumbersome trifles.

Sudhana awoke from his dream. The early morning grove was astir with birdsong. Sudhana went to a little stream, sipped water from his cupped hands, and left the place. He was prepared to meet the lady Maya. Ordinary people would consider any claim that a long-dead person was still alive to be a mere lie. But Sudhana believed firmly that the long-dead Maya was alive, and believed too that such belief possessed a power capable of making the thing believed become a reality.

At the thought of going in search of Maya, Sudhana felt a strong hesitation. He wondered if he wasn't being rash, setting off on such a quest. He paused on the road, considering whether to walk away. He was tormented by a hesitation he had never experienced before. Just then a yellow urunga bird flew away from a branch, causing one of its leaves to fall. At the same moment a voice echoed from the sky above the forest:

> The form of the lady Maya
> can only be seen
> with the eyes of Samantabhadra.
> I cannot see her,
> I cannot see her.
> Why should I go in quest of her?
> Shall I ever see her form,
> hear her voice,
> receive her teaching?

The voice echoed precisely the questions occupying Sudhana's heart. It was the voice of the divinity of the air, one of the spirits protecting Kapila-vastu. The spirit's words, transformed into petals falling from the sky, dropped onto Sudhana's head.

"Young pilgrim, come with me. Today your heart's true nature is to be celebrated."

Sudhana followed the spirit. He passed a host of spirits busy with various tasks, but each and every one stopped to encourage Sudhana.

Sudhana lost all notion of whether the spirit was leading him to

Kapilavastu or somewhere else. His heart had left reality and was passing into quite another world; he could not distinguish whether the places he was passing through were real or imaginary. Amidst the acclamations of the spirits, he arrived at a place where he could see the majestic form of an exalted lady. Sudhana felt dizzy. It was the lady Maya. Sudhana groaned.

Light was emanating from Maya, yet it was no ordinary light. Her pure body was not fixed and limited. She was capable of manifesting freely everything in the world and outside the world, for she was constantly changing. She appeared as a female demon, as a woman from the heaven of Paranirmita-vasavarti, then turned into a woman from the heaven of Nirmanarati before becoming a nymph from Tushita heaven. She transformed into a woman from Suyama heaven, became a woman from Trayastrimsa heaven, then changed into a woman from the realm of the Four Heavenly Kings, before appearing as a dragon, a Yaksha, a Gandharva, an Asura, a Garuda, a Kimnara, a Mahoraga, and a human yet not human woman. The lady Maya was the sum of all women. Ultimately, she was a woman who had formulated the desire to become the mother of all bodhisattvas who live for the sake of all sentient beings.

As Maya appeared in multiple bodily forms, Sudhana too manifested himself in numerous bodies, all of them advancing before the lady Maya and bowing in deep reverence. The Sudhanas addressed the Mayas.

"Sacred lady, the bodhisattva Manjushri bade me fix my heart on total illumination and untiringly seek for every kind of knowledge of what is good. Since then, obedient to his instructions, I have visited many places where knowledge of the good is available and after many wanderings I have reached here. I beg you, holy lady, speak for my benefit. How does a bodhisattva embark on bodhisattva works, and attain full bodhisattva wisdom? With this question alone I have traveled throughout southern India and will now travel all over the north as well. I beg you, speak."

The lady Maya smiled at Sudhana's words, and replied, "Faithful child, will anyone be so foolish as to advance and deny that, as I am mother of all bodhisattvas, you are my son? My own son, my truth. At last you have come to me, now listen to what I say."

The lady Maya had risen and was leading Sudhana by the hand. All the host of lovely maids who venerated the lady Maya stood in a circle around them, singing in clear voices matching their beauty. Their song brought clouds rising.

47.
IN INDRA HEAVEN

Now Maya and Sudhana were alone. Her appearance suddenly changed into that of an ordinary housewife from the villages in the great Indian plains. Her style of speaking changed as well.

"I left this world seven days after giving birth. When I died I felt so sorry for the baby that I could not even close my eyes. That sorrow matured into the compassion I needed to become a bodhisattva in the world into which I was reborn. First, I lived in one place in the Tushita heaven and one place in hell, encountering creatures with good and bad karmas. Now I have come into this world, where my child has grown up and become a Buddha. That is why I am sitting here with a child of truth like you.

"This is what I have to tell you, Sudhana: Never put compassion forward too soon. Compassion has to rise early, but should stay at the back, right back at the back of the end.

"By the source and wisdom of bodhisattva being, I received a liberation enabling me to fashion things as if by magic, bringing into being in the world things that did not exist. That is why I was able to become mother of bodhisattvas. I entered the pure-blooded governing clan here in Kapilavastu in the southern regions of Jambudvipa and bore a child from my right side. I gave birth in no house, but by the roadside. Then later I died by the roadside, at the age of eighty. I not only gave birth to that child. Every time any of the bodhisattvas were reborn, I had to become their mother.

"At the moment when I gave birth there in Kapilavastu, I saw how all the bodhisattvas of the ten-directioned worlds were filled with transformations and majestic glory. My womb is a dwelling where all the bodhisattvas of the world abide, coming and going freely. Yet when I am pregnant with all those bodhisattvas, I become no larger; and I become no slimmer when they are all outside in the world. So in the world I am known as 'mother of bodhisattvas' and 'mother of the Buddha.' They call me 'mother of trans-formations' too, because the transformation involved in receiving the bodhisattva seed and giving birth to a bodhisattva signifies all this world's transformations. I was always the Buddha's mother, from the moment when the first Buddha of the present aeon, Krakuchchanda, was born; after him came Kanakamuni Buddha, then Kashyapa Buddha, and finally the pres-ent Shakyamuni Buddha.

"I was merely their mother; I felt no attachment to that motherhood. If I left the world seven days after giving birth in Kapilavastu, it was because I did not want to be limited to being his mother. I have returned now to give birth to the bodhisattvas that have to come into this world. And also to meet you here."

The lady Maya underwent another transformation. She once again became a sacred bodhisattva, majestic in stature. Her voice took on the tones of someone reciting from sacred scriptures:

> Little pilgrim, Sudhana.
> I have been the mother of every Buddha:
> the Lion Buddha, the Great dharma Light Pillar Buddha,
> the Marvelous Eye Buddha, the Pure Kusuma Flower Buddha,
> the Marvelous Flower Omen Buddha, the Sage Buddha,
> the Temple Buddha, the Marvelous Will Buddha...

She continued on and on, reciting several hundred names.

"I was the mother of all these Buddhas. Throughout all the Buddha cos-mos in this present aeon, I have embraced motherhood. And each of those bodhisattvas coming to be born chose to have me as a mother as they pierced this world's darkness and pain with their compassion.

"Sudhana, there is a reason why I have recited one by one all the differ-ent Buddhas' titles in your hearing; the mere omission of even a single Bud-dha's name is like abandoning one of this world's myriad creatures. Little pilgrim, in this world more Buddhas than there are grains of sand on the shores of the Ganga are constantly hastening toward all living creatures, and you should hear the sound of their breathing. You should become famil-iar with that quietness."

A long time passed; the lady Maya pronounced the names of all the Buddhas again, one by one, teaching Sudhana. As she did so, she gazed at him with eyes full of tears, recalling with longing each of the Buddhas whose mother she had been.

"From here you must journey up into the heights of heaven above. When you reach Indra heaven's lofty realm, you will meet Surendrabha, the daughter of its ruler. She will inform you of bodhisattva ways with more vigor than I can. I have grown old with so much childbearing.

"Now, everything has been said. Off you go. As you hurry on your way, you will turn into a bird and fly up until you reach Indra heaven. Heavenly maids are the loveliest of all, so hurry off now, fulfill your happiness with their loveliness."

Maya rose and left for an unknown world. Sudhana set out on his new journey. From the parklands skirting Kapilavastu, Sudhana took the long road leading towards the city of Saravastha in the land of Koshala. Sudhana expected to be drawn up to heaven late at night, midway along the road that had been indicated to him. So far, Sudhana's journeys had all been situated on the Earth. Even the bleak brown and gray emptiness of the Deccan Plateau had been part of the Earth's surface, and therefore not outside of Sudhana's real world. But the maiden that the lady Maya had indicated was not to be found on Earth but in the heavens. To reach that Indra heaven, he was being called to make a journey far different from any he had so far made.

Along the road leading away from Kapilavastu, the red glow of evening set the whole heavens ablaze; the forests gleamed gold, then faded into the growing twilight darkness. The night passed; it was already early morning, but not yet dawn. All lay sound asleep; the whole of nature was plunged in solitude. Sudhana slept for a moment, then opened his eyes. A shooting star appeared in the sky, flaming brightly. Someone could be heard moving in the darkness. It was a woman. She whispered, "Follow me. I will guide you."

This was a celestial maiden come down from Indra heaven. Wings sprang from his shoulders; he turned into a bird and went flying up into the heavens.

There was no telling how high he had flown, but as night lifted from the face of the Earth far below, not a single detail could be distinguished clearly. There seemed to be nothing at all left on Earth, all was pure emptiness. Finally, the Earth itself vanished completely and the heavens grew dark;

from time to time they flew past stars in the bluish gloom, and various heavenly realms. Sudhana flew on without a trace of fatigue. It was only as they approached Indra heaven that the maiden spoke.

"I was charged to guide you from the world of Jambudvipa. I have guided many visitors, but I have never seen one make this laborious ascent as lightly as you, or follow me so precisely. You must have studied much in order to be able to reach the Indra heaven. The higher you fly, the more mere human strength is unavailing. I could never bring anyone this far before. Either they died for lack of breath along the way or they fell back onto the Earth where they had lived previously. Look, we have arrived."

She had no sooner spoken, than the gates of Indra heaven swung open. The gates were pellucid. The heavenly realm was situated at the topmost peak of Mount Sumeru, in the vastnesses of outer space, and constituted the second of the six heavens of the Realm of Desire. Also known as Trayastrimsa, at its center was the realm of Indra, around which in all four directions lay eight heavens, making up the full thirty-three.

The king's daughter Surendrabha came forward to welcome Sudhana.

"You have labored hard to reach this distant place. I welcome you with all this heaven's joy."

Surendrabha was of outstanding beauty. Her beauty was such that it inspired those beholding it with hopes it would remain eternally, in betrayal of the truth that everything changes. Her words only served to increase her loveliness. They were like drops of water spangling leaves that fall to the surface of a pond. Surendrabha led Sudhana to her room. It was full of the perfume of heavenly maidens. They sat down together, as if they had known one another for years, smiling at each other. The maiden spoke.

"Child, the only thing I have to tell you concerns the Precepts, revealed and not revealed. When they have become part of oneself, they serve to open the gates of emancipation as we practice the Buddha's dharma. Yet the gates of emancipation are not emancipation itself. Once within those gates, you still have to perform innumerable bodhisattva actions before attaining emancipation; thus the gates are not gates but the performance of bodhisattva incarnations, with repeated cycles of birth and death. Only so can there be the illumination in which the Five Accumulations, the Twelve Places, and the Eighteen Precepts are transformed and vanish. Then, practicing the dharma giving entry to the thirty-seven classes of wisdom, practicing the ten perfections and the first steps of all the observances, soon this world comes to perfect harmony. That perfection of harmony can only be attained, though, by one who has passed through all the ancient aeons of the past, the Utpala Flower Age, the Good Earth Age, the Wonderful Virtue Age, the Nameless Age, the Wonderful Light Age, the Inexpressible Glory Age, the Supreme Omen Age, the Sunrise Age, the Excellent Nature Age, and the Wonderful Moon Age, meeting as many Buddhas as there are grains of sand in several hundred rivers like the Ganga."

Only one of them was speaking, yet it felt like the most perfect of conversations. Sudhana felt able to hear more than what she had so far said. She continued:

"Every present moment is a moment that existed somewhere previously. The present moment is always a copy of the past, while the past lives by reason of the present. Once all this heaven and the world below show compassion, thanks to the emancipation you receive and the bodhisattva nature you attain, all will achieve newness, as a present containing countless past aeons. Child, young man, that time is inscribed in your future destiny. The world of that time will be ruled by its children; all the adults and old people will simply play chess, or sing, or yawn.

"In order to work for such a world, the time has come for you to return to Kapilavastu in the world below. Kapilavastu is a rare and wonderful place. True, it is a small, weak city, yet from it arises a fragrant smoke that spreads all over the world. I want you to go and meet the children there. One younger than you is waiting for you. They say that I am beautiful, yet I believe it is only because I reflect your beauty. At the very heart of all forms of beauty lies a beauty arising from liberating emancipation, as well as from illusion. All that is yours."

48.
THE BRAT

UDHANA opened his eyes. He was lying not in a heavenly realm, but somewhere in the middle of the Grove of Five Hundred just outside Kapilavastu! He got up and yawned, as if he had woken up in the same place he had lain down in the night before. He made his way from the grove to a village beneath the walls, where the vaysya people lived, to beg something to eat. He managed to collect some mango gruel, a few steamed roots, and three wild fruits. He gulped the food down quickly, like a bird. After planting the stones from the fruit, he went into the town and asked for the house of Vishwamitra the kid.

"Vishwamitra? That good-for-nothing? Isn't he back in prison again? Anyway, if you go down this alley, you'll come to a neighborhood whose people are a mixture of low-class and outcaste, *achut*, blood. Ask for that Vishwamitra trash down there. And where might you be from, might I ask? Very handsome, I must say...Odd company for a brat like Vishwamitra."

Sudhana felt that this was getting more and more interesting, as he headed for the houses where people lived whose blood was partly sudra and partly outcaste.

"I'm looking for a child called Vishwamitra."

"My, if a mountain hermit hasn't deigned to drop by. Vishwa! There's a wizard looking for you!"

As soon as the urchin called, a youth threw open the rickety plank door of a crumbling mud hut.

"What's up? What's all the racket about?"

It was Vishwamitra the kid.

"Are you Vishwamitra?"

"That's me. Have you come to arrest me?"

"No, I've come to learn things from you."

"What? Learn from me? There's a laugh!"

Sudhana looked puzzled.

"What fools there are! You're no better than a squirrel and look at you, roaming all over the place talking nonsense like this!"

"Vishwamitra! You're supposed to teach me all about Buddha's dharma and the laws of emancipation!"

"What? You fool! Idiot! Buddha? Is Buddha your dad? Your dad's whore! To think of there being people like you in the world. The world's too kind, a heck of a lot too kind. Get out of here. If you want another good fright, try those houses over there. There's a little kid there called Shilpabhijna. Go and get stoned with him, you wretched little pup! What filthy luck I have, today again, filthy. Yuck!"

Sudhana moved away with an acute sense of satisfaction, as if something had just burst. Vishwamitra the kid! Manjushri Bodhisattva? Samantabhadra Bodhisattva?

49.
A VERY OLD CHILD

HE INHABITANTS of Kapilavastu had to endure more sorrows and torments than those of any other city in all the northern regions. A minute city-state squeezed between a number of great nations, it had almost no territory of its own outside the walls. No one recognized the glory of its great families, which had come down from the Himalayan heights, apart from that of the Shakyas.

With the kingdom in such a position, its inhabitants never knew a day without hardship. The tensions with the surrounding nations, as well as within its own ruling class, were ancient in origin. Siddhartha may have been crown prince, but his father Suddhodana was not able to rule particularly well. Like most other rulers and princes, he oppressed his subjects. He merely ended up serving the interests of the rulers of the great kingdoms around his. He is said to have reflected deeply after his son's departure, but still he left no very remarkable list of achievements behind him.

In such lands, sorrows and pains make people far more deeply thoughtful than elsewhere. Pessimistic ideas, that this present world is bound to be bad, abounded; some people became vagrants, despising the world and mocking its folly. That may be why there was such a wide variety of eccentrics in Kapilavastu. Vishwamitra the kid was one. But was he simply an eccentric? Or was it that he reminded Sudhana of Manjushri, or an incarnation of Samantabhadra?

Immersed in thoughts of Vishwamitra, Sudhana walked toward the neighborhood where Shilpabhijna lived. Shilpabhijna was a true prodigy. He was only six years old, yet there was no aspect of worldly ways that he did not know. In particular he had unequaled knowledge of a philosophy

298   LITTLE PILGRIM

based on Indian phonemes. Part of the Buddha's own teaching was rooted in that same science.

Sudhana sat before the young scholar, without asking a single question. There were other visitors before him. They were advanced in age, obviously enlightened brahmans. It seemed that they wanted to hear more from the scholar, for they stayed sitting there although they had already heard his remarks to them. Shilpabhijna's voice was the only childish thing about him.

Listen to the sounds I make.
When I say "A," I enter deeply through a door of Wisdom,
called "Revelation by Bodhisattva Powers that the Essence of
All Dharma is unborn."
When I say "Ra," I enter deeply through a door of Wisdom;
its name is "Detailed Knowledge Appearing Far and Wide until
All Is Infinite."
When I say "Pa," I enter deeply through a door of Wisdom;
its name is "Detailed Wisdom Illuminating Far and Wide
the Equal Age of the Realm of Dharmas."
When I say "Cha," I enter deeply through a door of Wisdom;
its name is "Abolition of Distinctions of Light by Wide-turning
Wheels."
When I say "Na," the name is "No Period Can Be Relied on or
Remained in."

When I make the sound "La," the name is "Abolition of Defile-
ments with the Rejection of Reliance on Nominal Categories."
When I say "Da," the name is "Upaya (strategic skills) that Never
Surrender."
When I say "Ba," the name is "Training-place of the Diamond
Wheel."
When I say "Ta," the name is "Everywhere Perfect Wheel."
When I say "Sa," the name is "Ocean Brightness."
When I say "Pa," the name is "Everything Released and Dwelling
Peacefully."
When I say "Tha," the name is "Perfect Light in Moon and Stars."
When I say "Ya," the name is "All Distinctions Brought Together
in a Pile."

When I say "Shtha," the name is "Light Shining Bringing Passions to Rest."
When I say "Kha," the name is "Incessant Gathering of Clouds."
When I say "Sah," the name is "Great Downpour of Rain."
When I say "Ma," the name is "Rapid Manifestation of Rainbow Light."
They are like a host of mountain peaks.

Little Shilpabhijna had reached that point, when rain began to pour down. The stream running through the town, which had been like a rotting swamp, filled to the brim quickly with the new water. Then the sun came out again, as if to ask if it had really been raining, and all the town's white buildings shone dazzlingly. Sudhana reckoned that this was all caused by the mystic powers of Shilpabhijna's voice, and felt even more fascinated by him. The six-year old Shilpabhijna resumed his teaching:

When I say "Ga," I enter deeply through a door of Wisdom; its name is "Vast Accumulation of Wheels."
When I say "Taa," the name is "Light Without Distinctions, True Likeness Made Equal."
When I say "Ja," the name is "Pure Living after Total Immersion in the Ocean of this World."
When I say "Swa," the name is "Thought of All the Majesty of Buddhas."
When I say "Dha," the name is "Detailed Investigation of the Entire Accumulated Dharma."
When I say "Sha," the name is "Following the Glorious Wheel of the Teaching of the Buddhas."
When I say "Ka," the name is "Brightness of the Wisdom Appearing Before Causation."
When I say "Ksha," the name is "Brightness Yielding Wisdom when All the Oceans of Karma are Brought to Rest."
When I say "Stha," the name is "Unfolding of Pure Light Removing the Defilements of Lust."
When I say "Znya," the name is "Gateway of Wisdom Transcending the World."
When I say "Ha," the name is "Lantern of Wisdom Gaining All Creatures but Without Self or Others."

When I say "Pah," the name is "Majesty Perfecting All Palaces."
When I say "Tcha," the name is "Wheel Covering the Light of
Expedients Bringing Increase of Ascetic Accomplishments."

Then, when I say "Sma," I enter deeply through a door of Wisdom;
its name is "Glory of Seeing Buddhas in Every One of the Four
Directions."
When I say "Hwa," the name is "Splendor of Cymbals Yielding
Powerful Means to Scrutinize All Microscopic Beings."
When I say "Tsa," the name is "Unrestricted Entry into the Ocean
of All Virtues."
When I say "Gha," the name is "Splendor of Strong Cymbals Har-
boring all Dharma clouds."
When I say "Tha," the name is "Making the Sight of the Buddhas in
All Ten Directions Similar to Empty Space by Essential Power."

When I say "Nha," the name is "Entry within the Boundaries Not
Complete So Long As the Wheel of Letters Turns."
When I say "Pha," the name is "Utterly Perfect Place for All Living
Creatures Once Enlightened."
When I say "Ska," the name is "Wheel of Light Shining Far and
Wide Illuminating Every Place by Unimpeded Oratory."
When I say "Isa," the name is "Wisdom Expounding All the Bud-
dha's Dharma."
When I say "Scha," the name is "Entering All the Cosmic Realms
of Living Creatures and Shouting Everywhere the Great Sound of
Dharma-thunder."
When I say "Dah," the name is "Bringing Enlightenment to All
Living Creatures,
Opening Buddha's Frontiers by Speaking Dharma Selflessly."
When I say "Rha," the name is "The Distinctive Splendor Inherent
in All Dharma Vehicles."

Little Shilpabhijna spoke, then he yawned, just like a six-year-old ought
to yawn.
"While I was addressing you, the forty-two gates of Wisdom became my
foundation and all my words flowed freely, enabling me to enter deeply the
infinite, innumerable gates of Wisdom."

Sudhana stepped forward.

"Shilpabhijna, little sage. I want to know how to enter directly into those deep gates of Wisdom, those liberations. Can it only be done by means of those sounds?"

"Either you can attain liberation by using the sounds I have just pronounced, or you can try to practice the ten laws."

"What are they?"

"To possess wisdom; diligently to search after knowledge of the good; to be dauntlessly upright; to abandon lustful passions; to be ever pure in righteous works; to venerate right dharma; to see that the essence of dharma is emptiness; to abolish bad opinions; to practice righteous living; to observe sincere wisdom. Bodhisattva living is not an end to studies; bodhisattva living is the reason for studying."

The six-year-old child rose to his feet. Sudhana and his companions rose too. A crimson dusk was covering the green of the grove's trees with a layer of scarlet. The flocks of flying birds were tinted red and gold, and the whole sky soared aloft, as if formed of precious metals. Shilpabhijna spoke a few last words:

"You see, I have only a very little knowledge of the gates of liberation. Bodhisattvas and Mahasattvas combine the complex laws governing life in the world and away from the world with unusual powers and miraculous arts, sounds, writings, calculations, knowing them without lingering over them; they likewise have deep knowledge of prescribing medicines and casting magical spells, so if any creature has been possessed by a demon, fallen under an enemy's curse, or been struck down by black arts, or if they are being pursued by the dead, have gone mad, or been poisoned in some way, they are able to help them recover completely from all those mysterious afflictions. In addition, they know where to get mysterious gems and rare substances of great price—gold, silver, jade, pearls, gems, coral, sapphire, mani, mother-of-pearl, quartz, agate, copper, iron, zinc, stone, and fine incense—as well as knowing the different varieties and the proper price of each.

"The bodhisattvas keep constant watch over all the places where people live, be it cities or hamlets, fortified towns or royal palaces, gardens, rocks, springs, forests, or ponds. They possess within themselves six hundred and sixty-three different fine appearances. They establish by comparisons which things are more or less admirable. They know how to suffer and heal; they recognize good and bad fortune; they know whether a person will live long or die early, and although they possess so many fine appearances, they know that that is nothing compared with a fine voice, but they equally know that no voice however fine can be compared to true good fortune. They fully realize that the karma bringing a mass of good fortune into being cannot be changed, that the relationship of fruits and rewards is unchangeably decided. They are equally well-versed in astronomy, geography, prophecy, hidden mysteries, the dual principles of yin and yang, phrenology, fortune-telling, bad stars or disasters, catastrophic storms, the calls of birds and animals too. As for travel by land and sea, propitious and inauspicious omens, the rhythms of good and bad harvests, the world's peace and disorder, all the ways of the world are known and utterly familiar to them. They can also distinguish clearly between the various ways of escaping from this world, so that they speak with deep, precise deliberateness after scrutinizing forms and appearances, aware of wills and conscious of names, practicing and acting accordingly. Thereby they gain wisdom in the eyes of all, without doubting, without hindrance, without folly, without dullness, and without care, without failing..."

He finally reached the end of his phrase.

"Just outside the walls of the capital city of Magadha, you will find a small village. A woman named Bhadrottama is living there. I want you to meet her. I have grown very old now."

"What? How can you say you're old, when you're so young?"

"Oh, but I can. I'm six years old. Six-year-olds can be the oldest people in the world, too. Now be off. I have nothing more to say. You're taking all my sounds' gates of Wisdom with you; I'm dead broke. Be off with you."

Shilpabhijna the child sage left Sudhana standing there and walked away. Then Sudhana set off alone, for his companion had decided not to go to Magadha but to Khashi in search of a brahman sage, taking a different road. It was most odd. Quite marvelous, really. How on Earth could a six-year-old talk in that way about Buddhas and liberations of Earth and space? Where had he got that breadth of learning about sounds? And not only sounds; there could surely be no one who could equal him in erudition.

Once again he began walking tirelessly along a long-stretching road. Yet there were far more waterways than roads leading from Kapilavastu to Magadha, all of them impossible to cross without the aid of ferries. Compared with the endless overland routes he had taken in the south, a journey through a region like this, with its constant alternation of roads and ferry-crossings, was immensely more agreeable for Sudhana. First of all, he had traveling companions. Villages and towns followed one another almost without interruption, so that he never found himself in any kind of extreme hardship. He had no need to travel with a pack holding emergency supplies or reserve stocks. Whenever the moment came, he was always able to get a handful of rice in this region, since it had grown accustomed to offering hospitality to pilgrims.

He crossed the Srina River and spent the night sleeping under a tree. Then he crossed another river. Traveling in this way, it took him a full two weeks to reach Rajagriha in the land of Magadha. The moon had grown full and begun to wane in that time. Sudhana at once sensed that the nights in Rajagriha were full of music. Within the city walls, in the groves, and even in darkened houses, no one was to be seen; yet every single person was singing to the sound of an instrument or unaccompanied. Sudhana had once heard from a traveler that the people of Rajagriha recited and memorized not only songs but stories and poems too, passing them on from one generation to the next. Now the city's evenings were not only full of music, they throbbed with history, too.

Sudhana found the night in Rajagriha truly beautiful and he was so happy he could not get to sleep. Moonlight poured down from on high far into the night while the stars dipped close to the Earth, blazing brightly. The stars seemed to want to tell humanity something by their light. One who can grasp their meaning is a true sage. If this is true, there are words waiting to be heard everywhere in the world. One who can hear those omnipresent words is a servant of truth. Sudhana's ear was able to detect virtually all sounds.

On the following morning, leaving behind him the joy that had kept him open-eyed all night long, he left the city by the eastern gate. The fair-skinned woman was easy to find. Bhadrottama was glad to see Sudhana, as if she had been expecting him. She addressed him in a torrent of words:

"Young pilgrim, of all those teachers you've met, not one was fit to be anybody's teacher. You kept asking about bodhisattva ways and the gates of liberation. You've traveled hither and thither, and now all the way here, asking, asking, always asking exactly the same question, always trying to get a deeper understanding of your initial question.

"Young pilgrim, you've got nothing to ask me about. You've got nothing left to ask anybody. Those who ask have already found the answer for themselves as they ask the question. You know very well that your question returns to you as its own answer. If there is something that you still want to know even a single leaf's worth about, go south to the city of Bharukaccha where you'll find a man called Muktasara the wise. He's a goldsmith, so he's bound to have a lot of gold in his house. Yet you'll not find a single scrap of gold in his house."

Bhadrottama's heart contained a great store of affection. Sudhana left before he was able to see just how kindhearted she really was.

50.
CROSSING RIVERS

UDHANA CROSSED any number of rivers. On every ferry-boat, there were plenty of other travelers just like himself: truth-seeking travelers, hawking travelers, as well as homeless, roaming beggar-travelers. However, such a life of wandering was only possible for members of the warrior kshatriya caste or the vaysya caste. The lower castes and the untouchables had to obey orders and could enjoy none of the wanderer's freedom, never putting so much as one foot in front of the other freely, serving the noble classes, the brahmans and kshatriyas, the rulers and the administrators, generation after generation.

The truth about equality that Shakyamuni taught was intended to do away with that system. Naturally, his teaching provoked such intense opposition from the brahmans and kshatriyas that the crowd following Shakyamuni was quickly labeled "a seditious mob" or cursed as "a gang of mindless fools." One brahman youth from the land of Vaishalla had murdered Shakyamuni's disciple, Maudgalyayana. Brahmans swore at the members of the newly formed groups of Buddhists in exactly the same terms as they used for lepers: "That band of beggars, the trash of India!"

The more Sudhana enjoyed the freedom of being able to cross one river after another, the more convinced he became that the wounded existences of all those lower-class people unable to travel prevented his own freedom from being complete.

The waters of the Ubilla flowed deep and green. It would soon flow into the Ganga. As he crossed that river, Sudhana kept furthering his resolve that Shakyamuni's declaration of the equality of all people should be put into practice.

The ferryman was a hollow-cheeked old man from Punjab, his face black as earth. As the boat drifted downstream in the turbulent waters at the center of the river, a youth began to pour out a stream of abuse at him.

"You peasant scum! Just talking to a serf like you is an insult to the dignity of my class. You trash, why don't you drop dead? Old folk like you ought to die and get over into the world beyond or rest in peace, anyway. Why do you have to go on living so miserably, waving oars that you can't even row with? To think that I got into a boat steered by filth like you! It's a disgrace on me and on my father, too! Pshaw."

The youth drained a bottle of wine and tossed it into the river.

"There, that's how you ought to die," and he thrust the old ferryman over the side. Sudhana rose and was about to go to the boatman's rescue, but although old, the ferryman was strong enough to swim out and rescue the oar as it floated away. He grabbed the iron ring at the stern of the boat.

All the passengers clustered round the drunken young man. One traveling peddler advanced with a wild expression, grabbed the youth by the throat, and pulled him to his feet.

"I reckon today's a good day for me to die. You can't imagine how worthwhile it is to die ridding the world of a wretch like you," the peddler shouted. "You're less than an insect. You scorpion-scum born after a scorpion screwed your mother!"

He screamed his remarks and hurled the young man into the river. The ferryman, who had just escaped death himself, made a grab at the young man but the peddler forced him to sit down.

"Let him drown."

The youth came to the surface once or twice, before finally sinking out of sight. A few moments later, his dead body could be seen floating away down the river. All the passengers on the boat felt their hearts grow heavy.

The boat touched shore. Silently, people went their various ways. Sudhana remained alone, standing on the wharf. The boat they had come on was returning without passengers. On reaching midstream, the old boatman very gently slipped from the boat and vanished beneath the water. There was no time for even a single prayer. The empty boat floated off downstream, two oars and a pole hanging from its sides.

Sudhana touched the river that had just brought death to two people and bowed his head. What could be the use of all the truth he had spent his life searching for? He had been unable to say or do anything to stop those unnecessary deaths. He resolved to meet the teachers he still had to meet as quickly as possible, then get away from truth with all its high-blown words and plunge into the thick of human life.

He headed for the city surrounded by flat meadowlands. Muktasara's private guards were patrolling the streets. After going through strict formalities, Sudhana was led to the sage's house in a grove to the north of the city. The sage looked prosperous. Servant girls were fanning him with fans of eagle plumes; he ordered them out. His great girth made it hard for him to endure the heat.

He greeted Sudhana with a story. "In my youth I spent a full twenty years living underground. Down in gold mines, copper mines, tin mines, it's cool, never hot like this. At first, it was horrible, like being buried alive, but the horror vanished after about a month. One day I struck a light from flint to look for something and saw there were insects down there. They were emitting a pale light from their shells. Those insects are called hell-bugs; if an empty space occurs underground they never leave it empty, they settle there. Down below, it's not just solid earth, not all rocks and stones. There are the dry channels of ancient streams, and caves where the ground has split open. And there are living creatures down there, too.

"After I discovered those hell-bugs, I began to think that human beings could live down there for a long time, too. Once convinced of that, I dug out gold with much greater zeal. I lived a mole's life, or rather a hell-bug's, down in that gold mine. When I finally came up loaded with gold, I was so glad to be back that I rushed straight out and the daylight made me blind. I spent another three years working blind in iron and tin mines. Now I've come back to this upper world and live as prey to this wretched heat. And what possible cause might there be for you to have come visiting a fellow like me, young man? Did someone tell you to visit me?"

"Yes, Bhadrottama in the land of Magadha."

"Bhadrottama? Ah, you mean Bhadrottama the Best of the Good. I know that Amazon. She went off with all my gold. She took it without my consent, saying she had to build a monastery to house the Buddha and his disciples when they came to the land of Magadha in the future. A whole half cartload of gold. I'm someone who doesn't so much as nod if a cousin of mine starves to death beside me, yet I was completely bowled over by that Amazon's talents. I spoke to her, I did. I said: 'You brigand of a woman, won't you come and live here with me?' To which she replied that I was destined to go on living with gold and copper, so we'd better wait for some future existence.

"So what do you want of me?"

"I've come to learn bodhisattva works."

"Uh? Bodhisattva? What's bodhisattva? You've come to learn about such things from me? Everything odd seems to be happening today.

"Well, since you've come so far, take a scoopful of copper from over there as you leave. Use it to build yourself a house to live in and come to your senses. That's in return for having been sent by that Bhadrottama woman. Stop wandering around talking rubbish about bodhisattvas and I don't know what else, and once you're in your right mind again, just live a normal life."

Receiving no response from Sudhana, the rich man made a sign to the maid to take Sudhana into a separate building concealed deep among the trees. When he was inside, they bolted the door fast. Sudhana found himself in a dark room. From outside the door he heard Muktasara's voice.

"I thought I'd give you gold to take with you, but you're not interested in things like that, I see. So try eating the darkness in there instead!"

From the stale damp smell lingering in the room, Sudhana could tell that it had been unused for a long time. The floor was made of wooden planks. After a while he heard the sound of mice moving.

Sudhana whispered to himself: "In this world it's always a lie to say you're alone. It is utterly impossible for me to be alone in this world. That's it. I must go out into the very midst of the world. Going out into all those places will make me truly myself. Until now, I was becoming myself by my journeys to various places and teachers."

Locked in the dark room, Sudhana tearfully offered up fervent prayers for all the places he had been in. He began to feel hungry. There was no sign of life outside. He settled into a lengthy meditation. He entered a state of non-thinking, free of darkness and hunger. Plunged in deep meditation, Sudhana dimly heard the sound of the bolt being slid back and the door being opened. The old man called out in a loud voice:

"What have you been doing in the dark? Are you alive or dead?"

Sudhana emerged from his meditation. "I haven't enjoyed such a good moment for a long time," he told him. "Thank you."

Muktasara fumbled for Sudhana's hand and grabbed it.

"Little pilgrim. I am a very foolish old man, unable to enter so much as a single one of the eighty-four thousand doors of your mind. I may have gone south to the gold mines of Madras and Mysore and brought back all the gold I mined, I may have loaded myself with brass, the alloy of copper and tin, and sold it for a high price, but I've acquired no other wisdom since my ancient ancestors came from among the Dravidians. Why do you ask a man like me to teach you?"

"There is something I have learned from you already. I am deeply grateful to you. Beyond thanks, I am obliged to eulogize you."

"Don't drive me into yet further sin."

"Not at all. You are a hidden sage. Your hands may have been full of golden treasures, but you never forgot the treasures of the heart."

"Little pilgrim, I was intending to give you a mass of gold as I sent you on your way. I failed completely to recognize you. A visit from you is a blessing. It would not be right for me to be the only one to receive it. There's a man in this town called Suchandra. In his house there is always light, not at all like the gloom reigning here. Go and talk once with that man so rich in light. I treated you badly and made you starve; if you go there, you can be sure of a generous welcome."

"Not at all. I can never be hungry here. My heart is overflowing with joy, thanks to the virtue you have given me. I have come to realize that the darkness in this building is the best possible place for a person to study."

"It's true that last year a sage called Dharmapari came to practice meditation and yoga here for a while; when he left, he had been cured of a chronic sickness."

Sudhana realized that everywhere in the world, no matter where, is a place of meditation.

Sudhana prostrated himself before Muktasara with an overflowing heart, then set out again. Night was past, daybreak had come. He saw again the death of that old boatman. He thought of how he had taken his boat to come and visit the sage. Muktasara had revealed nothing at all of himself, he was so completely humble. All his words and deeds had been those of a gold miner, as if he had known nothing of the reason for Sudhana's visit. He had merely come into that dark room at daybreak and thrown out a few ambiguous words at random. All he had done was mention the passage of Dharmapari the previous year.

Sudhana's journey took him more than half the day. He obtained a few crab apples from an old woman selling them at the ferry landing. Eating two of them for his lunch, he boarded the boat, which was reserved for members of the warrior caste. Sudhana's class was not checked. With so much mixed blood around, there were bound to be any number of boys with Sudhana's looks.

Everything was behind the times in the lands of Anka and Magadha, renowned for their isolation. In particular, Magadha was never a brahman-istic region, and it quickly became Buddhist. The wealthy Suchandra whom Sudhana was on his way to visit had already heard the Buddha's dharma. Sudhana had a companion, an old man wearing a shabby turban.

"Ah, you wretched little *pratiya!*" he growled at Sudhana.

The word pratiya was frequently used to signify a base or wicked person. It was not unreasonable of Sudhana's companion to speak to him harshly as someone of lowly origin. He had no shoes on his feet and his clothes were certainly not made of any expensive cloth.

"You are a pratiya, too, I think," Sudhana growled back. It was enough to break the ice between them.

"Ah-hah, you're a smart little pilgrim."

"You are quite smart yourself, sir."

"Let's rest. Your feet are hurting."

51.
FRESH WATER FOR THE THIRSTY

ESPITE WHAT Muktasara had implied, Suchandra did not turn out to be a loveable person at all. He was not kind; he did not treat Sudhana like a guest. It was October and it rained every day; the sun had not shone for months in a monsoon season that seemed to know no end in the regions south of the Ganga. All night long there was no sound but the falling of rain. Yet Suchandra's reluctant attitude towards Sudhana was not entirely the fault of the weather. Of course, the arrival of a dripping wet visitor is enough to increase anyone's melancholy.

"Welcome to the lands of rain." The words seemed forced out, yet Sudhana was not worried.

"There is everything in India. It's a marvelous country," Sudhana replied.

"Hmm, there are even people capable of surviving unending monsoons every few months," Suchandra said "What part are you from?"

"Before I met Muktasara, the sage, I was in the north, and before that I made a pilgrimage through the south."

"Look, I didn't ask anything about before or after Muktasara the sage. That fellow is all the time sending me people I'm in no position to sit with making leisurely conversation. What region were you born in?"

"It was where the Jumna, the Son, the Ganga, and the Ghaghara rivers meet; but I lost my parents when the great kings occupied our lands in battle. I was orphaned when I was four years old. But I'm not an orphan now; my body is lodged in the truth taught by Shakyamuni, my home is the triple cosmos, my family the four forms of life."

Suchandra unconsciously rose to his feet, trembling.

"What's your name?"

"Sudhana."

"Sudhana, I've heard about you from the captain of a trading ship down in Kharak harbor. You're the child who walked all the way across the Deccan Plateau. Why, you're just the kind of first class fellow this country needs."

Suchandra's expression became intense. He took Sudhana by the hand and led him down a long corridor away from the entrance hall, deeper into the house. They came to the family's communal bathroom. Immersed in the hot water, Suchandra's ample beard swayed to and fro like water-weed. His body was twice the size of any normal person's, yet flesh and bone were so powerfully built that he did not look fat. It was a very long time since Sudhana had enjoyed a hot bath. Multiple layers of fatigue seemed to melt away.

They could not bring themselves to leave the steam-filled bathroom. Sudhana lingered in the tub, while Suchandra lay reclining on a couch, body and mind relaxed completely.

"Sudhana, I was by origin a brahman, but I know all the suffering my father went through; he was reduced to serfdom among the vaysyas after being left helpless because of the khsatriyas' loss of power. More than any other, the Indian world is marked by suffering. Because of this conflict of castes, I was without hope of ever escaping, thinking that I was doomed to die at the end of a lifetime spent plowing the lands of the warriors as a serf. My father died out in the fields while harvesting. I was only twelve at the time. I went to scatter his ashes in the river, then escaped down it as far as the port at Kharak.

"I got work at a fish store in the harbor. The owner's sister became my wife and I managed to get a small shop of my own. From that day on, I limited myself to one meal a day and began to save. I never so much as set eyes on shoes; I always went barefoot. By the end, I was in charge of six stores. I had sons. The elder went playing on the beach at low tide, the returning tide caught up with him, and he drowned; I don't know what became of the other one. He would have been your age by now. Once they were both gone I realized that the wealth I had acquired was nothing at all. I joined a group of ascetics who believe in the water gods of the Bengal Sea and became a wandering holy man, going with them in their boat. They spend all their time sailing the seas, practicing mortification.

"Two years of that kind of mortification were enough to rid me of grief

at the death of my son. Then I began to think of all the happiness those
two sons of ours had given me as they grew up, of all the love they had
inspired in me. That had been enough. Not even the grief of losing them
both could match that happiness. After that I was able to go back to where
I had come from. I left the port at Kharak, came here and took up farming.
I say farming, but I have no idea where my fields are; it's all in the hands of
my clerks and administrators and stewards."

"But for how long do you intend to hold on to all your lands and riches?"
Sudhana asked.

"What do you mean?"

"Can't you give your lands to Shakyamuni's groups of monks? Then your
wealth will serve to help people who are suffering. The sufferings of those
who have nothing are terrible. I have seen those sufferings in every place
I have visited, south and north alike."

"You are very bold."

"Not at all. Because you and I are here naked like this, we can see that
no matter what anyone in this world may have, they have nothing."

"That's exactly what I have been thinking."

Sudhana saw into the rich man's heart and spoke urgently. "You've
attained your goals. You became the richest man along the Bengal coast
and now you own most of the fertile fields in this region. What more do
you want? Now it's time for you to become rich in dharma, rich in truth."

"Rich in truth!"

"Yes, but in that case you first have to rid yourself of all your previous
wealth. Like rotten meat or a tattered rag."

"Like rotten meat!"

"Yes, only then can you start to amass riches of truth. After all, we have
lived through a multitude of lives before this present existence. What do
you have left from all those past lives? Nothing at all. It will be the same
with today's worldly wealth. Such things really are mere bubbles. Shakyamuni Buddha makes it utterly clear that they're mere foam, utter emptiness. It is a Buddha's task to fill that emptiness with compassion. You and
I, as Buddhas, have to perform that task."

Until this moment, Sudhana had always listened first to the words of his
teachers, but now he himself began to speak.

Suchandra seemed to be holding back his own words, in order to listen
to what Sudhana was saying. Or perhaps he had spoken of his past only in
order for Sudhana to be able to speak now.

"You mean I have to go and find Shakyamuni Buddha?" Suchandra asked.

"No. Not now, anyway. If you wish to join the ranks of Shakya's monks, that wish will surely be realized. After all, he can be found after only a ten day walk from here; there is no problem about it."

"Have you any idea what kinds of disciplines you have to observe if you become his follower?" Suchandra wanted to know.

"First you have to study how to arrive at bodhisattva ways and the gates of liberation. There are ten kinds of laws."

Sudhana got out of the bathtub. He was cooking in the hot water. He continued teaching.

> The ten laws are:
> never to refrain from good knowledge;
> never to forget the thought of seeing the Buddha;
> never to neglect to go in search of the good knowledge of Buddhas and bodhisattvas;
> never to neglect to serve and venerate them;
> never to turn away from those who preach knowledge of the good with much learning and wisdom;
> never to refrain from listening to the ways of perfection;
> never to refrain from listening to teaching concerning the practice of enlightenment;
> never to abandon the three gateways of liberation;
> never to refrain from the four laws where Brahma-deva dwells; and
> never to refrain from the essence of all wisdom.

"Can I gain present enlightenment?" Suchandra asked.

"Yes, surely. You need only experience the heart of the Prajñaparamita, the Perfection of Wisdom, and if you and it are in harmony, you will gain enlightenment into all that you see and understand."

"And if I simply hear talk of Prajñaparamita, can I gain present enlightenment?"

"Not immediately. You have to have knowledge of the true essence and nature of the whole dharma before you can gain enlightenment into the Perfection of Wisdom."

"You mean the *tathata*, the thusness, of supreme enlightenment? Can't we gain enlightenment just by hearing mention of tathata?"

"Oh, no. You can never gain enlightenment just by hearing. There's a story: one summer's day in a vast desert without springs or rivers, a man is walking from the west towards the east when he meets someone coming from the east. He asks, 'I am thirsty now; where can I go to find water and shade?' The one coming from the east replies, 'Keep heading east; you will find the road divides to the left and right. If you take the road to the right, you will reach a shady oasis, and a spring of cool water'. What do you think? Will that man be able to quench his thirst just by thinking of going?"

"Obviously not," Suchandra said.

"Right," Sudhana continued. "Bodhisattva living is just the same. You cannot gain enlightenment into the entire dharma just by hearing, thinking, and understanding by wisdom. The desert is the reality of birth and death. The man coming from the west is every living being, experiencing the three poisons of greed, anger, and folly; the one coming from the east dwells in all wisdom as Buddha, as bodhisattva, with an equal knowledge of the nature of the entire dharma and having received a sincere will. To take the cool water and be freed of thirst and heat is to be enlightened for oneself as regards that true path."

"That makes sense."

"Let's leave here now. You led the way in, now I will lead you out."

Suchandra was happy as a child. "Today I have at last been freed of the melancholy I have suffered from for so long. Thanks to your teaching, I feel infinitely happy."

Sudhana and Suchandra left the bathroom and returned to the entrance hall. Outside, the rain was pouring down as if it would never stop. The monsoon season's humidity soon soaked into Sudhana's refreshed body. They drank cups of hot tea.

Suchandra spoke: "You've already heard about my past, but there is something from even earlier that I want to tell you. There is something I can recall from a previous existence. Before being born here as an Indian in this present world of Jambudvipa, I was a human being, too. Only then I lived on the other side of the Himalayas, as a Tibetan.

"I was a shepherd in the Tamilta basin. Though I was a shepherd by calling, I played the flute so well that reports of my skill filtered out into the world beyond. I received my master's permission to go as far as the capital city, to take part in a flute-playing competition. While I was there, I met a peddler from beside the Indus who had come round the western end of the Himalayas, crossing the Pamir highlands. He invited me to go with him to see somewhere better than Tibet, so I went back with him over the Pamir highlands.

"We nearly died there but survived and reached a great city on the banks of the Indus. Alas, misfortune was awaiting the peddler who had brought me there. He was murdered by youths belonging to another tribe, in revenge for having killed a man from their clan in days gone by. So there I was, a complete stranger, a starving orphan, alone in that terrible heat, unable to speak or understand a single word of the language. Then a criminal who was on the run persuaded me to go with him to Simla in the Punjab. From there I fell in with people moving further and further east and journeyed on, until I fell sick in a cave somewhere and died.

"Yes, I died there. The life after that was this present one. I became an Indian in my new existence."

"You know, you were able to become an Indian in passing from one life to another," Sudhana told him, "but for a creature to become a Buddha and set out on bodhisattva paths is a matter of this present moment, once the heart has made a firm decision. That is why Shakyamuni, after his first sermon, caressed the disease-ridden body of an untouchable who had come to him. As he touched him, he said to his first three disciples, 'Behold, here is India's Buddha.' At once the sickness went out of the poor wretch and he became a follower of the Buddha."

"Fine words indeed."

"That man had already received recognition from Shakyamuni, but nonetheless, he insisted on starting his studies from the very beginning, as the most ignorant disciple would. He prepared the food for the community and did the washing up after they had eaten; he would go on lengthy errands at times when it never stopped raining, like here now; or enter forests teeming with poisonous snakes to gather rare mushrooms; or late at night, he used to draw water from streams when the mud had settled, all the time asking the Buddha's other disciples about how to study well. The ten kinds of law he asked about then are still remembered today."

"I would like to hear what they are."

"Since the bodhisattva way includes ten laws leading to liberation, they are the Laws of Liberation."

Suchandra sat upright, uncrossing his legs, listening to Sudhana's words.

"The first is to shun every law that does not lead to good; the second is to never fail to keep each and every one of the Precepts laid down by the Buddha; the third is to shun all lust and envy; the fourth is always to offer all veneration to the Buddha; the fifth is to practice every kind of virtuous work; the sixth is to pursue wisdom; the seventh is to cultivate all proper means of spreading the dharma; the eighth is the pronouncing of the great vow; the ninth is to observe fully all renunciations; the tenth is to culti-vate assiduity in devotion. If a bodhisattva practices these ten laws fully, a deep and far-reaching illumination of liberation cannot fail to arise."

Sudhana made a complete prostration before Suchandra, in sign of admiration. Suchandra likewise made the deepest prostration possible before Sudhana. The two of them remained with their brows pressed to the floor, as if unable to tear them away again. At last Sudhana raised his head and spoke almost inaudibly.

"Master Suchandra, indicate where I should go."

Sudhana spoke in what seemed a baby's fretting tone. Suchandra responded in a kind of lullaby.

"Be off with you. You are to meet Ajitasena, whose name signifies 'Form That Knows No End.' There you will find a bottomless ocean. Pour out water and fill it."

"I will. Here, too, the rain is falling into a bottomless ocean; perhaps in that place it will also be raining."

"I'm off to look for that Shakyamuni Buddha you told me about. Either in this life or the next; if not in the next life then in a later one, on another shore."

52.
A Night with Ajitasena

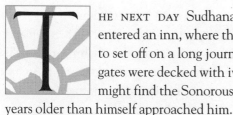

HE NEXT DAY Sudhana crossed the river Prana and entered an inn, where the carts of some merchants about to set off on a long journey were parked. The inn's huge gates were decked with ivory. He was inquiring where he might find the Sonorous City when a young monk a few years older than himself approached him.

"I live in the Sonorous City. Last night a great magnate there, Ajitasena, received a message from Suchandra in a dream; that's why I've come out here this morning. In the dream, Suchandra said that a child pilgrim was on his way, that he should not wait to open the door to him, but send someone to meet him at the river crossing and respectfully accompany him. Now and then Suchandra and Ajitasena meet in their dreams like that, in spite of the great distance separating them."

The Sonorous City lay a hard day's walk from the place where they had met. They walked with rapid steps, like scurrying animals, dust billowing up from beneath their feet. It was late at night when they arrived at the foot of the enormous city walls. As they approached, a murmuring had become audible and now the sound was loud. Yet the villages below the walls lay peacefully plunged in untroubled sleep.

The city gates swung open and Sudhana followed the young monk down the main street. Along both sides of the road, great fir trees stood in weighty silence. The street was spread with sand that shone white in the dark.

Ajitasena was extremely rich but he only took one meal a day. At first he had become rich by selling chariots and arrows, swords and spears to the neighboring cities when there was war between them and his home city of Shiapara. He had been a tight-fisted miser. When his uncle lay sick and dying, he refused to pay for so much as a single dose of medicine. Then one day, a young assassin from his home city broke into his bedroom and plunged a knife into the bed. Ajitasena survived because he always slept in an adjacent room, as a precaution in case anyone broke in. He hastily pulled at the bell cord and the assassin was caught in the garden.

After a whole week's interrogations, Ajitasena learned that the youth was the son of Sadaham, who had been like a sworn brother to him when he was a child. One month later, the young man stood before Ajitasena and spoke out boldly.

"You have made yourself rich by betraying your native city. The rich have no birthplace, no fatherland, I know. That's why I was given the job of killing you."

"How many other gangsters are there behind you, villain?"

"You get your power from wealth; I get mine from justice. Threaten and torment me as much as you like, trying to find out who is behind me. You'll not get so much as a single mustard seed out of me. You'd better hurry up and die. Die before you can kill me, and be reborn in another world as a nice little animal. Villain, you call me? You're the villain."

Ajitasena screamed at his subalterns: "Take him away and cut off his head!" They dragged the youth out, but along the way Ajitasena's men took to the city's sewers with the youth and escaped from the city through a drainage outlet. On hearing what had happened, Ajitasena received such a shock that he fell sick. He kept having nightmares, in which the young assassin appeared and plunged a knife into his throat.

When at last he was able to go out again, he'd repented for his past ways. He gave out food to the beggars and poor folk at the city gates, and to the untouchables, as well as setting up places where they could live in his vast forest domains. He sent numerous gifts to his original home city of Shia-para, together with titles to land and to farming rights.

He sent for famous brahman scholars, but as he was listening to their teachings, he heard that a new teacher, Shakyamuni Buddha, had arisen, who was more excellent than the brahmans. He made visits to a Buddhist monastery in the highlands where Shakyamuni was then living, learned the "Middle Way" of Buddhism, accepted the Precepts and became a deep believer in the dharma. Now, ten years later, his virtue in the Way had become as famous as his wealth. People generally gain virtue by disposing of their wealth, but he had gained virtue and wealth together and was considered to be at the same time master of wealth and master of the dharma; he came to be known as "Old Double Master."

Sudhana rested well in a guest room, then on the following morning paid a visit to Ajitasena, who was already an old man.

When Sudhana came in, the old man muttered, "Why, he's just like Sadaham's son. How long destiny stretches, to be sure."

Sudhana caught nothing of what he said. He showed absolutely no interest in the wealth that Ajitasena had accumulated but simply stood there in front of the old man and laughed innocently; truth so obviously had nothing to do with wealth and riches. Without even asking him why he was lying down, Sudhana remarked: "Yesterday I found my ears were no longer working, because of the noise from this Sonorous City."

"Surely it doesn't matter how much noise there is; it won't bother you once you're used to it. And then again, the Buddha's dharma is the same. Perhaps what we call the Buddha is something that we make in our own image."

Sudhana replied, "I have already heard all you want to say from master Suchandra. You always tell people to dispel everything that would shatter their thoughts of living justly, to banish to distant lands all that kills those who live justly. You also tell people to scold the idle and to get rid of women who dress in white. You teach ten laws of dismissing and banishing, but I think you tell people not to banish to distant lands creatures unable to rid themselves of their possessions? That means you teach eleven laws, not ten."

"Eleven laws, you say!" old Ajitasena mumbled, trying to understand Sudhana's words. He was an old sick man who had at last cast aside like a sloughed skin the authority with which he had for years dominated everybody. It was certainly hard to understand how he had had power enough to persuade even the lord of the Sonorous City to bestow riches on him.

Ajitasena did not send Sudhana away; they spent the rest of the day together. His eyes opened and closed while he lay there, unaware of the passing hours. Finally, he sent a servant girl to fetch the manager responsible for the daily running of his estate. He was out inspecting orchards and opium-poppy patches outside the main domain but he jumped on a horse and came galloping home.

"In the next few days I want you to distribute everything I own," Ajitasena told him. "Give some to my home town and the rest to the people in and around this city."

The major-domo started to protest but the old man silenced him.

"My lips have learned not to speak two different words; that includes not saying the same thing twice."

The major-domo glared at Sudhana, as if to say, "This villainy is all your work."

Sudhana considered that he had no reason to stay there any longer and rose to his feet. Ajitasena gazed up at him, then addressed him affectionately.

"If you go out of the South Gate, you will find Dharma village. Living there is the brahman Shivaragra. It does not matter if we meet once a year, once every three years, or once every four years, it's always as if we had met only the day before; he never changes. Most brahmans despise the dharma. They call it 'beggars' nonsense' and us 'seditious rabble,' but he's not like that. Nowadays, brahmans are like wild beasts; they swear that the dharma and Shakyamuni Buddha must be gotten rid of. The brahmans' days are over, though. Go and see Shivaragra. He's a far better teacher than I am. I'm mere straw compared to him. He's a butterfly flitting high above the straw."

Sudhana left the mansion unaccompanied, refusing any help in finding his way through the city. The estate around the house was so vast, he had to pass through nineteen intermediate gates and eighteen little gardens. As he emerged from the Sonorous City, the constant noise suddenly stopped. The people out working in the fields exclaimed that it could only mean that Ajitasena had entered the Paradise of Bliss. They had been convinced that the sound emanating from the city was in fact the sound of his breathing.

Dharma village was a haven for old people. Despite frequent epidemics and poor standards of living, there were more than thirty centenarians living there, while another ninety were over seventy. In contrast, children were few and far between.

Shivaragra emerged from his house during a break in his afternoon meditations. He was a hundred years old. Sudhana approached and observed the proper decorum by circumambulating about him once to the right.

"Sacred master, I beseech you to instruct me."

"How can the whole world be expressed in a few words? In the course of the lifetimes that have brought you here, you have already attained bodhisattvahood; what can an old brahman like me teach you? Just spend a few days here before you go on. Resting is a kind of study, too. You say you're Sudhana? I met Manjushri Bodhisattva once. In a grove on the banks of the Jumna River. He talked about you. He was worried to tears, wondering where your travels had taken you, what teachers you'd met."

"Manjushri Bodhisattva!" Sudhana's heart jumped.

Shivaragra didn't tell him that Manjushri had been so concenered about the little pilgrim that he had made some inquiries into his past. He found that Sudhana's name meant "good fortune" and it had been given to him because the villagers said that at the moment of Sudhana's conception, a jeweled tower rose from the ground in the courtyard of his parents' great mansion, sheltering a hidden treasure. When the child was born, again the tower with its treasure had appeared, this time a visible treasure of five hundred vessels bearing jewels, clothing, and food.

But there was no need for Sudhana to know this. Determined to draw the child's fortunes away from material wealth and toward the dharma, Manjushri had taught him the Buddha's commandments before sending Sudhana out on his interminable journey.

Shivaragra had a playful, impish grin on his face. "I made a joke with Manjushri back then, too. I said, 'You mean Sudhana's your son. After you left home and gained all that wisdom from the Buddha's dharma, didn't you make another kind of prayer and go with a woman? Isn't that how he was born?' That's what I said to him, but you know, he paid not the slightest attention. He just went on thinking about you, about whether you would be able to walk on the scorching roads, and whether you were wearing sandals, even if they were only tied on with string.

"I'm glad you've come. You must have walked over quite scorching roads on the way. Rest your feet for a while in Dharma village. Forget about hearing lessons from a worn-out old brahman like me."

But the centenarian talked on and on. "You know about this place. They say that if you once pass this way, you gain an extra ten years of life to practice your piety in. Won't you express such a wish, young as you are?"

He laughed. The old brahman was a master of vows. An initial yearning, banishing passion, leads to the blooming of a flower. Then by prayers and vows for the attainment of truth, each living creature advances towards bodhisattva truth. So the yearning grows vaster. That yearning is no illusion or fantasy, no mere night's dream. Or if it is a dream, it is the dream of every living creature. Sudhana felt convinced that the brahman Shivaragra knew absolutely everything about the stage he had reached. That was why the hundred-year-old brahman could be satisfied with nothing but heart-to-heart conversation. Sudhana limited himself to the exchange of a few words, as fish occasionally rise to the surface of a stream, then sink again.

Shivaragra pulled out an antique string instrument and played a tune. The bliss shining on his aged face suggested someone who never had to worry about getting milk as a baby, who never had to worry about food while growing up. Yet in fact he had been an orphan, and for long periods he was nothing but skin and bones on account of wars and droughts. He had never known anything that might be termed youth, until he had risen in caste, thanks to a distant relative who was a brahman, and had embarked on a life of ascetic observances.

His tune went on. Looking closely, it became apparent that the aged fingers plucking the seven strings had no nails. Sudhana recognized that even in this world's havens of bliss and peace, there is no one that does not bear a past history and previous lives marked by pain and struggles with poverty. The brahman sang, accompanying his tune:

> If there's a river, it can be crossed.
> Why say that river cannot be crossed?
> If there's a river, it can be crossed.
> I'll make a little boat—
> a big boat would take too long.
> If there's a river, it can be crossed.
> Ah, surely the loveliest thing of all
> is a newborn babe crossing a river
> at its mother's breast.
> If there's a river, it can be crossed,
> it can surely be crossed.

He stopped playing and closed his eyes. Soon, he had fallen asleep. Sudhana removed the instrument, then he climbed up on to the empty couch in the center of the spacious room and lay down. The couch was made of woven reeds and cooled his body.

The old brahman Shivaragra and Sudhana dreamt a single dream and took leave of each other.

"You have nothing more to learn, Sudhana. Just a few more visits, and the way of bodhisattva living will open before you."

"Not so, I am still far from that."

"Ha! Not at all. Until now, you have been traveling around in search of truth and the dharma, visiting various masters, but really you were paying visits to yourself, instructing yourself. How do you expect me at my age to speak empty words to you?"

"I am ashamed, deeply ashamed."

"Well yes, of course. In the presence of truth, in the midst of truth, we always feel ashamed."

They slept for a long time. Shivaragra normally woke early to begin his meditations but that hour had long passed. An elderly brahman from the adjacent room wandered in and shook Shivaragra. "Children sleep so soundly," he muttered.

53.
A CONVERSATION UNDERGROUND

ECEIVING HIS LAST LESSON from the old brahman, Sudhana found himself reflecting: "Ah, surely if my journey is once finished, I'll have nothing left to do? Not at all. Then I'll be one with every living creature in the immensities of the Buddha cosmos; I'll sing and dance with them all."

As he walked away, Sudhana thought of the wise people he had met who had managed to live as they had. Each had become his teacher, and had been like a flower in full bloom. It was as if Sudhana, in his journeys as a little pilgrim, had been visiting flowers rather than finding teachers. Yet it might also be true that the flowers that had appeared before his eyes could only be flowers because he had entered the way of bodhisattva living. Everything seen with bodhisattva eyes blooms as a flower of bodhisattva life.

Sudhana recalled a story one of the sailors had told him:

There once was a rich man who was hardened by greed. He ordered the wretched food his servants ate to be limited to one meal a day. Seeing that, the great god Indra transformed himself and took the rich man's form, while he was away enjoying himself. He entered the house, opened the storerooms, called all the servants together and tearfully addressed them: "I have treated you harshly all this while, but at last I have freed myself of my greed and repented for my treatment of you." Then he invited them to take anything they liked, be it jewels, land, anything.

After that, Indra, still disguised as the rich man, turned to the mistress of the house, their children and relatives, and the servants: "Soon the incarnation of the greed I have rid myself of is going to appear, looking just like me. You must beat the villain and drive him away."

The master of the house duly returned. The men keeping the gates beat him black and blue and drove him away. "You wicked pack of greed. Away with you!" Their shouts could be heard as far as the borders of his estate. The greedy master, full of resentment, went to find a friend and the two of them managed to enter the house together, only to see another master exactly like him sitting there.

Then his wife and children set about him with sticks and clubs, screaming: "You wicked pack of greed, can't we get rid of you?" Driven out a second time, he went to the king and appealed for help. The two masters presented themselves at the palace and the king spoke. "Let whichever of you is the true master produce some secret sign to prove it." The master of the house at once lowered his clothes to reveal a hidden mole. The disguised Indra showed an identical mole. The king thought of another test. He pretended to order the execution of the man's youngest daughter. Both masters burst into tears.

With that the king gave up, lamenting, "I'm just an ordinary mortal, there's nothing more I can do." He commanded them to go to the Buddha, who was reported to be travelling through a neighboring kingdom. So they went to present themselves before the Buddha.

As they reached Jetavana-vihara, the Buddha saw them coming and exclaimed, "A god in disguise!" At once, Indra resumed his true form and vanished. The greedy man was left standing alone. The Buddha told him, "Now go home." But he stood there lamenting, "Even if I go home, there's nothing left, so what's the point?" Then the Buddha said, "You can give all you have to others and stay with me, if you wish to make such a vow."

He made that vow, then returned home. There, he found that all his accumulated wealth had been restored. From that moment the householder cast off his greed and began to live for others.

The old brahman Shivaragra had given Sudhana only the simplest directions: "Look for some friends in Sumanamukha. They will be holier teachers than I am," and Sudhana had set out on another long journey. Crossing a region where the Ganga divided into numerous branches, he again headed southward. The city of Sumanamukha he had been told to visit would not be easy to reach. Although he did not know it, the road to the

city was not Sudhana's alone. Another young pilgrim, named Samantavyuha, whom Sudhana would never meet, was on his way there, too.

The old brahman had sent Sudhana on the same path as Samantavyuha
for a reason. In a world aeons before, Samantavyuha had witnessed the
virtues of a former Buddha and from him had received understanding of
the depths of concentration. In gratitude, Samantavyuha had composed
this song:

> Like a thousand suns rising
> and suddenly shining forth,
> dear lord of Boundless Light,
> you are difficult to meet
> even once in boundless aeons.
> I gaze up at you as at the sun.
> I stand here in your light
> and my anguish melts away like ice.
> What joy! High above all joys,
> the joy that fills my heart.

A Buddha of an earlier age, on hearing this song of praise, had said to
Samantavyuha: "You have done well, little Samatavyuha! The sentient
beings of all ages to come will rely on you. You will purify this world with
your light and your compassion. I am overflowing with joy, for a mind eager
for awakening, a *bodhichitta* mind, has arisen within you. I have only one
thing to add: You will only be able to complete your task by attaining the
power of assiduous devotion."

His teaching about assiduous devotion was virtually identical with the
main contents of what was to be Shakyamuni's last sermon in a later age,
contained in the pages of the Mahaparinirvana-sutra:

Everything in the world is heading towards destruction. You must fix
your minds, without negligence, on truth.

The old Brahman had seen that Sudhana's pure and innocent child's
heart was almost identical with that of Samantavyuha in that aeon long
ago, when the world of the Garland Sutra had revealed itself. In the same
way, with their equal possession of a child's heart, there could be no difference between Sudhana and his many teachers in the southern lands, in the
Deccan Plateau and along the course of the Ganga, apart from the difference of age and profession.

Sudhana's itinerary kept changing. He would travel by night for a few days, then by daylight for a while. Disoriented, at last he encountered a phantasmagoric guide. As they journeyed on together, he found he had left the surface world and was once again in the underworld. He descended deep, in a trance with no thought of how he would return.

This underground world lay hundreds of fathoms below ground and consisted of an enormous carnival. Humans and all kinds of creatures fraternized together down there. There bugs and ants, wild cats and monkeys living with Dravidians, and predators from the southern forests lived with the other creatures without harming them. Turtles stood erect like giraffes, having fun as they attempted to dance, most unskillfully. On closer inspection, swarms of ants all clustered together could be seen dancing, as well.

Glancing to one side, Sudhana found a group of snails and inchworms singing in harmony:

> You will see how majestic
> are the countless Buddha worlds
> that lie in one single atom,
> in a single pore;
> yet how like an illusion!
> Can lies exist in this realm of dharma?
> Can truth be like an illusion?
> How majestic, the countless Buddha worlds!
> You will see.
> After seeing,
> you will hear.
> After you hear
> eight thousand hymns sung in reality,
> you will know they are like an illusion.

In one place, a group of blind old men were dancing in a circle and singing:

> The future Maitreya
> dwells in blind darkness.
> Though it be darkness,
> Stars, moon, and sun are surely there.
> With eyes closed,

faraway places can be seen
as clearly as if nearby.
Buddha-tree flowers can be seen
blooming there,
lovely Buddha-tree flowers can be seen.
Ah, you come to put an end to every life's pain.
Today's true Wisdom,
putting an end to every life's pain.

Deeply moved by the blind men's dancing and singing, Sudhana noticed a group of fresh young girls and boys holding hands and dancing, a little way away. His guide had disappeared and Sudhana realized that this was a world peopled by illusory phantasms. After finishing their dance, the boys and girls split up and went in small groups to sit on the hills of their underground world. One girl emerged from among them and headed for Sudhana.

"You've come a long way!"

"This world of yours is a happy place," Sudhana responded.

"My name is Shrimati. Let's go over there, to where young Shrisambhava is."

"Ah, Shrisambhava, Shrimati," Sudhana spoke their names in tones of deep respect, "I have attained a heart ready for the ultimate awakening but I still am not clear as to how a bodhisattva should perform bodhisattva deeds to advance along the bodhisattva path. I beg you to instruct me."

Hearing his words, Shrisambhava replied so rapidly that his words nearly overlapped with Sudhana's question: "How can we know the full extent of your great pilgrimage after truth? Ours is merely the condition of phantasms, an incomprehensible condition of selfhood, one that goes roaming all over the country, concealed behind visible realities, united with reality's pain, distress, and sorrow, the facts of mortality, old age, sickness, and death. That heart of yours that asks the question is best equipped to become our answer. After all, even liberation is a phantasm. How could we know anything that is not a phantasm?"

The power contained within those few words was such that Sudhana abruptly grew taller and began to radiate light from every part of his body. He had a song poised on his lips, ready to express all he felt, but Shrimati whispered earnestly to him in a clear voice: "Master Sudhana, once you leave here, passing the swamps and plains to the south, you will reach the sea. On the shore, there is a vast garden known as Samanta-vyuha Park and in the midst of it is a tower called the Hall of Vairochana's Solemn Adornments. There resides Maitreya Bodhisattva. This underworld carnival is about to vanish; this place will turn back into a world of darkness waiting for the carnival yet to come."

Sudhana spoke, "But what about all these joyful dances and songs?"

Shrimati whispered again to Sudhana, smiling. "I wish I could follow you, but I have work to do with Master Shrisambhava. We have to reveal anew the invisible world of pure Buddha nature to all the creatures that have come here, before we send them on their way."

Sudhana took his leave, circumambulating three times round her. Observing that Shrisambhava was some way away, busily giving good advice to a number of people, wild beasts, and tiny creatures, Sudhana reckoned that it was not necessary to say good-bye to him, and left without further ado.

He set off up the incline leading out of the underworld without any guide. It was dark but he was able to find his way even in the dark, thanks to the light filling his eyes.

Emerging from beneath the ground, he stood for a while on the surface of the Earth with closed eyes. He found himself on a road lined with palm trees. The tang of the ocean had already begun to penetrate his nostrils. The sun was blazing strongly, but the burning heat was tempered to some extent by a breeze coming off the sea.

He had no sooner passed a white sandy beach and set off down the highway, than Samanta-vyuha Park appeared. As he entered it, he could see the Hall of Vairochana's Solemn Adornments, a tower soaring up until it touched the sky. It was not built by slaves at the command of some lord or rich potentate, or by the labors of prisoners of war. It was said to have arisen uniquely through bodhisattvas' virtues and wisdom, as they offered up the power of their thoughts and their vows, their unconditioned freedom, and their supernatural gifts for the sake of all living creatures.

This was the tower where Maitreya Bodhisattva resided. As soon as Sudhana pressed his brow to the ground beneath the tower in veneration, the tower's teaching communicated itself to him. Sudhana began a lengthy poem of praise to Maitreya Bodhisattva.

After Sudhana had finished reciting fifty-five poems, Maitreya Bodhisattva welcomed him and recited one hundred and seventeen poems in his praise. This Maitreya, who deigned to dedicate such lengthy poems to a lit-

tle disciple coming on a visit, was himself still very young. In his last incarnation, Maitreya had brimmed with the most prodigious premonitions,
like the blazing rays of the setting sun, more than any of the Buddha's other
ten great disciples. Shakyamuni had prophesied that the world that would
come after his, the Dragon Blossom World of the final Buddha Maitreya,
would be more sublimely beautiful than any other future age, thanks to the
sorrow occasioned by his own death.

On visiting Maitreya Bodhisattva, Sudhana was able, for a brief
moment, to experience in the present something that still lay five billion
six hundred and seventy million years in the future. He sighed deeply.

54.
A Teacher From the Next World

LTHOUGH SUDHANA had set out along a level highway the very foot of the majestic tower was swathed in a mass of clouds. Sudhana had slept through the night at the foot of the tower. An elderly man was busy sweeping up scattered fragments of cloud. Finding that to be an odd sort of employment, Sudhana cautiously ventured a question: "Are those clouds you're sweeping up?"

The man kept sweeping.

"They are clouds, aren't they?" Sudhana persisted.

"You sloughed off scab of a guest, can't you use your eyes? If these aren't clouds, what are they?"

Sudhana felt snubbed: "In that case, we must be up in the mountains!"

"You think this is a mountain? Not at all. This is the outer yard of the inner courts of Tushita heaven. The topmost pinnacle of the Hall of Vairochana's Solemn Adornments rises in this garden. You thought you were walking along an ordinary road, but it wasn't, it was the road to heaven. Clouds are sometimes called the shadows of wisdom, but sometimes they're just the dregs of obscurity."

Sudhana was completely at a loss. Could he really have taken a road leading up to heaven? During his travels in the south, he had heard a report that Maitreya had fallen sick and died while still only a child, after a short life marked by wonderful talents, asceticism, and compassion. So was the Maitreya Bodhisattva in this Tushita heaven a bodhisattva yet to be born into the present world? Or was he now a bodhisattva waiting for the next age, having already died one last time and returned to his home here? A voice, seeming to come out of one of the building's pillars, provided a response:

> This tower is a place drawing one aeon into all, all aeons into one.
> This tower is a place drawing one world into all, all worlds into one.
> This tower is a place drawing one dharma into all, all dharmas into one.
> This tower is a place drawing one creature into all, all creatures into one.
> This tower is a place drawing one Buddha into all, all Buddhas into one.

The little pilgrim ceased to consider it strange that he was up in the sky, here in Tushita heaven. Inspired by the voices emerging from the pillars, Sudhana became a poet and began to improvise a set of fifty-five new canticles.

Just as Sudhana had finished singing, Maitreya returned to the Tushita heaven from the world below. The young Maitreya came accompanied by a phoenix with golden wings and a snake-headed Mahoraga. He was surrounded on all sides by heavenly beings—dragons, the four heavenly kings who guard Indra's Brahma heaven, and a hundred thousand living creatures. The bodhisattva Sudhana had come to meet arrived after him and came to him from outside, not inside the tower.

Advancing before him, Sudhana fell at his feet. Immediately, Maitreya spoke Sudhana's praise in a thunderous voice, reciting no less than one hundred and twenty canticles. On first meeting this nameless, wandering child, he had responded to the child's praises by far longer hymns of praise. It was a moment of intense emotion.

"Bodhisattva, oh, bodhisattva," Sudhana kept whimpering and could not help breaking into tears. As he wept, he made repeated prostrations, innumerable prostrations. He had never made so many in his life before. Each prostration was full of multiple other prostrations so that in the end he must have made tens of thousands.

Sudhana could feel that Maitreya would one day emerge as the ultimate Buddha of Love. Then he would redress this present world and reveal it as a world made new, emerging as the Buddha of the Dragon Blossom World as it opens towards infinity in all directions, seated beneath the *Naga-pushpa*, Dragon Blossom Tree. For the time being, Maitreya would travel here and there, visiting every place, while the suffering of creatures grew more intense. The creation of a new world could never come about without wandering and fumbling. The chaos the cosmos experienced in its initial myriad of aeons was no different.

Maitreya Bodhisattva led little Sudhana toward the Hall of Vairochana's Solemn Adornments, the door of which opened at a snap of his fingers. There, everything belonged to the world of the innumerable. There are no words to describe the stately jeweled palaces and balustrades within it, while innumerable udumbara flowers, innumerable padma blossoms, innumerable kumuda flowers, and innumerable pundarika flowers bloomed in gorgeous profusion. There were drawings portraying the course of Maitreya's present and past lives, that could all be taken in at a glance, as well as portrayals of the innumerable forms in which he had manifested himself. And more. Far more.

Maitreya Bodhisattva at once included Sudhana among his followers, uniting him with them in one community by a blazing shaft of light. They breathed in harmony together, in such extreme joy that clouds of light blazed from his every pore, billowing forth like drifting clouds. Yet Maitreya knew he could not retain the young pilgrim at his side. He was obliged to send the wanderer on his way, for after this he still had to meet his first teacher one more time, Manjushri, the Bodhisattva of Wisdom, and his last, Samantabhadra, the Bodhisattva of Practice.

As Sudhana left Maitreya, first circumambulating him several times to the right and bowing to touch his feet, their two childhoods had become one. That oneness would bring about his meeting with Manjushri. Their relationship stretched far into the future, so now Maitreya, for whom this parting was far from easy, placed his beloved Sudhana in a cloud chariot and sent him back Earthwards.

As he approached the Earth, Sudhana gazed down at the Himalayas, spread in a majestic panorama below him. As he dropped towards the Earth's lacework of rivers brimming with pure water, Sudhana made a promise to himself: "In order to hear one single word of doctrine spoken by the Buddha concerning bodhisattva works, I am prepared to hurl myself into a Buddha cosmos full of flames and endure the torment of the fire."

The surface of the world was a sad and lovely place.

Sudhana's heart was beating faster than ever, faster than a sparrow's heart: he was going to meet his first teacher, the Bodhisattva Manjushri. At last! Maitreya had just returned from spending time with Manjushri and Sudhana had fully agreed, with nothing either to add or subtract, with all the praises of his first teacher he had heard during his time in the Tushita heaven.

The more Sudhana's mind was filled with thoughts of Manjushri, his first teacher, the more those coincided with thoughts of young Maitreya. Now that Maitreya Bodhisattva, his most influential teacher, had become his friend, Sudhana's heart grew increasingly alert.

Sudhana had reached the point where a meeting with Manjushri had become inevitable. A long-lasting affection had preserved the innocence of both master and pupil.

Sudhana recalled Maitreya's words in praise of Manjushri, addressed to the deep recesses of his heart.

"Good boy, little pilgrim. I will show you what kind of bodhisattva your teacher Manjushri is. I will show you how he has penetrated the practice of Samantabhadra Bodhisattva and become perfect."

Maitreya had caressed the little pilgrim's head and shoulders as if he were his own brother as he spoke. He had delivered a solemn eulogy, yet spoken in tones light as the sound of a babbling stream.

"The vow made by Manjushri Bodhisattva lies beyond the reach of the other ten thousand billion myriads of bodhisattvas. Ah, little Sudhana, his practice and perfect performance are amazing, while his vow has been so often repeated it knows no bounds. He is a bodhisattva indeed. His wisdom does not mean he is foolish in human terms; he is a bodhisattva in whom wisdom is exactly identical with physical reality.

"What person is there, no matter how senior, who can go down to the lowest place and fetch up the highest wisdom, as Manjushri Bodhisattva has done? Manjushri Bodhisattva has been the mother of ten thousand billion myriads of Buddhas, the teacher of ten thousand billion myriads of bodhisattvas. He was not content to stop at that degree of wisdom. From ancient days in times long past he has entered into a state of liberation and fulfilled all the works of Samantabhadra, until none can tell which is Manjushri and which Samantabhadra."

Sudhana recalled the sound of Maitreya's voice. It had made Sudhana's heart tremble, dropping ever lower at first, like a rushing stream, then like the whisper of the wind scouring mountain heights, or like raucous voices of farmers outside city walls as they celebrate with songs, after harvesting the corn, shaking their shoulders and dancing in circles.

Joy at the prospect of meeting Manjushri and sorrow at parting from Maitreya mingled in Sudhana as he boarded a skiff at twilight to cross the

Ganga, at a point where its width was not too great. The oar creaked and spread a pattern of ripples over the flowing water. Fish rose, made slurping noises, then sank again. They seemed to be bidding him welcome and he greeted the little creatures in return.

Sudhana headed for a village where lights were already shining here and there in the dusk across the silent riverside lands. He did not bother to go in quest of a place to sleep. He found a mound of straw, onto which he simply threw himself. When Sudhana awoke, a pair of eyes was gazing down at him; they belonged to the daughter of the nearby house.

"There are two empty rooms in our house, and yet you sleep here like this?"

The girl seemed to be reproaching him, even as she expressed her pity.

"Thank you for your concern."

"What concern? We deserve a severe punishment for not having welcomed a visitor correctly. I'm going to prepare breakfast for you; I beg you not to refuse. Come along. First you can wash your face."

He followed the girl into the house. It was a prosperous house, not brahman or kshatriya caste, but its tidy yard was full of the simple dignity of those frugal folk who treasure every last grain of corn, in the belief that it is theirs as a gift from above.

Sudhana hungrily ate the food he was offered. Sumanamukha was still far away.

55.
MEETING WHILE FAR APART

UDHANA SPENT one more night in that place. The daughter of the family inhabiting the main house was a cheerful girl, bubbling with memories of previous lives. She gave Sudhana new clothing as simply as if they had been brother and sister.

"Those clothes you're wearing are too shabby for someone going back to visit their teacher. You should have new clothes, ready to contain a new heart."

Sudhana was puzzled. Still, as soon as the girl had put the clothes down and gone out, he changed into them. They seemed to have been made for him. His body adjusted to its new dress.

"That's better. Now you are ready to meet your first master again. You met him before, by the stupa in Salavana, the sal tree grove necropolis near Kushinagara. When you are in old clothes, no fresh joy arises on meeting truth or teachers."

"What? Have you seen my master the bodhisattva Manjushri? How do you know that I am his disciple?"

The girl laughed. Sudhana took his leave of the girl and soon arrived in front of a huge dolmen, half a day's walk from Sumanamukha city in the land of the Universal Gateway. From the slope where it stood, there was a wide view out over any number of rivers, marshy swamps, and plains. The view was made more striking by the almost complete absence of trees. Sudhana wondered where the Buddha's monastic community of disciples might be now, that band of followers founded by the sage from the Shakya clan. No doubt his teacher Manjushri must be among them as they moved on, never able to stay in one place, like a ship on the river.

Sudhana awoke from these thoughts that seemed to rise echoing from the vast plains lying before his eyes. Now his heart's deep longing was all centered on his first teacher. His daily existence had always been directed toward the future, yet now everything else was powerless before the memory of that moment in the distant past when he had met the master, a tiny wartime orphan in a grove surviving alongside the ruins left by war.

He was longing for his teacher, when suddenly his master's hand stretched out from a far-off place, one hundred and ten *yojanas* away, and caressed his head as he stood there. A teacher is always in touch with his pupil, and the love between them has such power that it sometimes seems the master could caress his pupil's head from far away as if he were close beside him. Now that had become a reality—and not only his teacher's hand; his voice echoed from very nearby, between the sound of their breathing.

"Well done!" How Sudhana had been longing to hear those two words. "Well done, Sudhana. As long as you live you will be able to fashion skeletons with piles of stones and teach them the way of harmony. The day will come when one by one those stone skeletons will come to life and dance for joy at the law of the identity of all things you have attained."

Sudhana felt embarrassed but was obliged to hear his master speak his praises.

"If you had not possessed deep vows and belief, how could you have survived the long ordeal of visiting all those teachers in the southern realms? Surely, at some point, you would have turned aside and given up, overwhelmed with immense fatigue. Or you might have been content to make do with the few fruits harvested in the course of a small number of visits, giving up the ascent of the mountains on which the greater fruits are found.

"If that had happened, you would never have been able to do the works contained in the nature and principles of the dharma, never have been able to perform the works involved in coming to know everything, knowing a little, knowing deeply, and then knowing the essence so completely that you enter and possess it. Sudhana. Well done!"

Sudhana could never forget the initial jubilation with which he had begun his journey. It had been his life's first joy. There are ten lands that represent the ten stages of arduous formation required for a bodhisattva to attain the supreme enlightenment, and the first of them is *pramuditabhumi*, the Land of Joy.

However, to attain this first land of joy, there is no avoiding the strenuous ascent through the ten grades of faith, the ten steps of wisdom, the ten lines of action, the ten goals, and the forty steps. Sudhana had already fully reached this stage in previous lives; accordingly, he was able to enjoy so chaste a rapture at the very beginning of his earthly pilgrimage. At the height of his ecstasy of joy, he had truly seen every kind of flower blooming in the Avatamsaka realm, amidst the limitless expanses of the whole world's heavens, as far as the infinite horizons of the desert.

By the end of his pilgrimage in the south he had attained the second land, *vimala-bhumi*, the Land of Purity, the third, *prabhakari-bhumi*, the Land of Radiance, the fourth, *archismati-bhumi*, the Blazing Land, the fifth, *sudurjaya-bhumi*, the Land Hard to Conquer, and the sixth, *abhimukhi-bhumi*, the Land in View of Wisdom.

With the attainment of the sixth land, *prajña*, enlightening wisdom, is perfect and complete. In other words, perfection has been achieved through self-discipline to one's own great benefit. Beyond this point, by attaining the seventh land, *durangama-bhumi*, the Far-reaching Land, the eighth, *achala-bhumi*, the Immovable Land, the ninth, *sadhumati-bhumi*, the Land of Good Thoughts, and the final tenth, *dharmamegha-bhumi*, the Land of Dharma Clouds, it becomes possible to pass from self-benefit to the perfection of works of altruism. Immediately ahead of him, one step away and blocking his path like a vast abyss under a dawning sky, lay the ultimate state of buddhahood. Sudhana had now reached that stage.

Sudhana turned his mind from these abstractions and instead requested his master for further teaching, with an artless question.

"Master, how did you arrive at your present exalted position in the world?"

The question was less a question than a query full of his desire to share for a moment the love arising from all the truths that they had experienced together in one common heart as master and pupil, although they had never once met again. Manjushri was delighted with Sudhana's question, which came like flowers blossoming in a flowerless spot, it was so bright and clear.

"My dear Sudhana. Once any bodhisattva achieves the ten dharmas, they reach my world at the opportune moment."

Sudhana pressed him further: "What are those ten?"

"You know them already: the first is perfection by illumination in the unborn dharma; the second is the dharma that is never abolished; the third is the dharma that is never lost; the fourth is the dharma that never comes and goes; the fifth is the dharma that lies beyond words; the sixth is the dharma that can never be expressed in words; the seventh is the dharma spoken without conceits; the eighth is the dharma that cannot be spoken; the ninth is the silent dharma; the tenth is the holy one's dharma. Once any bodhisattva has perfectly mastered these ten, they enter my world at the opportune moment."

Sudhana drew from his unconscious mind images of the scene when Manjushri, obliged to leave the company of the Buddha, had spoken about the truth and the worlds to a gathering of two thousand or more at the foot of the great stupa in Salavana, the grove of sal trees to the east of the city of Punyaprasavas. He combined that with his own memories of his first meeting with the master as an orphan, soon after the end of a battle. He finally got an answer to one of his recurrent questions: the essential bodhisattva task and the things he had suffered were one and the same. He had another question for Manjushri.

"Master, what do you mean by your world?"

"It is the place where all bodhisattvas are."

"What is the place where all bodhisattvas are?"

"The first and fundamental principle is the place where all bodhisattvas are."

Until he had reached the fifth of the ten lands, *sudurjaya-bhumi*, the Land Hard to Conquer, Sudhana's confidence in his own grasp of the truth had often wavered. Once there, he attained a state in which there was no more wavering or turning aside. From that point it was possible to reach a position of self-perfection in a state where there was no more dwelling in cycles of life and death, and no dwelling in nirvana, either.

Sudhana could now fix his sights on the world of altruism, since he had entered the decisive state of awakening by the experience of a reality without birth and death, an absolutely irreversible state, the state of no-birth. From that moment all bodhisattvas made of clay and sand could crumble, because he now possessed the wisdom of a diamond bodhisattva that would never dissolve in any wind or stream.

Sudhana cast a glance towards the ancient stillness lingering along the lotus-studded edges of a little lake, then followed his master away from that spot beside the dolmen outside Somana city. Among all the thoughts flashing like lightning through Sudhana's mind, the foremost was the highest principle. Actually, that first principle itself was the teaching he had received from his very first teacher. It followed that Manjushri Bodhisattva must be the embodiment of the first principle.

It was late when they paused to take their meal; the sun was already setting beyond the network of rivers, canals, and marshes that stretched as far
as the eye could see. It could scarcely be called a meal, consisting as it did
of the sparse victuals Sudhana was carrying in his pack, yet master and pupil
considered it a veritable banquet.

"This is very good."

"It's food I got before coming here."

"Very good."

The master repeated the same words several times. As he did so, he gazed
at where before them the river ran white as if swollen by rain, perhaps
because they had made mention of heavy rain as they talked, for the
weather had so far been clear. Then he spoke to Sudhana very quietly. If it
had not been for Sudhana's sharp ears, only the void might have heard.

"There is just one person left for you to visit. After all, the search for
supreme awakening is not for yourself alone. Don't bodhisattvas seek it for
the benefit of all sentient creatures? But where will you go to seek it? I have
received food from your hands, now my work on your behalf is done. How
I have waited for this day."

His teacher spoke in sorrowful tones. Sudhana could not reply to such a
master in any brilliant ornate form of address. He might have lips, but no
words emerged from them. The sun had reached the western horizon. For
one last moment its disk blazed crimson. Then the whole world seemed to
have been dyed blood-red. Flocks of birds flew across the crimson sky in
orderly formation.

The master had stretched out an arm across one hundred and ten yojanas
from a far-away spot to caress his pupil Sudhana, then that one hand had
become a whole body accompanying Sudhana. Now he withdrew his hand
again across those one hundred and ten yojanas and Manjushri disappeared
from Sudhana's side, leaving no trace.

Time flowed on. Sudhana stood still, not uttering a word, facing the
place where the master had been sitting. The master had been there! Sudhana recalled the simple way his master had kept repeating, "It's good, it's
good, very good," as they had shared that makeshift meal in the light of the
setting sun.

On the following morning, Sudhana felt no trace of fatigue as he opened
his ears to the songs of the dawn's busy birds. He had been in such a state
of stillness that he could no longer hear the sound of the river fretting once
in a while in its course. He murmured to himself.

"Why, those water fowl have greater freedom than I have."

The complete thoroughness with which Manjushri had vanished from before Sudhana, leaving not a trace behind, had perhaps been intended as a kind of silent lesson, to the effect that now wisdom had to be transformed into love and practical care for all living creatures. Perhaps that was the final lesson.

Only one problem lay ahead of him. That was his meeting with Samantabhadra Bodhisattva. Sudhana himself was now advancing as a bodhisattva, no longer as a mere child seeker. Having successfully completed each and every stage of his quest, his bodhisattva way had begun. The end was the beginning.

His final meeting with Samantabhadra Bodhisattva would signify that his bodhisattva way had indeed begun. First, though, he could not avoid the experience of standing there alone, having cast off Buddhas, instructors, and all else. It was an icy sensation of solitude, like standing on the peak of a high mountain and being swept by a chill wind rising from below. Or rather it was like that new dimension of solitude felt when first we rise and stand on two feet, after crawling on all fours since birth.

In order to discover where Samantabhadra Bodhisattva might be, Sudhana first aroused in himself a new yearning for the world.

56.
ONE DROP OF WATER IN THE SEA

N THE BUDDHA's solemn assemblies, Manjushri's wisdom always shone out on his left, while on his right, Samantabhadra's will for action reached towards the darknesses of all living creatures. For the little pilgrim, encountering his first teacher, Manjushri Bodhisattva, at the end of his long journey through every kind of storm and vicissitude, came above all as the confirmation of the truth he had discovered. Sensing acutely how important it was, Sudhana's emotion was such that he was unable to make any distinction between the two bodhisattvas, uniting the wisdom of Manjushri with the practice and love of Samantabhadra. Great Wisdom, Great Liberation, Great Pity, Great Practice, if divided, always blend into one again.

When Manjushri, Sudhana's first teacher, advised him to meet Samantabhadra Bodhisattva, Sudhana was filled with a childlike yearning; Manjushri had given him advice not as a teacher but as a bodhisattva and an equal in bodhisattva standing. Samantabhadra Bodhisattva! At present he had no further need of hymns. This was bhutatathata, the essential thusness, beyond all words, that constitutes the fundamental enlightenment.

In this present world, Samantabhadra had been born as the son of a mixed-race family of farmers, the third grade of the vaysya caste, and he had passed through a number of ascetic sects before converting to Buddhism and becoming the bodhisattva of practice. He, the foremost of all bodhisattvas together with Manjushri, not only possessed all the virtues of practice and action, he could even lengthen lives. He was usually depicted mounted on a white elephant or meditating, sitting on a lotus flower throne.

It so happened that once, when the Buddha was already growing old, he was on the point of leaving the Sitavana grove that formed part of the cremation ground just outside the royal capital where he had been staying; it was a place inhabited by the low castes. Someone set loose two mad elephants outside the north gate of the city, in the hope that they would trample him to death.

Samantabhadra Bodhisattva had saved his teacher in that moment of crisis, uprooting an old tree and blocking the path of the maddened elephants as they came charging towards his master. A nightmare from the previous night had repeated itself in reality; Samantabhadra's very dreams were acts of samadhi.

By now, Sudhana's longing for his fifty-third encounter with Samantabhadra had reached such intensity that it began to shine in his heart like a bright beacon of fire. He saw Samantabhadra's image contained in the flames. Sudhana was filled with wonder, as he attained a new stage of bodhisattva life, *dharmamegha*, where the clouds of dharma drop endless dew.

Samantabhadra Bodhisattva now appeared before him, sitting on a lotus throne before the Buddha. The throne was the same as the one on which the Buddha sat, for he served the Buddha known as the cosmic Buddha, Vairochana, while he himself held the rank of a nirmanakaya, a Buddha incarnate in human form.

Samantabhadra Bodhisattva was surrounded by a crowd of some two thousand disciples. At the center of the crowd there were bodhisattvas, celestial beings, monks, nuns, and lay devotees of both sexes. They included a cluster of children even younger than Sudhana, gazing up at Samantabhadra as they sucked milk from their young mothers' breasts.

Sudhana stood in the midst of this assembly, as Samantabhadra delivered a sermon on the opening section of the Garland Sutra. As soon as he had finished, he stretched out a hand and caressed Sudhana's head.

"You've come at last! Good, very good boy!"

The words were accompanied with a smile full of love and joy. He climbed down from the lotus throne where he had been sitting, in token that he was welcoming Sudhana as a fellow bodhisattva. They and all the people assembled about them broke into rapturous smiles.

"Sudhana, Sudhana Bodhisattva!" Samantabhadra spoke the young pilgrim's name as if in confirmation. Then he murmured to himself, "How lovely the world is, with such a bodhisattva in it!" He turned to Sudhana. "When did you see me before?"

Sudhana was almost too immersed in joy to reply. His reply was his joy. "I saw you when I first saw Manjushri Bodhisattva."

"That is very true."

It was time to eat. The community only ate once a day, shortly before midday. With bodhi trees casting their shade across the dry grass, the place was not too hot. Samantabhadra gave Sudhana a share of the food, which members of the crowd had received by begging. It was rough fare, and there was very little of it, yet all—bodhisattva and monks and laypeople—began to eat contentedly. Sudhana duly followed suit and ate. The bodhisattva chewed each mouthful a hundred times before swallowing, and every time he swallowed, he looked at Sudhana and smiled brightly.

"While we are eating, there are many people starving. Helping them, giving them food, is part of the bodhisattva's task."

Until now, Sudhana had never heard such words. Bodhisattvas and teachers had all spoken about "dharma" and "truth" or "the universe." They had mentioned living creatures and the need to succor them, but talk like Samantabhadra's, of how creatures were starving, was certainly a great rarity.

"It would not be right if the so-called supernatural powers I have achieved did not bestow the ability to see where people are starving. What place can there be for truth if people have nothing at all to eat? Not that creatures can live by bread alone; there also has to be the food of truth, the food of dharma, the dharma's offerings of food."

Sudhana composed a very short poem in his heart:

> Without a mouthful of food to eat,
> how can compassion be received?
> How can compassion be given?
> How in mutual compassion
> can one flower emerge?

Samantabhadra had been given responsibility for delivering sermons, while the Buddha was away for a few days in company with his senior disciple, Kashyapa, the younger Ananda, and Subhuti. Now the morning sermon and the midday meal were finished, so he took Sudhana with him to a grove, where they rested their limbs and relaxed for a while.

Samantabhadra Bodhisattva pillowed his head on his arm, with a sign to Sudhana to do the same. Master and teacher had become the closest of friends, in a relationship completely unmarked by formalities. Every last trace of authority and deference had melted away.

"Little bodhisattva!" Samantabhadra spoke quietly. "Just as you journeyed for so long from place to place in the southern realms, meeting teachers and attaining bodhisattva status, so I, too, have been born and have died, been reborn and died, since long ages ago, through many lives, with enlightenment as my goal. Yet on reflection, the fact that I have completed my works and vows as a bodhisattva following the Buddha amounts to nothing more than a drop of dew brought into being by long practice of devotion. You must have seen how lovely a drop of water looks as it pearls in the heart of a lotus leaf. It amounts to nothing more than that. In all that time I have seen countless Buddhas; I have attained countless enlightened hearts, performing every kind of worship and offering, practicing every kind of good wherever I went, without pause, as our breathing never stops.

"Sudhana Bodhisattva, now you have seen me, you must also see my true Buddha nature. In that way you must be born again within my dharmakaya."

"But Bodhisattva, can I really be born again within your true nature?"

"Yes. For it is none other than Vairochana Buddha. Vairochana is the pure, essential Buddha nature."

At that moment Sudhana saw that every one of the pores on Samantabhadra's body, and all the minute pores hidden within his body, were each filled with innumerable Buddhas. Around each of those innumerable Buddhas, crowds were assembled like clouds. Sudhana had now become capable of seeing such microscopic realities with his ordinary, weak eyesight.

Samantabhadra Bodhisattva had almost nothing left to say to Sudhana. Perhaps that was his way of transcending the distinction between emptiness and being.

"Listen carefully. Pure essential Buddha nature cannot be measured against anything or likened to anything in any world whatever. Every comparison is just so much trash, for Buddha nature transcends all worlds, beyond emptiness and being alike.

"If anything, it is like a dream, or like a picture drawn in the void. Listen carefully. Even if you could count the number of drops of water comprising each wave that breaks on the shore, could you ever count a Buddha's meritorious achievements?

"I have one last thing to say, Sudhana. You are equal to the Buddha and all the bodhisattvas. Henceforth, the people you encounter will not be

Buddhas and bodhisattvas or any kind of teacher, they will each and every one of them be a living creature that you will have to meet with wisdom and compassion."

Samantabhadra Bodhisattva had spoken, breathing deeply between each phrase. Now he rose.

"I have finished."

He caressed Sudhana's head one last time, then resumed his place on the lotus throne. The light shining from the bodhisattva's back as he went out into the sunlight was not a mere reflection of the sun, for mingled in it was a light shining from within himself. The result was like dazzling sunlight and subtle moonlight. Clearly, bodhisattvahood was light.

Until now, Sudhana had always known where to go next on leaving a teacher. One master had invariably indicated the next. But now he had no further need of those directions and promptings. Sudhana's lengthy journey had reached its end.

Blessing of fifty-three teachers!
Blessing of having visited
innumerable places!
Now, with that blessing complete,
blessing of the road I must pursue for myself!

Samantabhadra was an ancient bodhisattva, adorned with the accumulation of the many sacrifices he had made in many different worlds. Sudhana would imitate him in turn. Samantabhadra Bodhisattva! In him were concentrated the compassionate works found in all bodhisattvas. Among the followers of Shakyamuni Buddha, he was always to be found working in the Buddha's shadow, while the light streaming from his body was such that even his shadow dazzled every eye.

It was Samantabhadra who finally accomplished the proclamation of the Garland Sutra in the course of eight assemblies, held in seven different places. The first and second were held in the plains of north India, the third in Trayastrimsa, the fourth in Suyama-deva, the fifth in Tushita-deva, and the sixth in Paranirmita-vasavarti-deva, all in the heavens. Once his teaching had established a metaphysics capable of uniting heavens and Earth, he returned to Earth in a final act of vicarious offering, and the seventh and eighth were held here, the last in the central Indian monastery of Jetavana, where the Buddha and the first community often sojourned.

This last section of teaching even included the tale of Sudhana's lengthy pilgrimage! Now Sudhana had attained all that had been prophesied about him in the final portion of the Garland Sutra. He had nothing more to expect from Samantabhadra, the originator of the Sutra, for he had reached the state of utter liberation and detachment.

Sudhana felt a wind blowing from every direction. When he faced east, it was an east wind; if he turned to face the north, it became a north wind. When he faced south, the wind came blowing from the southern regions he had traveled through for so long. His body was wrapped in winds from the four cardinal points, from all eight directions. Sudhana stood there in the wind, in such poverty that apart from his pure being itself, there was nothing anyone could hope to receive from him. Then the winds enabled Sudhana to hear their voices. By them he came to understand that he was being called for in many parts of the world.

He perceived that the wind coming from the east was laden with the tang of the sea. That was a smell he had grown familiar with in the course of his journey up from the south along the coast of the Bengal Sea. He gazed heavenward. The sky was completely empty, with no trace of the heavenly realms. Since there was nothing stirring within his heart, of course there was nothing visible in the sky. One huge bird floated by; it was a Himalayan kite, a species that had never been known to frequent those parts. It seemed to have no intention of ever moving away. It hung poised in one spot, unfamiliar, its huge wings spread wide.

With a child's curiosity, Sudhana wondered how a bird from the Himalayan regions could possibly have flown this far. He only knew that he had recalled the sea by its smell, and by the Himalayan kite he recalled the towering mountains, that soared up and up until they touched the sky. Then, instead of heading back towards the mountains, the kite flew off eastward. With a start, the little bodhisattva realized that the kite was indicating the direction he should go. He felt intensely hungry. For no apparent reason he also felt intensely sad. Too sad to cry. That sorrow spoke to Sudhana:

> Little pilgrim!
> Now
> your path
> has opened in heaven,
> has opened on Earth,

has opened in the midst of the sea
toward a greater land
toward a greater world
than any you have so far attained.
Little pilgrim!
How could your path
be limited to that alone?
Ah, your path
lies open before you—
as multiple as the grains of sand by the Ganga,
as long as an asankhyeya kalpa unending age,
an ayuta myriad in number,
an indescribable wonder,
infinite in quantity,
lasting a moment,
a split second,
one ksana flash—
your path lies open as zero quantity.
Ah, your path is yourself!
Can a single hair ever grow
anywhere on your body?
Little pilgrim!
For ever
and ever the same
little pilgrim, never growing old!
Will there ever be,
anywhere in this world,
samadhi awareness as deep
as that in your young heart?
You, little pilgrim,
are the first embodiment of truth.

Sudhana found himself completely alone. There was no teacher left for him to visit. His was a mature sorrow, caused by a state of masterlessness. In the end, the samadhi of Manjushri, his first teacher, and of Samanta-bhadra, his last, had been nothing but expedients to bring Sudhana to himself. Or had it all been nothing more than dreams?

When he had met the lady Maya, he had longed deeply to meet her son,

Gautama Buddha, but now he could wait for him no longer. It was almost as though the teachers he had met had all been the Buddha. Besides, it might be several years before the Buddha returned to the community now presided over by Samantabhadra Bodhisattva. He had left to go preaching in the west, where epidemics were reportedly widespread, the roads thickly strewn with people starving in a famine resulting from recent wars. The Buddha and his companions had gone into the midst of all that suffering.

Sudhana simply told himself that he would meet the Buddha and his followers some other time, not now, and set out on his own journey. He headed east. His path lay in exactly the opposite direction from the Buddha. As the river entered its lower reaches, countless tributaries flowed into it. Downstream, the water seemed to expand, surging against the banks as if it would overflow its bounds.

"Hey, little wanderer!" A voice called him from a boat out in midstream. "If you go that way, there's nothing but the ocean cliffs. You'd better come aboard my boat."

The speaker was an eighty-year-old boatman, his face deeply wrinkled. The boat touched shore and Sudhana climbed in. Beneath the glow of the setting sun, the boatman spread the sail and the boat hurried seaward.

57.

FOR THE UNKNOWING WORLD

RAIN BEGAN TO FALL as the little pilgrim recalled what Samantabhadra, his last teacher, had said. His last words had been, "I address you as nothing more than a single drop of water in the limitless ocean of buddhahood."

Through his lengthy journeyings, he had acquired an experience and knowledge of the world that those who have not made such a journey cannot imagine, no matter how hard they try. Sudhana's heart was firmly lodged. No one can look into the world's abyss and remain unchanged. In appearance, the little pilgrim was as young as ever, but soon his accumulated knowledge would begin to transform his physical appearance.

He felt a deep melancholy as this inward change began to effect an outward transformation. His earlier dream of setting off on a long journey and perhaps meeting the Buddha at some point in the future was growing dim. Wasn't he going in the opposite direction to that taken by the Buddha and his followers? What kind of fate was waiting for him in the eastern regions beside the Bengal Sea? His new encounter with sorrow meant that his memories of innocent joys seemed to be fading into a previous existence.

The boat bearing the little pilgrim sped down the lower reaches of the river, borne along in midstream by the powerful current. The old boatman simply held on to the rudder and nodded quietly, almost asleep. At the sight of the sleepy old boatman, Sudhana found himself able to put his sorrowful feelings to rest for a while.

Sudhana began to nod, too. The boat hurried onwards, while the two of them nodded themselves asleep, completely detached from the boat's speed and the current carrying them along. By the time Sudhana woke, they had passed the estuary where river water and salt water met, and he

was drenched by the moist ocean air. Behind him, the boatman was awake and was staring back at the distant coastline.

"Have you done with dreaming?" The old boatman spoke gruffly, "Even when you wake out of a dream, you're still in a dream. No matter how deep the life of devotion you led, was it anything more than games in a dream?"

The old man interrogated him insistently.

"So where do you intend to go next?"

Sudhana made no reply.

"Here we are, out in the open sea. If you don't want to go on living, you only have to give the sharks a chance. Bengal Sea sharks are famous for their ferocity. Once, a friend of mine fell sick; he asked me to take him on board. I brought him here and plop! he jumped in. The sharks' fins came racing along in a flash. Do you know why I'm telling you all this without you asking? It's because there are a few last words I want to say, before I offer myself as food for the sharks."

"What do you mean?"

"This is the end of me. Once we're dead, all our ancestors and all the people of the Ganga basin end up here in this ocean of death, floating down as scraps of bone or ashes, if not as naked corpses, all intent on taking leave of this world. I'm off to the home of the dead down under the waves. If you have somewhere to go, take this boat and go there; after all, you boarded it in the first place because you had somewhere to go, didn't you?"

Sudhana heard almost nothing of the old boatman's babbling. After his visits to so many different teachers, he was still in a stupor, with no real concern about what might be going to happen to him next. Even sacred sayings were like nothing more than mirages looming between the waves.

But when he heard the boatman say that he had come out into the middle of the sea to put an end to his life, Sudhana fixed his eyes on him. The boat they were in was not very old. Prow and stern, and the mast, too, all were freshly painted; there was nothing old or worn in sight. It was a boat that would last a hundred years, capable of surviving in any of India's rivers and seas.

A flying fish soared above the listless waves then plunged down. Again, there was nothing but the waves. Sudhana was gazing out at the point where the fish had vanished, when he felt the boat rock slightly and looked behind him. There was no sign of the old boatman, in the boat, in the waves, or anywhere. While Sudhana had been looking in the other direction, he had slipped into the water. There had been no splash. The rough stone that had been lying at his feet had vanished, too. He must have tied a rope round the stone, fastened the rope to his waist, and dropped with it into the sea.

Little Sudhana Bodhisattva made several circles in the vicinity, awkwardly manipulating the oars after raising the tiller. From now on he would have to sail the boat himself. He took a while to reflect on the death of the boatman. He sensed that he would have had something more to say about the way he was going to separate himself from life by dying. The man had gone as he had resolved to go. Now Sudhana was forced to be a very awkward boatman out in the open sea.

He soon acquired a certain skill in manipulating the oars, but he had great difficulty in getting the sail up. The boat kept rocking from side to side, but finally the sail was up and once it had caught the wind and was billowing nicely, he fixed it securely. The waves began to slap sharply against the boat's prow. Driven by the wind in his sail, he turned away from the sea and headed for the distant shore, visible as a mere white line with a trace of green above it, the green being all that could be seen of the coastal forests.

He entrusted the job of getting there to the boat and entered a state of deep concentration. A voice reached him from the depths of the sea, brought by his meditation.

> Sudhana, you have already witnessed one death.
> There was no trace of his impending death,
> yet there can be no doubt that the man who was with you
> has quit the world.
> Sudhana, you could not go after him as he died.
> No matter how great a bodhisattva you are,
> there has to be something in this world you cannot control.
> Suppose you set your mind on knowing everything in this world,
> then the fact that, all unbeknown to you, there is something
> or some place in this world you cannot know
> would veil completely your attainment of purification,
> on account of your misguided conception.
> If you were to penetrate rashly
> into the very core of the truth about life,
> how could you bring anything new into this world?
> You have to return from here onto dry land
> and set out towards the unknown creatures you will meet there.

Did that mean that little Sudhana would continue a life of wandering? Did it mean that before him stretched a life of traveling, on top of all the journeys he had so far made? Sudhana recognized at once that the words reaching him from the sea, rising from thousands of fathoms below the surface, were a message from the dwellings of the dead.

He abruptly realized that he was very hungry and thirsty. A wave striking the prow splashed against his legs and he came to himself. Looking up, he saw that the boat had come close to the shore, the east Indian coast with its vast stretches of sand, overshadowed with palm trees, mango trees, blossoming trees of all kinds, growing in such profusion that no matter how hard the east wind might blow, it was tempered into a gentle breeze by the time it reached the world beyond the ancient barrier of trees, with its paddy-fields, swamps, and meadows, its roads and rivers busy with carts and boats.

The little bodhisattva looked for a spot to tie up the boat; a harbor lay farther to the south. There he lowered his fine boat's sail and tied the painter to a bollard on the quay. The luxuriant woodlands behind the village were somehow summoning Sudhana urgently. Leaving the harbor behind him, he took a road leading into the forest.

He was weary from the hours he had spent adrift at sea, so once he was deep in the forest, he spread a layer of withered plants on the ground and sat down. Ferns and other delicate flowerless plants grew beneath the trees, never touched by sunlight. His heart felt utterly peaceful, as the young bodhisattva settled into the lotus position beside a tree and enjoyed a time of rest, deeply absorbed in meditation.

A little later he quietly opened his eyes at the approach of jabbering voices. A group of about thirty people belonging to the lowest, achut, caste appeared. They were despised untouchables, one passing touch from whom was thought to defile. Yet the Buddha had welcomed them as equals. Rising to his feet, Sudhana greeted them. They simply blinked their huge dark eyes, not saying a word. These were innocents, with no innate sense of the distinction between words and silence. They had big mesh bags full of fruit slung over their shoulders. Some were carrying long ladders, poles, and other implements.

Sudhana walked briskly past them as they stood there. His way lay before him. The little pilgrim had completed his journey. It had brought him to sublime heights. As a consequence of his immense pilgrimage, from Manjushri at the start to Samantabhadra at the end, he had attained bodhisattva stature. Now he had unlimited freedom, utterly unrestricted freedom of choice. He had crossed the sea to faraway worlds and encountered the creatures there. Until now, his teachers had been of various classes and kinds but each had been the same, a teacher instructing him. From now on, no matter where he went, the people he met would not be teachers but simply living creatures, and since the essential nature of every living creature is Buddha nature, in the end it meant he would be meeting a multitude of Buddhas.

On his first day through the forest, or perhaps it was the second, he came across a little boy about ten years old. The boy was crying. As soon as Sudhana asked why, the answer came: "My mother's died." Sudhana asked how long ago. The boy stopped crying just long enough to reply, "A while ago."

"Yesterday? Or the day before?"

The child replied he didn't know exactly, but about ten years ago. Sudhana was taken aback. Then, from within his heart, like a sudden slap on the knees, glee came surging up. It was characteristic of the people of India that when they said, "just here," they might mean anything up to a million leagues away, while "a little while ago" might mean ten years or it might signify several hundred aeons. For them, time meant primeval time, while time without the cosmic realities of primeval time was nothing more than the foam left by the waves that come crashing onto a sandy shore. Surely that is the unfolding of the cosmos of empty eternity, the coming into being of the infinities of cosmos and selfhood.

The little bodhisattva Sudhana would visit many places in the world, appealing for love. He would attain the gateway of universal union, where subjective and objective, active and passive fuse into one, entering into unrestricted freedom in the Garland Dharma Realm where the particular and the general, the general and the particular, active and passive, passive and active alternately fuse together and part again.

Yet whether at this high level or at the most basic level, the principle of the identity of differences which establishes unity between different natures is always the same. Unless the resplendent Garland is seen as both a madman's ravings and a Buddha's samadhi, there is nothing but hell waiting.

The little pilgrim and the weeping child emerged from the depths of the forest and headed for the harbor together.

"Come on," Sudhana said, his hand on the boy's shoulder. "Let's be off."

THE WORLD OF LITTLE PILGRIM

GARY GACH

All in one; one in all.
—The Avatamsaka Sutra

I discovered the secret of the sea in the dewdrop
—Kahlil Gibran

FORTUNATELY, nothing I could say could ever alter the story of Sudhana, the little pilgrim. So at this point in the tale, at its so-called end, I'd like to just add a few words which might enhance your appreciation, as it continues to unfold in your heart, of the Avatamsaka, its source, plus the remarkable author, Ko Un (say "go oon"), who has inscribed the text in his own blood.

For many readers, *Little Pilgrim* will be an initiation into the stream of Buddhism, known as The Way of the Buddha. And it's also known by the title of its primary text, the Avatamsaka (Sanskrit); also called Hwaom-gyong in Korean.

The Avatamsaka is a sutra, a teaching spoken by the Buddha. It's the longest of his teachings, eighty-one scrolls in Chinese, about 1,500 pages in English. The next-to-last chapter is a book unto itself, entitled the Gandavyuha. *Little Pilgrim* is based on this book.

Ko Un retains the structural elements from the Gandavyuha Sutra's beginning and end, and the fifty-three teachers in between, but it's a fairly free adaptation of the Sutra, more akin to the way Shakespeare drew from classical legends and tales and made them new—or, in our own day, similar to certain works by Italo Calvino, José Saramgao, and Derek Walcott.

The Avatamsaka Sutra ranks with other timeless journeys preserved in literature, from Gilgamesh to Ulysses. As an epic pilgrimage, it's reminiscent of *The Divine Comedy*, *Canterbury Tales*, and *Pilgrim's Progress*. Scholar D.T. Suzuki waxes rhapsodic, calling the Avatamasaka Sutra "the most remarkable thought system ever elaborated by people of the East." To sense this power, you have only to consider its influence in the 10th-century murals on cave walls along the Silk Route, at Dun Huang, in China, and the 9th century sculptures of the Borodobur Temple in Indonesia.

The truth at the heart of the Avatamsaka sounds simple. It is about the unimpeded interpenetration of all things. In a word, interbeing. All things, all beings, all moments, all realms, are all infinitely interconnected. A single drop contains the entire universe.

Welcome to the world of the Avatamsaka. This is the entry into the realm of the inconceivable, into ultimate reality, always available to us in our daily life. Indeed, the Avatamsaka reminds us that the ordinary and the extraordinary are one. It can take years of study for its profundity to become one with bone and breath, yet the illimitable magnitude of its conception is but the flip side of the smile born of everyday practice.

Here's a tale wherein we see an enlightened life as within our reach, as taught by its innumerable guides along the path. Indeed, there are always teachers in our own life, if we're ready to listen. To really hear, without pre-conception or judgment, like Sudhana. Truth is always right here; we need only to nourish the conditions for it to blossom within our scope. So Man-jushri doesn't sit down with him to explain the meaning of life, once and for all. No, after reviving him at the river, at the outset, he sets the boy's feet on the path. Full circle, the road leads back.

When the student is ready, the master appears. With the skillfulness of art (*upaya*), the teacher (like the teaching) can assume many forms, appropriate to the moment. Plain as well as smart. Outcast as well as saint. Male and female. Rich and poor. Child and spirit. Human and animal. Dreaming and waking. Once you've received the teaching, you'll be sent on the Way. Once you get the message, hang up the phone, and go on to what's next.

Enlightenment, like suffering, is not an individual matter. Our lives are all intertwined in a vast tapestry. That's the essential plot (but not the story) here. One ingredient that makes *Little Pilgrim* unique is the way the novel itself parallels Ko Un's own extraordinary life. Indeed, this book spans over twenty years, from when he first put pen to paper until the final period, full stop, so it reflects his own pilgrimage as well.

The seed of the book was planted during Ko Un's ten-year monastic life. He'd ordained following first-hand encounters with the horrors of war. As a mendicant he, like Sudhana, walked across his country. An elder monk suggested he write of Sudhana's journey. Ko Un later went on to become a

master, and was in charge of famed Haeinsa Temple. Yet he grew disillu-
sioned with the self-centeredness he encountered within the order and dis-
robed.

Back in the world of the householder, he experienced skepticism,
nihilism, and suicidal despair. Such despair was familiar to fellow Koreans.
Taking a job as a school teacher on the island of Cheju, he began asking
people about their lives, until the authorities hauled him in and gave him
a beating for doing so. He became an activist and was repeatedly imprisoned and tortured. Then came vindication; and marriage and fatherhood.
His attention returned to Buddhism.

While other writers were adopting the literary strategy of magical realism, Ko Un chose Buddhist realism. There's no beginning, no middle, no
end.

Where an author's tale leaves off, its reader's begins. Closing a book, we
open another, the one in our hearts.

Learning is experiential, made real in our own lives, not just something
to take on faith or be repeated by rote.

See for yourself.

Enjoy the journey.

SUDHANA'S LITERARY HOME

FRANCISCA CHO

THE FANTASTIC JOURNEY that unfolds in *Little Pilgrim* was first narrated in the Gandavyuha Sutra, which was folded into the momentous Avatamsaka Sutra in the late third or fourth century. There, the pilgrimage of Sudhana to fifty-three enlightening beings forms the last and longest chapter of one of the most influential Buddhist scriptures in China and Korea. The Avatamsaka Sutra, commonly known as the Flower Garland or Flower Ornament Scripture, is rivaled only by the Lotus Sutra in prestige, and both texts formed the foundation of major doctrinal schools of the medieval period.

It is puzzling, then, that it has taken this long for the tale of Sudhana to attain the level of literary adaptation that Ko Un now offers us. Buddhist personalities, both historical and mythical, have always been the subject of literary and artistic elaboration in East Asia. The sixteenth century Chinese novel, *Journey to the West*, for example, fictionalizes the pilgrimage of the Chinese monk Xuanzang (c. 600–664), who went to India in a fifteen year voyage to obtain Buddhist scriptures. Both tales share the element of the enlightening journey—that cross-cultural metaphor for the adventures and trials of life itself. In spite of this intrinsically appealing theme, the journey of Sudhana has remained confined to its canonical home, for the most part. The primary exception to this is the 129 relief carvings depicting Sudhana's tale on the galleries of the Temple Borobudur in Java, Indonesia, completed early in the ninth century. More recently, the 1994 Korean feature film *Hwaom-gyeong* (the Korean title for the Avatamsaka Sutra) updates the story into the tale of the boy Sonje searching for his mother in the social margins of contemporary Korea. A meager harvest, indeed, from such monumental origins.

Of course, a plausible explanation for the dearth perhaps lies in the original Sutra text itself. The Gandavyuha is a protracted work that inclines toward descriptive reiterations of an infinite universe beyond what the mind and words can encompass. The sheer power of enumeration, in which a simple list of all the bodhisattvas present for the Buddha's discourse can go on for pages, is marshaled in a hyperbolic display of the immensity of the universe that is contained even in a single pore of the Buddha's body. The grandiosity of the Gandavyuha's sense of space is part and parcel of the Avatamsaka's signature vision of the limitless interpenetration of all phenomena. As "there is nothing that is not your master, even the least grain of dust," the extraordinary compass of the Gandavyuha teases the imagination, but does not make for engaging storytelling. In its pages, Sudhana treks from teacher to teacher of deliberate variety—monks, artisans, courtesans, low-born, high-born, males, females—but his encounters consist of highly impersonal and enumerative conversations that are meant to exemplify stages of the bodhisattva path: the ten faiths, ten abodes, ten practices, ten dedications, and ten stages. These conceptual categories do not encourage an exploration of the fantastical, transformative world of Mahayana emptiness philosophy (*sunyata*) nor do they allow for the personal and emotional colors of Sudhana's pilgrimage.

Ko Un's *Little Pilgrim* at long last rectifies the lack. Sudhana is fully fleshed now, a boy orphaned by war and dispatched by Manjushri (the bodhisattva of wisdom, in traditional lore) on a journey for truth. The literary visualization here, however, is not that of the contemporary novel. For one thing, the story is a series of episodes rather than an integrated plot. One does not get the expected development, sense of growth, and culmination that a journey tale usually implies. Individual characterization and psychology are not the elements of traditional Asian narrative or of a popular Buddhist tale. Ko Un's *Little Pilgrim* is manifestly traditional, and it mends a gap in the East Asian literary tradition. At the same time, Ko Un's literary finesse—his sparing and individually poetic style—makes his realization of Sudhana an eminently contemporary achievement.

In accompanying Sudhana on his journey, the reader might profit from a short briefing on the elements of the popular Buddhist tale. To begin, there is the enlightening dream, so vividly rendered in Sudhana's erotic voyage with Hehua ("Love in the Mist"). In Asian fiction, depictions of the ultimate brevity and sorrows of romantic love are rendered in dreams, literalizing the Buddhist observation that the pleasures of life are as brief as a spring dream. Far from imparting a life-negating message, Ko Un weaves the dream tale into Sudhana's journey, as part and parcel of it, to suggest that if life is ultimately short-lived like a dream, its passions are nevertheless a part of the path to salvation. For Sudhana, it is in fact a gift given to him by the enlightening elephant that carries him for a portion of his journey.

If illusory dreams can accomplish such spiritual work, then so can the magical transformations that populate the book, such as the gender shifting personae of Sumera ("Sumera and Sanuita") and Vasumitra ("Sunlight Park"), and the horrific but unreal spectacle of King Anala ("The Executioner"), who is himself an illusory transformation of the enlightening hawk that appears in two separate episodes. The literary license of fantasy fiction can be found in most cultures, but its liberal presence in Buddhist tales performs metaphysical work: If life is a brief manifestation and the universe itself an expression of the divine play of the gods (as per traditional Indian cosmology), then fiction and life alike are chimeras whose primary values are to teach and liberate.

Buddhist liberation, especially in the Mahayana tradition, is doggedly non-developmental, for all its talk of stages and journeying. One's enlightenment is not something to accumulate, it is something to be reminded of. This idea is a persistent theme that sounds throughout *Little Pilgrim*. Well before the end of his journey, Bodhisattva Ananyagamin tells Sudhana, "Little Pilgrim, you have already learned all there is to learn, you are fully fed. My words will make no difference" ("The Song of Avalokiteshvara"). It also engenders the frequent suggestion that Sudhana's voyage is but a series of constant endings and beginnings that ultimately has nowhere to go. This gives rise to some of Ko Un's most poetic words: As Sudhana sets off on yet another quest, Ko Un observes "he knew the freedom of a child who has no direction. Going anywhere meant the eternal standstill of going nowhere. Such a standstill was the eternal motion of all journeying" ("Cloud-net the Giant").

Consider too, finally, the thought of Sudhana at the conclusion of one episode, as he realizes the enlightening hawk has departed: "Encountering is the mother of parting, and sometimes parting's son. The experience of meeting followed by parting is the shape endlessly taken by this world's unfolding course" ("The Executioner"). The joy of meeting and the sorrow of parting echoes the poetry of Manhae (1879—1944), a Korean Buddhist monk as famous for his poetry as for his actions in the world along the paths of his native land under colonial domination.

Little Pilgrim is a treasure trove of movements that embodies the themes and imaginations that have animated traditional Buddhist popular literature for centuries. In Ko Un's surefooted possession, the story of Sudhana's passage to enlightenment is liberated from its scriptural confinement into the full light of day.

THE AVATAMSAKA SUTRA
BROTHER ANTHONY OF TAIZÉ

LITTLE PILGRIM'S TITLE in Korean is *Hwaom-gyeong*, the same name as the huge Buddhist scripture known in Sanskrit as the Avatamsaka Sutra and known in China as the Hua-yen. Its full name in English would perhaps be best translated as The Teaching of the Garland of Buddhas.

The Garland Sutra exists in various versions. One of its fullest translations in English is *The Flower Ornament Scripture* by Thomas Cleary (Boston, MA: Shambhala Press, 1993). The final thirty-ninth section of the Sutra is really an independent teaching called the Gandavyuha, The Entry into the Realm of Reality, about a young boy's search for wisdom. In the course of a long pilgrimage, the little pilgrim Sudhana encounters fifty-three teachers. These teachers include holy men and monks, as well as several women of various social levels and people involved in worldly activities.

The Avatamsaka Sutra has played an extraordinarily important role in the development of East Asian Buddhism since its introduction into China in the sixth century. In Buddhist tradition, the Avatamsaka's entire contents are said to derive from a series of sermons preached either by the historical Buddha, Gautama, or by his disciple the bodhisattva Samantabhadra, in various locations, both earthly and heavenly. In the course of *Little Pilgrim*, Ko Un refers to this tradition and to the problem posed by the difference in contents and style between this and other, simpler, scriptures which also claim to transmit the teachings of the Buddha. One solution proposed is that the Buddha preached the Avatamsaka early in his teaching, realized that the contents were too difficult for people and preached the other scriptures at a level better adapted to their capacities. The Avatamsaka remained hidden until the time came when a few people could understand its contents.

Modern secular scholarship naturally discounts this kind of legend and prefers to see the Avatamsaka as an encyclopedic compilation of a whole series of originally independent works of high philosophy and spirituality, culminating in the story of Sudhana's pilgrimage. The first Chinese translation of a fairly full version of the Avatamsaka was done under the direction of an Indian monk, Buddhabhadra (359–429); a later Chinese translation of a longer version was directed by a Khotanese monk, Shik-shananda (652–710). Much of the original Sanskrit or Pali text has since then been lost. The powerful vision of the work inspired a major school of philosophical Buddhism in China, the Huayen school, and was equally important in the development of the Ch'an school of Buddhism, called Son in Korean and Zen in Japanese.

In contrast to other scriptures or other parts of the Avatamsaka, something dramatically human happens in the last section of the Sutra; a child meets individual people with specified names and occupations. For the time of its teaching as well as now, it is striking, even revolutionary, that the enlightenment Sudhana gains from his teachers is not the monopoly of monks and intellectuals. However, in the original Gandavayuha, the immense philosophical discourses which Sudhana's initial question provokes each time are not very accessible. Sudhana listens, says thank you, and is directed to his next teacher.

Ko Un's novel takes very little of its actual contents from the Avatamsaka, beyond the bare structure of the fifty-three encounters with people who often, though not always, have the same names as in the scriptural story and who sometimes live in places with the same name. There are also encounters with people who do not count among the fifty-three, and some parts of the novel take place in Sudhana's dreams. The encounters in the novel rarely lead to prolonged discussions of abstruse philosophy; exactly what Sudhana learns is often not explicitly stated.

The story is set in India at the time of the historical Buddha, a time when India was divided into many warring states. The work refers to the Buddhist reaction to the caste-system and at times suggests a Buddhist utopian society. As in the original sutra, the text frequently passes into poetry in order to transcend the limits of mere factuality.

It is not easy to summarize the main message of the Avatamsaka Sutra. One of its central concerns is the universal potential that exists everywhere for enlightening or awakening. Since this enlightening is what characterizes the nature of a Buddha, and since the potential is present everywhere as soon as there is any trace of enlightened compassion, every sentient being is potentially Buddha. This opens the way to an immense vision of unity and equality. Every being and every atom of every being is full of potential buddhahood.

The historical Buddha known as Shakyamuni plays virtually no role in this vision of reality. Time or history are not important since enlightened buddhahood is not attained by any techniques or cause-and-effect processes. The key question that Sudhana keeps asking is "How?" yet all the replies he gets tend to suggest that the bodhisattva way is not a matter of doing but of seeing.

The English language has no word able to translate the term "bodhisattva" that is so central to the Avatamsaka. Thomas Cleary uses the phrase "enlightening beings" to indicate that their wisdom is part of a continuous process.

One of the main features characterizing the bodhisattva is a concern for the good of all other beings. This aspect of the Gandavyuha is of great importance to Ko Un, whose life's vision is deeply marked by social commitment and concrete concern for the common good. The central vision of the Avatamsaka Sutra includes a strong call to altruism; life-for-others.

Another important aspect of the sutra is the theme of the interpenetration, the interdependence and oneness of all things. This reaches its climax near the end of Sudhana's pilgrimage, when he meets the future world-Buddha Maitreya outside a great tower, the chamber of the adornments of Vairochana, the illuminator. Together they enter the tower:

> Inside the great tower he saw hundreds of thousands of other towers similarly arrayed; he saw those towers as infinitely vast as space, evenly arrayed in all directions, yet those towers were not mixed up with one another, being each mutually distinct,
> while appearing reflected in each and every object of all the other towers.... By the power of Maitreya, Sudhana perceived himself in all of those towers.[1]

It is striking to find such an ancient work intensely aware of the immensely vast dimensions of the universe, and of the molecular tininess of its component parts. In the West, there is a somewhat similar pattern in the Platonic notion of microcosm and macrocosm, where each distinct

1 Thomas Cleary, *The Flower Ornament Scripture* (Boston, MA: Shambhala, 1993) p. 1489-90.

concrete temporal reality is seen as the reflection of an eternal idea; but in the traditional images of Indra's Net or of the tower of Vairochana, everything is a reflection of everything and contains everything while remaining itself, and there is no absolute reality giving origin and form to contingent realities.

For a novelist, whose raw material is mostly the difference between individual persons and places, it is not going to be enough to declare that "each thing is everything, each moment is every moment, each being is all beings." *Little Pilgrim* is not a *bildungsroman* in the usual Western sense, indeed I'm not quite sure that it should be considered a "novel" in the normal sense at all. For there is virtually no growth and development in the central character as one encounter follows another. Sudhana is never felt to get any older or any cleverer during his vast pilgrimage. He is always simply himself, a child.

It is only near the end of Ko Un's work that the narrator looks back over Sudhana's travels and explains that he has gone through various traditionally recognized stages in the passage towards awakening. One of the challenges to the novel as a literary form that Ko Un cannot avoid is the fact that the Buddhist vision of the nature of things virtually denies the reality of progress and the possibility of ending. Another challenge is that the deeply philosophical Buddhism of the Avatamsaka tradition does not lend itself to simplification.

As a result, the last third of the novel increasingly uses a technical Buddhist vocabulary of considerable difficulty. Yet the main narrative is quite simple, indeed almost austere. Like the sutra itself, Ko Un maintains a separation between Sudhana and the historical Buddha although the two are considered to be living in the same moment of time and on the same Indian subcontinent. They are destined never to meet. If all are potentially Buddha, no one Buddha stands above the rest. This kind of Buddhism lays little stress on the specificity of the historical Buddha.

In both this novel and his poetry, Ko Un writes about those who are usually considered insignificant people: children who died or were killed, village women whose only task was housekeeping, farmers and layabouts, a host of figures. He is convinced that history is collective, not the usual "history book" picture of famous men, important politicians and such.

Little Pilgrim is no simple allegory of the moral and spiritual challenges of ordinary people's daily life like the *Pilgrim's Progress* told by Bunyan, and yet it is a tale evoking a great variety of lives in a multiplicity of styles. To read a little at a time is the only option available to most readers, but it is not the way this work ought to be read; we really need to pursue our path through its lengthy text like Sudhana, nearly dropping with fatigue under the blazing sun, unsure if there is anything ahead of us waiting to be found, or not.

Because the novel was written over twenty-two years at different stages of the author's career, its style and its main concerns vary greatly. The early sections are lyrical, set in a delightful fantasy world. The central chapters develop more directly social themes, such as the need for the rich to free themselves of their accumulated wealth, the democratic nature of good government, and the need to abolish dictatorships. Towards the end, Ko Un introduces more and more explicit Buddhist terminology, not only the cosmological system with its multiple systems of heavens and worlds but also the traditional stages of the enlightening life.

Some Korean conservatives think of Ko Un as a "dangerous radical" or even a "leftist" yet he tells tales far removed from ideology and often closer to the idealism of St. Luke's Gospel. For a long time in the second half of the story, the characters that Sudhana meets are not human beings at all, but spirits of the night and spirits of the underworld, to say nothing of heavenly beings. Their messages are often pragmatic, about feeding the hungry and sharing wealth, for example, but always as a way of practicing compassion.

It is important to notice what happens at the end of Ko Un's work. In Bunyan's *Pilgrim's Progress*, Christian comes to the gates of the Heavenly Jerusalem. Christianity suggests that every journey, every human life has a goal and an ending. The West is deeply apocalyptic in its vision of time. There must be an end, which beyond death is expressed in Christianity as Heaven, union with the Eternal (usually called God) who is believed to be the origin and unending fulfillment of all that ever has been.

In Buddhism, as in modern astrophysics, there is not the same form of end. This might even help explain why Buddhism did not develop the narrative forms so popular in the West; you cannot have an endless book. So when we reach the last page of Ko Un's tale of Sudhana's pilgrimage, we are not surprised to find there is no end but instead a new beginning. If Sudhana has indeed attained bodhisattva enlightening, and there is no way anyone can be sure about that, it does not give him any kind of privilege. He has not in any sense "made it" and he will have to continue living even if he dies since it is in the nature of "enlightening beings" to remain turned towards those still caught in the sufferings of the illusory world.

What finishes at the end of the novel is the story of Sudhana's meetings with fifty-three masters, a story that had been related in the young Buddha's preaching of the Avatamsaka even before Sudhana was born! Sudhana is now free, since the essence of awakening is that it is a liberation from all determinisms, and he can go where he will. The bodhisattva's place is not on a podium in a temple or a university, though it may sometimes be there too, but buried deep in the living fabric of suffering humanity. The bodhisattva needs no teachers, but has chosen to stay on Earth, embodying great compassion. For Sudhana, the story is over; life can begin.

GLOSSARY

achut – *see* castes

Amitabha Buddha – The Buddha of the heaven called Sukhavati, also called the Pure Land in the West or the Western Paradise.

anuttara-samyak-sambodhi – Full perfect enlightenment, that is attained by a Buddha.

Aryans – Indo-European people who invaded and settled in India, particularly in the North, subjugating or forcing many of the indigenous Dravidian people south.

Asura – A god or spirit who is fond of fighting and subject to frequent outbursts of anger.

Avalokiteshvara – The bodhisattva of compassion and deep listening who hears the cries of the world. In India Avalokita is male, in the Far East, female (Ch., *Quan Yin*; Japanese, *Kannon*; Korean, *Kwanseum*).

Avatamsaka Sutra – The Garland Sutra; the Flower Ornament Scripture. An important scripture appearing at the height of the Mahayana which emphasizes interpenetration, the one is in the all and the all in the one.

avatar – (Skt.) A divine being born on Earth, free of karma and the sense of a separate self, aware from the outset of his or her divine mission.

avidya – (Skt.) Ignorance.

bhumi – (Skt. "land.") Ten steps on the path to enlightenment.

bhuta – (Skt.) Creature, everything that exists. bhutathathata – The true nature of everything. (tathata – Skt. "thusness)

bodhi – (Skt.) Awakening, enlightenment.

bodhi tree – (L. *ficus religiosa*) The tree under which Siddhartha sat to attain full awakening.

bodhichitta – (Skt.) The mind of awakening, the volition and the determination to go on the path of enlightenment.

bodhisattva – Literally "enlightening being," one committed to enlightening oneself and others so that all may be liberated from suffering.

bodhisattva nature – The potential in everyone to live in an enlightened way and act in the world with compassion.

bodhisattva vow (Great Vow) – The vow to awaken oneself and all beings, and not to enter nirvana until all have reached the shore of liberation.

bodhisattva way – The path of liberation from suffering, fear, and ignorance; the path of enlightenment.

Body of Transformation – *see* trikaya

Brahma – (Skt.) In Hinduism, the creator of the universe. The first god in the Hindu trinity of Brahma, Vishnu, and Shiva. brahman – *see* castes Brahman – (Skt.) In Hinduism, the absolute, eternal non-dualistic nature.

buddha – A fully enlightened being. Buddha – The "enlightened one," the historical Buddha, Shakyamuni, born in the sixth century B.C.E. and living for eighty years before passing into nirvana. Buddhas – According to the Mahayana tradition, there are countless

Buddhas and bodhisattvas throughout the cosmos. **Buddhas of the Past** – There are seven, each of a previous age. The most recent was Buddha Shakyamuni. **buddha nature** –The potential in every being to be fully enlightened.

castes – The heirarchical division of Indian society into four classes: *brahman*, priests and educated people; *kshatrya*, rulers and warriors; *vaysya*, businessmen and property owners; *sudra*, peasants, workers, and servants; and below this a class called untouchables (*achut*) who perform the least desirable and dirtiest tasks in society. The three highest castes have many rights and privileges not granted to sudras and untouchables.

deva – Celestial being, a god or goddess.

Devadatta – A cousin of the Buddha who became a monk in his sangha and later tried to murder him. As Devadatta was dying, he came to the Buddha and reconciled with him.

dharani – A long mantra or short sutra in verse which when recited has magical or transcendant power.

dharma – (Skt., "truth; universal law") The teachings of truth; the teachings of a Buddha.

dharma-wheel – (Skt., *dharmachakra*) "The wheel of the teaching." With his first teaching, the Buddha turned the wheel of dharma, setting it in motion. The eight spokes represent the Noble Eightfold Path.

dharmakaya – *see* trikaya

Dravidians – People living in India before the Aryan invasion, now predominant mainly in the south of India and in Sri Lanka.

emptiness – (Skt., *shunyata*) The nature of all things is that they are interconnected, always changing, and empty of a self-nature.

enlightenment – Realization of the highest understanding.

Four laws where Brahma-deva dwells (Skt. *brahmaviharas*) – The four practices of true love: loving kindness (Skt. *maitri*) – bringing joy to others; compassion (*karuna*) – relieving the suffering of others; – sympathetic joy taking pleasure in the happiness of others, without jealousy (*priti*); and equanimity (*upeksha*) – inclusiveness, looking on everyone with understanding and love, not giving up on anyone.

Gandharava – Heavenly musicians.

Ganga – The river Ganges, holy river in northeast India. It was in the kingdoms of the Ganges basin that the historical Buddha, Shakyamuni, walked and taught and had monasteries, especially in the kingdoms of Koshala, Magadha, and Shakya.

Garuda – Mythical birds who are half man and half bird.

Heaven of Indra – In Hinduism, the highest of the heavenly realms, presided over by Lord Indra who is the supreme deity in Hinduism.

Indra's Net – A limitless net stretching infinitely in all directions, with a jewel in each node of the net. These jewels are infinite in number, each reflecting in itself all other jewels. This image is generally used to illustrate the teachings of interbeing and interpenetration.

Jains – A sect of ascetics living in India who do not believe in a supreme being but in the divinity of all beings. Liberation is attained through right thought and right action; not harming any living being is particularly important.

Jetavana – The main monastery of the Buddha and his sangha, located in the Eastern Park near Shravasti in the kingdom of Koshala.

Kapilavastu – The capital city of the kingdom of Shakya. Siddhartha was a member of the ruling Shakya clan, and grew up in the royal palace in Kapilavastu.

karma – (Skt., "action") The causes and effects of our actions.

Kinnara – A mythical being that is a man with the head of a horse. Sometimes associated with the Gandharavas.

Koshala – A kingdom on the Ganges in the time of Shakyamuni Buddha, neighboring the kingdom of Magadha. The capital city was Shravasti.

Kumbhanda – A kind of evil spirit.

liberation – (Skt., *vimukti*) Emancipation from the cycle of samsara.

Lumbini Grove – Near Kapilavastu, it is the place where Siddhartha was born while Mahamaya was on her way to her parent's home in Ramagama, capital of Koliya, where she had intended to give birth.

Mahabodhi – Great awakening as a buddha.

Magadha – A kingdom on the Ganges in the time of Shakyamuni, neighboring the kingdom of Koshala. The capital city was Rajagriha (Rajgir).

Mahabrahman – (Brahman) In Hinduism, the deity representing absolute consciousness, ultimate reality.

Mahamaudgalyayana – One of the great disciples of Shakyamuni Buddha.

Mahayana – The flowering of a Buddhist reform movement in the early part of the common era, stessing the bodhisattva ideal over individual enlightenment.

Mahasattva – A great being, a bodhisattva, one who has realized awakening and illuminates the way for many others. Often occurs together with the word bodhisattva.

Mahasthamaprapta – The bodhisattva who escorts people to the Pure Land of Buddha Amitabha.

Mahoraga – Demon in the form of a great serpent.

Maitreya – The bodhisattva who will be the future Buddha.

Manjushri – The bodhisattva embodying the Great Wisdom which dispels the darkness of ignorance.

Mount Sumeru – The world mountain, the center of the world where are all the heavenly realms, according to both Hindu and Buddhist cosmology.

nirmanakaya – *see* trikaya

nirvana –The extinction of all views and concepts and the suffering based on them; having no attachments to the realm of birth and death. Refers to the ultimate reality.

prajña – The highest wisdom.

Prajñaparamita Sutras – A collection of sutras of the early Mahayana, around the first century AD, dealing with the nature of emptiness and the realization of transcendent wisdom. The Prajñaparamita literature preceeded the Avatamsaka.

Pure Land – The western paradise ruled by Buddha Amitabha.

Rajagriha (Rajgir) – City on the Ganges River, was the capital of the Kingdom of Magadha in the time of the Buddha Shakyamuni.

Realm of Formlessness – *see* Threefold World

samadhi – One pointed mind, concentration.

samsara – The cycle of birth and death; the cycle of suffering which continues as long as human beings remain ignorant of the interconnected nature of all things.

Samantabhadra – The bodhisattva of Great Action, associated with Vairochana, and protector of those who teach the dharma.

Shakya – Kingdom in the north of India ruled by the Shakya clan into which Siddhartha was born. **Shakyamuni** – lit. "sage of the Shakya clan". Refers to the historical Buddha whose awakening and teachings laid the foundation for the practice of Buddhism.

Shariputra – A great disciple of the Buddha Shakyamuni.

shravaka – (Skt., "hearer") A person on the way to enlightenment through listening to the teachings of the Buddha.

Siddhartha – Siddhartha Gautama, the given name of the one who would become the historical Buddha, Shakyamuni.

skandhas – (Skt., "aggregates") The Five Skandhas are the five aspects of a person: form (body), feelings, perceptions, mental formations, and consciousness.

Suddhodana – The father of Siddhartha Gautama, head of the Shakya clan, and ruler of the Kingdom of Shakya.

sudra – *see* caste

Tamil – A Dravidian people and language in the south of India and in Sri Lanka.

Threefold World – (Skt., *triloka*) The three realms in which existence takes place. The desire realm, where desire predominates; the form realm, where there is no desire but there is joy; and the formless realm, a purely spiritual realm.

trikaya – (Skt.) A Buddha is said to have three bodies: *nirmanakaya* (transformation body), through which a Buddha lives and acts in the world; *samboghakaya* (body of bliss or enjoyment) resulting from the accumulated merit of compassionate action; *dharmakaya* (body of true nature), the Buddha in the ultimate dimension, not dependent on incarnation in human form; the body of the dharma, what remains when the historical Buddha is no longer with us; the true and ultimate reality.

Tushita heaven – In Buddhism, the thirty-third or highest of the heavenly realms.

udambara tree – The appearance of a Buddha is said to be as rare as the blooming of the udambara flower, which happens only once every three thousand years.

upaya (Skt.) Skillful means; the many ways a bodhisattva guides people to liberation and the discernment to know what means are appropriate in a given situation.

Vairochana – (Skt.) The Buddha of the ultimate dimension, the dharmakaya.

vaysya – *see* castes

vimukti (Skt.) Emancipation, liberation from all fear.

Yaksha – Supernatural beings who are not violent, but sometimes live in isolated places and disturb the peace of practitioners of meditation.

yojana – (Skt.) A unit of measure, approximately one day's march.

FOR FURTHER READING

Cleary, Thomas. *The Flower Ornament Sutra: A Translation of the Avatamsaka Sutra* (Boston, MA: Shambhala Press, 1993). The one-volume edition includes Li Tongxuan's seventh-century guide to the Gandavyuha. The three-volume edition does not include Li's commentary, publishing it instead as a separate book.

Ibid. *Entry into the Inconceivable: An Introduction to Hua-Yen Buddhism* (Honolulu, HI: University of Hawaii, 1983). Four classical Chinese commentaries, with introductory survey.

Master Hua, Hsuan. *The Flower Adornment Sutra (Avatamsaka Sutra)* (Buddhist Text Translation Society, 1985). Master Hua supervised this translation of the complete Avatamsaka with a team of his monastics, and intersperses the text with his commentary.

Chang, Garma C. C. *The Buddhist Teaching of Totality: The Philosophy of Hwa Yen Buddhism* (University Park, PA: Pennsylvania State University Press, 1976). Arguably the first book-length exposition on Hua-yen in English, it remains a hallmark work in the field.

Cook, Francis H. *Hua-Yen Buddhism: The Jewel Net of Indra* (University Park, PA: Pennsylvania State University Press, 1976). Francis Cook manages to match Garma C. C. Chang's work and add some extra layers.

Nhat Hanh, Thich. *All in One One in All: The Nature of Interbeing* (Singapore: Kong Meng San Phor Kark See Monastery, 2001).

Ibid. "The Avatamsaka Realm" in *Cultivating the Mind of Love: The Practice of Looking Deeply in the Mahayana Buddhist Tradition* (Berkeley, CA: Parallax Press, 1996).

Sutra Translation Committee of the U.S. & Canada. *Samantabhadra: Supreme Vows.* (Sutra Translation Committee of the U.S. & Canada, 1995). The Gandavyuha comprises the 39th chapter of the Avatamsaka and concludes with this, the 40th. It is also considered the fourth sutra of numerous Pure Land schools.

Suzuki, D.T. *Essays in Zen Buddhism: Third Series* (York Beach, ME: Samuel Weiser, Inc., 1953). Suzuki was a pioneering exponent of Buddhism in the West, and this represents one of the first expositions in English of Hua-yen. The first half of the book includes four essays treating the Gandavyuha in relation to the book's overarching theme: the transformation of Indian Buddhism in China.

About Ko Un

Ko Un was born in southwestern Korea in 1933. A former Buddhist monk, he has published over a hundred volumes of poetry, essays, fiction, and drama. Widely acknowledged to be Korea's foremost contemporary poet, he has received many prestigious literary awards and was shortlisted for the Nobel Prize in Literature in 2002 and 2004. Ko Un's work has been translated into all major Asian and European languages.

About Brother Anthony of Taizé

Brother Anthony of Taizé was born in Cornwall, U.K. in 1942. He joined the Community of Taizé in France in 1969. He has been living in Korea since 1980 and is a professor in the English Department of Sogang University (Seoul). He has published numerous English translations of modern Korean literature, including Ko Un's *The Sound of My Waves*, *Beyond Self*, and *Ten Thousand Lives (Maninbo)*.

About Young-Moo Kim

Young-Moo Kim was born near Seoul, Korea in 1944 and died in 2001. He was a professor in the English Department of Seoul National University. He published three volumes of his own poetry and worked as co-translator with Brother Anthony on a large number of translations, including *The Sound of My Waves*, *Beyond Self*, and *Ten Thousand Lives (Maninbo)*.